A CIVIL ISSUE

A CIVIL ISSUE

CURT VON FANGE

FIVE STAR
A part of Gale, Cengage Learning

GALE
CENGAGE Learning

Farmington Hills, Mich • San Francisco • New York • Waterville, Maine
Meriden, Conn • Mason, Ohio • Chicago

GALE
CENGAGE Learning·

LIBRARY OF CONGRESS CATALOGING-IN-PUBLICATION DATA

Names: Von Fange, Curt, author.
Title: A civil issue / Curt Von Fange.
Description: First edition. | Waterville, Maine : Five Star, 2016.
Identifiers: LCCN 2016003807 (print) | LCCN 2016015053 (ebook) | ISBN 9781432832513 (hardback) | ISBN 1432832514 (hardcover) | ISBN 9781432832438 (ebook) | ISBN 1432832433 (ebook)
Subjects: LCSH: Gold theft—Fiction. | United States—History—Civil War, 1861–1865—Fiction. | BISAC: FICTION / Historical. | FICTION / Action & Adventure. | GSAFD: Adventure fiction. | Historical fiction. | Western stories.
Classification: LCC PS3622.O655 C58 2016 (print) | LCC PS3622.O655 (ebook) | DDC 813/.6—dc23
LC record available at https://lccn.loc.gov/2016003807

First Edition. First Printing: July 2016
Find us on Facebook– https://www.facebook.com/FiveStarCengage
Visit our website– http://www.gale.cengage.com/fivestar/
Contact Five Star™ Publishing at FiveStar@cengage.com

Printed in the United States of America
1 2 3 4 5 6 7 20 19 18 17 16

A CIVIL ISSUE

★ ★ ★ ★ ★

PART 1

★ ★ ★ ★ ★

CHAPTER 1

It started raining again. Big drops splashed here and there like someone tossing small pebbles into a quiet pond. It quickly increased to a steady downpour. A group of riders on tired horses came up to the main gate of the guardhouse. A man in a saturated uniform sloshed up to the entry, talked with the gatekeeper and passed some soggy papers over for inspection. The gatekeeper nodded and ushered him into a small wooden shack out of the rain. As he entered, he took his Confederate hat and placed it on a hook on the wall. Water dripped off the edges and collected in a puddle on the floor. His long, black hair matted the sides of his face. He pulled it aside and draped it across his ears.

The guard on duty scanned the papers under the oil lamp and asked in a quiet tone, "If these five prisoners were picked up near the Maryland border, why were they brought all the way down here to central Georgia?"

The man with black hair responded, "I don't know. The colonel in charge gave me orders to deliver them to the commanding officer at Camp Sumter near Andersonville."

The guard finished looking at the documents and replied, "Well, seems like everything is in order. Go ahead and bring them in and turn them over to the yard master. He'll orient them to the rules of the prison. I'll contact the commander and have him meet you over there."

The black-haired man took the papers from the guard. As he

9

turned to leave, he reached for his hat, smacked it against his thigh to remove some more water, and placed it on his head. He opened the door and yelled to the other soldiers on the horses, "Take them through the first fence and over to the yard master. It'll be the third tent on the left past the stables. It should have some oil lamps hanging outside the main entry."

The fenced gate opened at the gatekeeper's command and the group of ten horses plodded across the sodden, red Georgia earth to the yard master's canvas tent.

Captain Heinrich Wirz, a native of Zurich, Switzerland, rolled off his cot. The guard from the front gate had shaken him awake to inform him of the arriving prisoners. "So, why are you waking me up for these five men?" he asked as he sat up and put his feet on the moist ground.

The guard responded, "There was something strange in their papers. The officer sending them here gave strict orders that they be delivered personally into the hands of the prison commandant. You can see them yourself when you get over to the yard master's tent; that's where I sent them."

Captain Wirz rolled his eyes and struggled into his damp shirt. He was a veteran of the Confederate Fourth Battalion, Louisiana Volunteer Infantry, but was severely wounded in the right shoulder at the Battle of Seven Pines in Virginia. He had only been transferred to Fort Sumter a couple of days earlier. He finished dressing, pulled the tent flap to the side, and saw how hard it was raining. He quietly cursed as he trudged toward the yard master's tent.

The yard master's tent was rather large as tents come. It was hastily erected so the incoming prisoners could be processed. Since they came in by the hundreds, it needed the necessary space to check the new arrivals for identification, overall health, and to direct them to the stockade, hospital, or proper location for their tenure. The sergeant in charge was a short, stocky man who didn't smile but was efficient in his duties. Seven camp guards were stationed around the tent at strategic locations with their rifles leveled at the prisoners. By the time Captain Wirz arrived on the scene, the sergeant had already reviewed the new prisoners' papers, entered the pertinent information in the camp logs, and given leave to the escorts from the train depot. The man with the matted black hair stood off to the side waiting for his release so he could begin his trip back to his regiment. As the captain walked in, he snapped to attention and barked, "Master Sergeant Sam Rediger, 1st Cavalry, Alabama. I've been instructed to deliver these five prisoners to your care, sir."

The captain returned his salute and replied, "You have done so, sir, and are dismissed." He turned to the yard master and then said almost as an afterthought, "You might stop by the bakehouse on your way out and grab some grub. I think you have time before the next scheduled train is to depart from town."

"Thank you, sir," Sergeant Rediger responded. He looked over at the prisoners, donned his damp hat, and slipped out of the tent into the rain.

The captain took the papers, sat down on a stool, and started to read the contents. After a few minutes he looked up and asked in an almost fatherly tone, "Who are Frank and Fred?"

Two young men in their late twenties stepped forward.

"You two are brothers, I take it," the captain commented. They didn't respond, so he continued, "I have two sons fighting together in Virginia somewhere. One of them is named Francis; he looks a lot like you, Frank. He just turned twenty-five last week." The young men gave no response so he continued scanning the documents. He looked up again, searching for an older face. He directed his comments at a man in his mid-fifties. "You, sir, must be H. Mueller."

The third prisoner took his place next to the other two men.

11

"That is correct, sir. My name is Henri Mueller."

The captain continued, "Seems you are a building engineer of some sort. Let's see," he sifted through another page of documents. "Ah, yes, you construct bridges, roads, railroads, and have a working knowledge of explosives. That's quite a set of talents for these times." Henri merely nodded in acknowledgement. The captain continued, "Looks like you were reconstructing a railroad bridge near the Maryland border when you got caught in a skirmish with some of our boys. Only you five were left after the volleys were done. Don't you think it odd that you were sent all the way to Fort Sumter to be placed personally in my care?"

Henri did not respond.

The captain absorbed the balance of the papers. His wrinkled brow indicated an intent interest in what he read. He scratched his nose and looked up at the prisoners with puzzled eyes. Then he said, "Well, I'm not here to interrogate you, only to keep you interred until you are picked up in a few days by Colonel Baxter. The yard master oriented you to the rules and conditions of the stockade. Let me reiterate that the deadline is not to be crossed under any circumstances. To remind you, it is the line drawn about twenty feet from the stockade wall. If you cross it, you will be shot." He turned to the guards standing by and ordered, "Take them away."

CHAPTER 2

The rain had moved on by morning light. Large puddles of water stood on the saturated ground and drained via small rivulets toward the central creek flowing through the stockade. Fort Sumter had been hastily constructed as a prison to house the growing number of Union prisoners transported from northern battles. Construction began in January of 1864 using slave labor procured locally from plantation owners. It covered sixteen and a half acres and consisted of a huge stockade surrounded by a fifteen-foot-high, hand-hewn pine fence. Every thirty yards elevated guardhouses that the prisoners called "pigeon roosts" housed sharpshooters. They had orders to shoot anyone who crossed the deadline. Stockade Creek flowed through one side of the encampment and provided both water and latrine duty. The camp, though new, was already overcrowded and undersupplied. Sickness was compounded by the unsanitary conditions. Union soldiers died on a daily basis.

The spring cold front that passed through the previous evening had dropped the temperature to the lower fifties. Henri and his men huddled with a large group of prisoners around a fire that had somehow stayed lit in spite of the rain. He spent most of the night thinking about the chain of events that had transpired since he left Washington only three weeks earlier. He had met with Union generals to discuss the importance of rebuilding railroad bridges that had been blown up by the Confederates earlier in the month. One in particular had been carrying a Union supply train loaded with payroll. The Rebels had caught wind of the shipment and destroyed the train at a narrow bridge over the Maple River east of Cumberland. The entire payroll cargo, all in gold bullion, disappeared. The wreckage had been cleaned up and the bridge debris cleared over the past couple of weeks and it was Henri's job to rebuild the bridge.

Henri had taken a special crew of "organizers" with him to the bridge site. Fred and Frank were two select managers of this team. They were brothers raised in a farming community in a remote section of southern Indiana. When they reached eighteen and twenty, respectively, they had been given an opportunity from a wealthy benefactor to attend a school in the east. Though both studied engineering and had exceptional mechanical aptitude, it was their people skills that set them above their peers in obtaining advancement in the engineering community. Frank, the elder of the two, had a knack for convincing others to assist in difficult projects. His six-foot-four-inch frame, sandy-blond hair and brilliant-blue eyes marked him like a lone oak tree in a cleared field. His air of confidence, tempered by knowledge beyond his years, attracted men like metal filings to a magnet.

His younger brother, Fred, also possessed many of the same talents as his brother. But his drawing card was not his size. He was smaller, just under six feet, and had his mother's brown hair and gray eyes. Fred was not the showman that his brother was. A quiet peace about him made others feel assured and at rest with his abilities.

The other two men on Henri's team were from the west. Jack was from Welsh descent and had extensive training in deep-rock mining. He had helped his father operate a number of coal operations in Wales. In spite of his youth he was offered a position in California in the late fifties by a mining firm that needed his acquired expertise. Early prospectors in the California gold rush found the easiest gold in deposits along the riverbeds called placers. Sifting and panning the gravel beds could pick out gold in the form of pure nuggets. But, after the surface gold was depleted, prospectors theorized that deep-rock intrusions of mineralized, gold-bearing quartz were to be found as the source for the placer deposits. Few men had the knowledge of deep-rock mining so large corporate companies were formed who imported that deep-rock mining expertise in the form of mining engineers from the old world. Jack answered that call. It was unfortunate that the theory of deep gold-bearing strata was not the case in western California. The gold-bearing placer deposits were collected erosion debris laid down in ancient riverbeds from old mountains long gone. Deep-rock exploration revealed no gold-bearing mother lodes and many of the newly formed companies closed. Jack, one of the casualties of closure, eventually worked his way back East to be a part of Dobson Engineering, a subcontractor of Henri's firm. His cribbing and structural analysis abilities were a great asset to the group.

The last member of Henri's team was Mike. He was a young Englishman who seemed to have a knack for finding things. His short history was shrouded a little bit in mystique. He claimed to have lived a short time as a pirate's mate off the coast of Africa. The captain was mesmerized by Mike's ability to find virtually anything and to make use of almost nothing to make something happen. A raging sea battle with a British cruiser left his ship in tatters. But Mike managed to assemble a small raft out of scrap materials and float away unnoticed before the boat sank. He ended up along the coast of France where Henri, on one of his overseas trips, was introduced and drawn to the young man's resourcefulness. They became friends and he accompanied Henri home. He had been part of Henri's business as "the finder" ever since.

Once at the bridge site in Maryland, the crew was given a

work force of one hundred military men assigned to rebuild the railway bridge. Many of the workmen were escaped slaves who had made it to the northern side of the Mason-Dixon line and joined the Union army. Because they lacked schooling of any sort they were often assigned to labor intensive tasks such as the bridge rebuilding team. Henri had already designed the triangular ribbed structure to span the small valley. Jack was assigned to assemble moveable sections with his group. Fred and Frank worked with two teams in salvaging and rebuilding the foundational piers. Mike took a team and canvassed the surrounding countryside for timber and iron pegs. Everything was on schedule when a band of Confederates encountered the project and closed it down with a night attack. Some of the workers scattered in the dark of night. Others were killed in their tents by the rapid succession of rifle fire. Since it wasn't a protected military campaign there were few armaments for defense. The project was quickly overrun and prisoners taken. The Rebel captain seemed to know exactly who it was he was after. He picked out Henri's group of five and immediately had them transported under guard to Fort Sumter. The rest of the workers he had shot; the bridge construction that they had repaired was once again razed to the ground.

Henri's line of thought was interrupted by a voice. "Aye, mate, y'er new here, ain't ya?"

He turned his head to see a slender man about five and a half feet tall with a curly crop of hair addressing him. His face was ruddy and was deeply grooved with stress lines. Henri thought, maybe, they arguably could be laugh lines. The man held out his hand and said, "Ay there, welcome to Fort Stink. Name's Binky."

Henri's mouth curled at the ends in a smile as he looked the man over from head to toe, reached out and grasped his hand. "Hi, my name's Henri. Did you say 'Binky'?"

"Aye, mate. Binky, 'tis. My mates used to say I blinked too much in the sun so they nicknamed me Binky. Real name is Arnold. But I likes Binky better."

"Well, Binky, it's a pleasure to meet you. How is it you came to be here, at Fort Sumter?"

"I tell ya, cap'n, it's a long story. I'll shorten it by sayin' I was assigned to a Union boat a-tryin' to catch blockade-runners. Seems one of them little buggers was a little too smart for our skipper. Our boat ended up on the bottom of Wilmington Bay. At least he had the decency to pick up survivors, me being the only one. Next thing I know, I'm here. I tell you what, though, lemme fill you in on how this place works so your stay will be a little bit easier on ya."

Binky spent the next few hours giving Henri and his entourage the inside orientation of Fort Sumter.

Over the next few days they met many of their comrades from all walks of life. Some of their fellows were young kids who enlisted in the army with a hazed idea of romance and glamour. Others were farmers who had a high moral fiber and interest in preserving the Union. There were soldiers who had made a career out of war and some who thought it would be fun. Unfortunately, Fort Sumter gave a dose of war's reality. The young men would return with a chiseled expression of horror permanently etched onto their faces. Farmers counted the high cost of death, whether it be an animal or a person. Even seasoned soldiers could not forget the conditions found in the prison camp. All men were changed in some way.

CHAPTER 3

It was the fourth day of Henri's internment. As his men and Binky gathered around the fire pit eating their cold stew, three guards approached and ordered Henri to follow. Ten other guards bearing rifles surrounded the additional men of his team along with Binky and directed them through the gate into a courtyard.

Henri was directed to a tent, walked through the door and noticed a gray-uniformed officer sitting on a chair, his feet propped up on a wooden table. Off to the side was another man in uniform. "Must be his assistant," Henri thought. The man leaned against an upright dresser. The gray uniform he wore was frayed and worn. Brown teeth gritted a chew of tobacco as he smacked and licked his fat lips. There was a scar across his throat. A black regiment hat squashed down the dirty, red hair that framed his fat little face. His stocky body and short limbs belied a hidden strength that bulged under his tight shirt. His incessant wheezing made Henri wonder about his state of health.

The man sitting at the table cleared his throat and spat off to the side. He had thick, brown hair pulled back by a leather thong and donned a black felt hat with a red feather. He put a hand-rolled cigarette back into his mouth, drew a breath through it, and let the smoke unfurl slowly out of his mouth. His uniform was unkempt and dirty. In contrast to the camp guards, it appeared he had traveled far and fast to reach his destination. A holstered revolver was strapped to his side. His black eyes were viewing the papers that Captain Wirz had perused a few days earlier. They crumpled under his bony fingers and sounded like fresh pine popping in a hot fire. On his finger was a silver ring with an opaque stone embedded in the setting. Henri's acute vision could make out some circles around the stone but it was just beyond his focus to interpret their meaning. The man scratched his pointed nose, fingered his mustache, looked up at Henri, and squeaked, "My name is Colonel Baxter and I require the services of you and your men to blow up a bridge."

"And why would I do that?" Henri inquired.

Baxter continued as though he hadn't heard. "This is not an ordinary bridge, sir. It is of iron and stone construction. There is no wood in it. Its piers are anchored onto bedrock that is thirty feet in the mud. It has a length of three hundred ten feet. It is divided into five spans that are greatly reinforced. This makes it difficult to collapse. A very important train will be traversing this bridge in four days. Because of the advancing Union forces it is vital to the Confederate cause that this bridge be immediately eliminated after this train passes over it."

Once again Henri responded, "And why will I help you do this?"

Baxter continued to crackle the papers. "I went to great pains to capture you and your team. As you know, you are the most renowned explosive engineer in the country. You not only know how these bridges are built; you also know where the weak spots are for their destruction. You and your men are very resourceful in using what is available and convincing others to assist you. I have a limited force to work with and I require your expertise and creativity." He motioned to one of the guards to bring in the other prisoners. "Now, as to why you should do this for me. If you do not, I will shoot, one by one, each of your companions until you comply."

The line of men came into the tent and stood against the tent wall. Their hands were tied behind their backs. The guards stood with their rifles trained on the prisoners. Baxter looked at Henri and said, "Now, are you ready to cooperate?"

Henri looked at his friends, then at the colonel. He couldn't believe this man was serious. No one, especially an officer, would blatantly murder someone in cold blood.

Baxter rose out of the chair and stared into Henri's eyes. "I said, are you ready to cooperate?"

Henri still gave no response.

Baxter's fierce eyes squinted slightly. His right hand reached to his holster. He unsnapped it and pulled the revolver from its sheath. Without moving his line of vision, he raised the revolver to shoulder height and pulled the trigger. The loud report from the gun brought everyone to attention. All except Binky. The force of the bullet threw him into the side of the tent. He crumpled to the ground with a hole through his ribcage.

"Are you ready to leave now?" hissed Baxter.

Henri's mind recoiled at the horror. He could feel tears welling up as he whispered, "Yes, we are ready to cooperate now."

CHAPTER 4

Frank was jerked awake by a sudden shift in the railcar. He looked over at his brother and saw that Fred was still asleep. The past forty hours since the group left the prison were a jumble of forced walks, trotting horses, and clattering train rides. Now they were on a freight line moving in a southwesterly direction. The members of their group were under guard in a partially filled boxcar. Shrunken wood slats on the walls permitted a stroboscopic view of the surrounding countryside. It seemed like this section of the state was untouched by the carnage of war.

At the end of the boxcar, a small doorway opened. A guard pushed Henri through and motioned him to sit on the straw near Frank. He closed the door and left. Frank scooted over to Henri and asked, "Did you get any more information from our gracious host?"

"Yeah, afraid so," Henri responded. "Colonel Baxter is taking us to southern Alabama to a railroad bridge over the Tallapoosa River. He showed me the construction prints. It is quite well built for a bridge out in the middle of nowhere. Like he said, it is around three hundred-some-feet long, five spans, iron supports with limestone buttresses. He compelled me to show him the best location for the type of explosives that he is going to use. It's a little strange because I don't see why this particular bridge is so important to blow up. It doesn't seem to serve a vital interest to the Union."

Frank replied, "Tallapoosa River. Isn't that down in the direction of Mobile?"

"Yes, that's correct," Henri answered in a whisper. He furrowed his brow, thought for a moment, and then continued, "At my meeting in Washington a few weeks ago, I remember General Grant mentioning to me something about Admiral Farragut's plan to break the Confederate blockade at Mobile Bay. I bet this train is transporting valuables out of Mobile before Farragut's attack starts. If this were the case it would mean there is a leak of high-level information among Lincoln's generals."

Frank matched his quiet tone. "Do you think Farragut would drop troops at Mobile and then try to push up through central Alabama using the railroad for transportation? It would be faster than the river route."

Henri thought for a moment. "I suppose it is possible. I didn't hear anything about a plan like that." His eyes glazed over as he stared out the boxcar slats. "I wonder if we could rig the explosives on the bridge to go off but not do critical damage so the rail would be left intact? If Baxter has any knowledge of explosives it might be difficult to conceal, especially if he monitors our work."

"We could doctor the fuses so the ends in the explosives are neutralized," Frank thought out loud.

"You know if the bridge is left standing after the train goes over it, Baxter will probably have us shot," Fred whispered.

Henri and Frank both looked over their shoulders at Fred. His eyes were almost, but not quite, shut. "You ought to whisper a little quieter," he said. "It's a good thing the guards have to contend with the train-track racket or they might hear you."

"Your hearing always was too good for your own good," Frank piped in.

"In response to your statement," Henri continued, "they'll probably shoot us anyway. Unless, that is, we formulate a plan."

"How about if we make something up for when the explosives misfire?" Fred suggested. "It might be the most opportune time since no one will be expecting it."

"That might work," said Henri. "We'll find some time and see what Jack and Mike think."

The train began slowing down and eventually creaked to a halt. A few minutes had passed when the sliding door jerked open. Colonel Baxter peered in from a distance and ordered the men to get out of the car. A small collection of covered wagons lined the roadside. The group was directed into the middle wagon. The driver was dressed in the standard gray Confederate uniform. It was dusty and faded much like Colonel Baxter's. The soldier carried no sidearm. As he tied the curtains at the rear of the wagon, Henri noticed that the soldier wore a silver wrist bracelet. It was rather narrow with the exception of four spots where the metal flared out to accommodate four small precious stones. He thought it odd that an enlisted man would sport such an ornament during wartime. The guards mounted some horses and followed to the sides and rear of the middle wagon.

Toward the morning of the fourth day after leaving the prison camp, the caravan arrived at its target. The men were unloaded from the wagon, ushered down a small trail toward the bottom of a ravine, and directed into the entrance of a cave. Inside the generous opening, a tall, slender man was sitting at a makeshift table, sifting through bags of powder. Further back were boxes labeled "explosives," along with unmarked canisters and wooden containers of supplies. When he saw Colonel Baxter enter, he stood to his feet, saluted and said, "Everything is here that you required, sir."

Baxter turned and looked at Henri. "You have your instructions, Mr. Mueller. Please see that the charges are placed as you and I agreed." He pointed across the valley to a small rock

outcropping a few hundred feet away from the bridge end abutment. "The detonating plunger box is located just out of view
behind those rocks. Please apex the wiring to that point." He
pulled Mike and Jack aside and pushed them to the rear of the
cave. "These two men shall be my insurance that you will have
your task accomplished by four o'clock this afternoon. You will
be divided into three teams. Each of your men will be accompanied by two of mine: one to stand guard, the other to assist and report your actions to me. All necessary supplies are
here in the cave. My quartermaster, John, will issue what is
necessary. Please be careful of the canisters as they contain a
very volatile experimental fluid. I think that you, Mr. Mueller,
are acquainted with its use."

Henri squinted as he looked at the canisters. He carefully
picked up one of them, unscrewed the top, and slowly removed
a flask that was inside. He looked up at Baxter and commented,
"These aren't the explosives that you said we were planting."

"No, they aren't," was the stone-faced reply. "This is a sample
of a new kind of glycerin made from a solution of nitric acid. I
wanted to see its full effect on this 'impregnable bridge.' You
can handle it the same way as the material that I know you are
acquainted with. Just be more careful and don't shake it."

Henri glanced at Fred and Frank as he returned the flask to
its canister. They all knew how unstable the fluid was. Miswir-
ing the flasks would be impossible. Their original plan was to
cold wire the solid stick charges at the pier foundations so they
all wouldn't explode. The retarded blast would not have damaged the bridge significantly. The flasks, on the other hand, were
different. Once one flask went off, the violent vibrations
transferred through the bridge would detonate the rest. It created a problem for them that didn't have a remedy.

Baxter ordered the teams to get to work. Fred was to stretch
the ignition wires from the detonation point to the first abut-

ment, then across the bridge to each of the five foundational piers, ending at the other end of the bridge. Frank was to transport five canisters to each pier while Henri attached and wired them in series. Two additional flasks were wired in at each abutment end. Baxter intermingled with the teams during the entire process and had kept a close eye on all the connections. The teams started at six in the morning. By late evening, as the sun started to set in the west, it was all set up for the detonation.

Back at the cave, Baxter assembled his small army along with Henri and his men. "I've checked your work and have found it to be very competent," he started. "My congratulations to you and your men. I hope you don't mind if my men bind you for now so you don't try to do anything rash." He motioned for two of the guards to secure the arms of each of Henri's team. When they finished they placed Jack and Mike farther back in the cave where the passage was still fairly large. The other three were taken down to the river, put on a small rowboat, and taken to the other side. They were led up the pathway near the detonation site. But they were considerably closer to the abutment end and at a lower elevation below a limestone bluff. There the guards securely tied them to a stand of small maple trees. Baxter waved the guards back to the cave to gather up the remaining supplies and load the wagons.

"You see," Baxter started, "I didn't really need your expertise so much as I needed you at this bridge site. You, Henri Mueller, have acquired quite the reputation in the south not just for bridge building and explosive techniques, but for your intriguing work at the Treasury Department as well. Our cause has been well aware of your interest in the various gold shipments that have disappeared from the Union trains over the past months. I'm afraid that you were getting too close to discovering the techniques and patterns of how we choreographed our strategy. After all, we wouldn't want you interfering with our future endeavors, now would we?"

Fred interrupted Baxter's thought. "So, why bring us all the way to Alabama to kill us? You could have done it back in Maryland and saved a lot of trouble."

Baxter glared at Fred and started to respond but was cut short by Frank. "Well, Fred, who better to take the blame for blowing up a bridge than Henri and his team? Think how it will look to the Confederate cause when the headlines read that the world-renowned explosives expert missed the train and was killed instead?"

A sly, wicked smile coursed across Baxter's face, but he said nothing. He pulled out a small, gold pocket watch from his side cuff and checked the time. In the far distance a soft whistle could be heard. "Gentlemen," the colonel said, "I believe I have a train to catch."

CHAPTER 5

The guards finished moving the remaining boxes and extra items into the wagons. All that was left were three canisters of the explosive. Seth, Baxter's red-haired assistant, unscrewed the lids and carefully removed the flasks. He took a small pedestal, placed it on the ground, and fixed some rocks around it to hold it in place. The pedestal had a square top affixed to its vertical shaft. Seth balanced the three remaining flasks on the square top and carefully backed away. He casually spat a wad of tobacco juice from his fat little face. It hit the ground beside Jack. Seth started laughing at him but then started wheezing so badly that he doubled over in a coughing fit. When he finished his hacking, he straightened up and said, "When the bridge blows up it'll knock those flasks off the pedestal. You two will go up with it." Then he turned and gurgled in laughter as he waddled away.

Jack looked over at Mike for a reaction but he was already in motion. As soon as Seth turned his back Mike scooted himself over to a collection of rocks on the ground. He used his fingers to juggle a small, sharp stone into his grasp. He quickly wormed his way back over to Jack and told him to flip over on his side. Mike grunted next to him and started to work the stone back and forth over the rope binding Jack's hands.

"Hey, watch my wrists," Jack whined.

"Oh, quit your bellyaching and be quiet," he fired back.

Within a minute he had the rope sliced in two. Jack wriggled his hands free and unlashed his feet. Then he swirled around and untied Mike. Within five minutes they crept around the flasks and inched towards the cave's entrance. As they moved outside in the long shadows of dusk, they noticed John, the quartermaster, off to one side. He was down on one knee gathering up some leftover papers that had fallen out of the satchel he was carrying. A revolver was strapped to his hip. He was so occupied that he never noticed Jack's long arm reach out and grab him by the collar. An instinctive reaction, though, caught Jack off guard and he was caught full face with John's left fist. Mike quickly stepped in with a punch between the quartermaster's eyes and he collapsed on the ground. Jack's face was bleeding from the hit and he stumbled back. "He has mighty hard knuckles for a paper cruncher," he moaned.

Mike looked at John's hand and commented, "No, just a mighty big ring."

He held up the man's arm and showed Jack the silver ring with the huge opaque stone on it.

"No time to look for souvenirs," he said. "C'mon, we have to get to the others before that train reaches the bridge."

The two men raced to the river's edge and knelt behind some bushes. Baxter was high above the limestone bluff and a few hundred feet off to the side, out of view. Mike pointed at their companions struggling against some trees below the bluff right next to the abutment that was wired to explode. They both jumped into the river and found that it was only a couple of feet deep. The sluggish current helped to quicken their pace. There was the distinct shrill of a train whistle growing louder behind them. They reached the other side, grabbed some willow branches, and pulled themselves up the slick bank. It was easy for another sixty feet before the sides of the valley tilted upwards. Fortunately, there were plenty of handholds from trees to hasten their climb. About two-thirds of the way up the incline, they intercepted a pathway that led them to their companions.

Frank sarcastically called out, "About time you guys showed up. What took you so long?"

Without breaking the pace, Mike knelt and started to untie Fred's hands. Jack worked the ropes binding Frank's arms and quickly released him. It wasn't long before Henri was also free. He looked across the river and said, "Let's move it; the train is starting across the bridge. We've only a few minutes to get away before that lunatic blows this bridge sky high."

They ran down the pathway that led away from the bridge abutment. The heavy locomotive had just reached the last span when there was a series of enormous blasts. The first shock wave blew all five men off their feet. When the tiny glass flasks attached to the piers exploded, they took out all the supporting members that fastened the iron to the limestone. The abutments at each end of the bridge exploded into showers of rock and masonry shrapnel. Without support the iron bridge surrendered to gravity and collapsed in a sickening cloud of smoke and fire. The train, full of Confederate soldiers and freight, folded up like an accordion as it fell toward the river bottom in a shrieking conglomeration of iron and steel. Off to one side, in the cave where Mike and Jack had been detained, the violent shaking of the ground collapsed the pedestal that the flasks were balanced on. The glass containers fell and broke, igniting another monumental explosion that rocked the surrounding landscape. Rocks and debris flew across the river and pelted the unconscious group of five as they lay scattered but hidden among the timber on the hillside.

CHAPTER 6

It was well after dark when Henri aroused. Small blurs of light glowed from the few fires left burning in the debris field where the bridge once stood. His head pounded and his ears buzzed with an unending ring. He slowly shook his head back and forth hoping to clear his mind and sharpen his senses. He rolled over onto his side, scooted to a small boulder, and pulled himself up to a sitting position. In the valley below, the strong, full moon bathed the carnage of the two explosions in an eerie, ivory-colored light. He could just make out the shadows of a number of men moving in and out of the train wreckage. They carried oil lamps and seemed focused on one particular area in the debris. Every now and then he saw a flashy glimmer of something reflecting the lamplight. He watched the activity for a number of minutes and then was lost to darkness again.

Frank heard voices in the distance. The brilliant sunshine hurt his eyes so he opened them slowly. His body was covered with dust, dirt, and debris from the two explosions, but he had suffered no injuries. He rolled on his side and saw Henri a little way up the path leaning against a small boulder. Dried blood matted the side of his head but he appeared to be breathing regularly and deeply as if he was only sleeping. Once again he heard voices. He sat up and looked around. The surrounding trees had absorbed much of the flying rock and masonry shrapnel. The timber that faced the two explosion fronts was splintered and raped of much green foliage. Stone missiles that

30

did penetrate the natural canopy of wood were minimal. Henri, Frank, and Jack were around the edge of the bluff when the flasks ignited. Fred and Mike were not so lucky. They were still on the pathway below and to the side of the abutment and were partially buried in debris. Frank got up and hobbled over to Henri. He heard voices again, turned his head, and found that he could see the wreckage site through a cleared swath in the trees. A group of men climbed over the wreckage like ants on a discarded melon rind. They had pulled bodies from the twisted metal and stacked them like cord wood on the far side of the shallow river. Frank turned back to Henri and gave him a gentle shake. He immediately opened his eyes, looked at Frank, and then surveyed the situation. "At least my headache is gone now," he started.

"I can imagine the one you had," Frank commented. He reached up to Henri's head and separated the matted hair with his fingers. "With all the blood, I'm surprised it's such a small cut." Satisfied that Henri was fine, he turned to find his companions.

"Help me up," Henri said. "I can give a hand now."

Frank took Henri's arm and helped him to his feet. Then both men hobbled back up the path toward the bluff near the abutment. Jack was already stirring when they reached him. He had also just been around the limestone corner and was only knocked out and covered with dirt and dust. They helped him to his feet and the three of them rounded the corner on the path. One of Mike's arms extended from under the debris pile. The men started picking the rocks and tree fragments off of him.

Jack was the first to notice that he was still alive. "His arm is still warm," he began. "There, I see him moving his fingers."

They picked up the pace in removing the pile until they were able to extract him. Mike's legs looked broken. He was covered

31

with pasty, dirty blood. Jack carefully slapped his face a few times until he came around. Surprisingly, Mike opened his eyes and responded favorably. He was obviously in pain but did little to complain about it. The three men picked him up and carried him up the path and around the bluff out of view of the abutment.

Then Frank realized that Fred was missing. He ran back to the debris field and started to claw at the pile of rubble. Jack and Henri came around and studied the situation. Some large tree trunks, blown down by the shock wave, protruded from a mountain of limestone rock and dirt. Apparently, when the abutment end blew, it showered the pathway with stone.

Jack returned to tend to Mike while Henri moved forward and helped Frank move debris. After a half an hour they had made little progress. Frank noticed during a short break that the number of men working on the wreckage had increased. Some men had begun to move up the hillside toward their side of the bridge. Henri also saw what was happening. He put his hand on Frank's shoulder and said, "If we stay here much longer, we'll be discovered. Judging the size of this debris pile, it is very doubtful that Fred survived the blast."

Frank looked back at Henri in tears and said, "I know it. But I had to try. I couldn't leave him without trying."

They moved back around the bluff. Jack had splinted Mike's legs with some branches and some linen torn from his shirt. He looked at Henri and said, "Mike's in a bad way. I don't see how we can carry him out of here. He has a lot of deep lacerations and has lost a lot of blood. I've bandaged up what I could, but I'm afraid if we move him he'll not make it. I suggest that you two get moving and leave us here. I'll take care of Mike and see to it that he gets proper care."

"You know it will be difficult," Henri started. "Your odds might be better with us. There's a Confederate train in the river down there with who knows how many dead soldiers on it. You two will be the only Union men in the area to take the blame. I'd say your survival rate is minimal."

"Maybe so," he replied, "but I'm sure that Mike won't make it if we try to move him any distance. Besides, the two of us can be pretty resourceful. Now, you better get moving before you two are also discovered."

Frank and Henri quickly whispered to one another and agreed with Jack. They both gave Jack a bear hug. Then Henri knelt down and looked at Mike.

Mike understood the situation. He reached into his bloody pocket and pulled something out. It was hidden in his grasp so Jack couldn't see it. He pulled Henri close, put the item in his coat pocket, and whispered, "Here, Henri, I've got a souvenir for you. Now you two hurry and get out of here."

Henri nodded in understanding, rose to his feet, and waved Frank down the path.

Jack watched until they were out of view. Then he turned to Mike and made sure that he was comfortable. Mike cleared his throat, turned his head to the side, and spat on the ground. It was red with blood. He stared at it for a moment, pursed his lips in thought, then looked up at Jack with a sly grin on his face and asked in his worst aristocratic English, "So, how's yer suthern dialect, y'all?"

★ ★ ★ ★ ★

PART 2

★ ★ ★ ★ ★

CHAPTER 7

The view from the mine tunnel was incredible. Heavy timber draped the mountainsides like a dark-green curtain. Nearby, a mountain stream gushed with fresh snowmelt from the higher elevations. Up at timberline, the snow still covered gray fracture rock and made the barren peaks look like high-topped ice cream cones.

Derek Borden surveyed the beauty from his mine tunnel and took a deep breath of the clean, cool mountain air. He set the pick and shovel off to the side and sat down on a boulder at the edge of the debris dump. He opened a small box that he had set there earlier and pulled out a piece of jerky along with some dry bread. His supplies needed to be replenished and he planned on taking the next day to descend the trail into Silverton to visit the newly constructed general store. He had accumulated some promising samples of ore that he felt sure would assay high in silver. His hope was for enough of the precious metal to trade for adequate dynamite and fuses in addition to his regular monthly food rations.

Derek had come from the coal mines of western Pennsylvania. The dirty work and coal dust had caused his health to deteriorate. He was tired of the noise and smoke that the great industrial revolution had churned out during the Civil War. Near the end of hostilities, he decided to pack up and head west to seek his fortune in the newly discovered mining districts of the Colorado Territory. He also hoped to bring some health back to his bones by the change to a cleaner climate.

Derek was a small man, just over five feet tall. His round, jolly face with a short nose and long, fluffy beard made him look like a small elf. In spite of his size, he was strong, with limitless stamina. Derek was a professional coal miner, but the learning curve for working the mineralized veins of the high Rockies was trying his patience.

Early the next morning, Derek led his mule down the steep and narrow wagon road that followed Mineral Creek toward Silverton. In 1875 Silverton was a growing western mining camp situated high in the western slopes of the Rockies. Early prospectors had wandered into the area as early as 1871 and 1872 looking for gold color called "float" in the rivers that tumbled out of the high mountains. Rather than gold, they found large quantities of silver, enough to mine profitably in spite of its lower dollar-to-ounce value when compared to gold. When the Brunot Indian Treaty was signed in 1873 miners were given the legal rights to prospect the area. By 1874 and 1875 real mining took off and the town sites of Howardsville, Eureka, Animas Forks, Mineral Point, and Silverton popped up overnight. Derek's mine was still in a relatively virgin territory up Mineral Creek, north of Silverton, toward Red Mountain.

Derek followed the dry dirt road into Silverton and tied his mule to the hitching post in front of the Silver Heel saloon. The saloon had been around since the town first began. Though not the biggest, it seemed to have the freshest news of what was afoot in the territory. He walked in and saw his friend James sitting at one of the tables talking with a skinny, blond-haired man.

Derek had met James a number of months ago when he first came to the area. James was a good "people person," pleasant to be with and always willing to give a hand. He was a well-built man in his late thirties, about six feet tall with grayish-blue eyes.

Visiting with all the miners on a regular basis seemed to be one of his favorite pastimes. Another was investigating Indian writing that he found scattered about the county. Gus, the proprietor at the general store, provided him room and board along with a small payment in exchange for making deliveries to the mines in the areas. As a result James knew about everything there was to know about the Silverton locale.

James glanced up, saw Derek, and broke into a smile. He shook hands with the skinny man, pushed up from the table, and walked over to greet Derek.

"Derek, so good to see you. What brings you down out of the mountains? Is it time to restock already?"

Derek grasped his hand and received his warm greeting. "Yeah, I've run out of explosives and thought I'd restock my food supply at the same time. Say, you remember the last time I was in town you were asking me about some Indian markings that you were studying? I found some further up the creek from my workings a couple of weeks ago. I was returning from hunting over in Barrow's Park and took a short cut across the saddle at Red Mountain Pass. As I came down the Mineral Creek side I noticed a flat spot on a rock face that almost looked like it had been chiseled. It had some of those Indian markings you showed me last fall on that flat surface. I'm going hunting the day after tomorrow and was wondering if you wanted to go see them with me."

James's eyes glinted a little bit when he heard the news. "Yes, by all means. I'd like very much to see what you've found. I'll meet you at your mine a couple of hours after sunrise. Will that work for you?"

"That will work fine," Derek replied. "Maybe we'll get some elk up there and you can help me bring it down. Beats doing it myself!"

"You bet," James smiled. "I'll bring my rifle along. Hey, I

have to load a shipment to take to the Anvil Mine for Gus. I'll look forward to our appointment day after tomorrow."

The men shook hands and went their separate ways. As James left the saloon he accidentally bumped shoulders with a fat, little, red-haired man who was coming in through the swinging doors. "Watch where yer going," the man wheezed.

"I'm sorry. I didn't mean to bump you," James responded.

The man spat a sickly gob of chewing tobacco on the wooden floor. "Just make sure it don't happen again."

He forced his way by and waddled across the room to a table and sat down. James stared at him for a moment, and then went about his business.

CHAPTER 8

James was out early that morning preparing for the hunting trip. He went to the livery to borrow one of Gus's mules to ride up to Derek's mine. As he opened the corral gate the old colored stableman, Louis, yelled from the barn, "Hey, James, Gus told me to tell you to take Deer Jumper up to Derek's today instead of one of the mules."

James liked Louis. He was a small former slave who escaped from his Louisiana master in 1862. The Underground Railroad network smuggled him to northern Illinois. Then he slowly made his way west. He was uneducated but skilled in working with horses and mules. He never really had a name, but decided that since he had lived in Louisiana for forty years, he would take on the name of Louis. He had a way of becoming excited when he told a story, and his voice would pick up tempo and octaves at the same time.

James turned and responded, "Why is that, Louie?" Louis answered in his high, shrill voice, "Well, a man came in late last night and caught Gus in the barn while he was looking through the harnesses. He said he wanted to rent all the wagons and horses for the next four weeks. He was mean looking. And ugly. Had a big scar across his throat." Louis motioned a finger slicing across his neck and then continued, "Yes, sir. I was watching from the saddle room next to the harnesses when he come in. Gus, he said that he couldn't afford to rent out everything for that long because it would hurt his business. Well, the man, he took out of his coat a bag weighed down heavy. He untied it and dumped a bunch of gold coins out right there on the shelf next to the harness bolts. Then he says," Louis paused for a second to catch his breath, "he says, 'Will this be enough as a deposit? I'll give you the same amount when we bring the wagons and teams back four weeks from Tuesday. I want them harnessed up and ready to roll by tomorrow evening at five.' Well, Gus, he looked at the gold coins and then looked back down at the man. He was really short, you know. And then he looked back at the coins, put them back into the sack and said, 'Tomorrow at five. They'll be ready.' Imagine that, five wagons and ten mules. And what's a feller like that gonna do leading a train out that late in the evening? Hmmm? You tell me, what's a feller like that gonna do? Why, he won't be able to see once the sun goes down, and then there's been reports of . . ."

James rolled his eyes and cut Louis off. "I don't know, Louie, but it sounds like you got your work cut out for you. So, where's Deer Jumper anyway?"

The old man looked across the corral and said, "Over there. I'll get him for you."

"No, that's all right," James interrupted. "I'll go fetch him."

He got Deer Jumper, saddled him up, and was on his way as the sun peeked over the high ridge near Kendall Mountain. The cool, crisp ride up the valley reminded him that springtime came late in the high mountains. After two hours he could smell the fresh, smoky pine scent of Derek's cook stove. His cabin sat about eighty feet above the mine entrance. It was made from native timber that Derek cut and trimmed from the tailing site. He didn't believe in wasting material so he hand-cleared the site where he knew the over-burden rock from his tunnel would be dumped. The two-roomed building was placed a little higher and quite a bit further back into the mountain than the mine entrance. James rode past the mine and up the narrow trail to the cabin. "Yo, Derek. You ready to ride?" he yelled.

"Sure am," came the muffled reply from the cabin. Derek slammed the cabin door on his way out. "Did you remember to bring your rifle?"

"Sure did," James responded as he patted his saddle-mounted rifle. "Wouldn't miss a good hunt."

Derek mounted his mule and led James down the trail past the mine and toward Mineral Creek. Then they picked up the regular trail and headed up toward Red Mountain Pass.

"Looks like Gus let you use his good riding horse," Derek commented.

"Yeah, I thought that was quite admirable of him," James said as he looked at Derek's ride. "Sure beats one of those lumpy mules!" The rush of the mountain stream enveloped their laughter as they rode up the trail.

After a number of hours the great peak of Red Mountain came into full view. It towered thousands of feet above the surrounding landscape and could be seen for miles. Red oxides of iron tainted its sides and made it glow like a red ruby in the midday sun. The trail branched about one thousand feet from the summit of the pass and followed a series of small, shallow ravines on the lower flank of the mountain. They all looked alike to James and he became disoriented by the sheer number. Derek watched the trail intently, then stopped and dismounted. He climbed over some small rocks and debris to a rock face and pointed at a design on the wall that was covered by a gritty moss. James slid off his horse and scrambled over to where Derek pointed. It appeared to be a circle surrounded by four smaller circles. Derek said, "That's it. Not much to look at. Just those circles."

James wistfully replied, "Maybe so, but this is what I like to study. I have pencil and paper in a pouch in my saddlebag. I think I'll draw a diagram of it."

Derek replied, "You do that while I do a little hunting. I don't have much affection for gawking at old drawings on rocks. I'll throw your pouch to you."

He worked his way back to the horse, removed a small packet, and tossed it over to James. "I'll be back in about an hour; that all right with you?"

"Sounds good," James said.

He moved back over to the rock face and examined the markings. Derek was correct that they were chiseled into the rock face. He could see the shallow, even chip marks under the moss. He opened his pouch, took out a small brush, and gently wiped away the vegetation. With each stroke he realized that the circles around the perimeter reminded him of a compass rose. Contained in the top circle a small "R" and "M" were embossed in the stone. The other surrounding circles were empty. The middle circle was not really a circle but an oval shape. In the middle of it was the letter "Z." Five flat, deeply chiseled lines moved away from the oval toward the upper right. Three of those lines appeared to be followed by a dot; the last two had three dots each to the left of the line. Four shallower lines radiated from the oval straight down or opposite the "R" and "M." There was also a series of ten dots punched on the lower right of the oval along with one shallow and one deeply chiseled mark.

He pulled out a small notebook from his pouch and ruffled through the pages to one in particular. It was a diagram of another rose that he located a number of years earlier in the southwestern part of Nevada. It had the same peculiar circles, lines, and dots but in different directions and amounts. The center oval was embossed with an "N" and the top circle with the letters "D" and "V." He also had one other rose in his papers. A companion of his in the northern section of Nevada collected it near a vast inland lake.

James drew the rose with its particulars in the notebook and added some measurements and notes. He reassembled his pouch and climbed down the rocks to his horse. The peak of Red Mountain towered over him like an ominous wizard reluctant to reveal its secret. He turned around to see Derek coming back to meet him. He seemed quiet and serious.

"I saw some men watching you from the upper ridge," he started. "I was following some tracks near the summit when I noticed a reflection just beyond those boulders." He pointed back down the path to a large pile of boulders near the fork in the trail below the summit. "I couldn't tell how many of them there were, but I think we better head back toward Silverton. I wouldn't want to run into them after dark."

They remounted their animals and immediately headed down the trail in silence. Every now and then Derek glimpsed shadows and movement behind them. After a couple of hours of descent they came around a bend in the trail and saw a man on a horse approaching them. As he got closer James breathed a sigh of relief as he recognized the familiar outline of his friend.

"Hey, amigo," James chimed with a smile as he came within earshot.

Derek also grinned as he recognized the skinny, blond man that James had chatted with from the saloon.

"You don't know how glad we are to see you," James continued. "Do you have your rifle with you?"

His friend tilted his head and raised his eyebrow at the question and replied, "Of course I do. I never leave home without it. Why do you ask?" The breath from his puffing horse warmed James's leg as the horses brushed one another. The men locked eyes, their bodies tensed with a touch of fear. "Let's pick up the pace," James said curtly.

There was little conversation. Along the trail they decided during their whispered conversation that Silverton should be their immediate goal. But as they approached the trail to Derek's mine, rifle shots rang out. Wisps of dirt and dust erupted behind and in front of their horses. The only spot unscathed was the trail leading to the mine. They spun around and dug their heels into the horses' sides. Clouds of dirt from the hooves mixed with lead drove the men up the winding trail.

"When we reach the top, jump off and head to the mine," yelled Derek. "We'll be safe in there."

As the horses reached the plateau of the tailings pile, the three men jumped off, rolled on the ground, recovered themselves, and sprinted for the dark entrance. Bullets whizzed off the tunnel walls as they went deeper into the dark.

"Here, come this way!" Derek yelled. He slipped off to the side into another opening. Without pausing, he fumbled in the dark for something and a small flame lit up the tunnel and eerily floated to a cabinet mounted on the wall. A frustrated voice said, "Where did I put it." A pause, then, "Ahh, here we go." The match quickly grew as the wick on an oil lamp ignited. A dim, yellow light permeated the black. Cool air crossing James's cheek carried the oil lamp smoke down a side passage into the inky blackness. Derek handed off the lamp, then opened another cabinet on the wall. "This is my backup," he grunted. As the doors swung to the side they saw a row of fresh Winchester rifles. "Indian treaties don't mean a whole lot around here," he added. They took the rifles out, opened some cartridge boxes, and loaded the weapons.

As James loaded the rifle he glanced across the tunnel. In the dim light he saw something that froze his blood. A canister was balanced on a small pedestal where the passageway forked. Then he noticed movement along the floor as a small rope attached to the pedestal slowly grew taut. "Quick, down the passageway!" he screamed. He stretched out his arms and forced his friends into a run down the dark corridor. Derek barely kept the lamp lit as they stumbled and scraped their way around a sharp bend as an enormous explosion ripped through the tunnel and everything went black.

CHAPTER 9

Early morning sunlight pierced the mist like a comet tail in space. An old man and his son swayed back and forth on the buckboard of a freight wagon on their way into town for supplies. Late-night thunderstorms, common in southern Indiana during the spring months, left a patchwork of puddles along the roadway. Their horses slopped lazily along, leaving hoof holes in the softer spots of the muddy lane, and the wagon left deep, narrow tracks. The clean, fresh scent of early March filled the air.

As the creaky old wagon entered the town, the old man elbowed his son and said, "Hey, Johnnie, wake up. We're in Jonestown." His grizzled old hands pulled gently on the reins. The team of horses immediately responded and pulled up to the hitching post in front of the hardware and feed mill. "I'll tell you what, Johnnie. This time, you get the flour, feed, and bagged supplies from Ralph, and I'll get the mail from the post office and newspaper from the printer."

"Ah, Dad, give me a break," the boy whined. "We've been on the road for almost two hours. I think my breakfast is still undigested. You don't want me to cramp up and become an invalid do you? Besides, that sounds too much like work."

The old man detected a grin sneaking out from under his boy's wide-brimmed hat. Johnny always was a practical joker. He probably got it from his dad.

"Too much like work, eh?" his dad echoed. With that, he

bumped Johnnie with his hip and knocked him sideways off the buckboard. But the young lad was quick and grabbed his father's sleeve as he rolled off the edge. His momentum was too much for his father's weight and they both slipped in slow motion off the wagon and onto the soggy ground of Main Street.

Ralph, the storeowner, heard the commotion outside, ran to the doorway, and indignantly remarked, "Really, Gerhardt, you shouldn't fight with your youngest son."

Gerhardt looked up from the street and replied in shock, "Fight? Fight? I don't see any fight! Ralph, you know me. I would never get into a fight, especially with my own boy. He would probably win." He got up, brushed the sandy dirt off his clothes, and continued, "I've got some supplies to pick up for the farm. Johnnie and I made up a list and he will help you load the things onto the wagon." He walked over and handed Ralph a crumpled piece of paper with writing scribbled on it. He turned around and helped his boy up, and then they both went about their business.

The feed and hardware store was Johnnie's favorite place. He enjoyed the smell that was peculiar to the store. The scent of feedbags, salt, new clothes, boxes, and supplies mingled together to form a unique aroma full of friendly memories. He wandered up to the counter and eyeballed the jars of candy sticks. Ralph watched him out of the corner of his eye and said, "Getting a little big for candy sticks, aren't you, Johnnie?"

He was a large lad. At eighteen he was fully grown, at least in height. He stood a towering six feet three inches with blond, curly hair and hazel eyes. He also had the muscles that one gets from hard work on the farm. He had not started to fill out, as people tend to do with time, but was still lean and trim. His hands were large with long fingers like his father's and he had a strong grip.

"Oh, I dunno, Ralph," he responded. "You still like an occasional one, don't you? Why should I be any different?" He reached down and grabbed some feed sacks and began to load the wagon.

Gerhardt finished his errands by entering the post office. He waited at the counter for the postmaster. Like his sons, he, too, was a large man. He didn't tower above six feet but was muscular for his age. He had come to America in 1830, a young man looking for adventure and a new start. When he first arrived in the country, a young Austrian girl named Marie captivated him. They ended up being married in six months. The two of them homesteaded forty acres near a small German settlement called White Creek in southern Indiana.

They cleared the land and started farming. The property reminded him of Uffeln, his home in the eastern part of Germany. It was rolling ground along a small river. He spent a few years clearing the softwood timber off the bottomland and was rewarded with some of the most fertile cropland in the county. Over the years he purchased more ground and expanded his holdings to almost one hundred-sixty acres. His six sons were indispensable in developing the extra acreage. Over the years, though, two had tragically died. The others had created their own lives and moved on to other things in different states.

Johnnie, a pet name for Johann, was his youngest son. Gerhardt knew that it was almost time for him to set out on his own to discover his avenue in life. He had expressed intense interest over the past year in traveling out to Kansas to visit his older brother, Alvin. Alvin had moved out to the prairie back in the summer of 1865 with some other relatives from the old country. Eventually, he settled in the west-central portion of the state near a town built in the 1870s called Lincoln, Kansas. Last they heard he was doing well raising cattle and corn on his sixty-acre plot. Gerhardt thought, perhaps, next month he might give Johann leave to travel west and visit his brother.

The postmaster walked in from the back room and said, "Gerhardt, I didn't hear you come in. I'm sorry for the wait."

"That's all right," Gerhardt replied. "Do you have any letters for us this week?"

"Yes, I do," he responded. "I'll get them."

He disappeared into the back room again. Gerhardt could hear rustling of papers and the moving of boxes. After a few minutes the postmaster came back out with three letters and a small package. "Here you go," he said as he passed the items to Gerhardt.

He took them and thanked the postmaster. As he left the post office, he casually glanced down to see the return addresses. Two were typical letters from friends of the family back East and one was from Marie's family in Cincinnati. The small box, though, raised his curiosity. Its return address was from a town in the Colorado Territory that he had never heard of. He opened the package as he approached the wagon in front of the feed mill. Johnnie was tying down the last of the supplies in the back of the full freight wagon. As Johnnie finished the last knot he looked up to see his father drop some papers and fall to the ground.

CHAPTER 10

"Ralph, run for the doctor!" Johann screamed as he ran for his father. He sprinted around the wagon toward his father. As he knelt and took Gerhardt's head in his lap, the doctor came and ordered Gerhard transferred to his office. Once there, the doctor checked his patient's vital signs and propped him up, since he was reviving.

Gerhardt mumbled at Johann, "The papers; let me see those papers."

Johnnie asked the doctor, "Will he be all right?"

"Yes," the doctor said. "He got excited and was overwhelmed by emotion. He should be fine in a few hours. I will keep him here tonight so he can rest."

Johann was relieved. He assumed that something that Gerhardt was reading must have been the cause of his collapse. He rushed back into the street to find the package and letters. One of the Samaritans handed them to him as he exited the doctor's office. He sorted through the materials that were opened and found a number of items including a formal letter, a diary, and some maps of the western territories. The letter was addressed to Gerhardt Schreiber, White Creek, Indiana, and the return address read, "Sheriff, Town of Silverton, Colorado Territory." He started to read the letter.

"Dear Mr. Schreiber, it is with sincerest regret that I must inform you of the death of your son, Frederick James Schreiber, on the date of March 5, 1875."

Johann stopped reading and immediately knew what over-whelmed his father. The federal government had told them that Fred was killed in March of 1864 somewhere in Alabama. Johann remembered a government official arriving home with Frank to give a detailed account as to what happened. He was young at the time but remembered that it had something to do with a Union raid on a bridge in Alabama. The target was destroyed, but Fred and some others were lost in the process. Johann continued reading the letter.

"James was a valued member of the community of Sil-verton, in the Colorado Territory. He was killed in a min-ing accident along with another citizen, Derek Borden. Regrettably, the bodies were unrecoverable. I've enclosed what I thought were the valued contents of his holdings found in his room. Clothing articles and such were donated to the local church. Please accept my condolences. I am in your service, Sheriff Clayton Guston."

He refolded the letter and placed it back in the envelope. His attention went to the diary. The cover was locked but he located the key among the other personal effects and opened it. On the back of the cover in script was written,

"To Fredrick James Schreiber, July 3, 1864. May you always remember to dream, from Mike and Jack."

He scanned the diary entries and was surprised to see that they were written in the old German dialect that Gerhardt had taught them when they were growing up. His father felt that each of his children should be fluent in their native language so they never forgot where they came from. He went to the first page, noticed the same date as on the cover, and began to read. "I want to thank Mike and Jack for giving me this diary to record my thoughts. They have shown themselves to be men of high caliber and great integrity. I am honored to be in their debt." Johnnie wondered who the two men were who had had such an impact on his brother's life. He read a little further. "This is the first opportunity to write since our group left Washington in February. For privacy, I've chosen to script all my entries in Old German that Dad taught us. We have been on the privateer *Revenge* for a month now sailing for California via the horn of South America. The captain promises it to be a four-month voyage barring any inclement weather. To my chagrin, I found out there are two other men onboard with the name of Fredrick. Since I'm the newest of the crew, I am now known by my middle name, James. I shall try to recollect our activities and actions starting in February."

A voice from behind interrupted Johann's reading. Ralph asked if he could do anything to help, since Gerhardt was staying the night. "No, that's all right," Johnnie responded. "I can take the wagon back to the farm. Mom and I will come back in the morning for Dad. Thanks for the offer, though."

He went in to check on his father one more time before leaving. Gerhardt was sleeping peacefully, so Johnnie slipped out, settled into the buckboard seat of the wagon, and began the long trip home with the supplies. It was a slow, bumpy ride, but his interest in the diary was so great that he read more of it in spite of the road conditions.

"February 14, 1864. Our team assembled today with a small group of generals brought together to discuss the most recent gold theft. Henri talked at length with his friend, General Grant, about Confederate troop movements in the area of the most recent incident—in Maryland. Grant maintains that there were no Confederate bands roaming the area that were capable of exploding a bridge of the size and type spanning the Maple River. They discussed the possibility of Rebel renegades, but it didn't make sense. These operatives had an organized supply line, an escape plan, transportation for the bullion, and secrecy to carry it out to completion. Grant suggests an outside organization may have choreographed the Maryland site along with five others in the past eight months. Undersecretary of War Edgar Burns thinks that the idea is ludicrous and leans more toward an elite group of Confederates working privately under Jeff Davis. Our group is assigned by Burns to gather some factual information at the Maryland site while rebuilding the bridge."

Johann scanned a few entries, and then that for March 7 caught his eye.

"March 7, 1864. The bridge repair is ahead of schedule. Jack and Mike have been combing the countryside under the guise of looking for materials. A local merchant told them about a group of men well-armed and dressed in old, worn Confederate uniforms bivouacked approximately one mile downriver from the bridge. After the area was vacated, Jack and Mike searched the site and found the usual camping debris along with some strange empty canisters with screw lids. One other item in particular was a jeweled silver bracelet."

"March 8, 1864. Early morning, around two. The Rebels ambush our campsite under a full moon. Many of the black workers have scattered. We are taken prisoner and shipped away. We have the feeling of being recognized by reputation as the Rebel colonel in charge sought the five of us

55

out. We were bound, gagged, and put in a covered wagon. As the wagon pulled away from our encampment we heard a number of weapon shots as if the balance of the work party was executed."

Johann continued reading about their transfer to Fort Sumter, Binky, Colonel Baxter, and the arrangement to blow up the Tallapoosa River Bridge in Alabama. Once again he slowed down and reread the March 15th entry, which was the portion about Fred being buried under the explosion debris.

"Henri and Frank agreed with Jack's assessment of the situation and left the area to try and return to Union territory. Just after they left, Mike had the idea of obtaining two Confederate uniforms to try and pass as soldiers on leave fishing under the bridge when the explosion occurred. While waiting for dark to steal two uniforms from some dead soldiers, Jack went to the debris pile that I was under to pay his respects. Two trees had fallen over me when the bridge exploded. They fell across some rocks along both sides of the trail and created a cubbyhole that protected me from other falling debris. I was rendered unconscious for a number of hours and then was able to partially dig myself out. Jack heard me, and helped uncover me. I was unharmed but for a number of bruises that took a long time to heal. That night we stole three uniforms and were successful in pawning ourselves off as planned. We were able to get Mike and ourselves transported by rail to Mobile and into proper medical care."

Johann's wagon hit a large bump and he dropped the diary onto the floorboard. He reached for it and read the opened entry.

"November 9, 1865. My feet finally touched dry land since leaving New Orleans early last year. Mike, Jack, I, and two other able-bodied crewmen were transferred off the *Revenge* to the *CS Shenandoah* off the coast of California. The warship lost five crewmen to disease in transit from their last port of call in Australia. The captain wanted to replenish his crew before sailing to the Bering Sea. In August of '65, news of the war's end reached the *Shenandoah*. The captain decided to surrender his ship in England, a country known for its sympathies to the Confederates. Today we landed in England and I mailed my first letter home."

In the distance he heard his mother calling from the farm. He put the diary away and prepared to tell her about the unusual set of circumstances that would change their lives forever.

CHAPTER 11

Henri sat on a bench and idly tossed small pebbles in the pond. He casually watched the ripples as they spread effortlessly away from the impact point and gradually disappeared. It was his last day in Washington, D.C. He was moving his family to the Colorado Territory to work for a man who was building toll roads. After the Brunot Indian Treaty was signed in 1873, new mining regions popped up faster than hotcakes on a lumberjack's griddle. A young entrepreneur named Otto Mears had contacted him in the fall of 1874 requesting his engineering expertise. Come spring, when the last of the snowmelt was gone from the high country, Mears wanted to start construction on a set of toll roads to the new mining fields.

Henri had put the man off since November. But over the icy months of the New Year, he had grown cold to the limitations of his importance at the Treasury Department. At one time, years ago during the war, he was assigned to uncover information about Union gold shipments that disappeared. A series of misfortunes left his investigative team either dead or imprisoned by Confederate soldiers. He and another man managed to escape after weeks of foot travel from central Alabama to the northern lines in western Tennessee.

When he finally returned to Washington and presented his assumptions, he found that he quickly fell out of grace with the undersecretary of war, Edgar Burns. His repeated requests for an investigation into the events that led up to the bridge affair in Alabama were met with skepticism and indignation. In the spring of 1865, after Lee's surrender and Lincoln's assassination, it was impossible for him to obtain any aid in searching out the matter. The government was clearly more interested in putting the whole Civil War affair behind itself. Henri's role with the Treasury Department was shifted around a number of times until he found himself gradually demoted over the years to a nondescript position stuffed away in the marble halls of Washington.

Henri's thoughts were interrupted by a mildly annoyed girl's voice behind him. "Uncle Henri, I've been looking all over Capital Park for you."

Henri looked up with a smile and responded, "I was right here. You just weren't looking in the right spot!"

"Aunt Emily's going to be furious that you've been gone so long," she continued.

Henri looked up at the girl and replied, "Well, Sarah, I think she'll get over it." He gazed with a smirk on his face at his niece.

Sarah was orphaned during the battle of Cold Harbor, Virginia, in June of 1864. Henri's wife, Emily, was the sister of Sarah's mother. She immediately took the child into her home even though Henri was still missing in action. When Henri finally returned home in November of 1864, he embraced his new daughter and vowed to settle down to a quieter life. His conflict with cabinet officials secured his wish.

Sarah's false exasperation evaporated into a smile as she helped Henri to his feet. She was a beautiful young woman, on the verge of turning twenty. Her sandy hair fell into two disheveled braids that framed her round face. Her blue eyes sizzled with energy in anticipation of each life event.

She was a contrast to Henri, who was now in his middle sixties. Henri's silver hair was in need of a haircut and he stooped slightly. His square face was furrowed by wrinkles of time, laughter, and worry. He never lacked energy but his zest for life had waned over the years. Sarah had heard him whisper at times to Emily about the horror of the war and the pain it left in him. Henri found it difficult to rationalize his inability to help his friends and to follow up on their passage. It had been almost eleven years since his capture at the Maple River and Henri still felt the weight of their failed investigation and lost companions. Even with a friend in the White House, he was unable to locate them. Grant was knee-deep in scandals and his administration was overly cautious about extending favors to those of the Treasury Department. Over the years his gait grew slower and he leaned a little bit on Sarah for stability.

"I think the Colorado air will do you some good, Uncle Henri," Sarah commented. "Besides, this Otto Mears fellow thinks that you have a lot to offer him. It'll do you good to feel like you are accomplishing something again."

"Yes, perhaps so," Henri replied.

"Are you still planning on stopping in Kansas to see that old friend of yours on the way out?" she asked. "That town he lives in seems so far from the railroad. It'll add a week or more on to your trip to see him."

"Oh, most definitely," he answered. "I sent him a note a number of weeks ago that I wanted to stop in. I owe him my life, you know. I feel obligated to stop in since I'll be that close. Besides, I have something special I want to leave with him."

"Oh? And what might that be?" she quizzed.

Henri reached into his pocket and pulled out a large silver ring. It had an opaque stone embedded in the center with some circle designs around it. He rolled it around in his fingers before offering it to Sarah.

"My, what a gorgeous ring!" she exclaimed. "Where on earth

did you get it?"

"It's a long story," he answered. "One that is far from over."

CHAPTER 12

One of the main players in the railroad system of the mid-seventies was the Union Pacific Railway. Their rail system covered most of the transport going west from Omaha, Nebraska, and Kansas City, Kansas. Train terminals at the many small whistle stops across Kansas provided the only outside contact with a growing country for the small, rural communities. In return, the towns provided life-giving coal and water for the continued journey of the iron horse on its westward trek.

Such was the train that Henri and his family were on, as they became another number in the mass migration west. They boarded in Washington, D.C., and headed west on a railway that operated twenty-four hours a day.

Henri awoke on the third day of travel somewhere in the middle of Ohio. The morning mist put a chill into the air that made him shiver under the woolen blanket draped over his shoulders. Sarah noticed him awake and moved forward to the vacant seat next to him. "So, how did you sleep last night?"

Henri, usually in good spirits, grunted unfavorably. "I had a better bed in the war."

Sarah smiled but understood. She hadn't slept the best either. "I see we are in Ohio someplace," she began. "Look at the mist rising off of the fields." She pointed off in the distance. "It must have rained some last night."

Henri gazed out the window for a moment, and then responded, "Yes, I think it probably did." In spite of his grumpiness, Henri could appreciate the beauty of the pastoral scene. It was a mark of his inner character to always adapt his feelings to coincide with the beauty of a moment. After all, he would say, such moments come and go. To appreciate them to the fullest, in spite of one's mood, is the mark of a well-balanced individual.

Sarah and Henri watched the fields and woods pass by in silence for a while. Her eyes wandered down to Henri's hand and she remembered the beautiful ring that he had shown her back in Washington. "Uncle," she began, "you never told me the tale about the ring that you showed me back in Washington. Can you tell it to me now?"

He turned his head toward her and smiled. "Sure, I can do that." He reached into his coat pocket and pulled out the ring and handed it to Sarah. She rolled it over in her delicate hand and marveled at the unique stone setting fixed in silver. The stone was an opaque bluish color, not a turquoise color, but a deeper, richer blue. It was oval in shape and was affixed in a setting of silvery gold. Around the perimeter of the setting were eight small circles. Each circle had either a dot or a line through it except the top circle, which had a small star emblazoned inside it instead. The ring was molded with a peculiar design, almost like a leaf-like décor. It hadn't tarnished like silver sometimes does, but retained a never-fading luster and brilliance. She inspected the inner face that rests against the finger and noticed an inscription. It said in bold letters, "New Beginnings." She tried the ring on her middle finger, but it was hopelessly too large. She smiled and said, "Whoever owned this must have had large fingers."

Henri smiled and took the ring from her. "Yes, an old friend of mine got this ring back in the war. He gave it to me as a parting gift. I never saw him again. Looking at it reminds me of him, and some of the things we endured together."

Sarah could see that Henri was moved by his memories, and

started to get up.

"No, you don't have to leave," Henri insisted. "Really, it's all right. It was a long time ago." He cleared his throat and rubbed his nose, then continued, "It struck me as odd that a Confederate military man would have such a ring in his possession. In fact, it wasn't as unique as it looked. I actually noticed a similar, if not identical, ring on the hands of two or three other soldiers, one colonel in particular. I only caught a glimpse of it, but I'm sure it was the same design."

Henri sat in thought for some moments as his mind reached into the past. The ring rolled around in his fingers almost to the same beat as the pounding train wheels on the track.

"So, tell me, Uncle Henri," Sarah said, "what's the story about this ring?" Her blue eyes fixed on his and didn't waver or blink.

His gaze held hers for a moment. He then asked, "Do you remember back in the early 1800s when Aaron Burr was tried for treason?"

She blinked and pulled her head back a little as she responded, "I vaguely remember it from history class."

Henri continued, "In a nutshell, Burr, after finishing his term as vice president under Jefferson, became disillusioned with the way the new government determined policy. His intent was to separate territories of the newly acquired Louisiana Purchase apart from the United States and begin his own sovereign state. He wrote letters, met with men of influence, and found financial support for his idea. Unfortunately for him, one of his staunch supporters, General Wilkinson, changed his mind, sided with Jefferson, who was in his second term, and had him arrested. To make a long story shorter, he was eventually tried and found not guilty by Judge Marshall because his act of 'treason' was not actually carried out in a time of war. Anyway, the point is that Burr wanted to create an independent country within the borders of United States territory. Follow so far?"

Sarah nodded her head that she understood. "But what does that have to do with the ring?" she doggedly asked.

Henri grinned at her impatience. "Let me continue. During the Civil War it was rumored that a group of men were contemplating a similar event in the western states. Information was extremely hard to obtain. They were unknown until a number of gold shipments in the early 1860s began to disappear from both sides. At first, it was thought that the thefts were war efforts carried out by special operations. But it was discovered that the operatives wore neither a blue nor a gray uniform. They were operating in their own interests."

He pointed at the ring and continued, "One thing that seemed to stand out was that everyone we came across that was involved with the thefts wore a ring or a piece of jewelry that was similar to that one. Anyway, General Grant thought that the stolen gold was to be used to finance a new government someplace in the west. Undersecretary Edgar Burns thought the idea silly. He attributed the thefts to war efforts on each side. When hostilities ended in 1865, there was no faction or movement that emerged to implement such a plan. With southern reconstruction and then the transcontinental railroad opening up the western frontier at such a fast pace, the present administration considered the affair to be nothing more than a rumor and did nothing to follow up on it."

They sat in silence for some moments as Sarah absorbed the information. Finally she quipped, "But what of the gold?"

"Yes, the gold," Henri thought out loud. "By war's end there were many shipments that were unaccounted for on both sides. As far as I know none ever surfaced." He paused for a moment in thought. "I can't imagine how anyone could reintegrate so much precious metal back into an economy without it being noticed." His eyes narrowed and his voice grew cold. "But I'm sure there is someone out there who knows."

CHAPTER 13

A shrill whistle heralded the train's arrival into Indianapolis, Indiana. The schedule called for a one hour stop in order to restock supplies on the train and accommodate the exchange of passengers. A flurry of activity ensued as baggage handlers barked out names of customers, people disembarked, and reloading of the train with supplies, fuel, and new travelers progressed. In spite of the arduous trip, Henri and his family stayed in their seats and dozed. Punctual as ever, after exactly one hour had passed, the conductor called out his "all aboard" signal and the train once again resumed its westward trek.

As the train picked up speed, the conductor came through the end door of the car, leading a young man. "Here is a fine seat, sir," the conductor said in a fatherly tone. "You'll have an excellent view of the countryside." He helped him stow his gear in the overhead shelving unit and indicated his seat. The young man offered the conductor his ticket, thanked him, and sat down.

Henri poked Sarah in the side and nodded toward the man, who was seated five rows ahead of them. "Looks like you might have some fun conversation with that fellow. He looks about your age."

Sarah rolled her eyes. "Why are you always trying to hitch me up with someone?"

"I'm not trying to hitch you up," Henri responded. "I think I'm a pretty good judge of character by my first impressions, and he looks like a nice, easygoing type of guy." Henri's eyes squinted a little as he continued, "Judging from his appearance I would say that he comes from the rural part of the state. See how his clothes don't quite fit him? I'd say he's wearing hand-me-downs from an older brother. He probably wouldn't quit growing and his parents couldn't afford to buy him new clothes every four months."

Sarah giggled at his comments and chimed in. "Did you see his gear? It looked like someone had sewn some pieces of canvas and tied them together with rawhide. And look at his shoes." She craned her neck around the seat in front of her and stared down the aisle. "They look like large leather boots. Too big for his feet." She poked Henri back and said, "Or maybe his feet are too big for him." She started laughing a little bit louder.

Henri looked down at his own feet and said, "Maybe so, maybe so." Then he looked at Sarah and said sarcastically, "I didn't know you could be so cruel."

"Oh, I don't mean to be," she said. "You started it, you know. Talking about his clothes that were too big."

Henri paused for a moment and said, "Yeah, you're right. I'm sorry. I shouldn't have started poking fun at him. You know, he might be a really nice chap. He is only a stranger until you say 'hello.' "

Sarah looked Henri in the eye and smiled. "Perhaps," she said. "Perhaps."

Once again the train rocketed out of the city and into the farmland and forests of Indiana. After a few hours the regular clatter of the wheels on the rails lulled Henri back to sleep. Sarah gazed slowly around the cabin and smiled inwardly at the hypnotic nodding of the passengers in unison with the swaying of the car.

As evening approached, the conductor came in and lit the small kerosene lamps overhead, anticipating the coming night.

In the dim light her eyes eventually fell on the young man that she and Henri had been joking about earlier. He seemed focused on a small, black book that he held near his face so he could read in the fading light. As the conductor passed her, she pardoned herself and whispered a sentence or two in his ear. He looked at the young man, nodded, and proceeded up the aisle to his side. Then he leaned over and asked, "Would you like the light turned up a little brighter so you can read?"

The man looked up and smiled. "That would be great. Why not show me how so I can turn it back down when I'm done?"

The conductor smiled and explained the simple operation of the lamp and how to trim it if need be. The man got up, listening intently, and adjusted the light to his liking. Then he thanked the conductor and sat back down.

Sarah smiled again inside and nodded off.

The high plains of Kansas offered scenery that Sarah never thought could exist. To command the best view, she went to the last car on the train and received permission from the conductor to stand on the railed platform overhanging the cold, steel rails. She surveyed the scene from her safe perch. The tracks over which the train had passed stretched as far as her eyes could see. There were no bends, no hills; only two glimmering rails running to one focal point where the sky and land met. Off to either side, endless vistas of green grass raced to meet the overhead canopy of blue. Spotty cotton clouds floated lazily above and left their dark shadows on the windswept plains. In the distance, she could see a strange brown mass moving slowly toward the east. Bewildered, she spoke aloud to herself. "What on earth is that?"

A quiet, but steady voice responded behind her, "What is what?"

Sarah quickly spun around and saw the young man standing behind her. He wasn't looking at her, but had his eyes fixed in the direction she had indicated.

"What is what?" he asked again, this time looking quizzically at her.

She blinked a couple of times, and then slowly pointed back out to the east. "That brown shadow. Over there." She moved her eyes in the direction of her pointing hand. "It seems to be moving like it's alive or something."

"Oh, yeah, I see it now. I'll bet it's buffalo. I read that the high plains, especially in Kansas, have great herds of buffalo. It seems they are so numerous that they look like a brown sea on a green backdrop when they move."

Sarah looked at the buffalo for a moment, then turned and faced the young man. "My name is Sarah," she said.

"How do you do? I'm Johnnie."

There was that awkward moment when two people don't know what to say. Sarah turned around to the east and asked, "So, how do you know about buffalo?"

"I have a friend who owns a general store where I'm from. He also has a collection of books that tell stories and have photos of the West in them. I read them when I get a chance. Have you done much reading on the West?"

"Just a little," she replied. "Ever since my uncle decided to relocate to the Colorado Territory, I've done some reading on the area."

"Why is he moving out there?"

"A man who builds toll roads in the mountains hired him to work for him."

"Oh, I see."

"Where are you going to?"

"I'm going to see my brother. I haven't seen him since I was a small boy. Dad decided that it was time I got to know him better."

"Where does he live?"

"He lives on a farm in central Kansas. He moved out there ten years ago with a group of relatives who wanted to get a part of the cheap land before it was all gone."

And so the doors of conversation opened up. Sarah and Johnnie ended up chatting about many topics including buffalo, railroads, farming, and the West. Time flew by in the presence of newfound friends.

CHAPTER 14

Seven days after leaving Washington, D.C., Henri and his family arrived in Brookville, Kansas. The town, originally surveyed and platted by the Union Pacific Railroad in 1869, was a regional hub that serviced the rail line across Kansas. As the train pulled into the outskirts of the third-class city of 2,000, Johann and Sarah noticed the characteristic wooden water towers on limestone bases and the brick roundhouse that provided the repair stations for the overland locomotives. Roundhouses were set up by the railroads every fifty to eighty miles along the rail line so the steam powered engines had ready access to servicing facilities. The iron horses needed daily maintenance such as oiling and cleaning, and it was found to be cheaper to locate frequent service houses rather than risk potential breakdowns along the tracks. The semicircular, brick structure arced around a central turntable capable of handling the largest engines. Two men on the perfectly balanced wheel could rotate a typical 125-ton 4-4-0 locomotive with a forty-five-ton coal tender. The roundhouse had ten bays for servicing the engines and provided the most advanced technical repair facility in the central part of the state.

By the mid 1870s Brookville had become an important shipping point for cattle on the Union Pacific. Cowboys drove herds of cattle from points as far away as Texas to be loaded on the freight cars heading east. Great corrals and loading bins accommodated the masses of marketable beef. Deep wells powered by windmills sucked water from hundreds, if not thousands, of feet underground and stored it in the above-ground reservoirs, making available the amounts of water required to sustain the bawling cattle and screaming locomotives that would power the bovines eastward. Granaries nearby held tons of wheat and corn ready to be shipped east.

In addition to the bustling railroad and cattle industry, the town housed a number of businesses essential for a western town. Many brick and lumber structures lined the dusty main street. There was a furniture store, hardware store, flour and feed stores, a cigar and tobacco shop, grain elevator, restaurant, flour mill, two hotels, a livery and feed stable, two lumberyards, a Knights of Pythias building, and four general merchandise stores. Miscellaneous homes and an occasional empty lot filled in the balance of the area. On the western edge of town the magnificent single spire of a limestone church towered over the endless prairie. At the east end, the train station for passengers cozied up to the main roadways traveling north and south. Beyond the station stood the railway service hub and the switching and loading facility. Full employment in the local railroad shops, flour and gristmills, and downtown businesses favored the Brookville residents for a prosperous future.

Brookville was where Henri planned to separate himself from his traveling companions in order to see his friend for a few days. He had arranged with the railroad to have his family, along with their belongings, transported to Denver, where they had purchased a home through a friend of theirs. He would catch up with them in a week or so. Emily and Sarah were to spend the night with him in Brookville, then continue on to Denver the following day. It would give the family an opportunity to freshen up after nearly a week of train travel and to absorb the change of scenery to that of the western frontier.

Henri had made arrangements for them to stay at the Central

Hotel, the oldest housing facility in town. It had originally been called the Cowtown Café. The white clapboard building was built in 1870 and had acquired a reputation, at least in central Kansas, for making the best fried chicken in the country. Ironically, Johann's brother had made him reservations at the same establishment and was scheduled to pick him up the following day. The extended roofline of the Central Hotel overshadowed the wooden walkway that lined Main Street and provided some comfortable shade from the toasty midday sun. Henri, with his family, and Johann checked into their respective rooms, quickly freshened themselves, and then settled on two wooden benches and a few creaky rocking chairs on the front porch and waited for the girls to come down for a late lunch.

A steady wind blew in from the west and added a cooling touch to the shady front porch. Henri leaned back in his rocker and remarked to Johann, "Looks like you and Sarah enjoyed the ride on the back of the train coming in."

"Oh, yeah," Johnnie replied. "We seem to have a lot in common." He looked over at Henri. "I can't believe that Brookville was your destination, too."

Henri smiled and responded, "Seems like a pretty small world, doesn't it?" He paused for a moment to enjoy the breeze, and then continued, "Sarah said that your brother came out here a few years ago to farm?"

"Yeah, that's right," Johnnie answered. "I was only eight or so back then, so I don't remember a whole lot about it. Dad told me that when he got home from the war he wasn't the same. It probably had to do with my other brother getting killed. He was only home for a few months when he decided to head to the Kansas territory for a fresh start."

Henri furrowed his brow, looked over at Johann, and listened intently. He thought for a moment and added, "It was a difficult time for many people after the war. A lot of folks moved westward away from the memories of that time."

Johann nodded in agreement, but remained silent.

Henri's gaze wandered down the road and noticed a lone horseman slowly riding toward the hotel. The dapple gray horse held its head high, as did the tall man riding in the saddle. He wore a brown hat and a beige shirt. Dual saddlebags, one behind him strapped to the leather saddle and the other draped over the horse's neck, had a light coating of road dust on them. He steered the horse to the edge of the boardwalk in front of the hotel and stopped. His crystal-blue eyes scanned the patrons relaxing on the porch. When his eyes met Henri's, he squinted slightly, smiled and said, "Henri Mueller, I believe you've gotten a little grayer since I saw you last."

Henri cocked his head a little, paused for a moment, and then quickly rose from the rocker, smiled, extended both hands and exclaimed, "Frank, it's you! I didn't recognize you at first. It's so good to see you!"

Frank dismounted, bounded up the porch steps, and gave Henri a bear hug. "Yeah, it's great to see you, too! And who are your companions?" he quizzed.

Henri turned around, noticed that his family had joined them, and promptly introduced them to Frank. He then looked over at Johann, extended his arm and said, "And this young lad is a new friend that we met on the train. His name is Johann, but I regret I haven't caught his last name yet."

Frank turned to face the young lad and looked intently into his eyes. As if recollecting an old memory, he smiled and said, "Johann, it's me, your brother, Francis Alvin!"

Johann blinked a couple of times and enthusiastically responded, "Alvin, it is you! I'd never have recognized you after all these years!"

As they gave each other a bear hug, Henri's eyes doubled in size as he realized the connection. "Frank, this is your younger brother," he said. "I don't believe it! We traveled with you all the way from Indiana and never even . . ." His voice trailed off.

After the usual quick succession of questions, answers, and short tales that newly found friends talk about, they all settled down to a more casual exchange of events and stories. "Let's go into the restaurant and continue this over some chicken," Henri suggested.

Everyone on the front porch heartily agreed and the entourage worked its way inside to experience some of the best fried chicken in the country.

No one noticed the man on the bench in front of the mercantile exchange across the street. He seemed overly interested in the reunion under the overhanging porch of the Central Hotel. He slowly rose from his seat and walked next door to the telegraph office. Silver spurs on his leather boots made a distinctive jingling sound as his boots clomped on the wooden boardwalk and then faded as the office door closed behind him.

CHAPTER 15

Everett Steele looked through the small panes of his office window toward the mountains that hedged the city of Golden, Colorado. Late winter snow still draped the high peaks that surrounded the mature mining community.

Everett and his brother, R.W., had been mesmerized by the tales of gold for the picking in California back in late 1848. The two left their home in Virginia, took a ship around the horn of South America, and landed in San Francisco early the following spring. They migrated inland and located a rich placer deposit on the Yuba River. Everett's natural business talent helped to quickly develop the claim into a highly profitable and stream-lined operation. In only a month they had expanded to a number of other claims covering a large portion of the rich mining belt and had consolidated them into a corporation. By fall the brothers were able to move back to San Francisco and leave their mining interests to capable managers.

Their next venture was opening a series of hardware and mercantile exchange centers. These stores proved to be as lucrative as the mining fields because they supplied the tools and equipment to each new boatload of hopefuls heading to the gold fields. Good investments in property and the success of the stores and mining operations led the brothers to open the Third Bank of San Francisco the following summer.

As time progressed, the gold frenzy began to fade. The easy gold, removed by simple separation mining techniques, had exhausted the river gravel bars. Hydraulic and deep-rock mining were the only hopes of keeping the golden ball rolling. The Third Bank made loans to new corporations that developed hydraulic mining techniques along the gold-bearing rivers in hopes of finding new untapped placer deposits in the hillsides. They also wrote notes to companies that experimented in a new deep-rock technology designed to locate the veins of gold thought to exist further inland deep in the bowels of the High Sierra. Unfortunately, many of the companies went bankrupt when the elusive metal was not found. The bank retained ownership of a few of the bankrupt properties, but sold most of them in order to remain solvent.

In 1858, word came to Everett from John Gregory, a friend back East, that new prospecting areas in the far western edge of the Kansas Territory, just beyond Auraria, the future city of Denver, looked promising. He decided to grubstake Gregory and ordered him to keep him closely apprised of the results. In late May of 1859, Gregory informed him that the creek beds were rich in placer gold, ready for the picking. Hoping for another California gold rush, Everett and R.W. secured proper management for their interests and headed east as quickly as possible.

They arrived in the early summer of 1859 and settled in Mount Vernon, one of the leading areas of rich gravel bed deposits. John Gregory had already established claims for them to work in the now famous "Gregory Gulch." He had moved further into the mountains into the newly developed towns of Black Hawk and Central City. As in California, the rivers and creeks were rich in gold. But the deposits were not as plentiful as the 1849 rush further west. It was discovered that the placer deposits were wash-out debris from rich quartz veins buried high in the mountains. As a result, extensive deep-rock mining techniques were employed in the high country to excavate those rich deposits. Though the investment to remove the precious metal was expensive, the returns from the concentrated mineral veins were enormous.

Once again, Everett and R.W. were in the right place at the right time. Their luck in the placer beds, along with the knowledge of deep-rock mining management, property procurement, and the retail industry, placed them in the enviable position of duplicating what they had done in San Francisco. By late 1860, they had created a rich network that promptly propelled them to positions of importance in the newly developed territory.

It was a sudden blow to Everett when his older brother suffered a mental collapse in March of 1861. R.W. was moved to the rising city of Denver for extended treatment and Everett relocated in 1862 to Golden City, the newly designated territorial capital located midway between Mount Vernon and Denver. From there he was able to watch over their investments and make regular visits to his brother. He also started another bank, First Bank of Golden City, and became deeply involved in the governmental structure of the newly designated Colorado Territory under the governorship of William Gilpin. His political etiquette, business savvy, and financial prowess made him one of the most influential persons in the territory.

By the early seventies, Everett had built an empire that had fingers throughout the Colorado Territory, the States of Kansas and California, and many areas in between. He had offices in Denver, the territorial capital since 1867, the city of Golden (shortened from Golden City in 1872), and Georgetown, another booming mining community closer to the Continental Divide. Many of his peers in business speculated that Everett had enough influential contacts in Washington, D.C., that he might be after some political office in the near future.

As he gazed out the window in his Golden office, his private secretary came in with a folder full of telegrams. "Sorry to interrupt you, sir, but these telegrams need your immediate attention." She held the brown folder out for him to take.

"Just set them on my desk for the moment," he replied without turning.

She complied and left the room without further comment.

After a few minutes, he let out a deep breath, turned, and sat down in the leather chair at his desk. He reached for the folder and opened it. The first communiqué was from Thomas Patterson, one of two territorial delegates to Congress informing him that the president, Ulysses S. Grant, would definitely be visiting Central City, Idaho Springs, and Georgetown at the end of March. Everett's mouth curled into a small smile as he nodded his head in understanding. He had a lot to prepare for the president's visit as that was only a week or so away. The governor had put him in charge of the president's itinerary, travel, and lodging arrangements. Those weren't the only details he was responsible for, though. He also had to address the president's public relations with the mining communities. That, in itself, was a potential problem. Until recently, most of the mines in the region were large producers of silver. But, in 1873, the United States government passed a law that demonetized the silver dollar, making gold the sole legal tender coinage in the United States. This governmental decision created an angry atmosphere in the towns where silver out-mined gold by a large margin. Everett had his hands full preventing the angry mine owners from having a confrontation with Grant over this issue.

The second telegram was from an associate of his who was transporting a large cargo of valuable materials from the southern part of the territory. It requested a specific time of delivery at the Silver Plume Mine and Milling Company, just west of Georgetown. Everett thought for a moment, and then scribbled down some figures and directions for a reply.

He opened the third telegram, read it slowly and thoroughly, and then turned to gaze out the window. His earlier smile collapsed as he unconsciously sucked on his lips and contemplated a reply. Dark gloomy clouds of an approaching storm gradually covered the bright noontime sun. Long shadows high on the mountains over Loveland Pass stretched like dark daggers toward the cozy little town of Golden as hints of thunder rolled down the valley. He turned to his desk, inked a pen, and scripted a definitive answer. He put the two answered messages back into the folder, and then opened the center drawer of his desk. He pulled out some old style sealing wax, lit the wick, and dabbled some on the edges of the folder where the closing sheets met. When there was ample wax on it he took the large, silver ring from his finger and emblazoned the quickly drying wax with its impression. It left a large oval with eight smaller ovals around its perimeter deep in the brown wax on the folder. Then he called his secretary in and said, "Make sure this goes immediately to Sam over at the telegraph office. He'll know what to do with it."

She nodded her head and slipped quietly out the door.

CHAPTER 16

The blackness in the mine was total. James recovered his senses. All, that is, except his sight. Dust weighed heavy in the air and breathing was difficult. Sharp rocks littered the floor and cut his hands as he searched his perimeter. He could feel warm blood oozing down the back of his head, his back, and his legs. He heard something stirring ahead of him. "Mike, is that you?"

"Yeah, it's me," a shaky voice responded. "What on earth happened?"

"They put one of their signature canisters on a pedestal just like in Alabama," James jeered. "How about Derek? Can you feel him near you? He ought to be close."

"Yeah, here he is," Mike said. "He's still unconscious. I can hear him breathing, though. How long have we been out?"

James slowly felt his way to Mike's side, then leaned with him against the mine wall. "I haven't a clue." They sat in silence for a few moments as each regained his thoughts. Finally, James continued, "Judging from where I saw the charge, and how far we ran, I'd say we've got a long way to dig."

Mike sensed the grim futility in his voice and thought it best to change the subject. After a few moments he asked, "Did you find it?"

"Find what?" James said.

"You know, the compass rose. Did you find it?"

Mike sensed a ghostly chuckle. "Yeah, I found it," James said. "Lot of good it does now." Some more silent moments passed and he continued, "So, what did you find out in Silverton? You seemed anxious to meet us."

"That I was, dear friend," Mike started. "Around ten this morning, two groups of men rode into town. One had traveled over Stony Pass, the other from Durango. I counted twelve in all as they entered the Silver Heel. I wandered over that direction and peeked in the window. I saw him. Colonel Baxter. And I also saw that fat, little guy who wheezed a lot. The one who spat at me in the cave in Alabama."

James angrily cut in. "I knew it was him. When I bumped into that short guy at the saloon the other day I knew I had seen him before. And then when I picked up Deer Jumper, Louie told me about a man with a sack of gold leasing the entire fleet for four weeks. His description sounded like our tobacco spitter."

"Gus's entire fleet?" Mike quizzed.

"Yeah, all his mules and wagons." James related the incident with Louis that morning. He also told Mike about the trip up Mineral Creek, the compass rose and the patterns on it, along with seeing the men and their rush down to where they had met.

Mike listened with his eyes closed, absorbed in every detail. Then he said, "I saw some of those men head up toward Red Mountain Pass around eleven in a mighty big hurry. I'd put money on it they were looking for you and Derek. In fact, I'd also wager that our tobacco spitter saw you leave this morning and followed you up the mountain. He left the canister on that pedestal for us in the mine and ordered his friends to herd us in here with the rifle fire." They were quiet again, lost in thought when Mike continued, "You know, when we get out of here, we won't be able to go back to Silverton. Those guys were all over the town. I imagine that they'd shoot us on sight."

"*When* we get out?" James exaggerated. "Don't you mean, *if* we get out?"

They heard some stirring in the darkness behind them. Derek was shuffling around in the dark looking for something. "All right, where are they," he mumbled. "Scooted down in that pocket, did ya? Well, c'mere then." A match ignited and chased off the darkness. "Quick, look for the lamp before the match goes out," Derek said.

Mike chirped, "Here it is." He moved a few rocks and picked it up. It was a little more dented and the glass was broken, but it still held oil. Derek lit the wick as the other two watched in anticipation. The flame flickered and brightened as the sooty smoke lazily floated down the dark corridor. They looked around their crypt. The passage they came in had collapsed. Shattered rock littered the tunnel. Total darkness tends to amplify the senses and such was the case with their injuries. The warm feeling James had felt was only a little blood mixed with salty sweat. Other than some scrapes and bruises the men were physically fine.

"So, why did you say you couldn't go back to Silverton?" Derek began. His face was a dirty crimson in the amber lamplight. He continued, "And who, in thunder, tried to kill us. And why?"

Mike looked at James and then at the collapsed tunnel. "I guess you might as well tell him."

"It may take a while," James said.

Derek pointed at the cave-in with his inverted thumb and grumbled, "I'm not going anywhere."

James sighed and began his tale.

CHAPTER 17

"It really began back during the Civil War," James started. "Mike and I," he paused for a moment and looked over at Derek. "By the way, this is Mike."

The tense trip down from the saddle on Red Mountain hadn't left time for a proper introduction. Derek's gaze met Mike's as they each nodded toward the other.

After the brief interruption, James continued, "Mike and I were part of a group that was assigned by the Treasury Department to investigate the disappearance of a number of Union gold shipments. At first it seemed typical of the Confederates to take the gold for their effort. But one incident changed my mind.

"Our group was captured in early 1864 and through a series of circumstances was compelled to help blow up a bridge in Alabama. We thought that the man in charge, a Confederate colonel named Baxter, was taking the bridge out in order to keep advancing Union forces from using the rail system to transport troops from Mobile to inland locations. Instead, he blew up the bridge, along with a troop transport train that was crossing it, and laid the blame on us.

"Mike and I were hurt in the explosion. But, with the help of our friend Jack we disguised ourselves as Confederates and made it into Mobile for medical attention. I wasn't hurt bad so, while Mike was recovering, Jack and I discovered that the troop train was carrying a shipment of gold from Mobile to Richmond.

We also found that the gold was quietly returned to Mobile and was placed on the privateer *Revenge*. Thanks to Mike's quick recovery and fast sailor talk, the three of us managed to get passage as deck hands." James grinned at Mike.

Derek repositioned himself along the mine wall and grunted, "How did you find out that the train was carrying a shipment of gold?"

James replied, "Even in Mobile they have their saloons. Jack and I made friends with one of the crewmates of the *Revenge* over a bottle of bourbon. We found him along the waterfront late one night looking for something to do. After the first bottle, he loosened up. He told us that the Mobile city council wanted to transfer the treasury contents to Richmond for safekeeping and made arrangements for the train to be guarded by the Fourth Alabama Regiment. That in itself was no secret. But he also had a friend who was at the recovery scene. He said that they found no trace of the gold shipment. About two weeks later, our friend said that a Confederate colonel approached the captain of the *Revenge* about transporting a special cargo to California. He offered a large sum of money, in gold, to do so. The captain agreed, but said that he needed to obtain a few more hands in order to make the trip."

Mike cut in and continued the story. "I was out of the hospital by then and we used Richard, the man who was in the bar, as an icebreaker to get an interview with the captain. I told him that we were three Confederates without an assignment because our unit was wiped out in a battle. We all had good sailing experience and were looking for a quiet way to sit out the rest of the war. Apparently, he had a schedule to meet and was short-handed. With the threat of Mobile falling, he took us on and the boat sailed the following morning."

Derek nodded in understanding and then asked, "So, you were on your way to California, then?"

"Well, yes and no," James replied. "The boat sailed around the horn of South America and continued on to California. But the *Revenge* sailed beyond San Francisco and met another boat about one hundred miles north of the city along the coast. I'm almost sure that it was Union. There was no flag flying, but the crew wore tattered Union uniforms. Their insignia wasn't correct though. It was military instead of navy. And some of the men wore silver bracelets that definitely were not government issued. I think whoever was on that ship had killed the crew and taken over the vessel. Anyway, we were ordered to help in the transfer of some very heavy cargo. Four of the *Revenge*'s crew transferred to the other ship."

"The *Revenge* never did put into port," Mike interrupted. "It immediately set course for England with the balance of its cargo of cotton."

James butted back in and continued, "And, to make matters worse, a few months later, in October, just off the coast of England, the captain transferred us to a newly commissioned Confederate cruiser, the *CSS Shenandoah*. It was a huge boat, almost 1,200 tons. Its commander, Captain Waddell, had orders to disrupt the whaling industry in the North Pacific and Bering Sea. We traveled almost 60,000 miles and never saw port until he finally surrendered his ship in November of 1865 in England."

"Hard to believe that was almost seven months after the war ended," piped in Mike.

"And then," James said, "we had to find transport back to the States. We ended up on another merchant marine vessel, the *Tally-ho*, which sailed east. It traveled to India, China, and a number of ports in between. I don't think Captain Wainscott really intended to sail back to the States. But, in spite of that, we became good friends with the captain and ended up sailing with him for a number of years. He was generous in sharing the profits of his cargoes with us. In fact, the eastern trade was so lucrative that we kind of lost track of the time and never did travel back to the States. But last year Wainscott decided to take a shipment to San Francisco. The *Tally-ho* dropped off a large cargo of silk and fabrics, and was going to pick up additional goods for New York. We had planned on going with her as the final leg of our voyage when a peculiar incident happened."

Mike continued, "Our partner, Jack, ran into an old friend. His name was Don Penrose, and he was part of the company that had hired Jack back in the fifties to do some deep-rock mining up in the Sierras. The company went belly-up when no ore was found. Jack went east and Don stayed in the San Francisco area, ending up with a job working for the superintendent of the mint. One of his primary duties was to keep detailed accounts of gold and silver production for each of the mines in the northern part of the state. His figures were collated and put into a report to Congress once a year by the director of the mint.

"Anyway, over the years he noticed that one particular mine, the Atica Mining Company in the High Sierra, had an unusually high output of gold for its location. The reason it struck him as odd was because it was one of the spots that Jack and he had worked back in the fifties. He knew that there was no gold-bearing ore in the area, but, yet, here was an operational mine shipping large quantities of refined gold on a regular basis. On a visit to the location, he was not permitted access to the shafts, but was able to inspect the buildings and mill. The processing plant was a top-notch facility with a well-dressed and orderly work force. He noticed that the workers wore silver jewelry, probably a distinguishing mark characterizing the affluence of the mine. Nothing seemed out of the ordinary as far as the production process went and, since he was only there to verify the gold output, his investigation went no further. But the odd-ity of it stuck in his mind enough to share the information with Jack when he did see him."

James picked up the narrative. "Jack knew that the rock structure where the Atica was located could not produce the gold claimed. With the knowledge of a number of missing gold shipments on both sides from the war, the gold transfer years ago from the *Revenge,* along with the characteristic silver bracelets, we decided that the Atica might be a clearinghouse of sorts for reintegrating Confederate and Union gold back into the marketplace. It was decided that we should remain in the area and look into this new set of leads."

"We made friends with people in the towns near the Atica workings and obtained a wealth of information," Mike began. "Over time it was discovered that the mine was a closed operation. No one from the outside was ever hired. A skeleton crew carried on a maintenance routine on the buildings and provided a high security perimeter around the facility at all times. Once every six months a number of wagons, over a week's time, would enter the property. The mill would then be fired up for a couple of days, then, just as abruptly, shut down. The procedure repeated itself for as long as the Atica was in operation."

"One night," James went on, "Mike created a small landslide on the far side of the Atica's property. While the guards checked out the disturbance, Jack and I were able to sneak into the superintendent's office. I found a number of interesting items that we 'permanently' borrowed. One in particular was a collection of maps of the western territories. At certain locations on the maps were numbers corresponding to footnotes on their backsides. The footnote numbers were next to what appeared to be a collection of compass roses. There were ten total on the back of the first territorial map. All but one had been crossed out. One of the crossed-out roses was near the location of the gold transfer from the *Revenge.*

"A set of maps clipped under the main one had detailed routes laid out for travel from those ten roses back to the Atica. A separate, second collection of maps had the same type of system as the first. It also had ten compass roses on the back with corresponding footnote numbers. All but two of the roses on this set had been crossed out. The additional clipped-on maps in this set included routes laid out to a mine and milling facility near Georgetown, Colorado. A third collection of maps was of the eastern U.S. On it were circled locations that were identical to where war gold shipments had disappeared."

Derek interjected at this point. "It would seem that someone found a successful way to reintegrate stolen wartime gold back into the economy without being detected. And these 'compass roses' . . . That's not like the one . . ." His voice trailed off in thought.

"Yes," James filled in. "It is like the one you found on Red Mountain. I've been searching for that rose for quite a while. That section of the map was smudged so bad that I couldn't get exact directions to the rose itself. Apparently, these people have gone through a lot of trouble to choreograph a massive operation over a long period of time. I think each one of the twenty compass roses indicated on the maps represents a cache of stolen gold. The caches were buried in areas from which they could be transported to future rich mining locales where they could be reintroduced back into the economy as legitimate mining product. Judging from the maps, all but three of the caches have been reintegrated."

Light from the oil lamp grew dim. Derek stood to his feet and wiped the dirt and debris off of his pants. "I feel quite a bit better now," he commented. He reached down, picked up the oil lamp, and started to pick his way through the rubble deeper into the passage.

Mike looked quizzically at James for a moment and said,

"Where are you off to, Derek?"

Derek turned over his shoulder and replied, "I'm getting cold in here. Let's finish this story in the cabin." He turned, and, in the flickering light of the oil lamp, continued shuffling down the corridor.

CHAPTER 18

Mike looked wide-eyed at James as the light faded around a corner. They both jumped to their feet and stumbled blindly down the passage to catch up with Derek.

"What do you mean, 'Let's finish this in the cabin'?" Mike shouted ahead to Derek.

Derek responded in a casual tone, "You don't think a professional miner like myself wouldn't leave a back door to my tunnels, do you?"

James and Mike looked at each other again in wonderment. "You mean there is another way out of here?"

"Well, of course," Derek snickered. "Didn't you notice that the smoke from the oil lamp kept drifting further into the passageway? If it were closed off the smoke wouldn't travel. That tells me that my ventilation tunnel is still intact. I knew that there was a way out as soon as I regained consciousness. I just needed a little time to get my wind back and squeeze a story out of you two." Derek chuckled as he made his way deeper into the tunnel.

After another 150 feet, the tunnel took a sharp turn to the right. Above Derek's head was an adit, or a side spur, that angled sharply upwards. Smoke from the lamp slowly curled into the dark opening. "This is one of three ventilation shafts that bisect the side tunnels," he said. "I don't know if you noticed, but my cabin was actually built above the mine tunnel and further back into the mountain than what one might think.

This adit climbs at a fifty-degree angle toward the entrance to the mine, but surfaces underneath the cabin. I installed them not only for the ventilation benefits, but also as a way of escape from the cabin in case of Indian attack. It will be a tight squeeze, but we should be out in ten minutes."

Derek located another oil lamp hanging on the wall, lit it, and gave it to James. "I'm sorry I only have one backup light. One of you will have to walk in the dark. Why don't I lead the way? Mike, you are smaller than James, so you take the middle. James, you take the second lamp and follow. All right, here's a wood crate to give us a boost up."

Derek put a crate underneath the opening and pulled himself up. The passage was a tight fit, and the slope was uncomfortably steep. But the old miner had taken the time to chisel foot- and handholds in the culvert styled passageway to facilitate a relatively easy climb. As per his promise, in ten minutes or so, Mike and James could hear the bumping of wooden floorboards as Derek cleared some kick-outs and climbed onto the cabin floor. He helped the other two men out of the hole, reinserted the floorboards, and invited them to the table for a seat.

"I can't believe you held out on us," Mike smiled. "I thought for sure we wouldn't get out of that hole alive."

Derek grinned back and replied, "I never really thought I'd need to use that shaft as an escape route. I guess all the banged knuckles I got while putting it in paid off. Now, you mentioned that we couldn't show our faces in town again. Why is that?"

"These men have a very intricate intelligence system," James stated. "Who knows how long they've been trailing us. I would guess that they have people watching all the towns and busy spots between here and Georgetown. When there is as much money involved as we're guessing, they can't afford to take chances. And, the fact that they wanted to get rid of us tells me that we are too close to something not to be careful. Besides," he added, "we might have an advantage by being 'dead.' "

Mike walked over to the window and looked out. "I'm guessing they took our horses into town to report the tunnel collapse to the sheriff. He'll probably be out here with a team to investigate. If we are going to play 'possum,' we'd better be getting out of here soon."

Derek nodded in agreement and added, "As I recall, Horse Thief Trail runs across Red Mountain and along the divide. We can travel on it and eventually intersect the road that will take us in the direction of Georgetown. It is such a high trail that only a few people use it. Let's take some food and supplies from my stores to carry us through. I'll leave plenty here as evidence that no one has taken anything."

Derek loaded three packs with some foodstuffs and other supplies from the storeroom. In addition, he gave each of the men a pistol, along with some fresh ammunition. Other than what they could carry out, they left the cabin just as they found it, dirty dishes and all.

They exited out the back and started climbing up the heavily wooded mountainside. Progress was slow as there was no trail to follow and the grade was steep. Two hours later they topped a plateau and could dimly see the narrow road into Silverton. A grim trail of dust kicked up behind a contingent of horses and wagons moving up the pass. "Must be the sheriff," Derek thought.

A deer trail on the plateau made it easier for the trio to travel deeper into the mountains. After another hour they bisected Horse Thief Trail. Derek stopped at the spot and offered a piece of the trail's history. "The miners gave Horse Thief its name because Indians used it to transport stolen horses from Utah down to Mexico. It's not a big trail, but it follows the high mountains for most of its length and that makes it safe if you want privacy. We shouldn't run into anyone at these elevations.

So, which way are we going? South will take us a little east of Silverton toward Stoney Pass, and north will take us toward the Gunnison region."

James conferred with Mike for a moment and responded, "Perhaps we should double back and take a look at the compass rose we found on the saddle at Red Mountain. It will take some extra time, but if we can find out the secret to the code it might be valuable for the rest of the cache sites."

Derek responded, "Actually, it won't be that much out of our way. Baxter will undoubtedly have to take the wagons over Stoney Pass toward Del Norte, and then north toward Saguache. From there, he'll probably go over Trout Creek Pass and toward Alma. Then I would think the easiest direction for him would be over the pass to Breckenridge, across Georgia Pass and on to Georgetown. He's looking at a long trip over those roads. If we go north from here, we'll be heading toward the Gunnison area to begin with, so a side trip back to Red Mountain is almost on the way. If that's what we are doing, then it's north we go."

The men packed up their gear and headed north. Toward evening, they approached the compass rose. The men were unsure of how much time had elapsed since their entombment in the mine tunnel. James estimated that it was a couple of days ago. The mountain shadows lengthen quickly in the evening so the men were forced to make a quick camp. They located a depression surrounded by boulders up on a ridge above the compass rose. Here, they could make camp and start a fire without fear of its light being seen from below. Derek pulled some food from one of the packs and warmed it in an iron skillet. "Only one fork for each of us," he said. "Make it last the whole trip 'cause I'm not sharing mine!" The men hungrily ate what they had, leaned back on their backrest boulders, and gazed quietly into the sky.

CHAPTER 19

The travelers were at work long before the morning sun breached the towering peak of Red Mountain. Mike and James huddled around the pale lantern and re-examined the glyph chiseled on the rock face while Derek broke camp. "You can't remember any of the markings off the other roses or map?" Mike asked James.

"No," he fumed. "I made all those diagrams in my sketchbook so I wouldn't have to remember. But we do know that the riddle of the roses was only known to a very few; otherwise, anyone could reclaim the gold."

Mike stepped back from the rock face, swung the lantern around, and inspected the ground again. "I can't believe that there are no footprints, horse prints, or wagon-wheel marks of any sort. We know that this glyph is the final clue to where the bullion was buried, but there is no evidence that anyone was here to claim and load it."

"Yeah, that is odd," James thought out loud. "With all those men, wagons, and horses, you'd think there would be tracks everywhere." He rubbed his scruffy chin and slowly walked off toward the main trail, watching for tracks. Mike could hear him mumbling, "compass rose, compass rose" under his breath as he went.

James approached the main trail over the saddle of the pass. The meager light of dawn was enough to recognize the lack of wagon tracks in the main artery of traffic. In fact, there were no tracks of any sort on the trail. He walked back down the path toward Silverton with Mike following a short distance behind. After a quarter mile, he noticed a spot where wheel tracks from the freight wagons appeared. James turned and yelled to Mike, "They covered their tracks."

"Covered their tracks?" Mike quizzed with wonderment. "Why would they do that? They already have the gold. Why bother hiding where they got it from?"

"I don't know," James responded. "But, see for yourself. The tracks have been wiped out up to this point. Look, the horse and wheel marks just end."

Indeed, there was no indication that any animal or wagon had traveled beyond where the two men stood. It was as though the wagon train had fallen off the edge of the earth.

Mike shook his head in disbelief, looked at James, and said, "I guess we'd better make a run for Gunnison. We've got a long way to go."

James took one more look at the tracks, turned, and headed back up the pass. They returned to the glyph on the wall and noticed Derek looking at it with his head sideways.

"Derek, you're looking at it wrong," Mike snapped.

Derek ignored him and mumbled, "You know, this does look like a compass rose. Only it looks like it's sideways. Here," he continued, "if you rotate the oval with the 'Z' in it toward north, then the 'R' and 'M' face Red Mountain, but to our left instead of right. Now, let's imagine that the deep chisel marks are in increments of, say, one hundred feet; the shallow ones, fifty feet. Since the dots are pegged next to the flat mark, we can assume that they are a one-point additional deviation from the true degree of the oval pointing north. So, the first heading would take us three increments of one hundred feet, or three hundred feet, at a southeasterly direction of 136 degrees. When we reach that point we'll need to recalibrate our direction, subtract three marks, since they are to the left of the flat ones, and proceed another two hundred feet at a direction of 132 degrees."

Mike wondered out loud, "How do you know the deep chisel marks on the southeast quadrant are the first ones in the series?"

Derek replied, "I don't. But, judging from the fairly open line of sight in that direction, it would only seem logical to start in that direction."

Mike looked at the glyph again and saw that it was part of a sheer wall with no access around or up it. When facing the way Derek indicated, though, there seemed to be an open pathway leading the correct direction. "Go ahead and finish your line of thought," he nodded.

Derek continued, "When we reach that next compass spot, it looks like we change direction and continue on for 250 feet at a 270-degree angle. Finally, we go at 245 degrees for 150 feet."

"O.K., Derek," James began, "how did you arrive at that interpretation for all this?"

He looked over at James innocently and said, "Back in Pennsylvania, when the surveying crew mapped underground coal seams, they used a similar set of marks on the tunnel walls. Since there were no landmarks underground, they chiseled marks, not unlike these, on the wall whenever a tunnel would change course. It was understood that the lines and dots were always superimposed around an imaginary circle, or compass rose. The map drafters would follow them a few days later and note the markings on the walls, then transfer them to a survey map. It worked pretty well since each tunnel turn had a new heading and distance measure all in one spot. The only real difference here is that all the directions and distances are marked on one rose."

"Well, let's see if you're right, Derek," Mike responded.

Derek took his compass and started walking in the specified direction. James and Mike took a fifty-foot coil of rope that they had in the pack and started measuring off behind him.

Remarkably, the first sequence was fairly straight and without obstruction. They worked down the hill between some trees and ended up in an open spot where Derek took his next measurement. Once again, the direction was straightforward and offered no problem. They also noticed that the pathway was leading back toward the main trail, though on a lower level. The third and final segment directed them toward a rock cut in a small natural knob on a heavily wooded hillside. Derek made the final steps and looked around. "I'm guessing that we're in the neighborhood of their cache sight. Anyone see anything?"

The three men looked around, but saw nothing obvious. Derek then noticed a couple of horse prints in the soft soil where some water seeped out of the hillside. A little beyond the other side of the seep there was a large amount of brush stacked against an outcropping of rock. Derek moved the brush to one side and noticed a small tunnel underneath the ledge of exposed rock. "I think I've found something," he called.

James scavenged a fresh pine bough to use as a torch. He lit it and crawled into the opening. Fresh markings on the tunnel floor indicated recent activity. After thirty feet or so, the crawl way opened up into a larger chamber. He noticed that a number of ledges had been carved into the walls of the cave. One ledge in particular had rectangular impressions on it. As Mike and Derek squeezed into the chamber, James pointed out the markings. "I guess it's safe to say that this was where the gold bullion was stored. These impressions on the ledge and all the disturbed soil on the floor show that someone was here recently."

Derek looked around in the eerie yellow light. "It looks like this is a natural cave that was adapted just for storage. Don't see too many caves in this type of rock structure. Someone must have stumbled across it years ago. I guess it served its purpose, though."

They finished exploring the cave, and then returned to the main trail that led to the saddle. Derek suggested, "I had a thought. Let's take this trail on down to the valley beyond the pass rather than going back up to Horse Thief Trail. There is an Indian encampment there and the Ute chief, Ouray, is a friend of mine. I met him last fall while hunting along the divide. There's a chance we might be able to buy some horses from him."

The men agreed and headed north over Red Mountain Pass. Once over the pass, the trail descended into a wide valley dotted with beaver dams. Toward the end of the valley, the central creek dropped into a deep gorge. A small pathway meandered along the sheer walls hundreds of feet above the canyon bottom. Hayden Creek, named after the leader of the Geographic and Geological Survey team that explored the area the previous year, foamed and roared far below them. Their meager trail paralleled the gorge for two miles, then rose in elevation across the face of Hayden Mountain and then descended to Canyon Creek, just above the Ute settlement. In the distance they could see smoke rising from the campfires of the Indian settlement.

"I've never been to their actual encampment," Derek stated matter-of-factly. "I only know that Ouray invited me to visit and enjoy the water."

"Enjoy the water?" James and Mike replied in unison. "What on earth does that mean?"

"I don't know," he replied. "But I guess we'll find out." He nodded down the path at two Indians walking toward them.

CHAPTER 20

The two Indians were short in stature, maybe five foot two inches or so. Their straight, black hair hung freely on the cloth shirts that they wore. Baggy, brown dungarees covered the tops of their leather shoes, and each had a woolen blanket wrapped around his waist. They both held dirty rifles but showed no threatening signs toward the travelers.

Derek approached them and asked in broken words if Chief Ouray was at the encampment below. They nodded their heads in understanding and indicated that they would take them there. Derek acknowledged and the trio followed the Indians down the pathway to the valley floor.

The narrow trail dipped occasionally into the still, side eddies of an otherwise raging creek born in the massive snowmelt of the upper elevations. Large pine trees and boulders, violently swept down the mountains by avalanches, haphazardly littered the creek bed. The valley narrowed and forced the men closer to the cascading torrent. Water showered the trail and made the steep descent treacherous. The men grasped the low branches of the plentiful conifers to steady their footing as they delicately picked their way across the slick boulders. The trail meandered around a house-sized boulder, and then emerged into a clearing that overlooked the valley. Off to the side, almost hidden by mist, a large cleft in the bedrock swallowed up the angry creek. They could hear the echoes of water thundering hundreds of feet below them.

The men paused for a moment to survey the grand view before them. The Indian encampment lay in a bowl carpeted with tall, green pine trees a short distance below their perch. Except for a river flowing through a canyon to the north, the entire area was surrounded by towering mountains. To the east was brilliant yellow and red weathered rock of volcanic origin. Southwards, a light-gray wall, stripped of vegetation and color by a vanished glacier, offered stark contrast to the brilliant blue sky overhead and dark, verdant carpet on the terminal moraine at its feet. Three waterfalls on cliff faces popped from unseen sources and rumbled to the valley bottom. Hidden canyons, steep rock faces, and ghostly mountain sentinels closed the hidden valley off from the rest of the world.

The two Indians signaled to the men to continue their trek downward to the valley floor. Reluctantly, they turned from the spectacular vista and applied themselves to the task at hand. The pathway funneled along a cliff face for a few hundred feet, turned to the left, then sharply descended through a grove of ancient pine trees. They emerged from the heavy timber and came into a small clearing near the base of the box canyon that swallowed the creek from above. A number of Indian teepees littered the encampment. Cooking fires sent up signals of smoke to the upper elevations that a meal was in preparation. A small, stocky man, well-dressed in smoothly tanned, beige deerskin, sat on the ground next to one of the fires. As they walked toward him, the commotion of the other inhabitants of the camp piqued his attention. He turned around to see the visitors, smiled, and rose to greet them.

"Derek Borden," his eyes smiled out loud as he approached, "you've come to enjoy our water!"

James looked quizzically at Mike, then at Derek, who smiled, shook his head, and whispered to himself, "I can't believe this guy remembers me!" He extended his hand in greeting and continued, a little louder this time, "Chief Ouray, it's good to see you again. My friends and I are passing through, but wanted to stop and say hello."

The chief continued in articulate English. "Derek, it's good to see you, too. Introduce me to your friends, then join me for some lunch." He waved the Indian guides off to resume their hunting, shooed away the noisy children that had wandered up, then gave Derek his full attention.

Derek turned and, with courtesy and grace, introduced Ouray to his companions. They shook hands, then, at Ouray's urging, walked over and sat down near the fire. Ouray disappeared for a moment into his teepee, then reappeared carrying some additional utensils. He passed them to his guests, took a ladle, and filled their bowls with hot, thick soup.

"We gather many of the ingredients here in the valley," Ouray said as he dipped his spoon into the soup. "The meat might be elk, bear, or bighorn sheep that the braves hunt in the high country. It's really good, isn't it?"

"Yes, it is," Derek replied. He was the only one with his mouth empty as James and Mike were greedily eating theirs.

Ouray laughed heartily and carried on some small talk with the men as they finished their meal. When they were done he extended his arms and offered, "Now, you boys come down and enjoy the water for a time."

They looked at one another in dismay, but were so curious as to what the old chief meant that they offered no argument.

Ouray rose and led them down the hill toward the creek that exited the box canyon. Wisps of mist gently wafted from the gorge entrance. Over millennia the fast flowing creek had cut a deep slice into the soft rock over two hundred feet deep but only ten or fifteen feet wide. The canyon corkscrewed its way deep into the mountainside for hundreds of feet before the actual waterfall appeared. At the entrance, but off to the side, someone had dug a pool in the gravel to form a bathing tub of sorts. Ouray took off his clothes and motioned for the men to do the same. Then, he stepped into the pool of water and floated off to one side. The men followed suit and were pleasantly surprised at the warmness of the water.

"These are hot springs!" exclaimed Derek as he settled into the pool next to Ouray. "My, they feel really good." He stretched out in the sizeable pool and enjoyed the healing powers of the hot mineral water.

James and Mike also reclined in the hot springs, oblivious to the other natives milling around nearby. After the long hike and the incident in Derek's mine, the massaging water soothed their aching muscles and relieved any tension they brought with them from the high country.

"Now I know what you meant by 'enjoying the water,' " Derek said, smiling. He gazed at the colorful cliffs, thick timber, and tall mountains and wondered why anyone would want to venture out of this place.

In the course of enjoying the water the men talked with Ouray about a number of things. He enjoyed a good story, so James and Mike ended up telling him about some of their adventures on the high seas back in the war. Ouray had never seen an ocean and listened to their descriptions and stories with interest. They vaguely shared with him their urgent need to reach Georgetown, a mining town across the state. He was more than willing to let them have horses to carry them there. After all, they discovered, it was a Ute custom of hospitality to take care of one's guests, and to send them graciously on their way. Derek also asked him if he knew about any caves up on the summit of Red Mountain. Ouray responded that he did and he had shown some of them to a white man back in the late fifties. Their paths had accidentally crossed on Red Mountain summit as Ouray was hunting for grizzly bear. One of the frequent, violent thunderstorms cropped up and Ouray had offered him sanctuary in one of the caves nearby. He remembered the man as pleasant and thankful for his help.

James noticed that the shadows on the amphitheater, the gray mountain wall across the valley, were lengthening. He looked at Derek and asked, "You think we should stay in the area tonight? Looks like it's getting late."

The soaking in the pool had taken more than just a couple of hours. Ouray looked at James and interjected, "You may want to spend the night." He paused for a moment, then continued, "Try standing up."

James thought for a moment, rose to his feet, immediately got light-headed, and started to sway. Ouray laughed. "Effect of the Ute firewater. It tends to drain your energy. But tomorrow, it'll be back tenfold! Tonight, you can bed down by my teepee and enjoy the warmth and safety of my fire. I insist!"

There was no room for argument from any of the travelers. They did as Ouray had offered and enjoyed a restful night under the stars of heaven.

CHAPTER 21

Once again the men awoke early to get a good start on the day. This time, though, Ouray had already been up and seen to the horses and supplies they would need for their journey. He offered the men some breakfast before they left and, while they ate, gave them specific instructions for the trip. "I can offer you smooth trails only as far as the valley you call Arkansas," he told them. "The town you speak of is north of there over another mountain range, but I haven't traveled that direction, so I can offer you no guidance."

Derek understood and replied, "We should have no problem from that point on. There are plenty of people in the Arkansas Valley to give us direction."

The three men finished their meal, rose, and thanked Chief Ouray for his hospitality and gracious help. Then they mounted the three horses and followed the river north out of the isolated valley.

It only took a few miles for the nature of their surroundings to change. Once they passed through the narrow opening in the canyon, the alpine setting of the mountain bowl quickly gave way to a high desert environment. Scrub trees, cacti, and dryness replaced the refreshing mists of Ouray's oasis. The temperature climbed as the late-morning sun heated the sparsely vegetated mountainsides. They saw the jagged spires of the Owl Creek range to the east.

"Ouray suggested that we take an old Indian trail over those mountains," Derek said. "It's a high elevation but will be quicker than going north to the Colorado River and then east. It will drop us into the Cimarron Valley where we can skirt Sheep Mountain and avoid the Gunnison Gorge. Then we can travel east through relatively rolling mountain areas until we cross the divide at Monarch. From there we'll drop into the Arkansas Valley, where there are some settlements where we can resupply. Then we can follow the same relative route that I think Baxter will take. I figure that, if we push hard, we should reach Georgetown in a couple of weeks."

"I wonder if we'll run into Baxter's wagon train," James thought out loud.

"It's possible," Derek replied. "Once we get to the Arkansas Valley, we should probably find some way to change our appearance so we aren't recognized by any of Baxter's watchers."

"Sounds like a good idea," Mike agreed. "I'll give it some thought between here and there."

The men directed their horses up the gradual trail that approached the jagged spires of Owl Creek Pass. In the afternoon, as they approached the summit, they noticed ominous thunderheads brewing in the western sky. "Looks like it's about time for our daily bath," Derek joked. Indeed, the high country had its share of showers and thunderstorms that regularly cropped up in the afternoon hours. Intense sun evaporated any available moisture on the valley floor and condensed it into huge clouds. As the prevailing winds blew the clouds eastward, their collision with the high mountains disgorged their vast amounts of water like a sudden squeeze on a sponge full of water.

The rain came down in torrents, occasionally accompanied by hail or curtains of snow. The arcing brilliance of lightning followed by resounding cracks of thunder made the men and their horses nervous. Their pace was slowed by the slippery trails and blinding rain, but, by evening, they had crossed the mountain range and descended into the lush meadows of the Cimarron. They made camp in a stand of spruce trees along a small stream that drained the upper valley to the south of its winter snow melt. Mike made a roaring fire out of dead wood while James made a cribbing of saplings on which to hang their soaked outer garments.

The next morning found a heavy frost on the thick spring grass of the lower meadows. The fire had smoldered down to a few stray wisps of smoke and the men groaned at moving their aching muscles in the cold air. Stray rays of sunshine peeked around the summit of Sheep Mountain to their east. Rather than take time for breakfast, the party decided to load up their horses and get moving, hoping they would sight some fresh game for an extended lunch somewhere down the trail.

A few hours of riding heated up their bodies even as the rising sun warmed the outside temperature. Gradually, the scenery once again changed from the alpine timber of the high country back to the semi-arid environment they experienced after leaving Ouray's encampment. They never did find any easy game that day, so they resorted to a mix of dried meat provided by Ouray along with some beans from Derek's cabin back near Silverton. Toward evening, they crossed the Lake Fork River and made camp for the night on the eastern bank. The water was swift and cold, but some gravel bars a short distance downstream kept them from soaking their clothes and prevented a chill after they crossed. Once again, a hot, crackling fire warmed them and lightened their spirits.

The next two days were uneventful and somewhat repetitious of their passage around Sheep Mountain. The arid landscape stretched for miles in all directions and provided no shade from the sun. Fortunately, the springtime temperatures were still fairly mild and, other than the barren landscape and the brightness of the sun, it was comfortable to ride in. The miles fell behind them as they picked their way through the sagebrush-covered steppe, characteristic of the long Gunnison plateau.

They were able to circumvent the prominent feature of the plateau, that is, the dark, seemingly bottomless gorge through which the Gunnison River flowed. The gorge, a major obstacle to all travelers, sliced the earth into an impassable chasm for over fifty miles. In some places, its bottom cowered over two thousand feet below its rim, while its walls spanned a mere 40 feet apart. Captain John Gunnison, under assignment by Jefferson Davis of the war department, accomplished a survey and feasibility study of the canyon in 1853 for a railroad route to the West. His reports gave little encouragement for its use as a viable route for easy transportation in either direction. It was good that Ouray had given them an alternate route around this geographic anomaly.

By the fifth day of their journey, occasional stands of spruce and fir trees, indicative of higher elevations, heralded their ascent toward Monarch Pass. Toward evening the trail became steep and arduous, so they made an early camp part way up the long mountain trail on a flat spot surrounded by a number of large boulders. The following day at around noon, they reached the summit of the pass. They took some time to enjoy the views, rest the horses, and refresh themselves with some jerky. Afterward, they descended into the southern section of the Arkansas Valley.

The amber lamplights of Poncha Springs welcomed them well after dark. The small town had been laid out two years earlier by James True, and already had a number of buildings to its credit. The prominent feature of its location was the one hundred hot springs that bubbled out of ground seeps nearby. One entrepreneur had already built a bunkhouse and small bathing facility around a small pool he had dug to capture the advertised "Healing Mineral Water of the Rockies." It was here that the party found a place to bed down. They paid the proprietor, stowed their gear under their bunks, turned the horses loose in the corral, and made a beeline for the steaming hot basin.

As they soaked in the steaming waters, Mike looked at James and asked, "Did you notice all the horses in the corral?"

"Yeah, it seemed like quite a few," James responded.

Mike got out of the pool, wrapped himself in a blanket, and wandered over to the owner. He was a friendly sort, not too tall, brown eyes and a full head of black hair. As with most entrepreneurs, he liked people and wanted to make sure his customers were satisfied. Mike started a simple conversation commenting on how nice the water felt and the cleanliness of the facility in spite of its frontier location. James inwardly grinned as Mike put his arm around the proprietor and walked him slowly around the corner of the building. After some time he returned to the pool with a smile on his face.

He slipped into the bubbling water and mumbled to his companions, "I know something you don't."

James rolled his eyes and replied, "Okay, okay, what did you find out?"

Mike folded his hands, then extended his arms to full length in an exaggerated stretch, obviously relishing the moment of attention. "Four men came into town yesterday afternoon. They had ten horses that they traded for fresh ones. They agreed with the livery owner to return the stock in a week or so to swap for the horses they dropped off." He thought for a moment, then added mysteriously, "They paid in gold."

Derek's head appeared to float forward like a disembodied spirit on top of the steaming water. He quietly asked, "How could Baxter move those wagons so far in only five days? We've been traveling light for almost seven days, have been making good time, and have only gotten this far. He has those heavy freight wagons and a number of pretty high passes to cross!"

Mike lowered his voice, looked over his shoulder, and hoarsely whispered, "This guy set up a network of fresh horses every twenty or thirty miles. They've been traveling night and day to get this load moved. The owner said that the livery master also arranged another trade-off for the guy at Saguache, thirty some miles south of here, and at Nathrop, twenty miles due north. And, not only that, but listen to this: Some guy named Mears just finished building a toll road across Los Pinos Pass. That cut the trip to Lake City by a hefty mileage and saved them a lot more in time. Instead of going east to Del Norte, Baxter went north after crossing Stoney Pass and then cut across this new toll road to Saguache. He's ahead of us by a day."

James stared at the water and wagged his head. "I don't believe this. Unless we get back on the trail now, we don't have a ghost of a chance of catching these guys. I thought for sure we'd be plenty far ahead of them."

"I guess we don't have much choice," Derek sighed. He gazed at some distant phantom for a moment, and then continued in an authoritative tone, "Mike, see if you can make some arrangements for fresh horses from the livery master. James and I will get the gear together and pick up some additional supplies from the general store. We'll meet there in thirty minutes. Guess we'll be riding by night!"

The men reluctantly jumped out of the hot springs pool, dried off, and dressed, then went about their business. Thirty-five minutes later, fresh horses with tired riders made their way north into the inky black of night.

CHAPTER 22

The clackity-clack of the telegraph receiver reverberated through the small office in Fairplay, Colorado. A young man in his early twenties quickly scribbled down the interpretation to the erratic clicks coming across the wires, and then transferred the finished wording to a formal paper form to be delivered to the addressee. He precisely folded the paper, inserted it into an envelope, and marked, "To Mr. Joseph Baxter" on the front. Then he put it in the delivery box off to the side of his desk where the message runner would pick it up at noon, locate the recipient, and promptly deliver it.

Sure enough, precisely at noon, a small boy, probably around age ten, came into the office. He was dressed in some faded gray dungarees, a long-sleeved shirt, and leather sandals. He nonchalantly shuffled to the counter, stood on his tiptoes so he could look over the top, and smugly asked, "Watcha got for me, Dooley? Huh? Watcha got?"

Dooley, the telegrapher, peered over his right shoulder and saw some dirty blond hair, two curious brown eyes, and a couple of scrawny arms dug into the countertop for fear of dropping to his demise. He tried to contain a grin as he pointed to the desk with his thumb. "Hey, Corky. Just that note in the box to be delivered to Joseph Baxter. I think he's over at the Graball Saloon."

The small boy plopped down to the floor, walked around the towering countertop to the desk, and picked up the addressed envelope. He flicked it in his hand for a moment, then said, "He's that guy that came into town late last night, ain't he? You know, the one leading that wagon train?"

Dooley nodded.

Corky made it his business to know everything that was going on in the growing town. The product of a saloon girl romance, he had been on his own since he was eight. As a result, he had become adept at finding odd jobs. He was, unofficially, the town messenger boy of both telegrams and information, anything to make some money. Corky pursed his lips, and, as he sauntered out the door toward the saloon across town, said quietly to himself, "I wonder what they're carrying in those wagons."

Fairplay, Colorado, was located in the vast basin of South Park about 125 miles southwest of Denver. The basin itself comprised a huge grassy valley around seventy-five miles long and twenty miles wide. In the late 1850s, prospectors discovered some rich placer deposits in the slow-moving, meandering streams that originated in the higher mountains to the west. The discoverers named their town site Tarryall. But they became so jealous of their new location that they ran off any newcomers who tried to join them. The latecomers were so indignant at the policy that they dubbed the new camp "Graball" and pushed onward to locate some rich deposits in the slow-moving waters of the South Platte River twenty-some miles to the southwest.

A mining district was set up and Jim Reynolds, one of the founding prospectors, demanded fair play for everyone. Consequently, when a name for the town was adopted, Fairplay was the only one on the list. Because of its strategic location in the valley, it soon became a major trading center for the region. The growing town had the usual number of hotels and saloons and even had constructed some buildings of permanence. The courthouse, finished a year earlier, in 1874, was built out of solid sandstone blocks and was placed in the center of town. In the spring of 1875, only a month ago, a new bell was installed in the towering steeple of the large, white, gothic-style Presbyterian Church. In addition to church services, its loud ringing heralded community events and meetings, and also served as an efficient fire alarm.

Corky scrambled down the main street to the western edge of town where the Graball Saloon stood next to one of the liveries. Seven men with rifles in easy reach relaxed on the ground next to five wagons parked in the back corral. Corky skidded to a stop at the saloon and yelled through the front door opening, "Mr. Joseph Baxter. Mr. Joseph Baxter, I have a telegram for you, sir."

After a few moments, a tall, lanky man emerged from the smoky dinge of the room. He wore a long, black coat draped to his ankles. A gray, felt hat covered a shock of greasy, black hair that was pulled behind his head and secured with a leather thong. A thick, dark, and very long mustache drooped below his thin mouth. He looked down at Corky. "What do you have there, son?"

Corky held up the envelope and asked, "Are you Mr. Joseph Baxter?"

"Yes, I am," he answered. He reached into his pocket, pulled out a coin, and handed it to Corky, who gave him the envelope in return. Without moving, he read the note, nodded, and smiled. Then he scrunched it up and tossed it into the corral as he pivoted on his heels and went back into the saloon. Corky wandered over to the corral, picked up the piece of paper, put it into his pocket, and slipped away into the shadows.

In the saloon, Baxter reseated himself at the table with a group of men. One of them wheezed, "What was that about?"

Baxter picked up a tumbler of whiskey, downed it, and replied, "Looks like we get to spend the night here in Fairplay.

114

The mill in Silver Plume won't be ready for our shipment for another four days. We'll stay here tonight and head out in the morning."

A slender man looked at Baxter and added, "Might be a good opportunity to attend that town meeting tonight at the church. I hear they are going to discuss some issues that might be of interest to us."

Baxter's eyes squinted as he nodded his head. "Yeah, best to take advantage of every opportunity." He looked at the slender man and continued, "John, you tell the men in the corral to set up night shifts to watch the wagons. And, give them some extra money to have some fun tonight while you, Seth, and I attend that meeting. Make sure that at least two men are left on guard at all times and that they don't drink too much. No one here knows what we're carrying, but it is best not to take any chances."

John nodded in understanding and left the room. Baxter filled his tumbler from a bottle on the table and mumbled to himself, "Every opportunity."

CHAPTER 23

When the sun slipped behind the mountains over Weston Pass, the new bell at the church rang out assembly time for the community. Every available space in the church was packed with miners, merchants, and politicians, as well as men and women from Fairplay and the surrounding areas. A second ringing of the bell heralded the start of the meeting. A middle-aged man dressed in a brown suit with a bowtie rose and moved to the podium in front of the church altar to call the meeting to order.

"Welcome, citizens of Fairplay and surrounding communities, to this meeting," he began. He continued with recognition to several people. After the niceties were completed, he went to the heart of the meeting. "You all know that the biggest challenge facing our community and this area today has to do with the moving of our mined wealth to the coffers of the politicians in Denver and to the eastern states of this country. Even though our fair town is not solely based on mining, it does have a large foundation on the mining industry in the mountains that surround us. And that industry is largely dependent on the silver produced in our sister towns like Leadville, Alma, Como, and others. When the government devalued that silver, it devalued our standard of living. Because we have so many questions and concerns, your town fathers invited Norman Kroot, a member of the territorial legislature in Denver, here to Fairplay to give you some answers."

As rousing applause filled the church, no one noticed two

116

men enter the back of the building. They worked their way behind the last row to the stained-glass window where they could stand and observe. Their large hats were pulled down to their eyes and they kept their hands stuffed in the pockets of the coats that strained to keep their bellies from popping out through the brass buttons.

Norman Kroot began his oration as any skilled politician would do. He complimented the citizens for their high work ethic and supportive patriotism to a growing country. He expounded on the great and unlimited resources that were in the Territory of Colorado and how they provided a great contribution to the rest of the country. But, after a few minutes of patriotic zeal his message shifted to a different vein, one based on manipulated fact.

"Here's the facts," he continued. "The Territory of Colorado is midway between the Atlantic and Pacific Oceans. Many of the people in the United States Congress would believe that it is the Manifest Destiny of the country as a whole to possess and own all the land between those two great bodies of water. Such is the doctrine to admit Colorado as a new state in this coast-to-coast union. And what are the results of this universal administration? You will then have a national government that will continue to determine the value of your gold and your silver. Grant demonetized silver. With the swift stroke of a pen, he cut its value compared to gold, and now silver is no longer recognized as legal tender in the entire country.

"My friends, how does this affect your ability to pay your debts? How does this affect the reward for your labor? Silver is currently king in the Territory of Colorado, but our gracious government won't even let us use it to pay our bills! As a result, capitalistic tinhorns from the east—places like New York, Massachusetts, and other states—are buying up our hard earned and personally developed properties because they have the cash readily available to buy our debt. And where will it stop?

"Colorado has vast amounts of timber. It supplies abundant water resources to the farming regions of Kansas, Oklahoma, and other eastern states. Our mineral wealth is not limited to just silver and gold, but to rare earth elements that enhance all parts of our lives. When will the government decide that these commodities are of more value to them than to us? We are the frontiersmen, the prospectors, the developers, the keepers of these resources. My friends, this Union government is out to enslave you for its profit. It is out to make you the slaves of the Union!"

The audience, quiet and contained to this point, broke out in cries of anger and hate. The rise and fall of unified voices sounded like an angry wind blowing across the open prairies before a torrential thunderstorm. Baxter looked over at John, wickedly smiling at his associate, and said loudly in his ear to overcome the commotion, "He's got them now."

As the uproar died down, Kroot continued, "My friends, there is only one answer to this predicament. There is but one way that the citizens of Fairplay, the citizens of Alma, the citizens of Denver, and the citizens of every other city in this territory can protect what we have built. We must protect our heritage, our future, our children's future, and our ability to determine our own destiny. We need a State of Colorado. Not a state in the Union, but a separate, independent, and autonomous State of Colorado. Better yet, a Republic of Jefferson, named in honor of the man who had a firm grasp on the true meaning of independence!"

Cheers erupted from the audience and the deafening applause rivaled an outpouring of hail on a tin roof. The two men standing by the stained glass looked wide-eyed and concerned at each other as the commotion in the gothic church rose to a frenzied level.

"My friends," Kroot continued, "listen to the facts. In 1848, the patriots of Texas revolted against Mexico to create the Lone Star Republic of Texas. The Manifest Destiny of President Polk absorbed their concept of a republic and, through governmental manipulation, forced them into submission to the Union. In 1852, settlers in the northern part of California felt unrepresented by their state fathers. Profits from their mining and timber interests were being exported to governing powers that ignored their needs for transportation improvements and tax-subsidized town development.

"A push for a separate 'State of Shasta' presented to the California legislature was permanently tabled without appropriate consideration due to other business. The following year, independence was resubmitted as a push for the 'State of Klamath.' Again, it was conveniently pushed aside by a so-called major Indian uprising. In 1854, a new separate statehood movement began, this time centered in southern Oregon, and variously called by the name 'Jackson Territory' and the 'State of Jefferson.' A proposal to create such a state was presented before Congress and the agitation continued until, as a measure of relief, Oregon was granted statehood in 1859.

"The same problem ensued here in this great Territory of Colorado back in that same year, 1859. Prominent men of the era tried to establish the independent 'Jefferson Territory' that would be able to control the needs of the unique mining community in its local area. It was undermined and, once again, placed under the direct control of the Union, hence the Territory of Colorado.

"Listen, my friends. Look at the pattern. Texas, Shasta, Klamath, Jackson, Jefferson. Each time when the needs, wishes, and desires of the people who settled the area were expressed, an impartial government stepped in, consolidated the wealth and equity, and moved it to other portions of the country

119

without regard to the ones who produced it. Is this what we want for us? Is this what we want for our children? I think not. I believe we need this republic. A republic responsible for valuating its own resources. A republic centrally located between east and west, a transportation hub able to supply resources to both sides of the Union at a price that we set as fair. A republic that determines its own education and housing needs, and rises to meet those needs from within its own resources. We need to be in control of what our labor produces! We need a republic with a militia that can protect itself and its natural wealth. We have the riches buried in these mountains and the valuable timber growing on their slopes to create and finance development for our cities."

As Kroot continued on his soapbox, the two men by the stained-glass windows worked their way to the aisle and out the door. Behind them, they heard the rising chorus of a unified community on the brink of a crusade.

CHAPTER 24

Once outside, the two burly men quickly moved down the main street of Fairplay toward the outskirts of town. Commotion from the church carried throughout the community well into the surrounding valley. As they walked by the courthouse, they noticed a small boy sitting on a rock bench hewn out of solid sandstone. He lazily swung his feet in the strong moonlight. As they passed, the boy piped up, "How come you two ain't at the town meeting? Everyone else in town is. Except for a couple of guards over at the corral, that is."

The two men stopped and eyed the boy for a moment. One of them then replied, "I'm not so sure we liked the message from the pulpit." He smiled for a moment, then continued, "What are you doing out here by yourself?"

"I'm just sittin' here thinkin'," he answered.

"Oh, that's a good thing to do," nodded the other man. "By the way, you mentioned some guards not being at the community meeting. What guards might that be?"

The boy looked at the men for a moment, and then answered, "Sounds like you want some information. Gonna cost you."

The men looked at each other in bewilderment, then back at the boy. With a smile, one of them pulled some coinage out of his pocket and offered it to the boy.

Corky took it and checked it for authenticity. Then he put it in his pocket, hopped off of the bench, motioned the men to follow, and said, "C'mon, it's easier just to show you."

The men followed him up the street. The boy stopped opposite the Graball Saloon. He motioned them to sit with him under the overhanging eave of the hardware store across the street. His voice dropped low and he pointed to the corral as he spoke. "Right there. See them? There are two guards watching those five wagons."

The two men knelt down in the shadows with the boy and observed the corral. One said to the other, "That looks like them. Yup, there's five all right." He looked for a moment, then continued under his breath. "I wonder what's in them."

Corky whispered an unsolicited response. "That'll cost you extra."

The men gazed dumbfounded at each other and looked at the boy for a moment. Quietly they gave him another coin.

"I climbed in there earlier this evening to look around," he started. "Those two guys aren't much for guards. I didn't see anything but mining machinery and supplies. Looked like they were grubstaking someone or restocking a mine or something."

"Are you sure that's all you saw?" one man asked. "Just mining equipment?"

"Yup, that's all," he replied. "By the way, my name's Corky. As you probably figured, I sell information. And it's always accurate. Nothing in those wagons but mining equipment."

One of the men held out his hand and smiled, "My name's James. And this is Derek. I have no doubt that you are as honest as you are shrewd, my little friend. But you must promise not to let anyone in town know our names or that we were even here."

"I see," pondered Corky. After a moment he continued, "Okay, I can do that. But it will cost you."

James smiled, pulled out another coin and silently handed it to Corky. He matter-of-factly placed it in his pocket and, without looking up, quipped, "Your belly is falling out. That one is free."

James looked at his belly and noticed that the blanket he had stuffed in his shirt was slipping out over his belt. He quietly laughed, shook his head in wonderment and pushed it back in. "Why don't we go somewhere else so we can talk."

The trio slipped quietly along the walkway and moved down a dark alley to another street. Then they moved toward the edge of town and out onto the grassy land of the South Park. After walking for a half mile they looked over their shoulders for any followers and then resumed conversation. "You're quite an entrepreneur, Corky. Just what do you know about those wagons?"

Before he could answer, James pulled out another coin and added, "Why don't we make this a one-time payment for working with us, Corky? I'm running out of money!"

This time Corky was the one who laughed and replied, "Okay, I know when I've squeezed the udder one time too many." He stopped and looked up at the men. They politely squatted down to his eye level before he began. "They came into town yesterday morning about six. I could tell the men and horses were tired, like they had been traveling all night. They pulled into the corral, lined the wagons up, and unhitched the horses. A tall man named Joseph Baxter went over to the telegraph office as soon as it opened and sent a cable to Golden, then waited for an answer at the Graball Saloon with two of his companions. When the message came in around noon, I took it to him."

"I wonder what it said," Derek mused to himself.

Corky continued, "Here, read it for yourself." He pulled the crumpled piece of paper from his pocket and held it out for Derek to take.

Derek's eyes got big as he slowly reached for the paper. "You, young man, are full of surprises!" He took the note, flattened it, and read it aloud. "To Joseph Baxter, Fairplay, Colorado. Joe, the mill won't be ready for another four days. I know you pushed to stay on schedule, but there were complications. Arrange for delivery at eleven in the morning four days from today. Also, have to make final plans on greeting Grant. Think on it. E.S."

James and Derek looked into the dark and pondered the message. After a minute, Corky piped in, "So, where are you going?"

James blinked a couple times, rose up, and said, "Back to camp, I suppose. Why not come with us?"

Corky shook his head in response and said, "No, I have responsibilities in town tomorrow morning. If I don't show up, I'll lose the work."

"Tell you what, Corky," James said. "You keep your eyes on Baxter and his friends. Let us know if something else happens that we should know about. We'll be in town again tomorrow night."

Corky scrunched up his nose for a moment as if trying to remember something. "Oh, yeah," he started. "Baxter said that they were only staying tonight. Guess that means they're leaving tomorrow morning."

Derek thought for a moment, and then responded, "I guess that means we'll be leaving, too. Corky, we appreciate the information that you gave us. If you find out anything more before tomorrow morning, would you come tell us? We're camping just beyond the tree line about a mile from here on the road to Breckenridge."

Corky pursed his lips, thought for a moment, and responded, "Yeah, I'll do that. But it will definitely cost you!"

CHAPTER 25

Some heavy clouds from the west covered the moon as Derek and James finished off some beans and bacon they had cooked over the fire. "What, none for me?" a voice echoed.

They looked across the campsite and saw Mike walking up to the fire. "We didn't know when you would be back," James said. "In fact, we didn't even hear you coming."

Mike grinned and replied, "You were more interested in your food than in listening to what was going on around you!"

"Hey, glad you made it back. What did you find out?" Derek asked.

"Baxter is in town. The five wagons are parked next to a saloon and boarding house on the south side. Two guards were watching them, but when they eventually dozed off, I was able to work my way into one of the wagons. At first I thought it was just full of mining supplies, but then I noticed the powder and water barrels were empty and most of the equipment was lightweight. I pried up one of the floorboards and found the gold in a hollow place underneath. I imagine each of those wagons is rigged with a false floor. Here," he tossed a shiny shard of something at James. "Thought we could use a little extra money."

James reached down and picked up a fragment of a gold bar. "What's this? You took one of the gold bars?"

"Nope," Mike replied with pride. "I only cut off a piece of one with my knife. It was soft, you know, almost fell off on its own. Couldn't just leave it there. Besides, I figured that since we were following Baxter all this way, the least he could do was help finance the trip."

James grinned appreciatively and put the gold shard into his pocket.

Mike looked at the fire and continued, "I wonder why they pushed so hard to get to Fairplay? There is no mill here or rail terminal or anything."

"I think we can answer that," Derek began. He then told Mike the details of their evening. As Mike scanned the crumpled note, Derek asked, "I wonder who E.S. is. You know, the initials at the bottom of the telegram."

"I've no idea," James replied. "Maybe, in time, we'll find out. All we really know is that Baxter will be delivering this load of gold to a mill in four days. Well, actually three days, now. And, according to the map we picked up in California, it's somewhere near Georgetown. I suppose the best we can do for now is to continue following them."

"You're probably right," Mike said. He threw a couple of pieces of wood on the fire and added, "And what's all this noise about a Republic of Jefferson that I heard in town?"

"That I don't know," James replied. "I've never heard of such a movement. Would seem that the messengers, like this Norman Kroot, are a little shortsighted, though. Mining only lasts for so long. Eventually, the resources dry up and one has to either move along or find a way to work with others around to keep things going. We see that now in some of these little mining camps and towns that are here one day and gone the next. How about you, Derek? Is this idea new to you, too?"

"No, not really," he answered. "There was some talk of it in Silverton last fall, but nothing came of it. Many of the miners there were, like myself, from the east. The way the government ran things seemed to be in everyone's best interests, not just a select few. I kinda figure, what works there can work here. Besides, I don't think a separate country in the middle of the growing Union would last. Eventually, it would need to become a part of the whole in order to survive."

"At any rate, our interest is in following the gold," Mike quipped. "And that doesn't have anything to do with the politics of Colorado. I'll leave that up to the territorial legislature. In the meantime, I'm going to grab some beans and go to bed. I imagine Baxter will be pulling out early."

The meeting at the church continued into the wee hours of the morning. Norman Kroot patted himself on the back for giving such a moving speech. The town fathers had really jumped on the bandwagon in lending support to the concept of an independent republic. In fact, the people had even volunteered and committed to a local militia sworn to defend their rights as free people. As Norman prepared to leave the church, Baxter came up behind and tapped him on the shoulder. He turned around, nodded his head in acknowledgment, and held out his hand. "Joe Baxter. Good to see you. I noticed you in the audience when I first came in. What brings you to Fairplay?"

Baxter cordially responded, "E.S. closed down one of the southern operations and I'm moving the extra mining supplies back up to Silver Plume."

"That's a good idea," Norman said nodding his head. "Would be good to consolidate right now."

Baxter then asked, "How are the meetings up north going?"

Norman knew what he was talking about and quickly responded, "We have a lot of support. All the major mining communities west of Denver are ready to act. I tell you what, Joe, Grant made a big mistake when he devalued silver. Those people up north are furious. Silver is about the only thing the mines up there are producing. The tension over the economic

127

troubles is a powder keg with a short fuse. It won't take much to spark it, either."

As Baxter walked Kroot to the door, he asked, "Has E.S. decided when he's going to make a motion at the legislature to create the new republic?"

"No, he's not told me yet," Kroot replied. "But the time is ripe. If something doesn't happen soon, he'll lose the momentum of meetings like the one we had tonight. The people are ready to act now. The timing for the devaluation of silver couldn't have been better. But there is talk of repealing the action. If that happens, it would give new life to the people wanting statehood. I just hope he doesn't wait too long."

The moon had disappeared behind some thick clouds. The night was black as pitch. Oil lamps from the church reflected off of Baxter's face like a dim pumpkin at Halloween. He grinned slyly as he shook Kroot's hand. "Not to worry. I think E.S. will time it about right." He bid Kroot safe travels, and disappeared into the darkness.

CHAPTER 26

The fried chicken at the Central Hotel was the best they had ever eaten. Even Johann, who ate like a horse, had his fill. A stack of bones on the plate in front of him faintly resembled one of the cordwood piles he was accustomed to splitting back in Indiana. As the natural grogginess resulting from a large afternoon meal crept in, Henri suggested moving to the front porch for some fresh air and a comfortable rocker. Only Frank agreed to the idea, as the rest of the party seemed more intent on an early afternoon nap in the comfortable beds upstairs.

As expected, the two rockers on the front porch and the warm sunshine provided a relaxing atmosphere for Frank and Henri to catch up on the past.

"So, tell me, Frank," Henri began, "has Kansas given you the peace you were looking for?"

Frank shuffled his feet on the painted pine floorboards, looked over at Henri, and replied with a faint smile, "Yeah, it's been good. It took a couple of years to forget about the war and everything that happened. Or, I should say, as much as one can forget something like that. My wife and I built up a little ranch northwest of here. We have a small sod house, a barn, and a couple of outbuildings. Even have a windmill for pumping water. My two boys are big enough to help out with the work. It's been good." Frank paused and reflected on the last decade of his life. Then his brow furrowed like a freshly plowed field. He looked off at some distant object and rhetorically asked, "How did James end up in a Colorado mining town like Silverton?"

Henri slowly turned his head and locked his eyes onto Frank's. "What are you talking about?" he asked.

"Perhaps I can fill you in," a voice from the doorway said. Johann was standing behind them with a book in his hand. He walked forward and sat down on the steps at Frank's feet. Johann handed him the worn book. "This is James's diary that Dad wired you about, Frank." He turned to Henri. "James wrote down the events that happened with you, Frank, and the others during the war. I had no idea that you were the leader of the operation, Henri. This morning, when I saw that Frank knew you, it all fell into place. This is the first chance we've had to talk about it."

Henri was dumbfounded by the strange change of events. "You mean James is still alive?" he stammered.

"No," Johann responded. He took the diary from Frank, opened the back, and retrieved Sheriff Guston's letter. He opened it and read it aloud. After he finished he said, "It was decided that Frank and I should go to Silverton and find out the details of what happened to James. Dad wired Frank so he would make arrangements to go there with me. We still have no idea why James would have been in Silverton."

Henri was quiet for a few moments as he absorbed the information.

"There's more," Johann said. "There were some maps included in the packet that Sheriff Guston sent to Dad." He pulled one set of three maps from a leather pouch, shuffled through them for a moment, and then picked out one in particular. The brown, almost leathery, paper crinkled as he unfolded it for Frank and Henri. "This one has the states of Maryland, Georgia, and Alabama on it. A number of locations are circled, but I've no idea what they are for."

Frank and Henri looked intently at the map. Henri's index

finger slowly floated from one spot to another as he mumbled to himself, "Mohekan Pass, Wildwood Junction, Maple River." He paused, then his eyes lit up as he hoarsely whispered at Frank, "These are the spots where gold shipments disappeared!"

"What are you talking about?" Frank replied.

Henri's excitement grew as he pointed at specific spots on the map. "This map has all the locations where Confederate and Union gold thefts happened. Look, here is the Tallapoosa River, in Alabama. And here's the Maple River in Maryland." He looked at Johann and inquired, "What other maps have you, son?"

Johann opened the pouch and pulled out another packet of three. Once again, he shuffled through them and then unfolded and stretched one of them out. Frank's finger immediately fell like a dagger to the compass rose. "Look at this, Henri."

Henri's eyes focused at the end of Frank's finger. Then he reached into his jacket pocket and pulled out the ring that he had shown Sarah on the train as they traveled through Ohio. Johann watched as he placed it next to the rose on the map. They were identical in nature. Henri looked at Frank and said, "Nothing else on this map makes any sense except this rose. Look, it's the same as the ring. What is the connection?"

"Perhaps I can help to answer that," a voice resonated from the edge of the porch.

The three men hastily looked up in alarm at the sound of a voice. At the corner of the porch was an extremely well-dressed man. His perfect posture complemented the dark-blue three-piece suit. In one hand was a magnificent cane that had a headpiece of silver. His other hand rested lightly on the porch banister. A unique silver ring with a bulbous, pale-blue stone glinted in the late afternoon sun.

Henri moved his gaze to Johann and indicated with his hand to put the ring, maps, diary, and papers back into the leather pouch. He flicked a look at Frank before locking his eyes on the stranger. "And how, sir, may you do that?"

CHAPTER 27

The stranger smiled and stepped forward. "Perhaps I should introduce myself," he said in an aristocratic English tone. "My name is Sydney Williams."

"Sydney Williams?" Henri interrupted. "You're a friend of Edgar Burns."

Johann whispered in Frank's ear, "Who is Edgar Burns?"

Frank whispered back, "He was undersecretary of war during part of Lincoln's term. He disappeared shortly after Lincoln's assassination."

Williams tipped his head and remarked, "Your memory is good, Mr. Schreiber. As is Mr. Mueller's."

"How do you know our names?" Henri inquired.

"Oh, I know a lot about you," Williams responded. "I know about your efforts during and after the Civil War. You might say Mr. Burns, while he still held public office, was an associate who kept me informed about your movements. One thing puzzles me, though. Why would a man of your stature and political position take on such a small role as a bridge designer for Otto Mears?"

Henri didn't respond, but, instead, redirected an explanation toward Frank. "As Mr. Williams said, he was an associate of Mr. Burns. To be more precise, I was suspicious that Burns had more allegiance to Williams than to Lincoln's cabinet. Mr. Williams is a wealthy banker from London who likes to support unpopular causes, for a profit, of course. I suspect his support of the Union cause was about equal to that of the Confederates. Would that be a correct assumption, sir?"

Williams's eyes grew cold as he articulated a precise, icy response. "I am a businessman, sir. It is my charge to return a profit to a bank's investors." After a pause, his demeanor returned to that of the English gentleman. "But, please, I didn't come here to belabor historic and economic differences. Actually, my train was detained last night on its way to Denver, something about repairing leaky seals for a drive rod. But I am now promised an immediate departure at my call. It has been requested by an associate of mine that I expedite your trip by providing you quick and safe passage to his office in Denver."

Henri's eyebrows raised in response. "An associate?"

"Yes," Williams answered. "He is most interested in talking to you and your companions. Why, Henri," he continued in an excited and congratulatory manner, "I believe, in the strictest of confidence, that he has a most intriguing job offer to make you."

"I'm sorry, Mr. Williams, but I have already made a commitment to Mr. Mears and his company. And our travel arrangements are fixed in stone, so to speak."

Williams pursed his lips, looked at the dirt, and ground the end of his cane into the sandy earth in a leisurely manner. He continued in an apologetic and whispered tone. "I am sorry, Mr. Mueller. But, you see, I must insist that you agree to my offer." He paused. Then, like the striking of flint to steel, he fixed his eyes on Henri's, and remarked, "You see, my friends behind you don't like troublemakers in their peaceful little town."

The three turned their heads and saw four men with Winchester rifles cocked, but loosely hanging by their sides. Henri's shoulders drooped slightly as he noticed the bright silver star of the sheriff. Across the street, two more deputies stood casually next to the telegraph office. Their hands calmly rested on their silver studded holsters as they nonchalantly watched a tumbleweed blow down the main street of Brookville.

Williams continued chatting as he rolled the silver cap of his exquisite walking stick in his palm. "I believe you'll find your companions and your luggage already loaded on my private coach, which, by the way, is comfortable. It's a uniquely designed Pullman made by a master craftsman from Germany." He cocked his head as if thinking deeply. "Lauff is his last name, I believe. Quite a charming man.

"I also have my own private cook and a full rack of the world's finest wines. I believe my steward is offering your friends some premium after-dinner refreshment. Now, why would you refuse an excellent offer to travel in luxury, at the quickest pace, and without further delay?"

After a pause for effect, Williams gently chastised their indecisiveness. "Gentlemen, gentlemen. If we stop this tomfoolery, we can be in Denver by early tomorrow morning." Williams stretched his arm toward the roundhouse, and, with the graceful cunning of a skilled chess player who recognizes an impending checkmate, ordered, "Now, please, without further ado, let's board my train."

Henri and Frank looked at one another and weighed the odds of the situation. After a full minute, Henri looked back over at Williams and quipped, "Did your men bother to load my shaving kit?"

"Oh, excellent! Capital! I am positive that they have, Mr. Mueller. Come along, now. The engine is up to pressure and ready to travel."

The three men followed their new host across town to the roundhouse and boarded the train. Williams offered them some plush seats next to their companions, gave some orders to the steward, and excused himself for the time being. Frank noticed two gunmen at each end of the luxurious, handcrafted Pullman car. The train gave a jerk and began its trip to Denver.

CHAPTER 28

Sydney Williams's train was a fantastic prototype of speed and power, well ahead of its time. Unlike the standard workhorse 4-4-0 of the West with its prominent smokestack, bulging boiler, and square engineer house, Williams's engine was sleek and smooth. It was patterned off of a locomotive still on the drawing board at the Baldwin Locomotive Works that wasn't to be put into production until 1878. In order to build the rail line over Raton Pass near New Mexico, the survey crews on the New Mexico and Southern Pacific line calculated "switch backs" two and three-quarters miles long, having six-percent gradients combined with curves of sixteen degrees. The extremely steep grades and tight bends required a locomotive of exceptional power and agility, and innovation yet unknown at that time. Williams provided substantial financial support to the Baldwin Locomotive Works, but required operational schematics of their proposed engine before releasing a contract. As a result, he used their research to build a working model of the engine, enhanced by his own changes and refinements.

The engine was a monster. Williams had steel panels bolted to the sides of the functional systems, which gave a smooth appearance. The engineer's box was integrated into this design along with an exhaust system for the smoke derived from the combustion process of a new type of fuel source, a black, gooey substance called petroleum. The locomotive, along with its fuel tender, two custom Pullman cars, and caboose, could reach speeds approaching an unheard of ninety miles an hour in between water stops. Needless to say, when Williams's train was on the tracks, all other traffic was diverted to side rails until it passed.

As Williams promised, the Pullman car that his unwilling companions traveled in was the epitome of luxury. Plush, thick-piled carpet covered the insulated floors. Large, cushioned seats were positioned much like the interior of a library or sitting room in a stately English manor. Assorted panels, shelves, and desks divided the large coach into autonomous areas defined specifically for meals, smoking room, a reading area, study room, and recreational lounge. Large windows permitted generous amounts of light. The night gloom was chased away by an unusual style of oil lamp resembling something from Arabia. A number of globed lanterns hung from walnut paneled walls. Ornately carved designs made from various woods covered the ceilings. The embellished motifs contributed a gorgeous three-dimensional aspect to the upper areas of the coach.

The shadows of dusk extended across the empty expanse of western Kansas as the train rocketed toward the setting orb of the sun. Henri and his companions rested in the velvety seats and watched the countryside race by at unbelievable speeds.

"Isn't the view extraordinary?" a dignified voice asked.

Henri turned in his chair to see that Williams had silently entered the coach and stood behind him.

"I've always marveled at the vast and endless expanse of the western part of Kansas," he continued. "It is so flat that one can see, it would seem, the very ends of the earth itself."

Williams moved to an empty seat and sat down next to Sarah. He folded his hands in his lap and stared quietly at the horizon as the sky and land gradually blended into one in the growing darkness. Sarah glanced at the silver ring on his finger, looked up at Henri, and smiled slightly. Then she asked, "That is a gorgeous ring on your finger, Mr. Williams. Where did you acquire such a magnificent piece of jewelry?"

"Ah, you noticed my ring," he replied pleasantly. He removed it from his hand, rolled it between his fingers, and handed it to Sarah. She immediately recognized the pale blue stone in the center and quietly gasped at the beautiful small diamonds set into the ovals surrounding it.

"The ring is patterned after my family crest," he said. "The stone in the middle is a rare transparent blue sapphire. It symbolizes the unity and strength of the Williams family. My ancestor, Roger Williams, who discovered Rhode Island in the mid 1600s, integrated the crest into a ring to honor his grandfather, the investor and supporter of his explorations. Roger's son expanded the design to include the eight ovals, one for each of his children. The original ring design included a star at the top of the ovals, symbolic of the eldest son, then a dot or a line for the girls and boys. I had the diamonds implanted over the oval designs. The raised leaf patterns point to the fruitfulness and bounty of the new land that my forefathers sought." He took the ring from Sarah, slipped it back onto his finger, and concluded, "It has a high gold and silver content with a touch of nickel, which keeps its luster bright and shiny."

After Williams finished his remarks, Frank asked, "You said that there was a connection between the ring and the insignia on the maps that we looked at back in Brookville?"

"Yes, but of course," Williams said. "A number of years ago, just before your American Civil War, some men of stature from both sides of your Union came to our facility requesting financial support for a plan to bring peace to your divided nation. After listening to their business plan my board felt it was an idea worth investing in, with potentially high returns. At that time, Edgar Burns was highly instrumental in setting up the initial design of the network. His plan included the use of men from both sides. In order to differentiate between them, they borrowed the concept of my ring to bolster a feeling of unity with their comrades. Their board of executors, so to speak, wore similar rings while subordinates had silver bracelets or other unique discerning jewelry that made them recognizable to others in the network. The ring design was incorporated into all their transactions and mapping techniques, kind of like a trademark or logo that gave it authenticity to the ones involved. The maps you looked at in Brookville were a part of that design and network."

"So, what was this plan of 'peace'?" Johann inquired.

"Put simply, young man, it was the belief in the concept that two bankrupt nations would stop fighting each other. Part of the plan involved finding creative ways to liquidate the financial reserves of both warring parties, then forcing them to the peace table in order to work together to avert widespread panic and depression, and to reunify the nation."

"So, that explains the gold shipments that disappeared from the north and south," Frank interjected. "But, since the plan to reunify the country through negotiations obviously failed, what happened to the gold and the men who arranged for its disappearance?"

"That, sir, is not information you are privy to at this time. Let's just say that the original business plan submitted to my institution was modified, and the length of term was extended to include longer-term profits." Williams turned his head and gazed out the window. "My, such a wonderful sunset," he commented. "The rainbow of pastels in the sky reminds me that each day can start the same way as it ends, in a multitude of promising colors and hope for the future."

Williams got up, bowed to his guests, and remarked, "Ladies and gentlemen, I hope you'll excuse me, as I have pressing business to attend to in my other coach. I encourage you to rest, as we will be arriving in Denver on time, just after midnight. I request that you stay on the train until six in the morning when, Mr. Mueller, I will introduce you to the executor of the board." He looked at Johann and faintly smiled. "Not to worry, young Schreiber. My steward will be most prompt and generous with your morning breakfast! I think pancakes, bacon, and eggs will be adequate, sir?" His faint smile waxed congenial as he departed. "Until then, good night."

CHAPTER 29

As promised, the train rolled into the Denver rail terminal shortly after midnight. The black iron monster idled past the standard unloading areas and proceeded to the far side of the switchyards, where it screeched to a stop alongside some cottonwood trees. In the distance, the night lights of downtown Denver twinkled in the pale moonlight. Sarah and Johann strained their eyes in an effort to see the mountains in the murky distance. Emily dozed on a couch across the coach while Frank and Henri whispered amongst themselves. Their attention was broken by Sarah's loud gasp as she jumped back from the coach windows. "Did you see that?" she exclaimed.

One of the guards quickly exited the coach with his rifle as her companions drew to attention and came to the window. "No, we didn't," Henri said. "What was it you saw?"

"A man looked in the window at me," she replied. "Right there." She pointed at some smudges left on the outside of the window. "He had a beard and long hair. His hands were cupped around his eyes so he could see in. I couldn't see much else than that."

Two rifle reports echoed outside the coach. A few moments later, Williams entered the coach, and with his usual aristocratic pomp remarked, "Nothing to worry about, my good folks. It was only a vagrant looking in. My guard ran him off with a couple of rifle shots." He looked at Sarah and voiced a little concern. "Are you all right, my dear? You seem a little upset by the incident."

Sarah politely answered, "I'm all right, now. He just caught me off guard, that's all."

"The rail yards house a number of drifters who wander the rails looking for handouts," Williams continued, "They are relatively harmless, but one can never be too careful. My steward will bring in some refreshments." He excused himself, walked to the door where the guard had resumed his station, whispered some instructions to him, and departed.

Ten minutes later, the steward entered the coach with juices and breadsticks and offered them to the guests, who gratefully took them to quiet their late night excitement and rising hunger pangs. The six companions sat comfortably in their sofa seats, sipped their drinks, and gazed silently over the quiet landscape as they pondered their situation. Frank noticed that the guards were yawning and rubbing their eyes. After some moments, Sarah put her glass on a side table, looked over at Henri, and whispered, "What are we going to do now?"

Henri, cautiously looking over his shoulder toward the guard at the far end of the coach, said in a low voice, "Unfortunately, I'm afraid there's not a whole lot we can do, Sarah. Our keepers seem to be well armed."

After a few moments, Frank tilted his head to the side, looked at Henri, and said, "I've been thinking, Henri, about a way to disarm the guards. These two have been watching us since Brookville and appear sleepy. That means a slower reaction time. Listen, the toilet is located in the second coach, near the front. If one of us asked to use the facilities, we already know from earlier in the evening that one of the guards will be an escort. That would leave only one to watch the rest of us. Perhaps I could work my way closer to him, distract him somehow, then overpower him before he gets a shot off."

"That's a possibility," Henri agreed. "Perhaps Sarah and Emily should make that request together. At least that would remove them from any possible gunfire. We better do it soon, though. I'm becoming sleepy myself."

Henri leaned over and whispered in Sarah's ear, then settled himself back into the plush couch. He nodded slightly at Frank, who slowly rose and idly strolled from one wall to another, casually looking at the décor of the coach. After a few moments, Sarah also got up, extended her arms toward the ceiling in a makeshift stretch, and went over to where Emily was seated. She reached down, tapped her on the shoulder, and whispered, "Aunt Emily, would you go with me to the lavatory, please?" Emily didn't respond. Sarah gently touched her shoulder and shook her softly. "Aunt Emily?" She bent over to look at Emily's face but, before she could focus on it, suddenly felt the room begin to spin.

In the reflection of the coach window, Frank saw Sarah fall into Emily's lap. He automatically turned around to stride to her assistance, but felt that his legs had become weighted with lead. He looked down at his wobbly legs, lost his balance, and started to fall. He grabbed onto a sturdy library chair and looked over at Henri and Johann. They were out cold. As darkness closed around his peripheral vision he saw the guard at the end of the coach; one corner of his mouth was scrunched up in a mocking smirk. He secured his rifle to his side, rose up from his padded seat, turned, and exited the coach. Frank did not feel his body impact the floor.

Henri smelled the fresh scent of a powerful cup of fresh-ground coffee underneath his nose. He automatically reached up to grasp the tin mug that danced like a ghostly waif in his blurry vision. A deep voice encouraged, "Here we are, Mr. Mueller. Just as you like it. One lump of sugar, two tablespoons of cream." Henri scrunched his burning eyes together in hopes of solidifying the apparition floating in front of him. Once again, the aroma of the coffee took precedence over his grogginess and brought him to an awareness of his surroundings. He focused on the mug, took it, and appreciatively sipped the hot brew. He was seated on a comfortable couch, designed for two people. In front of him were some large draperies, closed for the moment. Oil lamps hung from the ceiling. To his right were a large oak desk, some cabinets, three well-stocked bookshelves, and a couple of chairs. On the wall, some beautiful paintings of the rugged mountains accented the finery of the office. A man walked over to the draperies and opened them to the bright light and a majestic view of the eastern face of the Rockies filled the natural frame of the window.

"I hope you slept well," Mr. Williams said as he finished opening the drapes. "I was afraid, after Miss Sarah's ordeal, that you and your companions would be awake all night. I took the liberty of adding a sleep aid to your juice last night so you would be well rested for your visit with Mr. Steele this fine morning." He looked at Henri with a warm smile. "You may trust me, sir, that your companions will be enjoying an excellent breakfast in another hour or so." Williams went over to a table by the door, picked up a tray, and brought it over to Henri. "Please, help yourself to some pastries. My steward was up early baking them fresh for your pleasure."

Henri wasn't particularly in a pleasant mood, but he recognized the need to have some food in his stomach. He placed the mug of coffee on a nearby stand, surveyed the tray, then picked out a scone along with a few pieces of cheese. He placed them on a cloth napkin, leaned back into the couch, and slowly nibbled on the food. After a few moments, he asked, "Mr. Williams, you've gone to a great deal of trouble to get me here. What is this all about?"

Williams returned the tray to the table by the door and picked out a pastry for himself as he responded, "I've told you, sir. Mr.

Steele has had his eyes on you for many years. I do believe he wishes to make you an offer you cannot refuse." He turned around with a smile, took a bite, and uncharacteristically continued with his mouth partially full. "Isn't this simply marvelous? I brought my chef in from Koblenz, Germany. He makes all this food from scratch with only the finest of ingredients."

Henri wondered at his seeming lack of focus. "Yes, it really is good." He took another bite, finished chewing, and nonchalantly asked, "Who is this Mr. Steele?"

"Ah, forgive me," Williams apologized. "I should have explained on the train." He took an additional scone, walked toward the massive oak desk and continued, "Mr. Everett Steele is one of the most powerful men in this territory. He has interests in mining and milling, timber, and extensive holdings in the railroad." He pointed a finger at Henri and laughed heartily. "Why, it is he who clears the rails for me whenever I have a notion to visit him. How else do you think we can travel so far in such a short time?"

He turned to look out the large-paned window toward the mountains. He put his napkin on the desk and folded his hands behind his back as he continued. "Everett was one of the first men to bring operating capital into this area. Yes, he expanded on his fortunes from the natural wealth he found in these hills, but he also brought a private sum of investment resources with him from California. His drive and ambition translated into a personal, almost obsessive, interest in developing the infrastructure of the isolated towns that sprung up from the mining boom. He helped construct transportation routes to remote areas, provided guidance in setting up town corporations, and worked on building a system of economic stability for the mining industry through sound banking practices. Along with other ideas favorable to this unique, resource-rich area, he brought leadership throughout the territory in uniting the miners, merchants, and laborers. He is a highly influential and respected member of the territorial legislature and hopes to lead this area to a distinctive and protective role in the development of this country."

"That sounds intriguing," Henri responded. "But what has that to do with a simple bridge engineer like me?"

Williams pursed his lips, looked emphatically at Henri and answered, "A simple bridge engineer? Why, Mr. Mueller, you do yourself a disservice. You underrate yourself, sir." He fished a pocket watch from his vest and clicked it open to view the time. "Ah, Mr. Steele should be here momentarily. Perhaps you might address the rest of your questions to him."

Soft, but distinctive, footsteps could be heard outside the heavy, oak door. The brass handle turned and the door silently opened.

CHAPTER 30

An extremely well-dressed man entered the room and closed the door behind him. He was tall and muscular for a man of maturing years. His graying head was held high by impeccable posture. Confidence and determination etched his face. His steel-blue eyes momentarily locked on Williams's and immediately invoked a warm and gracious smile. He extended his hand and said congenially, "Sydney, how good to see you!"

Williams reached for his hand and gave it slow and deliberate shake. "So good to see you, too, old friend."

Steele continued speaking without looking over to Henri. "Except for your unexpected stop in Brookville for repairs, was your trip safe and uneventful?"

"Yes," Williams responded. "My engineer may have broken a new speed record. Other than picking up some passengers, it was uneventful."

"Good, good," Steele replied. He turned to look at Henri, studied him for an instant, and then readdressed Williams. "Perhaps you could leave Mr. Mueller and me alone for a few minutes while we discuss some business."

"Absolutely," Williams answered. Steele put a fatherly arm over Williams's shoulder and gently escorted him to the door. He leaned over and spoke some directions into his ear in a quiet, low voice. Then he pulled back, nodded, and patted him on the back as he left.

Everett Steele closed the heavy, oak door, then pivoted on his heel to face Henri. His probing eyes locked on Henri's for a full minute. Then he stepped over to the desk and leaned calmly on the hard wooden top. "Mr. Mueller, you have presented me with somewhat of a challenge."

Henri tilted his head slightly and responded with a simple, "Oh?"

Steele's eyes narrowed slightly as he continued, "Your incessant meddling in affairs that don't concern you has put my itinerary behind schedule."

"And what meddling might that be?" Henri inquired.

"Oh, come now, sir. Don't act so naïve. You've been hounddogging my operation for almost ten years. Ever since you presented your review of the incident on the Maple River to Edgar Burns, we've been trying to silence your investigation. If you had just stayed tied to that bridge abutment in Alabama . . ." His voice trailed off in mock disappointment.

"I'm sorry to have disappointed you," Henri replied sarcastically. After a moment's consideration, he added, "It was fortunate for you that your organization hid its operation so well. If I had had better facts to present to Grant back in 1864, you would have been out of business long ago."

Steele picked up on the compliment. "Yes, it was fortunate for us that we covered our tracks well." He idly looked around on his desk for something to toy with. "You know, after Grant was elected, it was difficult to create all those distractions to occupy him so he wouldn't notice the obvious. Corruption in government is as natural as the sunrise, but to orchestrate so many disruptions at one time and have them all point at the newly elected president was by design. It worked out well for us. That, along with Johnson's impeachment proceedings, kept both Grant and Congress in the dark about what we were doing and what you were reporting."

Henri thought for a second, then asked, "So, whatever happened to Burns?"

"You might say that he was removed from internal affairs." Steele's eyes flashed cold as he continued, "I'm afraid you spooked him to the point where he became a liability." He reached across the desk, picked up a pencil, and indifferently played with it. "He was becoming sloppy in his work. If he had been discovered, he would have been shot for treason. And who knows how many others he would have taken with him? I like to think that we provided him with a valuable corporate service and avoided a lot of embarrassment for both him and ourselves." He paused for a moment, then straightened to look out the window at the mountains. "You know it took me five years to get you demoted to that redundant treasury position? I had to call in a number of favors in Washington. You had a decent reputation."

"Well, that makes me feel real sad," Henri answered sarcastically. Plying for more information, he altered the subject somewhat. "Williams told us about your master plan to heal the Union through financial attrition. But, tell me, because the conflict resolved itself by other means, you had to alter your ideas. What did you do?"

Steele turned to face Henri, then calmly walked over to the chair behind his desk and sat down. He put his elbows on the oak top, folded his hands, and met Henri's stare. "We had a viable plan to reunify the North and the South. It would have worked."

"And, of course, all that 'lost' gold would have made you extremely rich, I imagine," Henri said.

"Yes, it would have," Steele quietly replied. "But the gold that was diverted from the North and South now has a greater purpose."

"What are you talking about?" Henri quizzed.

Steele leaned back in the chair and folded his hands behind

his head. He contemplated his response. "The original plan when the gold shipments were taken was to hide the bullion in secret caches across the West. Each location was thought by our geologists at the time to be close to future mineral-rich gold producing areas. After the country was reunited, our plan was to reintegrate the gold bullion back into the economy through falsified mining reports from the mines to the processing mints. We had planned on using the investment capital for a private rebuilding of the South at a great profit.

"When Johnson assumed the presidency after Lincoln's assassination, his sympathy for the South, along with Lincoln's already established reconstruction policies that Johnson determined to follow, in a sense threw our organization out of the investment arena. As a result, it was necessary to redirect our intent and design a new course of action. A second major blow to our itinerary happened when it was discovered that many of the cache sites ended up near mineral areas rich in silver, not gold. Only three locations could make viable covers for our gold reintegration policies. One of those, in California, ended up as a total falsification of all records because, in actuality, there was no gold at the mine at all.

"The geologists we hired misinterpreted the geologic formations of the area. It turned out that the only gold was placer gold deposited in the river gravel and the striated beds exposed by hydraulic blasting. Our deep-rock mining efforts were worthless. As a result, it took enormous additional amounts of time and manpower to manufacture and keep secret the misinformation campaign to even use that site. Even then, there were a few touchy incidents when the mint in San Francisco doubted our reports. Fortunately, the reputation of the gold fields of the 1850s was still prevalent in the area and we were able to build on that rush of excitement and plant some fresh gold scrapings in the deep mine shafts.

"The second site, in Nevada, became a problem because of the way the new mining laws were written when it became a state in 1864. We didn't realize the difficulty until we tried to reprocess the redirected gold bars from back East. The documentation for accurate production was overseen by a federal agency that prohibited us from slipping in any outside contraband. As it turned out, only the facility in Georgetown, a short distance west of here, was useable. It was still under the territorial control that I had a direct hand in establishing, so the laws for gold production and documentation were favorable. Plus, some of the surrounding mines still had the reputation as large gold producers. It has taken a number of years to secretly arrange the transfer of the buried caches all the way to our facility near Georgetown. There are only two left, one of which is in transit as we speak."

"You said that the unforeseen end of the war changed your purpose for the gold," Henri commented. "What changes in your plan did you make?"

Steele shifted in his chair and sat up. "Have you considered that the greatest hindrance to embarking on any new venture is the availability of operating capital?" He didn't wait for a reply. "To put it simply, Mr. Mueller, my intent is to create a new country out of this Colorado Territory. The gold currently in storage will be the financial impetus for success. And there is a very positive benefit thanks to the self-interest of the Grant administration.

"As you know, there is a so-called silver panic currently in progress. When Grant devalued the mineral two years ago, he created a number of backlashes. The first was that he fueled the growing discontent of the miners in this entire region. Silver, the main economic fuel for this area, has been tremendously devalued. But that is beneficial if you have gold. Previously, one grain of gold could be exchanged for nine grains of silver. Now the ratio is sixteen to one, and it will rise.

"My intent is to purchase large amounts of silver with the gold I have in storage. Now, through my persuasion of certain people in Washington, I have encouraged a movement to repeal the silver devaluation act of 1873. I'm guessing that by fall of 1878, Congress will pass a law requiring the government to buy back a certain amount of silver at a set price. The silver in my possession will more than double in price. My conservative estimate is that the gold we cached back in 1865 will be worth six times its bullion value by the end of that year. That amount will provide an abundance of reserves to properly develop the timber and mining industries of these fabulous mountains along with providing proper education, infrastructure, and community expansion to make the growth a long-lasting and profitable venture."

Henri shifted his weight on the couch, crossed his legs, and politely asked, "And what type of support do you have in this area for implementing such a plan?"

"Enough," Steele responded. "A number of my specialists have been working on my political agenda over the past few years. Many of the mining communities are supportive of the issues that have been raised. They recognize the need to keep the mineral wealth of this land in the control of a local and autonomous government. This territory is ripe for setting up this plan. In fact, Grant's devaluation of silver provides the fuse necessary to set it all in motion. All that is needed is the match to ignite it."

"And what is that match?" Henri asked.

"That, sir, is something that requires your assistance," Steele replied, without emotion.

CHAPTER 31

As Mr. Williams had promised, the breakfast served in the Pullman coach to the "guests" was magnificent. The table was spread with multiple plates of assorted fruits, pastries, and breads. Platters with fresh sausages, ham, bacon, and two types of eggs accented the silver tableware and cloth napkins. As with Henri, it was the fresh aroma of strong coffee that woke the sleeping passengers. They seemed oblivious to the events of the previous night and, after performing some necessities customary to rising in the morning, were seated around the table eating the morning meal.

"I guess Henri is meeting with Mr. Williams's associate," Emily commented as she seated herself at the table. "I noticed he was gone when I woke up. Funny, but I don't remember falling asleep on the couch last night. I must have really been sleepy."

"I don't remember a whole lot either," Frank added. "All I know is that I seemed to sleep well on the chair by the window. I wonder how long Henri has been gone?"

"I left him with Mr. Steele about an hour ago," Williams said loudly as he closed the entry door to the coach. The "guests" turned to look at him as he entered. "He is having a pleasant conversation about his future opportunities," he added. He placed his coat on a hook and walked over to the dining table.

"I see you are enjoying the breakfast I promised you." He smiled and folded his hands as he continued, "I hope you'll take this as an apology for the manner in which you were brought here. You see, Mr. Steele is on a tight itinerary, and it was necessary to have a chat with Mr. Mueller. It was fortunate that my train was in Brookville so I could expedite your trip out here. Mr. Steele had planned on meeting with Henri when he arrived in Denver, but circumstances accelerated so quickly that he needed to see him sooner."

There was no response from anyone. Their abduction and involuntary confinement spoke for itself and was understood. The necessity of conducting themselves in a friendly manner with their captors did not overshadow staying aware of their situation.

"Well, I hope they work out an arrangement soon so we can be on our way," Emily said as she reached for some fruit. She knew, too, that it was important to be relaxed and seemingly unaware of what was happening. It might give them an element of surprise should the occasion arise. "I've a household to set up in Denver."

"And indeed you shall," Williams responded. "It might only be delayed for a short time, that's all. Now, if you'll excuse me for a bit, I have some business to attend to at the station depot." He took his coat from the hook and exited the coach. Three guards stationed themselves at the two doorways and sat down on bench seats. The party resumed their meal in silence, each lost in thought concerning the next move.

It wasn't long after breakfast was finished that "the next move" happened. The train lurched and began creeping down the tracks toward the edge of the switchyard. "Where are we off to now?" Sarah thought aloud.

They watched out the window as the train pulled onto the main railhead, and accelerated on the rail tracks pointed west toward the mountains.

★　★　★　★　★

Everett Steele replaced the pencil on the oak desk, and walked over to one of the bookshelves along the wall. He perused the edges of the thick volume titles and reached out for one in particular. He opened it, shuffled through the pages, stopped, and began to read a short section to himself. Then he looked up at Henri. "Are you aware, sir, that some great events in history have started as a result of small, almost insignificant pivot points? Let me give an example." He looked at the book and paraphrased, "The battle at Gettysburg began when some Confederate soldiers went into that small town to look for some badly needed shoes. They rounded a corner and ran into a Union patrol. That began one of the bloodiest battles of the war and may have turned the tide to the Union effort." He closed the book, returned it to its shelf and asked, "Don't you think it strange, sir, how the smallest incident can turn the tide of history? Just imagine what something really significant might do."

Steele returned to the seat behind the oak desk. He pondered a moment and said, "What our endeavor needs is a significant event to light the fuse." He fixed his eyes on Henri and continued, "You were good friends with Grant during the war. He respects you. Did you know that he is coming here for a visit in a few days?"

Henri's eyes narrowed a little as he focused on what Steele was saying.

Steele picked up the pencil and doodled on some paper. "He's coming partly to campaign for his next term, partly to see the area. It's his second visit in only three years, you know. He likes it here. But Grant is a little unpredictable. On his visit to Georgetown in 1873, he came to the town a day early. The city fathers were rather upset, as they had a hoopla planned for the following day. Needless to say, the merchants would be thankful if someone was able to persuade Grant to follow his schedule on this visit. Perhaps you, Mr. Mueller, would be kind enough to accompany the president to Georgetown from Denver this next Friday? I imagine a visit from an old friend, such as yourself, could persuade him to keep his itinerary."

It was obvious by Steele's patronizing voice that there was more to his plan than Henri chaperoning the president. He shifted on the couch, looked Steele in the eye, and casually replied, "Mr. Steele, what would prompt me to offer you my assistance?"

Steele's eyes wandered to the desk as he ground the pencil he was doodling with into the pad of paper and snapped off the end. He looked at the broken end and tossed it in the waste can next to his chair as he repeated under his breath, "What would prompt you?" He glared at Henri and stated, "How about the safe return of your associates?" He paused, swung his chair to look out the window and continued, "You see, they are no longer in Denver."

"What do you mean, no longer in Denver?" Henri asked, startled.

"Let's just say that Mr. Williams invited them on an extensive tour of one of my mining facilities," he replied. "I can assure you, Mr. Mueller, that they have accepted his invitation. I do hope they are careful, though. Mining is such a dangerous occupation." Steele turned around, leaned on the desk and sneered, "Now, what was that you were saying about being prompted?"

CHAPTER 32

Mike, James, and Derek rose early in the morning. An overcast sky spat a mix of icy drizzle and sleet that added no enjoyment to their breakfast of cold, hard jerky. It was difficult to see the edge of Fairplay in the foggy distance, so Mike had climbed a huge fir tree bordering the forest line so he could scan the town's perimeter along its northern flank. There were only three roads that Baxter and his team could travel on. One went toward Denver, the second toward Alta, and the third by his perch toward Breckenridge. A bitter blast of mountain wind caused Mike to shiver as he focused with no small trouble on the three roadways. "Are you sure that Baxter was leaving this morning?" he piped to his comrades at the base of the massive tree.

"That's what Corky said," Derek answered. "Maybe the nasty weather changed his schedule."

"I doubt it," James interjected. "Baxter seems to be on a tight time schedule that doesn't allow for delays." He folded his arms and stamped his cold feet. "It's hard to believe the weather turned so foul overnight. I wonder if the passes at the upper elevations will still be passable?"

Unexpectedly, a small but distinct voice emanated from the tree line. "I kinda figured you guys would still be here." It was Corky. He was dressed in an oversized woolen coat with an ill-fitting toboggan affixed to his head. His clothes blended into the trees like natural camouflage.

"Corky?" James asked. "We didn't see you. Why are you out

here so early?"

"Not early enough," he replied sarcastically. "Simmons, the hardware store owner, told me this morning that Baxter woke him up around three to pay his storage bill. He then pulled out with the five wagons and headed east toward Kenosha Pass. He probably saw the ring around the moon last night and figured the weather would turn sour." He scanned through the low clouds and pointed toward the horizon where the eastern mountains should be and continued, "I suppose he took the road over Red Hill Pass, across Como Park, Kenosha Pass, and on toward Denver. You shouldn't have much trouble catching up to them as long as they don't reach the turnoff to Guanella Pass first."

"Guanella Pass?" James quizzed.

"Yeah, Guanella Pass," Corky replied. "It's another route over the mountains to Denver. I hear it's rough and gets snowed in easy. It goes north from Grant and skirts the backside of Mount Evans. Then it descends into Silver Plume and ties into the new wagon road going east toward Georgetown. From there it's only a few miles to a station on the railroad that connects Central City to Golden. You might have trouble figuring out which way they took if it's snowing up there."

"You certainly have a lot of knowledge of the area," James observed.

Corky looked down and slowly kicked his feet in the dirt. "I listen to the miners as they tell stories at the saloon. They come through Fairplay on their way to the newest strike, and give trail and weather reports about the passes. They also give all the news from back East. It's really the main way we find out what's going on back there."

James nodded his head, turned, and said to Derek, "Better get the horses." Then he looked up toward Mike and barked, "And you, get down outta that tree! We got some miles to travel." Then he turned toward Corky and continued, "We really appreciate you coming out to tell us." He reached in his pocket to fish for some coins.

Corky shook his head as he watched James's hand searching for money. "No, this one is free. I couldn't stand to see Mike turn blue in that cold wind up in that tree."

"Well," Mike graciously replied, "let us at least give you a ride back into town. No need for secrecy anymore. Let's move out."

The three men mounted their horses. Mike reached down, lifted Corky onto the back of the horse with one arm, and the group headed toward Fairplay at full gallop.

It wasn't long before they reached the telegraph station. Mike lowered Corky to the ground as James reined his horse in and faced the young boy. He caught Corky's attention just as he flicked a shard of something toward the boy. Corky, a little caught by surprise, cupped his two hands together and pulled the object toward his belly as if he were catching a ball. James wheeled the horse around, looked over his shoulder as he spurred his horse, and quipped, "Your information is worth its weight in gold, Corky. Use it wisely!" With that, the three men raced eastward to catch up with Baxter and his wagon train.

CHAPTER 33

The road, rendered slick by sleet, headed east across flat but slowly ascending steppe land. Off to the left of the road at a short distance was a narrow, turbulent mountain stream. It twisted like a snake through the thick carpets of grass, but was clear and crisp and radiated a little steam in the cold surrounding air. At a greater distance, patches of heavy timber dotted the landscape like pieces of dark cloth on a large green quilt. Above the trees, the high mountains stood like stark sentinels girthed in layers of striated clouds that covered their lower flanks. Behind them, to the west, streaks of freezing rain slashed to the ground in stripes of gray. Before them lay an ominous mix of unsettled weather reflected in the dark heaviness of low clouds full of snow.

James pulled up the collar of his coat and pulled his hat low over his ears as he urged his horse to continue its rhythmic canter. After a couple hours of travel, the high altitude of Red Hill Pass caused the sleet to turn into a thick, wet snowfall. It accumulated rapidly on the rocky roadway and forced the men to slow their pace to keep the horses from slipping. The bitter westerly wind pelted their backs with icy snow and reduced their visibility substantially, but they continued as quickly as was safe. The road descended rapidly on the eastern edge of the pass, and the snow once again turned into a slushy mix of rain and sleet. They continued riding eastward across barren land spotted with sagebrush and a prickly sort of bush and, after another two hours, began their ascent up Kenosha Pass. They noticed the snow line about two thirds of the way up the pass and braced themselves for more slippery travel. Sure enough, the sleet changed to snow, as if on cue, but this time built up quickly, covering the roadway and making it treacherous. The men got off their horses and led them over the snow-covered rocks and holes of the mountain saddle, and to the eastern slope. The leeward side offered a little more protection from the howling wind and blinding snow, but the reluctance of the horses to continue eventually forced a temporary reprieve at a collection of huge boulders. James led the small party to a relatively flat area protected on three sides by the massive granite cairns to give them all a rest out of the bitterly cold wind and snow.

"How far do you think we've come?" Derek asked.

After a moment, James responded. "I think Kenosha Pass is only a few miles from Grant. I can't believe Baxter got his teams over this pass before the storm hit. He must have really been pushing his horses."

James lined up the three horses to help as a windbreak and added, "And to think that Guanella Pass is a thousand feet or so higher than this one!"

"What makes you think Baxter took that way?" Derek queried.

"You heard Corky," James replied. "It goes to Georgetown. So far, Baxter has taken the shortest and most direct route possible regardless of the road difficulty. I'm confident that's the route he's taking." He wiped some snow off of his saddle, rubbed his hands, and pulled his collar up again. "I imagine we'll be catching up to him soon. He's got a lot of load on those wagons and can't make as good a pace as we can."

Snow continued to fall, though gentler in the confines of their open vault. They could hear the screaming wind a short distance above their heads, as they were not far from the pass itself.

"You know, this storm could go on for a number of hours," Derek said. "I know that down by Silverton these freak spring storms can dump feet of snow overnight above timberline. There's also not much wood up here to start a fire. Maybe we should risk it and continue on down the mountain. Grant has to be quite a bit lower than here and, perhaps, it is only raining there."

"I think that may be a good idea," James responded.

Mike nodded his head in agreement, cleaned the snow off his horse, and said, "I'll lead the way this time."

He moved his horse back onto the trail and the men began their descent. The roadway wasn't as steep on the eastern slope and the trio swiftly entered into an area that had more timber that protected them from the icy wind. Pine tree boughs collected the crisp snow and draped the roadway like large fluffs of white cotton.

"It's hard to believe that these trees break the wind so much," Mike noted. "It makes traveling this road a lot easier."

The roadway eventually descended below the snow line again and, sure enough, the mix of sleet and light rain resumed. A short time later the troupe saw the few buildings of Grant in the distance. They approached the small town and tied their horses up at the only store. It was a little general hardware that had a small amount of tools, groceries of a sort, and general merchandise pertinent to a small way station. They kicked the slush off of their feet as they opened the door and entered the store. In spite of the nasty weather outside, the interior of the building was warm and cozy. A large potbellied stove in the corner radiated a crackling heat from its cast-iron sides. Two men casually played a game of checkers next to the shelves of dry goods. They turned to see the entrance of the shivering travelers.

"Here, warm yourselves up by the stove," a baldheaded man said as he ushered the visitors in. "Elmer, move the table over and let these men sit in those seats. C'mon now, get a move on!"

Elmer did as he was told, albeit rather slowly. James and Mike scooted the chairs closer to the stove; Derek cozied up to the open stove door and held his hands near the flame.

"Here, give me those coats," the baldheaded man said. "I'll hang them up to dry over in the corner." He took their wraps and put them on some coat hooks on the other side of the stove. Steam soon wafted off of them like wisps of mist. Then he turned and added, "My name's Harry. You fellows shouldn't be out riding on a day like this." He wildly gestured with his hands and swung his arms around like a monkey as he walked toward the coal bin. "It's nasty out there. I can't believe there are so many crazy people cavorting about in such weather!"

James looked over at Mike. Mike smiled and politely asked, "What do you mean by so many 'crazy' people?"

"Well you three are not the only ones." He reached for a lump of coal and tossed it to Derek with a motion to stoke the stove. "About two hours ago a wagon train of miners came through town. Stopped to warm up for a while, and then headed back out again. Bought a few supplies, you know: some blankets, food, and some oil for their lanterns. They were a quiet bunch, but friendly and good-natured considering the elements outside. Said they had to get over the pass before dark. Can you believe that? Why, it's already . . ." He paused to get a breath of air and pull out his timepiece. He looked at the watch and continued like he'd never stopped. "After three. Can you imagine just how much snow is going to be up on the Guanella? Why, I'd venture to say it's already in the feet. Gotta be crazy to take a group of wagons up there in conditions like this."

Harry's face turned red and his voice trailed off at a higher pitch than when he started. Derek, his back to Harry, tossed the coal into the stove and smirked at Mike as he tried to contain his laughter at the ramblings of the store's proprietor. Harry concluded his tirade by asking, "So what brings you boys out in weather like this?"

James looked at Mike, who blinked a couple of times, then looked at Derek, who looked back at James. Finally, James replied, "We're traveling with the wagon train. We stopped to wait for a message in Fairplay and are now trying to catch up with them."

Harry threw up his hands in disgust, wagged his head in disbelief, and cried, "Why, you're all crazier than a grizzly bear eating a bee's honey nest!" He paused, looked at the cash register, and added, "Is there anything I can get you while you warm up?"

Mike sniffed in a mock reply. "Is that soup I smell?"

Harry jumped at the opportunity. "Yes, it is. Fresh vegetable soup that's been simmering for half the day. It's good and cheap. I'll get you each a bowl." He turned toward the kitchen, then added, "If you'd like, I can have Elmer here give your horses some fresh hay and brush them out."

James gave him a nod to do so.

As Harry dredged up some soup bowls, and Elmer reluctantly went outside to perform his chores, the three men quietly discussed their situation amongst themselves.

"The snow line has moved down the mountain," Derek remarked. He pointed out the window at the large flakes of slowly falling snow as he continued, "If Baxter picked up relief horses before ascending the pass, he feasibly could get across it tonight. That guy has determination in what he does."

"That's true," James added. "Seems like he'll push through

any situation to accomplish a goal." He pursed his lips and thought out loud. "I suppose we'll have to continue the chase or we'll lose him on the other side. We know he's close to his destination, but we don't know what that destination is." Derek and Mike nodded in quiet understanding. James went on. "Let's warm up for an hour, get some food in our bellies, then head out. I think the horses will be fine after some fresh feed and a short rest. If the snow is really deep on the pass, then perhaps even Baxter will have to pull off and wait out the storm."

"That sounds like a good plan," Mike said. He reached around behind him and pulled the small table toward him that Elmer had moved. "In the meantime, anybody want to play some checkers?"

CHAPTER 34

Their hour of rest passed quickly, but it gave them the second wind they needed to continue their pursuit of Baxter. The snow had not let up, but the winds had died down in the valley where Grant was located. They headed north toward Guanella Pass, their horses kicking up snow.

"Looks like Baxter has almost a two-and-a-half-hour head start on us," Derek said.

"I'm hoping that any deeper snow further up the valley will slow him down," James responded.

The roadway wasn't too bad to travel on. It was smooth and well graded and, although the snow had accumulated to around ten inches, the heavy timber on either side shielded them from any wind. They cantered their horses along at a steady gait and made good headway up the mountain. On occasion the trees would part and open up a view across the open range hundreds of feet below. The valley meadows, white with a blanket of fresh snow, stood out in contrast to the stands of deep-green trees. Low clouds, filled with snow, blocked the mile-long vistas, but opened here and there long enough to see the distant high peaks. As the roadway continued its climb upwards, it became increasingly narrow and rough. The tree stands became thinner and the wind speed increased. They rounded a bend where the road was almost pinched closed by two rock projections. On the other side, a small group of aspen trees had a natural open spot in the middle about the size of a large barn.

Mike, who was leading the troupe, reined in his horse and said, "Looks like one of their wagons broke something here."

Derek moved forward, dismounted, and walked up to investigate a small pile of debris in the middle of the clearing. Although the snow was over a foot deep, a spot that was trampled down had some timbers and miscellaneous parts scattered about. "Looks like one of their wagons broke an axle," he said. "There isn't much snow on the debris. And look," he pointed ahead on the ground. Fresh horse and wagon tracks were still defined in the snow. Derek added, "I'd wager they are less than an hour in front of us. This snow is only an inch or so deep on the broken axle transom, and their wagon tracks haven't filled up that much. We should take care, now, how close we get." He gazed up the mountain as far as the clouds permitted, and continued, "If this snow wasn't falling, we could probably see them on the shelf road above timberline."

They resumed their climb up the pass. Snow and wind immediately picked up in force as they emerged from the trees above timberline. The gnarled roots of the last stand of protective trees, small and deformed because of the high altitude, grasped at any form of bedrock to secure themselves from the raging winds on the mountain. Beyond was a steep blanket of white that could've been either ground or cloud. Deep snow hid the shelf road and completely covered the hidden holes, crags, and slippery, loose talus rock, making a firm footing difficult. To their left, the mountain fell away in a sheer, vertical drop. To their right, the cliff rose just as dramatically and vanished into the clouds. The men hugged the inner edge of the roadway as they led their horses through the heavy, thick snow. On and on they trudged, climbing higher and higher on the mountain. At last they reached the pass. It was barren and cold. Thick clouds closed off any view. It was difficult to distinguish between the snow-covered ground and the snow-filled sky. The one consolation was that the wind had actually kept the top of the mountain almost clear of snow, as its depth was only a couple of inches. The men took advantage of that and quickly picked up the pace, although it didn't last long.

After a few hundred yards on the leeward side of the mountain, the snow almost doubled in depth. The roadway, steeper and laced with switchbacks, disappeared in and out of the terrain like a frightened snake. As the trio slowly descended, the howling wind sounded like men screaming at the unrelenting elements. It was hard to fathom a man bringing five wagons of equipment over these mountains under these conditions. James wondered out loud why he and his companions had ventured into such a dangerous spot.

All they could do was continue their descent. Eventually, and gradually, they fell below timberline and entered the safety of the trees. Where the standing timber blocked the wind, the tracks of Baxter's wagons showed up clearly in the snow. After a short distance, Derek came up to James and asked, "Did you notice anything unusual about the tracks?"

James stopped and looked down for a moment at the roadway. The snow depth was less than a foot now, and the tracks were fresh and plain. He cocked his head a little to the side and said, "There're not as many wheel tracks."

"That's what I thought," Derek responded. "It looks like there are only two wagons instead of five."

They rounded another bend where the trees opened up; they could dimly see below in the valley two wagons moving across an open park. "There they are," Mike said. "There are only two left. Something must have happened on the pass to the other three."

"They may have split up on a turnoff that we didn't see," Derek theorized. He squinted his eyes for a better view. "I can't believe how fast those heavy wagons are moving. We better pick up the pace or else we'll lose them again."

The roadway leveled out where the horses could resume a steady trot. The snow had thinned and it was beginning to warm up. "Harry said this road goes by the Silver Plume mine and mill and then down into Georgetown, didn't he?" Mike asked.

"Yeah," Derek replied. "It shouldn't be too much further. I think he said it was only twenty miles or so from Grant."

"That's good, because it is starting to get dark," Mike added.

In spite of the inclement weather, they made quick time over the mountain. They left Grant around four and it was starting to push eight. From Fairplay they had been traveling over fourteen hours and it was showing on them and the horses. The storm deceived them by covering all the shadows that one usually sees in order to gauge the time, so it was a sudden realization how late it really was.

"We had better close up the distance between us and the wagons before all the light disappears," James said. "If we lose them now, it will be hard to locate them in the morning."

They picked up their pace down the path and noticed that the wagons had taken a turnoff. "Looks like they're about home," Derek observed. "I think this is the road to the Silver Plume mine and mill." In the distance they could just make out some lights in the window of a number of buildings a short distance across the mountain. "I think it's safe to say that this was their destination," he added.

They pulled their horses well off the main road into a stand of dense fir trees near and above the mine complex. "I guess it's cold jerky for dinner and a cold bed to sleep on tonight," Mike grumbled. The snow was barely falling now and the ground only had a trace of white on it. "I do hope it warms up by morning," he added as he unrolled his bed.

But James didn't lay out his sleeping pack for the night. He was intently watching the building complex. After some deliberation, he said, "You two stay here with the horses and try to get some sleep. I'm going down to the mill and look around."

"What? Are you nuts?" Mike exclaimed.

"No," he replied. "We followed these wagons all the way from Silverton. Now's the best time to see what Baxter is up to. It's night, there's a storm going on. I imagine he's really tired."

"Yeah, just like me," Mike quipped. "Okay, I'll go with you. Wouldn't want you to find any trouble."

"No, you two stay here. I think there is less risk of being seen if I'm alone. If I do get caught, I'll have an easier time explaining why I'm out in a blizzard by myself."

Mike and Derek could tell that he was serious by his tone, so didn't try to change his mind. Mike said, "Well, be careful. Double back to the fork in the road so you don't leave footprints leading to our campsite. I guess if you're not back by morning we'll come looking for you."

With that, James disappeared into the dark of night and headed for the mill.

CHAPTER 35

Sydney Williams's train thundered down the well-used tracks toward Golden. Rocky Mountain foothills grew in size as the plains of Denver fell behind. The mountains loomed ahead like an impenetrable barrier stretching from north to south as far as the eye could see.

"It's a fairly quick ride to Golden," Williams promised. "And it is scenic, though not as scenic as the narrow gauge run from Golden to Floyd's Hill."

Sarah pulled herself away from the window to look at Williams while she asked, "What is a 'narrow gauge'?"

"Ah, the narrow gauge," Williams wistfully replied. "The narrow gauge is what made railroad traffic in the mountains possible." He walked over to Sarah and sat down next to her as he continued to explain. "The type of rail that we have been traveling on since Kansas is called a standard-gauge track. It is four feet eight and one-half inches center to center, and provides a good degree of stability for speed and long range hauling of freight. But when the railroad needed to reach the mines, the tighter curves and steeper inclines required a lighter and more nimble type of engine. In addition, the cost of blasting a bed wide enough to accommodate the standard rail trains was prohibitive. General William Palmer, director of the Denver and Rio Grande, decided to set the standard for his mountain rail system at three feet, thus the term 'narrow gauge.' It made the easy and inexpensive transportation of equipment and supplies into the remote camps possible." He looked out the window and continued, "This train will carry us to the switching yard in Golden, where we will transfer to a narrow-gauge train that will take us west, part of the way toward Black Hawk and Central City. A switching device six miles this side of Black Hawk, at Fork's Creek, will then allow us to travel west toward Georgetown to the end of the tracks at Floyd's Hill. The Colorado Central owns the wagon and stage line that will then take us through Idaho Springs, Georgetown, and on to Mr. Steele's mining facility at Silver Plume. It is a most fantastic trip through some unbelievably narrow gorges."

"Why are we going to a mining facility at Silver Plume?" Sarah queried.

"Well," Williams answered, "part of Mr. Mueller's job offer involved extending the rail line on to Georgetown and then up the mountain to Silver Plume. The production at the mine and mill is extraordinary, and Mr. Steele thought that an appropriate tour of the facility, showing its great wealth and potential, might have some sway, as we say in the banking industry, on Mr. Mueller's pocketbook. He also thought that his family should see its beauty since that would be Mr. Mueller's residence."

He resumed looking out the window at the spectacular scenery. The train finished climbing the first gradient that extended over the top of Tabletop Mountain. Denver and its surrounding communities disappeared into some haze from the industrial section of the area. Miles and miles of empty plateau land, interrupted only by an occasional gorge, stretched on to the north.

Williams's train kept a quick pace all the way to Golden. The foothills and early grades of the higher mountains had little effect on the huge capabilities of the prototype engine. Less than an hour had passed before the train rolled into the switchyards on the outskirts of Golden. They stopped well away from the standard depot and waited for a smaller, stockier engine to approach on a narrower rail line located next to theirs. After a few moments, an almost toy-like engine with a white "58" painted on its side slipped next to Williams's much larger unit. A common bridge was slipped between the two passenger cars and the guests were led across. The first thing the group noticed was the plainness of the car. It was a long rectangular box with wooden benches attached to the floor. In one corner stood a cast-iron stove with a pipe extending through the roof. There was some wood, probably from the previous winter, stacked in a neat pile next to it. The windows had been removed for the summer months, which, on one hand, provided ample ventilation, but, on the other, permitted the sooty smoke of the engine to enter the car depending on the wind and angle of the train. They took their places in the middle of the passenger car, once again with two guards at each end of the aisle.

With a customary jerk, the train started moving. It wound noisily through the switchyard and headed toward the edge of Golden. The town had been the territorial capital until 1867, when the legislature moved it to Denver. As a result, the heyday it experienced was already a thing of the past. But the large buildings made of brick and clapboard siding were made to last. In spite of its political inferiority, it still maintained the status of a town with a bright future as a rail hub and primary supply station for the mining towns to the north and the west.

The narrow-gauge train skirted Golden's perimeter and continued west up the valley toward the turnoff to Black Hawk.

For a group of folks from the East, the panorama was magnificent. After only a couple of miles, the rail bed drew close to the raging river carrying volumes of water from the snowmelt of the high country. Gradual slopes of the mountains radically changed to steep, craggy walls plunging vertically out of sight. Boulders the size of houses littered the riverbed from the flash floods of spring. The railroad meandered parallel to the watercourse as it flowed between granite pinnacles. Where the gorge was narrow, the builders had blasted a horizontal bed out of the vertical mountainside and used the rubble as fill material for the railroad base. It was an engineering marvel that fascinated the travelers in the car.

The train soon reached the turnoff at Twin Forks. The gorge had broadened somewhat and opened up enough to accommodate a massive wooden bridge across the roaring watercourse. On one side of the river, just before the bridge, the rail forked, with one set of tracks continuing up toward Black Hawk, and the other crossing over to follow another river that gouged a path through the granite up to Floyd's Hill and Idaho Springs. The engine slowed for the bridge crossing, then climbed the consistent grade, belching black smoke and blowing steam.

It was a little over three miles from Twin Forks to the end of the line at Floyd's Hill. At that point, they were transferred from the train to a couple of stagecoaches for the ride to Georgetown, some fifteen miles further. The wagon road ascended through another canyon from the rail terminus, then over a steep hill, and finally into Idaho Springs. From there, it was a relatively easy road into Georgetown. It was there that the ladies adamantly requested a lavatory break from their travels. Strangely enough, Williams had already arranged with his drivers to stop in Georgetown at the Hotel de Paris, which had only recently opened. He seemed excited about the prospect, and aroused the curiosity of his confined guests.

CHAPTER 36

Georgetown was far from the typical Colorado mining camp. It was unique in that it was a town of homes, to which the miners and merchants brought their loved ones and tried to reflect the customs and style of their heritage back East. Many of the larger buildings were not just made to last, being built of brick and masonry, but carried in their architecture the nostalgia and dignity of a Victorian era more conducive to New England than a frontier mining community. An occasional cast-iron hitching post reminiscent of New York City, or a carriage block at the little park possibly inspired by a Vermont village green, added to the distinctive feeling that this was a mining community with "class."

Part of that class included the Hotel de Paris, which was owned by an eccentric Frenchman named Louis Dupuy. He had migrated to Georgetown sometime in the late sixties, intent on cashing in on the easy gold pickings he had heard about. Instead, he found hard work in prospecting the steep mountainsides. He had planned on moving to greener pastures, but an injury in a mine explosion involuntarily lengthened his tenancy. After his recovery, he lacked the strength to continue in the rigorous occupation of mining, so he drew on his natural talent for cooking and was hired at Delmonico's Bakery and Restaurant on Alpine Street. It didn't take long for him to become sole owner of the establishment and expand his operations.

A short, black-haired man with high cheekbones and a neatly

trimmed mustache stepped from the massive front door, warmly held his arms out and exclaimed, "Sydney, my friend! It's so good to see you."

"And you, too." Sydney smiled as he gave Louis a friendly hug. "I have some guests in my care that I would like to introduce to you," he continued. With aristocratic pomp, he commenced with introductions of his courteous captives, who quietly understood that an attempt at sanctuary at the Hotel de Paris would be futile. Afterwards, he added, "I would be most indebted to you, sir, if you would accommodate the immediate needs of my friends and also prepare them one of your fine midday meals. Afterwards, we must continue on so as to beat the setting sun."

"But of course," Louis graciously smiled. He turned to his concierge and whispered some instructions, then extended his arm hospitably. "Please, come in and allow me to show you my establishment."

Louis ushered the party into the grand hotel and saw to it that their needs were fulfilled in every capacity possible.

After a lavish lunch, Williams announced that it was time to continue their trek up the mountain to the Silver Plume. Sarah and Johann requested a final use of the facilities and were permitted such use without a guard. Johann took his leather pouch and knapsack with him.

At the top of the stairwell, out of sight from below, Johann whispered to Sarah, "I saw another door at the back while Louis was showing us his kitchen. If we sneak down the back stairs I think we can escape out the back without being seen."

Sarah narrowed her eyes, looked over her shoulder and responded, "Let's do it."

The two crept to the back stairwell, descended, and slipped through the hall door to the kitchen. The three cooks on duty raised their eyebrows as they entered, but made no attempt to question them. In a few seconds, they had exited the back door and dashed through a courtyard used to hang beef to dry and down the alley behind the hotel. Where the alley met a main street, they slowed their pace and nonchalantly walked toward the center of town, where they thought the sheriff's office might be. After walking only three blocks, Johann noticed two men with rifles closing in rapidly from the direction of the Hotel de Paris.

"Come on, Sarah, they've seen us," he exclaimed as he jerked her arm and broke into a run again. They sprinted to the middle of the block, then rounded a corner and ran down an alley. After a half block, they cut through the yard of a large two-story home with brown shutters and an unusual pink porch lattice. Johann, out of the corner of his eye, saw the hinged, wooden doors of a cellar and halted Sarah. "Here, let's hide in here. Hurry!" They clambered into the dark, dirt-floored cellar and closed the doors. In the dim light, Sarah saw a shovel leaning on the stone wall. "Here, put this in the door catches," she urged. Johann took the shovel and forced the long square handle into the retracting loops of the swinging doors. Then they backed deeper into the gloom to await the outcome.

Outside, the men chasing them found that two young adults can sprint a lot faster than they could. Sarah and Johann had long disappeared when they rounded the corner of the alley. One of the men waved at two additional men a few blocks away in a manner to indicate they would have to search for the runaways block by block.

Back at the Hotel de Paris, Williams remarkably kept his composure at the sudden disappearance of the two truants. "It is all right, Louis," he encouraged the concerned hotel owner. "My men shall find them in due time." He pulled out his pocket watch, saw the time and continued, "We really must be on our way, though. I wish to reach the Silver Plume by dark." He put the timepiece away and continued talking with Louis. "I have but one more favor to ask you, dear sir."

"Name it," Louis responded.

"My men will escort the two young adults to Silver Plume tomorrow morning. If you would bring them something to eat at the jail this evening and in the morning, I would certainly be more so in your debt."

"But of course," Louis smiled. "But why at the jail?"

"Sheriff Lyons is a good friend of mine," Sydney said. "Apparently, Sarah and Johann will be easier to watch if they are confined for the night."

The men warmly shook hands as two guards assisted Emily and Frank back onto the stage. The balance of the trip up to the Silver Plume mine was long and quiet. Even though Williams desperately tried to create conversation with his two remaining captives, there was no interest or response. The complacency of their captivity had reached the end of the line.

CHAPTER 37

A hoary halo surrounded the moon as the stage pulled onto the grounds of the Silver Plume Mine and Milling Company. A dark collection of buildings hidden in shadows created by the rising orb on the mountainside gave a ghostly appearance to the idle camp. A lone light, probably from a solitary oil lamp in the superintendent's house, pierced the gloom and gave direction for the tired driver and his horses. The stage pulled up to the building and stopped. The driver got off the coach and disappeared through a door with an "office" sign nailed above it. A few moments later, some additional lights appeared at the windows and some voices could be heard. A man with only one arm came out of the office with the driver. He motioned for Williams to come inside. The driver, along with the other two guards, stood watch over Frank and Emily.

Williams exited the stagecoach, went up to the one-armed man and shook his left hand. "Hi, Bill, it's good to see you again."

Bill returned the greeting, and motioned for him to enter the building. He led Williams down the entrance hallway to a room on the right, and offered him a Spartan wooden chair. Then, he walked around a table to the opposite side, pulled up a similar chair, and sat down. Bill shuffled papers on the table into a haphazard pile and scooted it off to the side. He reached behind his chair to a short dresser, opened the top drawer, withdrew a watch, opened it, and set the timepiece on the table. He looked

180

at Williams. "There's been a change in the schedule."

Williams cocked his head a little to the side and politely asked, "How so?"

"I got a telegram from Baxter about an hour ago. He thinks that a storm is building so he's decided to leave Fairplay as soon as he can. He's going to try and arrive by tomorrow night in case the passes get snowed in."

"I see," Williams commented. "Will you be ready to process the load at that time?"

"I'm not sure," Bill responded. "I was going to let the men sleep for another few hours before I rouse them. They've worked extra long these past few days trying to keep on schedule. We've got enough coal brought up for the boilers, but we're still lacking enough dry mix from the shaft. We were planning on blasting it out and processing it over the next two days."

Williams interrupted. "I have two important guests that need to be attended to."

Bill stared at Williams for a moment. "We need every man available to transport the blast rock to the mill before I can process any of the gold."

Williams pondered, then asked, "Is there a secure place we can put them so they won't have to be watched?"

Bill leaned back on his chair and scratched his nose. "We could put them at the end of tunnel number three. It's across the workings from where we'll be blasting. It has a lockable gate, so we could confine them."

"Is it a dead-end passageway?" Williams asked.

Bill paused. "It has an airshaft at the end of tunnel, but it has a heavy grate over the entrance to keep animals out."

"You seem reticent, my dear boy," Williams chided.

Bill leaned forward in his chair. "It might be a wild time because they'll still experience the vibrations and dust from the blasting." He rocked back on his stiff-legged chair and stroked his chin. "I suppose we could pressurize that tunnel with air lines from the compressor to put a positive pressure on it; that would keep the dust to a minimum. But many of the timbers and cribbing were moved to other sections of the mine because that tunnel stopped producing. The shaking might loosen some of the ceiling or wall rock; I just don't know."

Light from the dim oil lamp cast a shadow on Williams's hardened face and without further thought he replied, "That will work. I'm not so sure a rockfall might not work to our advantage. Confine them there. In light of this news, I have to return to Georgetown, but if you have a fresh horse, I'll leave the stage and my three men with you. Hopefully, I'll be returning tomorrow afternoon with some additional tenants."

CHAPTER 38

Sarah's and Johann's eyes adjusted to the dark cellar. Stone steps from the entrance were each a huge granite slab and looked heavy. The stone work of the cellar was equally spectacular. Rather than a montage of smaller stones laid in a mortar compound, these were sizeable slabs of hewn granite stacked and held in place only by their sheer weight. Collections of wooden crates were stacked in one corner amidst old furniture and miscellaneous stuff that is generally found in a cellar.

Sarah drew close to Johann and asked, "Okay. What's our plan?"

Johann replied, "If we can get to the sheriff's office without Williams's men catching us, then I think we'll be in good hands. We should probably wait a few minutes, though, before we try again."

"You might wait a bit longer than that," a voice whispered behind them.

Sarah and Johann spun around to see an elderly woman leaning on one of the wooden crates for support. They backed up a couple of paces but, when they realized she was no threat, moved forward and started to apologize for their intrusion into her cellar.

She put her hand up and waved off their feeble attempts. "No, no," she began. "Don't apologize for hiding. I saw you arrive with that old crook, Sydney Williams. I figured you and the other folks you were with weren't willing 'guests' by the guards and rifles he had protecting you."

Sarah cocked her head and quizzed, "Why did you call him a crook?"

"Who, Williams?" she cackled. "Why he's the biggest fraud in this area. His bank owns most of Georgetown. Loaned money out left and right as the mines started showing some promise. Everybody needed start-up capital and he provided it. Then he and some other snoot horn feller from Golden filled everyone's mind that the money the mines made should stay in this area for development of a separate state that could control its own resources. He talked many of the miners into putting their money into what he called an escrow account at Williams's bank that would help finance this so-called new republic. And, of course, he's the one in charge of it.

"And if the merchants and miners didn't donate to it, his riflemen came around and encouraged them to, if you know what I mean. But, generally, because of his smooth tongue and manner, that didn't happen too often. Ahh," she coughed in disgust. "Sounds like a bunch of rubbish to me. Why, any fool would know that, eventually, mines all over the territory will dry up and then the folks will move on. But Sydney, with his pomp and flair, somehow persuades everyone to put their trust in his ideas and to continue investing in this area." She pursed her lips, looked at the two, and continued, "Come on upstairs, now, and let's talk about what we're going to do with you."

She led them across the cellar to the far wall. Behind some cabinets was a staircase leading upwards that Johann had missed in the dim light. "I saw you from the upstairs window when you slipped into the cellar," she said. "Also saw a couple of men with rifles walk down the alley looking for you. Didn't take long to figure out what was going on."

At the top of the staircase, she turned the corner and ushered them into a sitting room. A medium-sized bay window let the sunlight in, but it was heavily filtered through a coarse, burlap type of drapery that prohibited anyone outside from looking in. Two velvety couches faced each other with a low, mahogany table between them. Some tall bookcases lined two of the four walls and were filled with old, brown books. She bade her visitors to sit, whereupon she pulled up an ornate rocking chair from a corner and sat close to them, presumably so she could hear more easily.

"Now, tell me," she began. "Where on earth were you trying to run to?"

Johann looked at Sarah, then slowly replied. "We thought if we could get to the sheriff we'd be in good hands."

The old lady snorted, shook her head and looked down. "It's a good thing you didn't make it to the sheriff. Old Sidney Williams has him on his payroll and wrapped around his thumb. You wouldn't have been in good hands with him." She got up and walked across the room to a pleated cord hanging from the doorway. After giving a tug on it, she shuffled back and sat down again.

A small, middle-aged woman entered the room and walked silently up to the old lady's rocker. "Ah, my manners," she continued. "Would either of you care for something to drink? I'm afraid my disdain for Mr. Williams and the sheriff has clouded my hospitality. How about some cool lemonade from the icebox?"

Sarah and Johann nodded in agreement. The younger woman gave a courteous nod of understanding, made eye contact with the old lady, nodded again, and left the room.

"My name is Evangeline," she said. "And you are?"

"My name is Johann, and this is Sarah, a friend."

Sarah continued the conversation. "We are traveling with my aunt and uncle. Uncle Henri accepted a position in Denver and is moving us out here to live."

"So, what kind of trouble have you and your relations gotten yourselves into?" she asked.

Sarah and Johann looked at each other, shook their heads, and Sarah replied, "We don't really know. Sydney Williams abducted us back in Kansas and transported us here on his personal train. He left Uncle Henri in Denver with someone who was supposed to make him a great job offer, but I don't think that was the real reason. He was too vague in his explanation. All we really know is that he was taking us to a mine called 'Silver Plume,' up on the mountain west of here for a tour of the facility."

"I see," Evangeline said. She turned around and said, "Ah, here's Irene with your lemonade." As the lemonade was passed around, she dropped her eyes and softened her voice. "Irene has been with me for almost ten years, even before my only son died in a mining accident. He discovered a rich lode of silver north of town and developed it by himself for a number of years and borrowed heavily against it to form the Pelican Mine back in the early seventies.

"The following spring, after he incorporated the Pelican, he built this house, but then was killed in an explosion later that fall. The sheriff said it was an accidental detonation of a blasting charge. I think it was a competing mine, the Dive, which had illegally bored a tunnel above the Pelican and deliberately set off a charge so they could move in on the rest of the silver vein." She raised her eyes and darkly added, "Sydney Williams owned the Dive at the time of the accident. He also was the one who bought the note for the Pelican after my son died." Evangeline got up from the rocker, walked over to the bay window, and gazed out the window at the mountains. "Williams is only interested in making money. All the pomp and circumstance with him is the way he persuades people to do what he wants. He's a fraud that somebody should expose."

She walked back toward the rocking chair, but stopped short next to a small wooden desk. She idly looked at the desk for a moment, then raised her eyes toward Sarah's. "There are some people in town who feel the same way I do about Mr. Williams. I hope you don't mind, but I took the liberty of sending Irene to arrange for us to meet one of them. I think he can be of help to you and your family."

Sarah replied, "But how will we meet him since the sheriff and his men are searching for us?"

Evangeline's voice fell and she responded in a whispered hush, "You just leave that up to me, dear."

CHAPTER 39

The sun had been down a long time when Evangeline woke Sarah and Johann from their slumber. The two had spent the last few hours sleeping in two of the upstairs bedrooms, while Evangeline kept watch in the library for any unwelcome guests. Bluish light from the moon illuminated the rooms so fiercely that no additional light was needed to adequately see. Sarah followed Evangeline into Johann's room, wandered over to the window, and looked out between the linen draperies. "My, the moon is spectacular tonight," she whispered.

Evangeline came over to her side, looked upward at the sky, and added, "Yes, and look at that marvelous ring around it! My guess is that we'll have some rain or snow later today."

The three slowly made their way downstairs to the kitchen, where Irene had prepared them a Spartan but nutritious meal of dried fruit and nuts mixed with oats and honey. She had also prepared three small packs with additional food and some flasks of water. Next to the packs were three unlit carbide miner's lamps, some gloves, and light coats. Across the table, the flames from two glass oil lamps flickered delicately and cast a dim amber light on the chairs and walls. As they sat and ate, their shadows danced eerily on the walls behind them.

Evangeline scooped up some food in her hand and nonchalantly said, "Irene made all the arrangements. As soon as you get a bite to eat we'll be on our way."

"Where are we going?" Sarah asked.

"It's kind of hard to explain," Evangeline replied. "It will be easier to show you than to tell you."

They quickly finished, put on the coats and gloves, took up their packs and lamps, and followed Evangeline down the hallway. She opened the basement door and descended the steep steps with the aid of the oil lamps from the kitchen. Upon reaching the dirt floor, she walked to the back of the cellar and asked Johann to move some crates stacked in the corner. "Take care with the last one," she added. "Lift it straight up instead of sliding it sideways."

Johann followed instructions, lifted the final crate into the air, and moved it to the side. As he did, he noticed a small black hole in the floor. He started to take the second lamp that Irene was carrying, but she pulled it back a little bit and pointed to Evangeline. Johann turned to see the elderly lady set her lamp on a small table and take one of the carbide lamps and unscrew its brass base. She reached into her pack and pulled out a small tin can, popped the lid off of it, and poured some fragmented pieces of stone into the chamber of the brass base. Then she screwed it back together. Next, she popped a cork out of the top of the lamp, took one of the flasks, and poured some water into the second top chamber. She reinstalled the cork, and pivoted a turnscrew on the top of the water chamber.

After a few moments they heard a faint hiss from the front reflector of the lamp. She polished the shiny surface and held it up to the flame of the oil lamp. After a moment, a small orange flame ignited from the center of the reflector and cast a warm beam of light on the wall of the cellar. Sarah and Johann cocked their heads at the amount of light from the little lamp. Evangeline grinned. "The rocks I put in the bottom chamber are a calcium carbide compound. When mixed slowly with water from the top portion of the lamp, it forms a flammable gas called 'acetylene.' The little tip in the reflector makes the gas build up a small amount of pressure that helps it to ignite when lit with a spark or flame. Many of the miners use these carbide lamps because it puts off a reliable light for three or four hours at a charge."

She lit the other two carbide lamps. "This hole leads to a tunnel that runs from this house all the way across town. It connects with the workings of the Pelican mine that I told you about earlier. The original tunnel followed a silver vein that petered out just inside the town boundaries. My son continued it to the house so he could have easy access to the inner workings of the mine. I've never gone all the way through it. He told me that it was locked from the other end so that no one could come in unless he had a key." She smiled and showed them a silver key dangling on a small chain around her neck. "We'll have to take care at the other end since that portion is still active. I don't think there will be a problem, though, since the Pelican isn't running third shifts right now. Anyway, this will get us outside of town and hide us from the watchful eyes of the sheriff and his cronies."

Evangeline handed the oil lamp to Irene, took her carbide lamp, and descended a wooden ladder that was flush with the top of the hole in the ground. Johann and Sarah took their belongings and followed. At the bottom of the ladder, they noticed that Irene had stayed behind, and had quietly replaced the wooden crates that covered the entrance.

The tunnel was cool and dank, but the carbide lamps illuminated the stone walls. A small passage three feet wide and five feet high extended slightly downwards into the darkness. Evangeline looked at the floor and commented, "There used to be some rails on the ground where the mining carts would travel. I guess they pulled those up when this part was abandoned." She led the way; Sarah followed immediately behind her, and then Johann.

They followed the tunnel for a few hundred yards. At times its dimensions would widen and become higher where more material was mined, presumably from the silver vein that it originally followed. For the most part, the passageway had been hewed from solid rock. But here and there, huge mining timbers supported a crosshatch of boards designed to keep loose rubble from falling and causing a cave-in. Those fracture zones permitted ground water to seep into the tunnel. As a result, small rivulets of water appeared on the tunnel floor and lazily flowed further into the blackness. Their progress was slow as they picked over fallen debris and tiptoed between the pools of water. The darkness behind and before them was intense and they were glad they each had their own light source to radiate the way.

A little over an hour had passed when they came upon a wooden door framed into the rock to fit the tunnel. It had a finely decorated silver doorknob and insert for a key. Evangeline took the key from around her neck, placed it into the slot, twisted it, and turned the knob at the same time. The door silently opened into the side of a larger, main passage that was fully developed as a transport route to the surface. Fresh steel rails laid on new timbers extended in both directions down the broad passageway. Large steel pipes that carried compressed air for machinery in the deeper workings hung suspended from bracing on the ceiling. Permanently lit oil lamps hung every forty feet or so from iron pegs driven into the rock walls. Each side of the passageway had a small ditch that carried the mine water to a lower level, where it either was pumped out or drained through an adit to empty into a waterway outside the mine workings.

"Let's travel to the left," Evangeline said. "There is a faint breeze in that direction. Usually these mines act like a chimney of sorts where the air flows toward the outlet."

Evangeline re-secured the door, and the trio started hiking up the tracks. The tracks led only slightly upwards, so the hiking was not arduous. Occasionally they came across other tunnels that angled off of the main trunk line. It was easy to tell which way to go, though, since they all merged in the same direction.

After an additional thirty minutes of slow traveling, the tracks came to an end at the main vertical shaft. "This is where the elevator takes the mine carts upwards to the top of the mountain," Evangeline remarked. "Looks like we'll have to climb up from here."

She moved her lamp around in a circle at the base of the elevator and found a series of ladder rungs nailed to the vertical cribbing. "This is the service ladder that the maintenance men use to lubricate and repair the elevator tracks," she continued. "We'll have to climb up it since the lift is not running."

Sarah aimed her lamp toward the ceiling and asked, "How far of a climb do you think it is?"

"I'm not sure," she admitted. "We should be almost a half mile from the house in a northwesterly direction, I think. If that's so, then this would be the second lift station out of four that bisect this tunnel along its length. That station, if memory serves me, is around three hundred feet higher than downtown Georgetown. At any rate, it'll be a good challenge!"

Johann glanced at Sarah as they watched the elderly lady start to climb the wooden ladder rungs. Their original perception of Evangeline was that of an older, feeble woman ready for the grave. They were surprised to see her climb with a steady pace and determination toward the top. After a few rungs, she looked back down at her fellow travelers and said, "Make sure to extinguish your lamp when you get near the top so it's not noticeable to anyone." Then she looked up and continued her climb. Sarah took off next with Johann following a few rungs behind.

After a number of stops for rest, they peeked over the safety rails at the shaft entrance, shut off their lamps, and climbed out onto the staging platform. The night was almost spent, and thick clouds had covered the moon. Falling snow glistened in the yellowish light emanating from haphazardly placed oil lamps littered around the compound. "Quickly now," Evangeline motioned. "We need to conceal ourselves in those shadows behind the tool sheds. There may be a night watchman wandering the property."

They rushed between the vertical timbers of the lift and stopped in the deep shadows behind the buildings. Evangeline led them quietly along the back of the sheds, from one to another, then into some tall bushes. Soon they came to the main roadway and continued westward.

"We can relight our lamps now," Evangeline said. "It is still another ten or eleven miles to where we'll meet my friend. He has a cabin up along the rock dikes about halfway to Central City. He was in town yesterday, and when I sent Irene to find him, he told her that it would be the safest place for you two." She looked behind her and continued, "It should be getting light soon. We'll stop and take a break then. How are you two doing?"

"Fine, I suppose," Johann wheezed. "I don't understand why I can't keep up with your pace, Evangeline."

She stopped and smiled. "It's okay, Johann. You're not used to the altitude."

"The altitude?" he asked.

"Yes, the altitude," she said. "We're probably a mile or so higher than what you are used to back in Indiana. The air is thinner up this high, and you have to breathe harder. I've lived here for years and have become accustomed to it. I'm afraid you and Sarah haven't. It's not good to stop here, but we'll take a short rest in a little bit so you can let your lungs catch up!"

Evangeline continued down the main road. After a while she turned off on a trail that forked to the north. The snow continued falling, but melted on contact because the ground temperature was still warm. They continued for another fifteen minutes, walked around a bend, and discovered a collection of large boulders. She stopped, scanned the surroundings in the dim morning light, sat down, and opened her pack. "Now, let's see what Irene packed us for breakfast."

CHAPTER 40

Another explosion shook the mine tunnel. Emily and Frank watched the ceiling shake as the seismic ripples dissipated above and below them. Frank shook his head and said, "I'm surprised this roof hasn't caved in yet."

Emily nodded in agreement.

The two were lying on some cloth-covered straw that Bill had laid down for them in the passageway. Next to them a steel gate with a new chain and lock prevented their escape back into the main tunnel that led to the surface. Although they were dressed properly for the temperature, their inactivity made their joints stiff and their extremities cold.

Frank pulled out his timepiece and held it up to the dim oil lamp hanging on the wall. "Well, we've been here almost a full day now." He reached over and dug a water flask out of the pack that Bill had given them. He opened it, took a little, and offered some to Emily.

"Thank you," she replied as she took the flask. The water was cold and fresh and raised her level of awareness.

During the hours of their captivity, they had managed to thoroughly examine the passageway where they were confined. It continued another two hundred yards, then angled sharply upwards for eighty feet. Handholds were chiseled in the stone so Frank could climb up the shaft without much difficulty. It ended at a steel grate that had been anchored to the rock outcropping where the shaft exited. It was firmly fixed and could not be moved or dug around without some steel tools to work with. One consolation was that it was warmer in the mine tunnel than it was outside. Frank had noticed a raging snowstorm beyond the grate and was glad that he wasn't in it.

They had spent the balance of the day huddled under some blankets, snacking on the provisions they found in the packs. Regular blasts from deeper in the mine shook their surroundings every two hours or so, but didn't spread any dust their way. Compressed air leaking into their adit from a valve in the overhead air line kept enough pressure in the tunnel to push the contaminated blast air toward a different exit.

One hundred yards to the east and four hundred feet deeper, Bill was examining the results of the most recent blast. Each detonation would crumble a section of granite about ten feet deep, and wide enough for two men to walk side by side. Four men had methodically cleared and sorted the fresh debris and began the arduous process of pushing the ore carts back toward the vertical lift. Bill stepped up to the newly exposed walls and ran his hand along the hard, gray granite. At waist level, his eye caught the porphyry layer of igneous rock that was pockmarked with the crystalline structures of sylvanite and calaverite, the feldspar-like crystals that contained the chemically bonded gold compound. This auriferous vein was different in structure than the other local gold-producing mines. It was rich in gold, but, because the crystals were refractory, or difficult to melt, a special chemical extraction process had to be developed. As was typical with Sydney Williams, the process was complicated and years before its time.

Bill gently brushed aside the thin layer of dust from the rich vein, and followed it toward the face of the tunnel. Halfway toward the end of the blast zone, he stopped abruptly. He backed up a few steps, relocated the vein, and then moved forward again, but instead of finding the continuation of the porphyry, he found only an angled fracture zone and then nothing but granite. He turned around and yelled to the old man pushing the cart toward the lift, "Harry, c'mere and look at this."

Harry turned and came down to where Bill was standing.

"Harry, look at this and tell me what you see," Bill urged.

The old man stretched out his gnarled hand and gently stroked the crystalline vein. He deliberately moved closer to the fracture zone. Harry's old eyes squinted and examined the rock face. Then he stooped down to the floor, furrowed his brow and ran his hand across the ground, brushing away the loose dirt. He continued up the other side of the tunnel and then overhead. He frowned at Bill and grunted one word. "Fault."

Bill's countenance dropped as he realized the significance. Eons ago the mountains were thrust up by extraordinary geologic forces. Intrusions of melted rock, rich in minerals and under tremendous pressure, haphazardly spiked into the solid rock and cooled, becoming the highly mineralized veins sought after by miners. But the mountains continued to expand and their growth stretched the rock beyond its structural capacity. The hard granite cracked and slipped along weak spots called faults. Some faults created well-defined lines of rubble deep in the mountain. When the mine tunnels ran across the crumbled rock zone, the miners braced and supported the weak sections with timbers and cribbing. Other faults were only noticed by the sudden change of rock structure. In this case, a slip fault had moved the porphyry vein elsewhere. And therein was the problem. Bill understood that the vein was lost, possibly for good.

He looked over at Harry and whispered, "What should we do?"

Harry thought a moment and responded, "I remember this same thing happened back in 1859 in the 'Old National' mine.

I set overcharges in a ring around the face and blew a huge hole in it. When I cleared the debris out, I was able to relocate the vein about ten feet off to the side." He looked into Bill's eyes for a long moment. "It's dangerous because the larger charges can collapse the tunnel network in the entire mine." He scratched his nose and added, "Just depends."

"Depends on what?" Bill asked.

"Depends on how many other debris faults there are in the mountain. A charge big enough to blow out a hole that big puts out a lot of vibration. If there are other debris faults near any tunnels, they'll collapse. The only other way to locate the vein is to run a number of exploratory holes to see if you can find it. It's trial and error and takes a lot of time. And then there's always a chance that you won't find the vein. It might be anywhere in this mountain. At least with the 'big blast' method you either find the vein quickly or you don't."

It didn't take Bill long to weigh the matter. "Clean up the exposed vein and drill the holes," he quietly said. "Then make the big blast."

Night had just fallen when Harry came up to Bill's office. He rapped lightly on the door and entered. Bill was finishing his daily report on the quantity and quality of the day's tonnage. He put the pencil down and looked at Harry.

"It's ready," was all Harry said.

Bill closed his report book, put on his coat, and headed to the lift station with Harry. Newly fallen snow sparkled in the bright lights of the oil lamps that Bill had lit. As they got into the lift, they heard the noise of galloping hooves and the rattle of wagons. The men turned to see two freight wagons racing into the mine compound at full speed. The drivers were barely able to stop the teams of horses before they barreled into one of the warehouses. Bill opened the lift gate and ran to the first wagon. The driver was covered in wet snow and shook uncontrollably in the wind. He tried to talk, but was incoherent in his mumblings. The driver of the other wagon was in the same condition. Bill motioned for Harry to assist the other man off the wagon and into the warm office.

They helped the two men through the front door and into the main room of the office. They collapsed onto the floor in front of the stove. "Get some more wood for the fire," Bill snapped to Harry. Bill opened the woodstove door, took a rod, and stirred up the coals. Then he helped the two men out of their frozen clothes and pulled them close to the source of the radiant heat. Harry returned, re-stoked the stove, then went to a black trunk in the corner and pulled out some heavy woolen blankets. He covered the men and patted them softly to help circulate their warmth. After twenty minutes the first man had stopped shaking enough that he could utter some words.

He reached up, took Bill's collar in his hand, and croaked, "Baxter slid off the pass."

Bill's face paled in shock. "Slid off the pass? Where? How far up?"

The man struggled to answer. "Two miles up. Lost three wagons in the canyon. Couldn't stop sliding."

Bill looked up at Harry and barked, "Get the rest of the men out of the mine and saddle the horses. We have to hurry."

Harry sprang to his feet, but then turned and asked, "What about the charge?"

Bill thought for a split second and answered, "Set it."

Frank and Emily were alarmed by the commotion. They could hear the lift elevator rising in the shaft. But it was the feverish pitch of the men's activity in the lift car that grabbed their attention. It stopped for a moment at their level. An old man quickly came out of the lift car, ran up to their gate, and stopped. He blankly looked at them, obviously not knowing what to say. He glanced at the lock on the gate, and then at the dark tunnel behind them, then locked eyes with Frank. Frustrated, he shrugged his shoulders, pointed to the blackness behind them, and shouted, "Run!" Then he pivoted and did the same back into the lift.

Emily turned wide-eyed at Frank. "Run? Run where?"

Frank scooped up the blankets in one hand and grabbed the oil lamp in the other. "Come on, Emily. Follow me! Hurry!"

The two stumbled down the black tunnel as fast as they were able. After many falls they made it to the angled shaft of the air vent.

"Quickly, Emily, grab the handholds and climb." Frank urgently pushed Emily up the shaft as she groped for the handholds. She moved fast and disappeared into the blackness of the vent.

He had just grabbed the first anchor point when the entire mountain shuddered. It seemed as though the tunnel they had just come through was whacked with a giant sledgehammer. Giant slabs of granite, jumbled together with dirt, stone, and debris, crashed to the floor behind them. A strong, dirty wind blew out their oil lamp and rushed up the ventilation shaft. Frank struggled blindly to pull himself up through the gritty darkness behind Emily, who had reached a small, flat, level spot in front of the grated vent. The rumbling mountain shook loose a small slide of snow outside of the grate, but the force of the wind from the blast and falling debris blew the snow away from the grated opening like the cork out of a Champagne bottle. Frank and Emily pulled as close to the grate as possible to ride out the explosion and collapse of the Silver Plume mine.

CHAPTER 41

The snow around the Silver Plume Mine and Milling Company glistened like little diamonds in the yellow light of the oil lamps stationed around the various buildings of the complex. The snow had slowed to light flurries, and the wind had calmed considerably at the lower elevation of the Silver Plume. James picked his way delicately as he moved toward the facility. He stayed off of the roadway to hide any tracks left in the snow by his passing. As he drew closer, he could see the two freight wagons that they had followed from Fairplay parked in front of a freshly painted building. Dark smoke mixed with an array of sparks belched from a stovepipe jutting through the tin roof and lazily floated toward the east. An assortment of activity flowed through the camp like a gypsy carnival. Two men by one of the barns seemed to be in a hurry to harness two horses to an empty freight wagon. Another man ran back and forth from a small storage shed. On one trip, he threw some bundles in the wagon and then returned with some tools. Another man rushed from a small building with an armload of wood towards the office, obviously for the stove inside. An additional man worked on saddling two large horses that were tied to the vertical posts of the mineshaft elevator. As if on cue, the men simultaneously mounted the horses and, along with the wagon, galloped down the road toward Guanella Pass.

Within minutes the camp was deserted. The jangling chains of the freight wagon disappeared in the cold air, leaving only the crackling embers spitting from the stovepipe in the office roof to break the silence of the slowly falling snowflakes. James scanned the buildings of the compound. Two dark warehouses stood like sentinels on either side of the inbound road. An additional tool house and blacksmith shop stood between the warehouses and the main office in the middle of the complex. About fifty feet to the left of the office towered a massive shaft house and elevator to the lower workings of the mine. A laid track from the landing at the lift merged with an additional line. One set of rails traveled to the large stamper and mill near the edge of a steep valley; the other set traversed the complex in a wood-covered tunnel until it disappeared into the mountainside. Miscellaneous buildings and barns for housing animals, supplies, and machinery were dotted among some boulders. Sets of oil lamps with foul-weather covers illuminated the scene with an eerie yellow light.

The only interior light was in the office. James listened to the silence, and moved toward the wooden house. Without warning, the ground rippled and shook as the mountain moaned. He swept his arms and shifted his legs as he fought to keep his balance. Immediately, a subterranean rumbling rolled from deep in the earth and grew into an intense explosion of dust and debris that shot from both the shaft and covered tunnel of the mine. The door of the office flew open and two men stumbled onto the porch and off into the snow like a couple of drunkards. They staggered to the frozen freight wagons and grabbed onto the large wooden wheels for stability. One man collapsed unconscious on the ground, while the other snatched glimpses left and right of the catastrophe unfolding before them. Soon he, too, closed his eyes and slumped to the ground. The quake lasted for a full minute before settling into an uneasy quiet. A dark cloud of dust descended on the camp and extinguished the snow sparkles that had hovered around the oil lamps. The white blanket that covered the Silver Plume Mine and Milling Company rapidly turned gray, and the lamplight that had given an almost cheery flavor to the remote camp swiftly changed to a muddy-brown haze.

James edged up to the two men on the ground next to the wagon. He stooped over them and noticed the wisps of frosty air from their beard-encircled mouths. He knew one of the men, a small, fat, red-haired fellow with a bushy, bright beard. James winced as he heard the man's wheezing breath as he struggled for air. He left the men alone, surveyed the grounds, and then proceeded to the mining office.

James entered the main office where Bill and Williams had met the previous night. He picked his way over debris to the upturned table and sifted through the disheveled documents on the floor. The stove was still in place, so he straightened a chair and sat next to its warmth as he read. After perusing the contents of the desk and table drawers, he worked his way back out to the courtyard. From there, he followed the ore cart tracks to the milling complex, entered the building, and studied the layout and content of the operation. After some time, he followed the tracks back toward the covered mine tunnel. As he went by the shaft house he salvaged one of the oil lamps from the ground, relit it from a burning fragment of wood, and carried it with him into the dusty passageway. The walls and ceiling were intact, but everything was coated with a thick layer of gray dust. After he had walked fifty yards or so, he discovered that the tunnel was blocked by debris from some failed cribbing. He retraced his steps, noticed a tunnel to the right, and followed it. It forked after a few hundred feet. The passage to the right was heavily gated with a fresh lock and chain. He held the light high before him and saw that the tunnel beyond the gate had collapsed. As he turned to leave, he cocked his head when he saw a thick pile of straw with two open packs lying on the ground beyond the grid. After only a few steps he came to the vertical shaft of the lift. The shaft below swallowed the feeble lamplight in a static cloud of dust. Above he could make out some bluish light from the moon as it started to break through the clouds. A wooden service ladder extended upwards and James opted to climb out. At the top of the ascent he found himself on the staging platform next to the elevator. He thought it best to head back to their makeshift camp for the night.

As he stumbled through the boulders above the roadway, a freight wagon drawn by two horses barreled by. He could see a man in the back holding an oil lamp and securing a long bundle of blankets underneath him. James thought he saw a snow-white face sticking out from one end of the bundle, but he wasn't sure. As fast as he saw the wagon, it was gone. He continued without a sound to their camp in the timber.

CHAPTER 42

Sunlight streaked through the pine boughs, danced on James's eyes, and woke him up. He was stiff from sleeping on the cold, hard ground, but the brilliance of the sun and the clear, blue sky gave him a breath of cool freshness. He slowly got up, stretched, and surveyed his surroundings. The snow was already starting to melt in the warm sunshine. The small stand of gnarled trees that they had camped in seemed to be the only protection on the mountainside. Small scrub trees dotted the slopes along with shoulder-high tree stumps that must have been cut when there was heavy snow on the ground. Apparently, the trees where they hid were so twisted and bent, maybe from some distant avalanche, that they were of no use for lumber. Behind their makeshift camp, the horses pawed away the white cover to get at the sparse vegetation underneath. Below them, the buildings of the Silver Plume Mine and Milling Company loomed beneath a strange mantel of gray and brown dust.

James roused his two companions and helped them break camp. As they worked they discussed how they should proceed.

"You said last night that the mine tunnels exploded," Derek began. "I wonder if they blew them up on purpose to hide something, or if it was an accident."

James shook his head. "I don't know. The men that came out of the office seemed oblivious to what was happening. They were terrified by the explosion."

205

"And you said that the tonnage reports that you read in the office seemed high on waste rock and short on ore?" Derek asked.

"Best I could interpret them," James replied. "I'm not a mining engineer by any stretch of the imagination, but it seemed as though the tonnage had been increasing steadily while the ore output was declining."

"Why not do this?" Derek suggested. "I'll see if I can slip into the mine through one of the ventilation shafts and root around a little bit. Maybe I can get a better idea of what's going on. It shouldn't be too hard to find one, since the dust from the explosion seems to have come out of all the mine exits. I'll take one of the horses around the far perimeter out of sight and see what I can find."

"Okay," James said. "Mike, why don't you make your way back to the mill. I couldn't see a whole lot in the darkness last night. Maybe you can see more in the daylight. I'll get back to the office and see if I can't pick up some conversation. Let's break camp here and meet further up the road, maybe a mile or so from where the road forks off toward Georgetown. I'm sure there will be a good place to make camp. That way we can start a fire tonight for warmth."

The three men agreed on the plan and went their separate ways, one with a horse, the other two on foot.

It was easy for Mike to enter the lower wooden door into the mill, as there were no men around. He worked his way up the long staircase that followed the mountain slope. The milling process used gravity to carry the ore from one process to another. The rock chutes were at the top, then the five huge stamps. Below that was another chute where the pulverized ore slid into a large iron canister where it was rotated and made into a coarse powder. It was here that Mike noticed a mound of something underneath an oil tarp. He pulled it to one side and raised his eyebrows at a neatly stacked pile of gold bars. He picked one up, and rolled it over in his hands until he saw the stamped identification markings. His eyes traveled from the bars to the iron canister on his right. The equipment wasn't operating, and a hatch on the drum had been removed and leaned against a support timber. He looked into the opening and, as his eyes became accustomed to the dark, he saw the rough shards of a number of gold bars mixed with the rough gravel and iron balls of the rotating crusher. Mike moved back down the staircase to the outlet of the drum, sifted some of the pulverized ore in his hand, and was able to pick out a number of large gold flakes. He put the coarse dust in his pocket and slipped back out of the mill.

James was slow in heading toward the office. There was no cover of night this time and, apart from a building or a piece of machinery, the courtyard was exposed in the morning sunlight. He took an indirect way to the office, starting behind one of the warehouses nearest the entrance to the facility. He moved along the rear of the framed structure until he could safely sprint across the open area to the back of one of the stables. From there he moved to the shaft lift, then beyond to the mine tunnel. He approached the rear of the office. Along the northern wall he crouched beneath a window that was cracked to let smoke out of the small room. Even though he had no real cover, he could plainly hear the conversations inside and could also make out anyone walking on the wooden floors as well as the sounds of doors opening and closing. James felt he could shift to a more secluded location if he heard footsteps moving toward the front porch. He distinctly smelled the fresh aromas of coffee and cigars. Three voices carried on a slow and deliberate discussion.

"I don't see how we can," said a low, gruff voice.

Another man responded in a high-pitched squeak, "I don't

believe we have a choice in the matter. The shipment has to be processed at the smelters and traded for silver by Saturday noon. It cannot be changed." There was a pause, and then the tapping of what sounded like a thick lead pencil on a desk. The man continued, "Now, how can we make it happen?"

"How long do you think the boys will take retrieving the rest of the gold off of the pass?" a third voice asked. It was a strained, raspy voice with a distinct wheezing. James immediately recognized to whom it belonged.

"My guess is that by noon they should return," the gruff voice answered. "I wish we hadn't lost those two men." There was another moment of silence, before he resumed.

"Okay, here's what we can do. We'll process the gold that is in the mill with the balance of the ore from the vein. Then we'll freight that to Golden over the ridge road along with the unprocessed bullion. I know it's rougher, but it's shorter by mileage, and will be less noticeable than trying to ship it through Georgetown, Idaho Springs, and then to the train. If we leave by midnight, we should be able to make it to Golden by Friday night or early Saturday morning, depending on the snow in the high country. When we reach Golden, we'll have the high grade processed as normal, and then file the paperwork for the silver trade. We can telegraph the smelter so he knows that we have a load to be processed first thing on Saturday morning."

"What about the bullion?" the raspy voice asked.

"That's where you come in, Seth," the gruff voice continued. "After the ore is processed, the workers usually take a long break for lunch, drinks, or whatever. I'll keep them occupied, and I want you, Seth, to ask Mr. Bailey, owner of the smelter, to verify the refined content of the smelted gold. Then, arrange an accident for him. Afterwards, go to his office and adjust the paperwork accordingly. Since it will already have his signature and seal on the documents, it shouldn't be a problem to alter them to show more tonnage brought in and more bullion processed. Make sure to also change the trade documents. Those will be located in the safe behind his desk. He keeps a key on a chain wrapped around his neck. You'll only have an hour to do this, so it will have to be quick and quiet. I would suggest disposing of his body in the smelting furnace. When we get back, you can say that he left on urgent business."

"I believe that will work," the squeaky voice said. His voice faded a little as he spoke to the other man. "Work out the details and fire up the mill. We leave at midnight."

"What about your arrangements with Steele concerning Grant?" the wheezy voice asked.

"Change of plans," the high-pitched voice responded. "Mr. Steele wired Bill this morning saying that he would take care of it from his end. Seems that Mr. Grant didn't keep to his itinerary." There was a shrill noise from the room as if a steel door was opened. The voice continued, "Seth, would you mind carrying some more wood for the stove? The fire is dying."

James retreated from under the window as he heard the screeching of a chair and the heavy footsteps toward the door. He moved swiftly toward the safety of the covered mine tunnel; then, after many minutes, retraced his path back toward their camp above the road where his horse waited.

Derek moved around the backside of a knob on the far side of the Silver Plume. He grimaced and wagged his head as he looked at the brown and gray streak stretching across the snow from a rocky overhang. He tied his horse to a nearby stump, got off, and trudged through some deep drift snow up to an iron grate embedded in the hillside. He grasped on to it, gave a number of sharp tugs, and was able to remove it from its foundation. He then went back to his horse, removed a candle from his saddlebag, and returned to the gaping, dark hole. The opening was littered with fresh ceiling debris, but Derek was able to slip into the shaft and down to the main tunnel. The candle danced in the breeze from deep in the passageway. Derek noticed that this section of tunnel was heavily reinforced with large timbers and cribbing. He advanced steadily into the gloom and pondered what he would find.

After forty-five minutes of climbing over rubble and debris, Derek came to an apex in the tunnel system. A system of tracks ran either way down the intersecting chambers. He turned to the left, but was soon blocked by a rock fall. Splintered timbers protruded from the base of the rock pile like fractured matchsticks. He turned around and shuffled down the other tunnel. A few hundred feet later, it stopped in an enormous pile of rubble that had collected under a gigantic chamber. Derek held the candle close to an exposed wall at track level and could make out the chisel marks on the tunnel face where the cleanup crews had removed ore pockets from the parent rock. He worked his way up the walls of the newly opened chamber and examined the ceiling. The newly fallen stone had exposed a small section of vein about twenty feet up. As he picked at it with his fingernail, a portion of it crumbled off in his hand. He rolled it over in the candlelight, smiled, put it in his pocket, and returned back toward the airshaft.

Derek left the grate lying on the ground in front of the opening. He mounted his horse and continued around the perimeter of the mine property. After another quarter mile, he located another grate, but the tunnel had completely collapsed. He moved further on to the west for an additional quarter mile and topped a ridge overlooking a valley. Below, he saw another dirt streak extending across the snow. He leaned back on his horse and stretched his legs. The ore sample in his pocket poked him in the side, so he pulled it out to examine it further in the bright sunlight. "Rich," he murmured to himself. He tossed the sample into the air, caught it in his hand like it was some immensely valuable coin, and returned it to his pocket. His gaze moved back to the dark streak below him. Derek pursed his lips, shook his head, turned his horse around, and started the return trip back to the Georgetown road.

CHAPTER 43

Bright sunlight mirrored on the snow cover and threw an almost blinding reflection onto Emily's face. She scrunched her eyebrows and squinted. Her body was rolled into a ball with Frank behind her. He had protected her from any large falling debris but the two of them were still covered in dirt and dust from the explosion. Heavy frost from her breath during the night coated a cross section of the cold iron grate. She stirred and gently poked Frank with her elbow. "Frank," she croaked. "Frank. Are you hurt?"

Frank cracked his neck muscles and opened his eyes. "No, I'm okay. Just have a splitting headache. How about you?"

"I'm stiff and I'm cold, but I'm alive," she responded. "Now, how do we get out of here?"

Frank worked his arms and legs around and kicked the debris around him down into the tunnel below. Then he clawed the loose dirt and light rock underneath him and worked it down the shaft also. He made a spot large enough where Emily and he could trade places. "You know, Emily," he said, "if you work more of this debris down the passageway it will warm you. In addition, we'll have more working room so I can try to dig around this grate."

After twenty minutes of digging the two of them were feeling better and had made enough room in the chamber for Frank to move around. He braced his back against the far wall and put his feet on the grate but was unable to move it. He reached to

212

the sidewall and flaked off a loose piece of stone. Then he reversed himself and started to scrape the walls where the grate was fixed to the rock. "They did a good job of molding this thing to the rock," he said. "Looks like they mortared it in place from the outside. I can't reach through the grate to scrape at it. Emily, how far can you slide down the shaft?"

She looked behind her into the gloom and replied, "I don't know; let me try."

Frank heard loose rock and dirt slide down the slope as she descended. He turned around in the chamber and cautiously lowered himself downwards.

"That's about it!" she cried. "Your feet are just touching my shoulders."

Frank stopped, turned to the wall, and managed to flake off a larger section of stone. He grasped it firmly in his hands and threw it as hard as he could at the grate. The iron responded with a dull thud. Frank pulled himself back up, grasped the rock, retreated as far as he could down the shaft, and threw it at the grate again. "I'm hoping the rock will jar some of the mortar loose," he relayed to Emily. "Maybe then I can work it out with my legs."

Frank repeated the process for another fifteen minutes. The dull thudding echoed up and down the valley with each hit. Then he pulled himself up to the grate to see if it had loosened any. He grasped it with his cold hands and jerked it back and forth a number of times. It didn't move. He flipped around, put his feet against it, and smacked it with all his weight. Nothing happened. He let out a long sigh and said to Emily, "I'm running out of ideas. There has to be a way to dislodge this thing."

"How about a horse?" a deep voice called from the other side of the grate.

Frank twisted his head around and saw a smiling face with a

bushy beard looking at him. "Where did you come from?" he said.

"I should ask you the same question," the man replied. "The name's Derek. I heard your pounding up on the ridge and thought I'd come see what it was." Derek heard the murmur of a woman's voice behind Frank. "Is there someone else in there with you?"

"Yes," Frank replied. "We're okay, but we want to get out of here. What did you say about a horse?"

"Hang on a minute," Derek replied.

A few moments later he returned with a rope. He tied it securely to the hard iron and then disappeared again. In a moment the rope grew taught and jerked the grate from its foundation. Frank climbed out of the hole, reached back to help Emily, and then turned to thank his rescuer.

Derek handed the two of them some blankets from his bedroll and helped them into the sunlight. He retrieved a container of water and some food from his saddlebag and gave it to them. They relished the refreshment as they warmed themselves in the sunlight and breathed deeply of the fresh mountain air.

"What were you two doing in the mine tunnel?" Derek asked.

Frank studied his face before responding. He didn't recognize him from any of their experiences. He decided to take a chance and tell him the truth. "Sydney Williams locked us in the mine tunnel a couple of days ago." Frank pointed at the now open ventilation shaft. "When the tunnel collapsed last night, we managed to get as far as the grate before passing out. I seriously doubted getting out at all until you came along. Thanks for helping us."

"My pleasure," Derek replied. "I don't know this Sydney Williams you mentioned, but if he is associated with what's going on at this mine, I'm sure he's no good. I have some friends around the mountain that have made camp along the Georgetown road. I'm sure they'll have a hot fire started and some warm food. It'll be dark by the time we get there, but we can warm you up with some more blankets for the ride. As I said, my name is Derek; what are yours?"

They traded first names and general information as Derek helped Emily onto the horse. After rolling up the blankets and coiling the rope, Derek took the horse by its reins and led his new friends back to the camp on the Georgetown road.

CHAPTER 44

The trail Evangeline referred to was steep and rough. The mild drizzle didn't help their footing either. From the boulders where they had some breakfast, the trail ascended eastward as it digressed away from the roadway. Many boulders and other obstacles in the trail slowed their progress and threatened to turn the trip into an entire day affair. Although they were wet, their strenuous climb kept them all warm.

"I've actually not been up this trail before," Evangeline said. "I had no idea it was so rough."

"I guess the scenery compensates for it somewhat," Sarah politely added.

They rounded another one of the unending turns in the trail and started the steep climb up an immense course of rocks. It was already after noon, but the heavy clouds and intermittent drizzle made it seem later in the day. Halfway up the slope they stopped for a breather. The view was astounding to the young adults who had never seen the mountains before. A swift river coursed hundreds of feet below them through a narrow canyon. Rugged landscape dotted with scraggy scrub trees and prickly brush lined the near-vertical canyon walls. The cliffs across from them extended higher than their present perch, so all they saw was the mountain face extending to the clouds. Behind them in the distance, the outline of the higher mountains was draped in snow clouds.

Evangeline cocked her head a little bit and said, "Do you hear that?"

Sarah and Johann listened in the direction she indicated. Sarah narrowed her eyes and said, "Yes, I hear a train whistle." She pointed down the canyon to the south. "And there. I see the smoke plume from its stack."

"That's right," Evangeline agreed. "It's the train that runs from Golden up to Central City."

They peered over the edge of the ridge and could see the approaching column of steam and smoke from the narrow-gauge engine. It was pulling a number of freight cars, including one bright yellow one for passengers. "Are those men on top of that yellow one?" Sarah asked Evangeline.

She looked intently for a moment at the train winding its way up the gorge and replied, "Yes, that is probably one of Sydney William's personal cars. The men on top are some of the riflemen I told you about earlier." She paused a moment, then added, "He must have some important cargo aboard." Then she pivoted around, rose, and started up the trail again. "C'mon, we have a ways to go. I hope we can make it before dark."

They continued their hike for the rest of the day. Late in the afternoon, they topped a ridge and saw a small collection of trees in a gently sloped valley below them. They sighted a small and primitive cabin next to a rushing creek along the side of a large boulder. Evangeline said, "That's his cabin. Should be there in another twenty minutes or so."

The trail was still steep and slippery. The top of the ridge where they stood was right at the snow line. They could see a thick blanket of white above their location, but down lower it abruptly changed to only a light rain. The trail was neither wide nor frequently used, but as they descended further into the meadow surrounding the cabin, it broadened out and turned into a dirt trail cutting through a carpet of thick grass.

As they approached the cabin, Evangeline noticed that there was no smoke rising from the chimney. "It could be that he's not here yet." She walked up to the simple, wood-plank door and kicked it a couple of times with her boot. There was no response, so she opened the door and peeked inside. It appeared to be a typical miner's cabin. A wooden table with two chairs was next to the stone-laid fireplace. In one corner was a straw bed with a couple of unkempt blankets on it. Next to that were a couple of stacked wooden crates used as cabinets for storing supplies. A pan on a stool contained some tin dishes that waited for a cleaning. A pile of straw was in the other corner of the cabin with some blankets folded next to it.

Evangeline wagged her head and commented, "Typical man. Just the necessities and nothing else." She entered the cabin and invited Johann and Sarah to follow her inside.

"I don't know how long we'll have to wait for him to return, but let's do something to pass the time." She turned, pointed at Johann and ordered, "You go outside and carry in some wood for a fire. Sarah, you bring in some fresh water from the creek and wash these messy dishes. I'll clean up his cabinets, make his bed, and sweep all the trash out of here."

Johann and Sarah smiled at each other as they listened to Evangeline mutter to herself about how untidy and cluttered men can be. "Well, go on," she commanded as she grabbed a broom and started an exaggerated sweeping of the floors. They did as they were told.

The atmosphere of the little cabin in the trees had changed remarkably in only a couple of hours. A cozy fire in the stone fireplace warmed a kettle of stew that Evangeline had prepared from food in the cabin larder and the bundles that Irene had packed. The floors were swept clean of an accumulation of dirt and debris. Sarah had found an old rug under the bedding, had taken it outside and beat it for ten minutes, then placed it underneath the table and chairs. The bed was made and, in addition, Johann had spread out the straw in two piles in the corner of the cabin and spread out the blankets that were stacked to the side. He found some small glass oil lamps, which he lit and placed in three locations: one at the doorway, one over the dishpan on a stool, and one on a nail over the table. Johann packed some additional wood in for the fire, and rolled in a larger sawn piece of wood for an additional chair at the table.

"I hope you like the stew I prepared," said Evangeline. She went to the kettle and filled one bowl at a time and placed them on the table. It smelled good and their mouths watered.

They had sat down and started to eat when the cabin door crashed open and a man with a bushy beard and a heavy bearskin coat entered the cabin. His wild eyes rapidly scanned the cabin and then settled on the older lady. Sarah's eyes grew wide and she blurted out, "You're the man I saw looking in the train window in Denver!"

The man switched his glare to Sarah for a moment, narrowed his eyes, grunted something and then returned his angry gaze back toward Evangeline. After a moment he squawked like a rooster with laryngitis, "Evangeline, what have you done to my cabin?" Then he smelled the aroma of the stew and saw the full bowls on the table. His eyes grew wide and he smacked his lips, smiled, and added, "Any left for me?"

CHAPTER 45

Everett Steele was not happy. He held in his hand a telegram from one of his men at the Longmont station about forty miles north of Denver. He crumpled it as he cursed under his breath to his secretary. "This is so typical of Grant," he fumed.

"What is the problem, sir?" his secretary asked.

He looked at her with angry eyes, then regained his composure and replied, "He's changed his schedule. Apparently, Grant wanted to take a ride through the mountains, so he disembarked at Longmont and took a buggy to Central City over the toll road. The telegram says that he'll be in Central City on Thursday night, late." He turned around, walked back to his desk, and sat down. He picked up a pencil and doodled on some scrap paper. "It goes on to say that he's requested a private trip for early Friday morning on one of the railroad pump carts from Central City to Golden so he can see the scenery without the noise and smoke of a locomotive." He shook his head and thought for a moment. Then he reached for some paper and scribbled down some instructions. He folded them and put them in the brown folder that the original telegram had come in. "One of these telegrams goes to the Silver Plume mine; the other one to Ted Walker at the Teller House in Central City. Get these over to Sam at the telegraph office. Then arrange to have our Mr. Mueller brought to my office."

An hour later Henri was ushered into Mr. Steele's office. "Ah, Mr. Mueller, so good of you to come on such short notice.

We seem to have had a change of schedule. I've made arrangements for you to ride the train to Golden and then on to Central City. Your train leaves in thirty minutes."

Henri offered no response or reaction.

Mr. Steele continued, "This man, Mr. Thomas O'Malley, shall accompany you on your trip and explain the details of what I require of you when you reach Central City."

A short, husky man entered the room and stood quietly by Henri's side. He was probably in his early forties with stone-hard muscles and a face that looked like rawhide.

"I don't expect that we'll see each other again, Mr. Mueller. I hope you enjoy your ride." Steele motioned for O'Malley to escort Henri out the door.

As they left, Henri turned around and added a postscript to Steele's last comment. "Remember, Everett, I didn't stay tied to the Tallapoosa River abutment, either."

O'Malley led Henri down the hallway and out of the building. They got into a waiting carriage and rode to the nearby station, where they boarded one of Sydney Williams's personal cars. Henri sat down by the window in a casual wooden chair while O'Malley sat across from him in one of Williams's plush, cushioned rockers. After a few minutes, the train jerked and began the journey to Central City.

Ted Walker was busy. As manager of the Teller House, his hands were always full. After all, the Teller House was the premier hotel west of the Mississippi.

The last time President Grant visited Central City in April of 1873, it was Ted Walker who had the sidewalk in front of the hotel lined with silver bricks. They were "borrowed" from the Caribou Mine and returned after Grant left. Visitors from all over the country came to Central City to enjoy those parties. They also came to see the stunning scenery surrounding the town and, usually, they ended up at the Teller Hotel for one or more nights. Grant was one of those guests, and Ted Walker was hastily getting the president's room cleaned and prepared. He had only received a telegram late that morning from Mr. Everett Steele, the president's host for his territorial visit. As with Grant's previous visit to the area, his arrival had been altered somewhat to accommodate his impulsive change of mind.

Ted paced the office. "What time did the telegram say the president was to arrive?"

"It only said sometime late tonight," his secretary responded.

"What else, what else?" Ted removed a handkerchief from his coat pocket and dabbed his forehead. "Tell the chef to alter the menu for a late night snack. Rearrange the ornaments in the front lobby. Move the flower pots with the columbines to the front door. After his last visit that will be anticlimactic but that's what we have to work with. Let's see," he continued dabbing his head like a woodpecker. He looked at his secretary and whined, "Mr. Steele said something about two additional guests?"

"That's correct, sir." She flinched. "A Mr. Mueller and a Mr. O'Malley are arriving on the train this evening. Mr. Steele requested a room for them separate from the rest. One with an inside lock on the door."

Ted stopped what he was doing, scratched his head, and muttered, "I guess the storage room downstairs by the coal furnace is the only one with an inside lock. I'll send Leo to clean it. Don't tell anyone else that someone is using it. It's not good for business."

The ride to Central City was uneventful except for the extraordinary scenery. Unfortunately, Henri was not interested in that aspect of his trip. Mr. O'Malley had proved to be an able companion, as he neither left his side, nor uttered more than a "yes" or "no" to any questions Henri asked. The train rolled into Central City in the evening, on schedule. As they got off, Henri did take note of the uniqueness of the town. One side was situated on a number of terraces, each somewhat higher than the other. Mines and mills lined the lower end of the valley and littered their way up the slopes. An assortment of buildings clung to the mountainsides as if they had been glued. Some built because the mine tailings created spots flat enough on which to erect a structure.

Central City, once larger than Denver, had its beginnings in the mid-sixties but, unlike many other mining communities, grew into a rich mining and cultural section of the state. Many of the buildings were relatively new, constructed from stone and brick after the disastrous fire of 1874. Currently, many of the town patrons were seeking the addition of a theater and opera house to enhance its growing reputation as a cultural center of the territory.

Mr. O'Malley guided Henri to the Teller House and down into the basement through a side cellar door. He had obviously been there before, as he knew where the oil lamps and iron shackles were to confine Henri to the wall. "I have some errands to run for tomorrow," O'Malley grunted. "Make yourself at home." He let out a snicker as he lit another oil lamp and set it on the table. Then he took the first oil lamp, closed the door, and left Henri to his thoughts.

CHAPTER 46

Evangeline rolled her eyes and said, "Yes, Jack, there's plenty here. But first, introductions."

She introduced Sarah and Johann to Jack. He grasped their hands with what looked like a bear paw and asked, "Did you do this to my cabin?" Without waiting for an answer he added, "Thank you. It didn't look this good when I built it."

Evangeline interrupted him. "C'mon, Jack. Eat up before it gets cold." She thrust a full bowl of stew into his hands.

Sarah and Johann chuckled at each other and continued eating. After some general small talk between Jack and Evangeline, Sarah struck up the courage to ask, "Why were you looking in the train window in Denver?"

"Well," he mumbled as he swallowed his mouthful of food, "it's kind of complicated." He wiped his mouth on his sleeve. "You see, I know one of the men that was in the coach with you. Henri Mueller."

Sarah dropped her spoon. "He's my uncle! How do you know him?"

Jack's bushy eyebrows disappeared into his long hair. "Henri's your uncle?" He set his bowl down on the table. "We worked together during the war. I last saw him during a mission when we were separated by an unfortunate incident."

"The bridge," Sarah whispered.

Jack looked blankly at Sarah. "You know about the bridge?"

"Uncle Henri told me about the incident on the Tallapoosa

in Mississippi; how it blew up, some of his friends were hurt, and he had to leave them behind."

"Yes, that's correct," he said. "Three of us were left behind."

"Fredrick," Johann blurted. "Fredrick was one of those left behind. And you were his friend, Jack."

Jack's eyes widened as he looked at Johann. "Who are you again?"

Johann straightened his back and tilted his head. "I'm Fred's younger brother."

Jack stumbled in reply. "So, you're Frank's brother, too?"

"Yeah, we're all brothers," he stated. "Frank was on the train, too."

Jack took a couple steps back as he tugged his beard. He looked over at Johann and continued mumbling to himself. "It was a quick glance. I didn't notice Frank there." His eyes moved to Sarah. "I didn't know that Henri was there either until I looked in the window. I have this friend at the telegraph office that keeps me apprised of the messages that come in and out, especially those that pertain to a couple of men. He told me, must have been a week or so ago, about instructions sent to Brookville, Kansas, to abduct a group of people and bring them to Denver. One, in particular, was to be brought to a Mr. Steele."

"That was Uncle Henri!" Sarah exclaimed.

"Yup, that's right," Jack said. "I knew what train to look for and when it would be in so it was easy to take a look in the window."

"You knew Fred?" Johann asked.

Jack turned his eyes on Johann and replied, "Yes, I do. We are good friends. He's doing some investigative work in Silverton, but I haven't been in touch with him recently."

"You haven't heard," Johann's face sank. "My family received a telegram from the Silverton sheriff a couple of weeks ago saying that Fred and another man were killed in a mine explosion."

Jack's hand fell from his beard. He leaned heavily on the cabin wall. With a deep sigh he said, "I'm really sorry to hear that, Johann. He was a good friend." He wiped his eyes and said as an afterthought, "You don't know who the other man was, do you?"

"Yes," Johann answered. "It was Derek Borden."

"Derek Borden," Jack echoed. "I've not heard that name before. I wonder why Mike never mentioned him?"

Sarah changed the subject. "Mike is the third of your party, then?"

"Yeah, that's right," Jack replied. "He was in Silverton with Fred looking for some glyphs that we found on a map in California." Jack stared off into space. "I guess I've not heard from him either."

"Hold on a minute, Jack," interrupted Johann. He got up from the table and went to the backpack that Irene had prepared. He opened it up, removed his leather pouch, and brought it to the table. After unlacing it, he removed one of the maps from the stack of paper and gently unfolded it.

Jack smiled as he recognized the map and its markings. "Unbelievable," he sighed. "I haven't seen this in over a year." He scooted the map around where he could view it better. "When we found this map, along with the others, we knew that the gold shipments from the war had been cached at various locations around the western territories. It was relatively easy to find the general locations, but the exact spot was harder. Each hoard was concealed and only when a chiseled glyph nearby could be found and interpreted could the gold be recovered."

Jack went over to his bed and dug a small book out from the straw mattress. He brought it back to the table, opened it, and laid it next to the map. They were almost identical. "I copied as much pertinent information from the maps as I could before we went our different ways. Mike and Fred went east from California and I worked my way north up toward Oregon. I found out some interesting information about Everett Steele that convinced me to come to this area to keep an eye on what he was doing. In fact, that's what I was doing when you came here this evening."

"What do you mean?" Sarah interrupted.

Jack replied, "I was talking to a friend in Central City. He relayed a message to me about a change in President Grant's itinerary."

"President Grant is coming here?" Johann asked.

"That's right," Jack responded. "He loves the scenery of this area. He was supposed to arrive in Denver, but he got sidetracked and decided to come through the mountains by buggy. I got the message late this evening. I imagine Steele won't find out about it until tomorrow morning." He pulled his watch out, looked at it and added, "Which is now. It's three o'clock already. We have to sack out because I need to return to Central City at first light and see if there are any updates." Jack's voice grew deep and quiet. "I have a feeling that Steele has something arranged for Grant. Don't know what, but I feel it in my bones."

CHAPTER 47

Jack left for Central City before the sun rose on Friday. The early morning was crispy cold with patchy frost on the meadow grass. The stars shone with extraordinary brilliance, their dim blue light illuminating the trail. By the time he reached Central City, the sun was high and had melted the frost into patchy layers of vanishing mist.

The first thing Jack did was visit the telegraph office at the edge of town by the railroad station. The office had already been open for three hours and Jack was sure that Monty, the chief telegrapher, would have some current news. Monty was a short, barrel-chested man with a black mustache to match his eyes. His jolly persona belied his deep disdain for Everett Steele's policy of moving away from territorial support. He inwardly supported statehood, but realized the dangers of vocalizing those persuasions.

Jack entered the little telegraph house and closed the door behind him. Monty looked up from his desk, beamed a huge toothy smile, and said, "Jackie m' boy, so good to see you this fine morning." Jack casually turned to look out the front window. "It's a chilly morning; would you like some coffee, dear boy? Come here and warm yourself by the stove while I get you a cup."

Jack smiled, walked across the room, and stood next to the small woodstove. It felt good to warm his face and hands. Monty came around the desk and poured him a mug of hot coffee off of the stove. The fresh aroma reached Jack's nostrils, and added to his warmth.

The door opened and a man walked in. Monty met him at the counter. "Johnson, good morning. Let me get your telegram." Monty disappeared behind a wall and came out a moment later with a piece of paper. As he handed it to Johnson, he asked, "Will there be a reply?"

Johnson read the note, thought for a second and replied, "Yeah. Send a message back that it will be ready by morning."

"That's it?" Monty asked as he scribbled on his memo pad.

"Yup, that's all," Johnson replied. He tossed a coin on the counter and turned to leave. He paused for a moment as his eye caught Jack's watching him from the stove. Jack gave him the customary nod that strangers tend to do. The man did likewise and left the building.

Monty took his own mug of coffee, and stood next to Jack facing the windows.

"That's the third time Johnson has been in this morning," Monty said.

"What's going on?" Jack asked.

Monty checked the windows before saying anything. "Steele wired him three times in the last three hours. I gather that President Grant was supposed to arrive in Denver tonight, but he changed his schedule and is coming here instead. He's requested a couple of rail carts tomorrow morning so he and his entourage can pump down the tracks to the Twin Forks junction and view the scenery. He wanted a train to pick them up at the Forks and take them the rest of the way to Floyd's Hill."

"That is a pretty trip down the gorge," Jack said. "Steep, but pretty. I hope they have good brakes on the flat cars."

"That's not all, though," Monty said. "Steele is sending two men from Denver tonight to accompany Grant down the gorge.

I know one of them. He's a burly guy named Tom. He has a reputation for doing much of Steele's dirty work."

"I see," Jack nodded. "Who is the other man?"

"Henri . . ." Monty paused and scratched his head for a moment. "Let's see, what's his last name . . . Molly? Miller? I don't remember, but, anyway, they did ask the manager at the Teller House to prepare a special room for the guests. I suspect that means one of the Teller House's basement rooms. Those are generally used for detainees of Steele's."

"And what of the president?" Jack asked. "Where is he staying?"

"Oh, he always stays at the Teller House," Monty said. "He has his own room that he sleeps in. His bodyguards stay in the room next door. It's been that way each time he's come. Ted, the manager at the Teller House, always knows to prepare those rooms, although this time it's a couple of days early."

"I see," Jack thought out loud. He finished his coffee, set the mug on the floor, and said, "Listen, Monty, I think I'll wander down to the rail yard and see just what kind of pump carts the president is planning on taking tomorrow. Maybe I'll drop back by on the way to the cabin."

"Sounds good," Monty said. "Here, let me get the door for you." He rose and went to the door, but, as he reached for the knob, he stopped and added, "Listen, Jack. There is something else. It might not be anything, but I thought I'd mention it. There have been a number of other telegrams coming in this morning for people that are supportive of Steele and his ideas. They all say the same thing; that there is going to be an emergency session of the territorial council on Saturday morning."

"The territorial council?" Jack wondered.

"Yeah. They govern this immediate area. They are meeting in Denver at ten o'clock Saturday morning. Why, I don't know."

"I'll keep that in mind," Jack said as he left the building and started for the track yard. As he walked down the boardwalk he turned and added, "Thanks for the coffee."

The rail station was near the telegraph office, only a few buildings away. On the other side of the station and down the tracks a few hundred yards was the stone building where engine repairs and maintenance were done. Jack worked his way along the base of the hillside where he wasn't as noticeable. When he arrived at the repair facility, he noticed that the main wooden doors were closed. He walked around the perimeter and was dismayed to find that the tall glass windows were painted black on the bottom half, thereby restricting anyone from peering in. At the back, though, he noticed a smaller wooden door that was open. It was used to shovel coal into the boiler room in the basement. Jack looked around and entered the doorway.

The basement was dimly lit with a couple of oil lamps affixed to some vertical timbers supporting the main floor. Jack was able to make his way between the coal piles, wooden crates of parts, and assorted debris without any noise. He found the main stairwell upstairs and quietly climbed the heavy oak treads. Near the top, he peered over the threshold and heard some men working in one of the corners of the warehouse. Two engines and some other machinery lay between them. Jack climbed the rest of the way up the stairwell and crawled under one of the locomotives. He recognized one of the workers as Johnson, the man from the telegraph office. He didn't know the other two. He couldn't quite see what the men were working on from his vantage point, so he crept across the opening between the engines. The workers were ahead and off to the side of the second locomotive, so Jack took the risk of actually climbing on top of the rear of the second engine for a better view. He moved silently along the top of the cab and pulled himself behind the massive smokestack. From here he could see that Johnson and his fellow workers were altering the braking shoes on one of the flat cars.

"Come on, Roy, drill those rivets out deeper," Johnson ordered. "They have to break off together."

Roy put more pressure on the hand drill as more metal shavings collected on the floor. Johnson glanced over at the other worker and barked, "Hurry up and get those rollers back together. We're running out of time. And make sure those cap nuts are loose."

The other man nodded his head in affirmative response.

Johnson walked over to the workbench and reached for an odd-looking piece of metal. It was tapered on one end and had a wedge clamp on the underside. He took it over to the cart and fastened it underneath the wooden platform with two butterfly screws. Johnson let out a gurgled laugh as he said, "They should really flip over this one." The other two men joined in grotesque laughter.

Jack took a good look at the pump cart, backed away from the scene, and retraced his steps out of the building. Once back in the sunlight, he made a beeline for the Teller House.

The four-story stone hotel sat across from the newspaper office near the center of town. Jack thought he'd stop there first and see what news there was. A stack of fresh newspapers was at the doorway, so he tossed the secretary a ten-cent piece, took a paper, and sat on the wooden bench on the porch. He didn't see anything about the president coming to town. He thought that odd, so he walked in and asked to speak to the editor. An older man with a white shirt and tan checkered vest appeared.

"Yes, he is coming," the editor said. "I believe it's scheduled for Saturday. I didn't put anything in the *Register* about it because I was requested not to."

"Who requested that?" Jack politely asked.

"Well," he began, "the last time Grant was here, the community made such a hooplah that the president was almost embarrassed. Along with the miner turmoil over the low silver prices, his secretary, Mr. Steele, suggested that we keep his visit downplayed so as to not draw undue attention to it."

After a short discussion, Jack thanked the editor and walked across the street to the Teller House. There was no one at the front desk, so Jack wandered around looking for someone to talk to. He rounded a corner and collided with Ted, the manager.

Ted apologized profusely. "Oh, excuse me, sir. I'm sorry, I didn't see you."

"That's okay," Jack responded politely. "What's the hurry?"

"I just have too much to do, that's all," Ted replied.

"Anything I can do to help?" Jack offered.

Ted looked bewildered for a second then blurted, "Well, since you offered, yes!"

Jack smiled and said enthusiastically, "Tell me!"

Ted sighed and said, "My maintenance man didn't show up for work this morning. The boiler downstairs needs a fresh stoking. If you would do that, I'll let you have any dinner you want tonight, on the house."

"Sure, I can do that," Jack answered. "Where is the basement?"

Ted showed him to the stairwell, told him where everything was, and rushed off to the kitchen. Jack smiled to himself and descended the steps into the boiler room and basement. He found the shovel and stoked the boiler with smaller chunks of coal. He checked the steam pressure gauge, adjusted the supply valves, and then swept the floor. As he replaced the broom, he saw some wooden boxes stacked in one corner. A small wine rack in the corner furthest from the boiler housed some fifty bottles of wine. Jack noticed a room next to the rack with the door ajar. He took one of the oil lamps, opened the door the rest of the way, and looked in. On one side of the small room was a bed and table. An oil lamp hung unlit on the wall. The back wall was hand-cut blocks of granite. The thing that caught Jack's eye were the shackles firmly embedded in the walls. His eyes narrowed as he remembered the special room that Monty mentioned. Jack thought for a moment and muttered to himself, "Mr. Tom, I think I have a surprise for you!"

CHAPTER 48

Henri sat on the bed and looked around. The dreary, yellow light from the oil lamp cast flickering shadows from the table and bed onto the granite floor, reminding him of a dungeon. As he replayed the conversation with Steele, he heard a mouse-like squeak from the door knob. It jiggled back and forth a few times, fell to the floor with a clink and was brushed aside by the opening door. A large man in a dark, hairy coat with a huge, bristling beard loomed before him. Henri cringed and asked, "Who are you? What do you want?"

"What do I want?" the large man said in a deep, throaty voice. "I want to know if I get back pay for the last eleven years!"

Henri cocked his head and stared dumbfounded for a minute. Then he whispered, "Jack? Jack, is that you?"

"Hey," Jack replied, containing his excitement rather well. He came up to Henri and gave him a bear hug.

"I can't believe it's you! What on earth are you doing here?" Henri asked.

Jack hushed him and urged, "We're short on time. We'll talk about that later. Right now, let's get you out of here."

"Wait," Henri quickly replied. "I can't leave. This man named Steele is holding my family and friends hostage. If I disappear, he'll have them killed."

"How many of them are missing?" Jack asked.

"There's my niece, Sarah; my wife, Emily; Frank, and his brother Johann," he answered.

"I've got Johann and Sarah at my cabin," Jack said. "I don't know anything about Frank or Emily except that Johann said they were taken to the Silver Plume mine. What do you want to do?"

Henri paused to absorb the information. "So Sarah and Johann are okay?"

Jack nodded in response.

"But you haven't heard anything about Emily or Frank?"

Jack's countenance dropped. "I'm sorry, Henri, no."

Henri paced the room. "Do you know what Steele's plan is?"

"Yes," Jack said. "President Grant is planning an excursion down the gorge in the morning on one of the pump carts to see the scenery. He's supposed to be picked up at the Twin Forks Bridge by the train and taken the rest of the way to Floyd's Hill, where he'll continue to Idaho Springs. I discovered earlier today that the cart has been sabotaged by some of Steele's men. I'm assuming that Steele is going to have Grant murdered on that ride."

Henri narrowed his eyes and said, "Now it all makes sense. Steele said that he was looking for a trigger for his plan of territorial independence underway. Grant's death would certainly do that."

Jack butted in. "That explains the emergency council meeting on Saturday."

Henri's eyebrows rose. "Council meeting? What council meeting?"

Jack's eyes met Henri's. "There's going to be an emergency territorial council meeting Saturday morning at ten o'clock in the legislature building in Denver. Mr. Steele put out notifications this morning."

"I see," Henri whispered. After a moment he continued, "Tell me, how was the pump cart sabotaged?"

"They fixed it so the brakes would fail," Jack answered.

Henri pondered and thought out loud. "With no brakes on the hand cart on that steep of a grade, I would guess the cart would reach speeds in excess of forty miles per hour." He tapped the table and furrowed his brow. "But I didn't see any curves on the way up that would cause the pump car to jump track, even at that speed." He looked at the floor and intently thought some more.

Jack broke the silence. "At that speed it would be suicide to jump off because of the narrowness and heavy boulders along the track. But if the cart hit a train traveling that fast, it would be sliced right in two by the track scraper on the front of the locomotive. Did you see any place on the way up where the train wouldn't necessarily see something small like a pumper cart coming down the track?"

Henri rubbed his chin and tried to recall the ride up the gorge from Twin Forks. He unconsciously scrunched his nose at the musty smell of the stone-encased room. "I've got it!" he exclaimed. "There is a tunnel about a quarter mile before the bridge, on the Golden side of the grade. It was probably two hundred yards long. I remember it because the train made what Mr. O'Malley called a regular stop while the engine was still in the tunnel. The smoke and steam from the engine were annoying. I still can't imagine why the train had to stop, but if a pump car was coming down the grade and it hit the train while it was in the tunnel, it would be totally destroyed. And because of the weight difference between the cart and train as a whole, nobody would really notice the impact. It would just feel like a typical train lurch." Henri turned his head and looked Jack in the eye. "That train stayed in the tunnel for a full fifteen minutes. If that is a normal part of its schedule then I would wager that Steele figured the exact time it would take for the pump cart to get there on that grade with no brakes." Henri turned his head and stared off into space. "Let's see; is it correct that the train makes two runs each day?"

"Yes," Jack replied. "The first one is in the morning; the train goes to Floyd's Hill. Then it backs up beyond the Forks and into the tunnel while the track is changed. Then it proceeds to Central City. It arrives around eleven in the morning depending on the weight of the freight it's carrying."

Henri concurred. "I'd wager that is Steele's plan. That train is going to wait for Grant's cart in the tunnel." Henri's face took on a serious look. "Looks like I'm going to be on that cart, too. Along with Mr. O'Malley, my guard. I wonder how he is planning to get off?"

"I'm sure he has figured out a way," Jack replied. "Now, the question is, how are we going to rescue you and Grant and still make it look like you were killed?"

Henri's face lit up and he grinned at Jack. "I've got an idea."

CHAPTER 49

James found a good place to camp for the night, much better than their first campsite above the mill. The road to Georgetown ran through some boulder fields about two miles below the Silver Plume mine. To the right of the road, beyond a grove of large pines, stood a grouping of large, wagon-sized boulders with a natural area of thick humus and soft lichen at their base. They created a superb campsite with a natural windbreak and an abundant supply of wood nearby. He tied his horse to a tree, gathered a supply of dead wood, and started a nice hot fire. The surrounding rocks trapped the heat in the basin, making the area warm and cozy. He removed the saddlebags from his horse and started to prepare some of the food that was left.

Sometime later, Mike came up to the site, leading his horse by the reins.

James turned around and asked, "Everything okay?"

"My horse threw a shoe on the way down the grade," Mike replied. "I'm not going to be able to ride him until it gets replaced."

James could see that the horse was favoring one hoof. "That's not good," he said. "Especially when I tell you what the Silver Plume Boys are up to."

Mike tilted his head and snickered. "Silver Plume Boys? What are you talking about?"

"I decided to call the men at the mine the Silver Plume Boys," James laughed.

"Okay," Mike chuckled, "Silver Plume Boys, it is. Now, what do they have planned?"

James stopped laughing and continued, "They are planning on taking the gold bars and ore to Golden for smelting. They're leaving tonight at midnight." James told Mike the rest of the plans they had made about murdering the smelter owner and falsifying the trade documents. "They said it all had to be done by noon on Saturday."

"I wonder why Saturday?" Mike wondered out loud.

"I don't know," James replied. "But one thing is for sure; we have to follow them and stop whatever plans they've made." He glanced at Mike's horse, and observed, "Your horse going lame isn't going to help things either. There's no way we can keep up with them once they start moving."

There was a long silence before Mike spoke. "Why don't we move the playing field?"

"What do you mean?"

Mike grinned. "I found some play toys at the mill." He pulled a long, round stick out of his pocket and tossed it to James. Caught off guard, James reached frantically for the object and shuffled it from one hand to the other before securing it in his lap. He raised it into the light and gasped. "Dynamite! Where did you find dynamite?"

Mike sheepishly replied, "In the mill. I found a full box of it. You could say I borrowed some. I thought it might be useful." His eyes grew cold and icy. "I say we take advantage of the element of surprise and change their plans for a trip to Golden."

Straightaway, they heard the sound of horse hooves coming into camp. In the dim light of the dying fire, Mike and James strained to see Derek leading a horse with two hunched forms in the saddle. They jumped to their feet to help.

"Derek, what happened?" Mike asked.

"Found them in one of the ventilation shafts," Derek

answered. "They would have died if I hadn't come along." He stopped the horse and directed, "Let's bed them down for the night. Keep them covered because they're cold and exhausted. I think a good night's rest will be the best medicine for them. We'll find out more in the morning."

Mike and James helped the riders down and half carried them close to the fire. "Here, Mike," James said. "Roll these extra blankets up for some pillows. They're both shivering pretty bad. Derek, there's some more wood over by my horse, if you wouldn't mind."

In a few moments, the two visitors were asleep under a comfy layer of blankets and in the radiant heat of a toasty fire.

"Frank and Emily are their names," Derek stated casually as he removed the saddle from his horse. "A man named Sydney Williams locked them in the mine. When it exploded, they were able to make it as far as the ventilation grate." He shook his head and continued, "They were trapped. It was fortunate that I had a rope and a horse. Never could have removed that grate without them."

James and Mike nodded and then changed the subject. "Listen, Derek," Mike began. "Here is how things stand right now." He explained what he and James had discussed earlier: the freight transfer, the smelter conspiracy, and the transportation problem. Derek nodded as they explained the situation.

"Yeah," Derek agreed. "I think we should get in there and disable any chance of them going anywhere with the gold. What did you have in mind?"

Mike's teeth gleamed in the firelight as he lowered his voice. "This ought to rattle their cage."

241

CHAPTER 50

Later that evening James, Derek, and Mike returned to the mill. They tied the horses to the gnarled trees at their first campsite and moved like shadows to the warehouses alongside the road. They surveyed the grounds of the mining camp and then proceeded to the tasks at hand.

Mike crept around the back of the largest warehouse, toward the stables. He noticed that a number of horses were hitched to four loaded wagons. Two men were putting some miscellaneous supplies from the office under each wagon seat. Mike assumed correctly that the wagons were already loaded with the gold ore and bars. He lay down in the shadows and waited for the two men to return to the tunnel. When that moment came, he unsheathed a knife from under his pant leg and swiftly moved to the harness straps of the first horse team. He sliced the thick leather straps securing the horses to the drive-timber. "We'll find you boys later," he whispered to them. Then he moved to the other three wagons and did likewise. In a matter of five minutes, he had regained his position in the shadows behind the warehouse. He pulled four sticks of dynamite from his pack, checked the short fuses for integrity, opened a box of matches that he had in his coat pocket, and waited impatiently in the snow.

In the meantime, Derek moved to the bottom of the mill, entered the door, and climbed the long staircase to the tumbler and loading chute. The mineworkers had already cleared out the gold and dry mix from the tenders, but had left the oil lamps aglow. Off to one side, Derek noticed a wooden case with a loose lid. He moved the lid aside and smiled at finding Mike's source of dynamite. He pulled out his pocket watch and noted the time.

James had worked his way around to his previous hiding place under the window of the office. He felt more secure this time, since the side of the building sheltered him from the light of the oil lamps hanging from the shaft house and office porch. He could hear voices inside, but the conversation seemed centered on gathering essentials for the wagons' departure. He opened his pocket watch, but couldn't quite see it because of the dark. He moved to a crouching position, then lit a match and covered it with his body so its light couldn't be seen. The time was eleven thirty. He moved the match to a fairly long fuse stuck in the end of three sticks of dynamite tied together. It immediately started a muffled fizz. He put it on the ground, covered it with the lid from a wooden barrel, and ran to the other side of the covered mine tunnel.

The detonation of the dynamite crate blew the Silver Plume mill into a raging fireball. Even though Derek was a safe distance away, the concussion from the blast knocked him off his feet. Bits of shrapnel from the machinery and shards of wood showered the camp compound with a rain of blazing fire and smoke. The horses harnessed to the freight wagons recoiled in terror, broke any remaining restraint, and bolted to the south. The men in the office ran out the door and viewed the inferno with bewilderment. At that instant, the charges that James had planted exploded and took out the side of the office building. All four men were thrown to the ground by the shock wave.

When Mike saw the location of the "Silver Plume Boys," he rapidly lit the short fuses on his dynamite sticks and then lobbed them into each of the wagons. He had just enough time to dive behind the warehouse for safety before each wagon disintegrated in its turn. After the final explosion, he peeked around the corner of the warehouse at the devastation, and then looked at the men on the ground in front of the building. He saw James emerge from the shadows of the mine tunnel with his gun drawn and some rope in his other hand. Mike sprinted from behind the building to give him a hand. Out of the corner of his eye he saw another man running in from the entry road.

James was first to reach the four men on the ground. Two of them rolled around in confusion from the stun of the blast. James tied the hands and feet of one man as Mike reached him. He removed a coil of rope from his pack and immediately started to secure a second man. He was dumbfounded for a moment as he realized the man was minus an arm. He improvised, finished the job, took his gun, and moved on to the lifeless third man. Two unexpected shots rang out from the shaft house. A piece of glowing red lead sheared the gun from James's hand and he shouted in pain.

"Hurry, Mike!" James yelled. "Grab that man and drag him behind the office rubble."

Mike holstered his gun, jerked the arms of a short fat man to the side, and dragged his unconscious body to some cover. Three more shots rang out and ricocheted off the remnants of the stove. Another bullet whizzed by Mike's head from a different angle.

"Someone is behind us!" Mike yelled. "We're in a cross fire."

"Get in the building!" James bellowed as he yanked Mike's arm. They heard a series of shots from the warehouse directed at the mine tunnel. A hunched-over man staggered out of the dark passageway into the pale moonlight and collapsed on the snow. A series of powerful rifle bursts chewed at the warehouse siding. A sudden lull in the storm of gunfire enabled Mike and James to seize the moment and, stumbling through the wreckage of the office, seek safety in the shell of what remained. Shattered window glass crunched under their feet as they hugged an interior wall and stumbled over framing debris and plaster. Mike tripped and, as he fell, he sliced one hand on a piece of broken glass. His other hand caught something round, which he automatically grasped. It was a Winchester, loaded and ready. He swung the barrel toward the broken window, aimed below the oil lamp, and pulled the trigger. He re-cocked, aimed, and fired in quick successions. A yelp from the shaft house indicated a hit.

Mike heard a report from behind him, and felt a searing pain like a scythe slashing at his thigh. As he collapsed, he whirled around and fired his rifle at a shadow standing where the window next to the stove had been. A man recoiled backward with a bullet through the head.

James crouched down next to Mike and took the Winchester from his hands. He checked the chamber, looked to his right for any more shadows in the opening, then spun around toward the shaft house and unloaded the rest of his magazine. Then he frantically searched the loose debris for more shells or another rifle to use.

Three more shots penetrated the thin frame walls of the building, but didn't pierce through the interior wall that concealed Mike and James. Back in the jagged opening of the building rent by the explosion, James heard some shuffling and movement. He froze as he saw the slender outline of the fourth man that they had left in the courtyard. James watched as the man raised his pistol to eye level, squeezed the trigger, and looked surprised when the gun clicked. The empty chamber gave James the chance he needed to grab the first thing within reach, a wooden shard of flooring. He slung it with all his might at the shadow, but it flew wide to the right. The man swung sideways in response, and aimed the gun again. A deep, throaty crack rang out. James jerked, and then watched the man shudder and fall to the ground. It seemed to James that the report had come from above the warehouse. He shifted his head and looked out through what remained of the front door and window. As he watched, a series of flashes and booming echoes rolled across the hillside. He crawled back to the shaft house, and gazed at the planks on the landing area as they splintered into small fragments under the barrage of rifle fire.

Abruptly, the onslaught stopped. A weak voice from the shaft house yelled, "Stop shooting! I'm hit and need help. Here's my weapon." A long rifle somersaulted out of the mineshaft. "I'm coming out!" the voice cried. A man crawled out of the shaft onto the staging area and feebly held up an arm. "I'm the last one!" he screamed. "Help me before I bleed to death!"

A long silence ensued. James roused himself and looked at Mike. "Are you okay?"

"I'm alive," he responded. "But I'm bleeding bad, and it hurts."

James crawled over to Mike and examined his wound in the feeble light emanating from the burning fragments left in the aftermath of the explosion. A bullet had entered his thigh about eight inches above the knee. James took off his coat and tied the sleeves around the wound to control the bleeding. "I'll be right back," he said.

He slowly stood to his feet and looked for any sign of movement around him. There was none, so he began to work his way over to the large opening in the side of the office building. Two men were lying in the snow. One was face up with a hole in his forehead. The other sprawled across a pile of debris. "No helping them," he thought to himself. He wandered to the edge of where the porch had been and looked around the remaining front wall. The man at the shaft house was still lying on the staging platform, writhing in pain. James looked to his left and saw the two men that he and Mike had tied up. He walked over to them and saw that they were still unconscious. James then moved to the side of the warehouse where Derek had been. James found him leaning against the wall with small shards of wood sticking out of his face and neck. A bullet had grazed his upper right arm, and another had gone through the calf of his right leg. He had controlled the bleeding by tying some dynamite fuses around the leg and by layering some cloth on his arm.

"Wow, what a firefight!" Derek croaked enthusiastically.

"Looks like you got it kind of bad," James said as he kneeled next to him. He reached up and jerked a piece of wood from Derek's cheek.

"Ouch, let me know next time!" he yelled.

James looked up from tending his friend to see another man standing near him with a rifle at his side. He could just make out Frank's silhouette in the flickering light from the fire at the mill. It reminded him of something, a memory long ago. "Frank? Is that you, Frank?"

"Yup," the man replied. "It's me." He paused a moment then added, "It is definitely me, Francis Schreiber."

James's blank stare washed away in tears of remembrance. "Francis? Francis, Frank. Of course! You're my brother." He stood up and held out his arms. "It's me, Frederick James. What on earth are you doing here?"

Frank leaned his rifle against the warehouse. "Why, looking for you," he replied with a smile.

CHAPTER 51

Friday morning dawned bright and blue over the mountains surrounding Central City. A mantle of white graced the high country, thanks to the recent snowstorm. The lower valleys, on the other hand, were warm and sprinkled with new spring growth.

At the rail yards, two flat cars with pump handles stood anchored to the tracks, waiting for their occupants to begin the beautiful ride down the river gorge toward Golden. The first cart had two seats bolted to the front of the platform so the riders could enjoy the scenery without obstruction.

A small entourage of men departed the Teller House at about fifteen minutes past sunrise. A small, stocky man with a full beard and some ranking general's stars on his coat led the group. They followed the boardwalk past the telegrapher's office, by the rail station house, and stopped at the end of the yard where the carts waited.

"What a gorgeous day!" President Grant exclaimed as he inspected the first cart. "I can't wait to see the gorge."

"Yes, Mr. President," one of his advisors replied. "I understand, sir, that Mr. Steele has graciously provided two of the railroad men to pump your cart for you. He telegraphed me this morning to say that he also has provided you with a companion for your excursion." He paused a moment as he read from a slip of paper. "A Mr. Henri Mueller?"

The President turned his head to make eye contact with his

advisor and reiterated in surprise, "Henri Mueller? Why I've not spent any time with him for a number of years! Now, how did Everett manage that?"

At that moment, Henri, Tom O'Malley, and Jacob Johnson walked up to the cart. "Mr. President, may I introduce myself? Tom O'Malley, your guide." He motioned to Johnson. "And this is Jacob Johnson, a long-time employee of Mr. Everett Steele and general manager of the rail yard here in Central City. And a friend you already know, Mr. Henri Mueller, who will graciously accompany you on your ride to Twin Forks."

The president shook hands with Tom and Jacob and then approached Henri. He held his arms out wide, sported a wide smile, and gave him a warm embrace. "Henri, it's good to see you after all these years."

"You, too, Lyss," Henri replied with an equally warm expression. They locked eyes for a moment as if to exchange an unspoken secret. "I see your beard has gotten a little grayer since the last time I saw you," he quipped.

"Yeah," Grant replied, "comes with the territory." He put his arm around Henri's shoulders. "Come now, sir, let's get this show started, and we can visit on the way down the canyon."

Grant led Henri to the cart, climbed onboard, and sat in one of the bolted chairs. Henri took a seat next to him as Tom and Jacob took their places on either side of the pumping handles. The president's advisor and security agents, along with two additional railroad men, boarded the second cart. Tom and Jacob began to pump and the platform cart gently rolled out of the rail yards and onto the main track to Golden.

Henri smiled at Grant's enthusiasm for the ride. Henri observed how the simplicity of a joy ride could relieve the pressures and tension from a man whose administration was rocked with numerous scandals, many of which were the result of Grant's inherent trust in a man's good word.

As the ride progressed, Tom and Jacob gave the president pieces of information about the area. "Last time you were here, Mr. President," Jacob commented, "these tracks were still under construction. You probably remember traveling by horse over the unfinished bed before the ties were laid."

"Yes, I do," Grant responded. He turned around and pointed back at Central City before it disappeared around a bend. "I see that much of the town has been rebuilt after the fire last year."

"That's correct, sir," Tom yelled above the hum of the rails. "Only six buildings resisted the flames. All of them, like the Teller House where you stayed, were built of stone."

"I see," Grant said.

The cart started to pick up momentum as the valley narrowed and the grade increased. The rail bed, built in places on rubble fill blown from the mountainside and leveled out, was situated alongside a rushing river. The rails closely followed the river's descent as it cascaded down the valley in small waterfalls and created whitewater rapids. Large boulders and rubble debris lined this section of the railroad and, as they whizzed by, the rails seemed to sing to them like the wind blowing through a wooden fence on a blustery spring day. Cold air from the higher elevations rushed down the valley and provided them with a wind at their backs that offset the wind in their faces that was generated by their rail speed.

The speeding platform car hurtled around a bend so fast that Henri and Grant had to hang on to the bolted chairs for support. At this point, Jacob moved to the rear of the cart, hung over the back, and removed an object that had been previously fastened underneath. He glanced to the front of the cart, but Grant and Henri were too enthralled with the speed and scenery to take notice. Jacob took the item in his hand, reached down to one of the rails speeding by, spread the wedge like a claw, and dropped it onto the shiny steel ribbon. Upon contact with the track, the wedge immediately clamped itself closed and, in spite of the speed, ground to a halt on the rail.

The second cart was moving too fast to notice the wedge on the track. As it came around the bend the left roller hit the wedge and ramped the side of the cart into the air. The men on board bounced like rag dolls as the flipping cart split into fragments upon impact with the sharp rocks and boulders along the tracks.

The first cart slipped around another bend right as the second broke up. The rail noise covered the screams of the dying men behind them. Jacob smiled at Tom as he took his place at the front of the pumper unit. Then he reached down along the vertical pipe that the pump rod was connected to, popped loose a clip, and removed a large safety pin holding the drive rods together. Tom and Jacob then lifted the pump bar up and threw it over the side of the cart.

Grant heard the ring of steel hitting rock, turned around, and yelled, "You there, what are you doing?" He started to rise from his seat, but another turn in the track forced him to secure himself.

Tom smiled back and hissed, "I hope you enjoy your trip, Mr. President." At that moment the cart sped over a bridge that crossed a tributary of the main river. There was a large pool of quiet water, the only pool they had seen on the trip thus far, under the fifty-foot-long structure. Tom and Jacob leapt from the cart as it roared across the small trestle. Tom cleared the ties and hit squarely in the pool with a large splash. Jacob wasn't so lucky. He didn't clear the bridge as his foot caught on a cross timber that spun him crazily in circles, and landed him too close to the rocks. The water wasn't deep enough to break his fall and his body split open in many places before it lifelessly slid to a stop on the rubble of the track berm.

Grant worked his way out of the chair, grasped onto its backing, and made his way to the mechanical mechanism that propelled the cart. Henri joined him and yelled above the clatter of the rollers on the track, "There's no way to use this without the pump handle!"

Henri reached behind him and pulled on the brake lever. As predicted, the wooden pads to the shoes flew off the moment they touched the wheel. Worthless sparks trailed as the metal fasteners ground uselessly against the steel drum. In a moment, the handle broke under the frictional heat and dropped to the rails with a clang and a crash.

The cart continued to accelerate on the downward grade. Grant looked at Henri and said aloud, "Okay, what next?"

"Hang on best you can," was his reply. "Help will be here soon!"

Two miles down the grade, just before the Twin Forks cutoff, Jack and Johann waited along each side of the tracks with the two fastest horses in Central City. The excavators of the roadbed dug further into the mountainside at this point in order to obtain extra material to create a foundation for the bridge that spanned the river. As a result, this harbored the only level spot on the line that was long enough to run a horse parallel with the tracks.

Jack checked his pocket watch. "The train should be entering the tunnel right about now," he theorized. He scanned the track toward Central City. "They should be here any minute. Get on your horse, Johann, and do exactly as I said."

Jack heard the telltale noise of the platform cart screeching down the tracks. "We've only got one chance at this." He mounted his horse, turned it down track, and waited.

Henri spied the two horses as the cart roared around a bend. He reached for Grant's hand and yelled, "Get ready, Lyss, we're going to have to jump onto those horses while they are at a dead run. They'll still be four feet or so from the cart, so just take a dive for the front of the saddle and the rider will keep you from falling."

Grant's gray eyes showed no fear as he rose to a crouching position and nodded his head in understanding. Henri did likewise, but facing the other direction.

The cart closed in on the flat roadbed. Jack gauged the distance, then shouted at Johann, "Now, move it!"

The two horses took off at a full gallop, paralleling the tracks and kicking up twin clouds of dust. Halfway down the graded zone, Jack looked over his shoulder to see the platform cart gaining substantially on their horses. "Kick that horse!" he yelled at Johann. "Get every ounce of speed you can!"

The cart rolled toward them at a quicker pace than the horses could run. Jack saw the president's eyes as he weighed his timing. Grant leapt from the wooden platform just as the cart passed Jack's saddle. He landed exactly in Jack's lap, but his weight carried him beyond. Jack grasped the president's clothing as he started to sail by his perch. Grant's coat ripped at the seam, so Jack scrambled to latch onto the president's leather belt. Jack pulled his foot from the stirrup and caught Grant's collarbone with the top of his boot in an endeavor to hold his head away from the horse's legs. He pulled back hard on the reins and brought the horse to a stop. At that moment, he lost his grip, and the president of the United States fell heavily to the ground.

The platform cart screamed out of control beyond the rail intersection at the Forks and around the bend out of sight. Jack looked across the tracks and saw Henri and Johann smiling at him from a most unusual position. As the cart passed Johann's horse, Henri jumped a little too soon and knocked Johann out of the saddle. Henri, in turn, grabbed Johann by the belt around his waist to hold him onto the racing horse. Each man grasped one of the horse's reins, and together they managed to stop the animal. As Jack watched, the horse circled unwillingly as the two men worked to untangle each other from the reins. Johann fell on the ground with Henri close behind.

"Well, it worked!" Johann cheered.

They rushed to help Grant to his feet. "Yup," Grant grunted as he got up and brushed himself off. "It definitely worked."

CHAPTER 52

The president stretched his back and grimaced at Henri. "Henri? What is going on here?"

Henri smiled and answered, "Well, sir, as you probably figured, this was an assassination attempt on your life."

"Oh, c'mon, Henri," Grant growled as he rolled his eyes. "Anybody can see that. Fill me in on what's behind it."

Jack stepped forward and interrupted. "Mr. President, I have two more horses in the ravine. We need to leave this area before the search for you starts."

Grant stared at Jack and asked, "And who are you?" Their eyes met and communicated a level of trust. Recollection came to Grant's mind. "You're one of Henri's men." He paused again as he searched his fine-tuned memory. "Jack, isn't it?" He hurriedly inspected his surroundings and continued, "Okay, I trust your judgment. Let's saddle up and you can tell me further up the trail." He puckered his lips and added, "Where are we going?"

"Up to that ridge," Jack replied as he pointed to an overlook high above the tracks. "It's not a long ride from here, and it will be a safe place where we can discuss our options."

Grant took another smack at his thigh to remove some dust, then took a good look at Johann and offered his hand. "My name's Grant," he began. "My friends call me Lyss. You did a brave thing here, son. Thank you."

Johann offered his hand in return. "You're welcome, sir."

255

Jack gave a shrill whistle toward a hidden ravine. Evangeline and Sarah appeared, leading four horses. They hurried to the party and were rapidly introduced. They mounted the horses and moved up the ravine toward the high mountain trail that paralleled the tracks.

At the top of the cliffs, Jack signaled the party to rein in the horses for a breather. Everyone dismounted and collected near an overlook above the Twin Forks Bridge. "You remember seeing this view the other day, Sarah?" Evangeline asked.

"Yes, but now there is a lot more going on." Sarah pointed to a number of men who appeared small as ants far below by the intersection of the Twin Forks Bridge.

"I imagine they are looking for me," Grant surmised. "I'm sure it didn't take too long for my Secret Service to figure out that I didn't make it to the train." He caught Henri's eye and said, "Okay, tell me what's going on."

Henri pondered for a moment, trying to decide where to begin. "You remember the gold shipments that were stolen back in the war."

Grant nodded in affirmation. "Of course. I assigned you to that case back in 1864." He stroked his beard and continued, "I believe there were a total of twenty-two gold bullion thefts between the North and the South during the last two years of the war."

"That's right," Henri agreed. "To condense a long story, Everett Steele and Sydney Williams were behind the original thefts. They originally were going to use the stolen gold to force a peace through financial attrition on both sides. Then they were going to invest in Southern reconstruction. When that idea fell through, they came up with the plan of creating and financing a self-serving federation, separate from the Union, and carved out of the Colorado Territory currently in place. Steele hoped that your assassination would bring a unity to the unhappy, silver-rich, but gold-poor mining communities across the area. Current silver devaluation fueled support for that bad attitude toward your administration among many territorial mining towns. Word of your death will give cause for Steele to call an emergency meeting of the territorial council tomorrow morning. He plans to announce the formation of this new entity and drum up support for a withdrawal from Union territorial status."

"The man is crazy!" Grant grunted as he shook his head. "Everyone knows that a separate country in the middle of the United States is ludicrous."

"Maybe so, Lyss," Henri said. "But the numbers indicate that he has the local support and financial infrastructure in place to try to pull it off."

Grant turned toward the view below and contemplated his options. "What do you suggest, Henri?"

"I think there is a way we can resolve this crisis," Henri said. "But we have to move fast." Henri looked at his pocketwatch, glanced over his shoulder, and asked, "Jack, how long is the ride to Denver from here?"

Jack pursed his lips and said, "A good rider could get there by late evening. It's a lot of mountain travel, not much level ground."

Henri nodded his head in understanding and continued, "I take it you know the roads that will take us there?"

"Certainly," Jack responded. "I just rode them the other day when I saw all of you in the rail yards."

Henri furrowed his brow as he organized his thoughts. "Evangeline, can you take Sarah and Johann back to Central City and discreetly contact the president's Secret Service men?"

She nodded and mimicked a question, "And tell them . . . ?"

President Grant interrupted. "Give them this." He pulled a ring off of his finger and handed it to Evangeline. "This ring is," he paused for a moment for the right words, "I guess you could call it 'an arrangement' that I have with my agent in charge. His name is Ambrose McHenry. Show him this and tell him that 'Lyss expects compliance.' He'll listen and do whatever you tell him to."

Evangeline took the ring and stared oddly at it. The president continued, "Ambrose was my right hand man during the war. He saved my life on two occasions and I trust him implicitly. He understands the chain of command, and this ring will be as good as my verbal orders. He will carry them out without question."

"But won't Ambrose be somewhere on the tracks looking for you?"

"No," Grant replied. "He'll be near the telegraph office. It's the best place to be during a crisis. All the search parties can relay messages to him by tapping into the wires along the tracks. It's from the communication base that he can manage everyone involved." He turned to Henri and added, "Tell Evangeline what you need."

Henri's voice instinctively grew low as he narrowed his eyes and laid out his plan.

Then Jack, Lyss, and Henri mounted their horses and headed for Denver, while Evangeline, Sarah, and Johann turned toward Central City.

CHAPTER 53

The Silver Plume Mine and Milling Company had sustained heavy damage. The intense explosion from the dynamite crate in the mill had sent a mix of timbers, equipment, and shards throughout the camp. One side of the office building had crumbled into a pile of rubble, and the warehouses were splintered from gunfire. The vertical lift and platform were still intact, but the shaft underneath the towering complex was partially filled with debris from the earlier blast deep in the mine tunnels.

Emily, who had arrived with Frank, stumbled across cotton packing cloth that had blown out of a warehouse in the explosion. Her instincts kicked in as she separated it from the pile of debris. She then turned to James, who was leaning against the nearby wall.

"Frank," she called, "put pressure here. I need to stop this bleeding." With an expert hand, she packed the wound with cotton wadding, then wrapped it in a ripped shirtsleeve. The hand throbbed, but the pain was tolerable. As Frank helped, he blurted out, "How come you never wrote home?"

James looked up and retorted, "I did."

"I don't recall any letters from you." James winced as Frank added undue pressure to his hand.

"Really, Frank, I did. The first time I wrote was when our boat reached England in '65. I wrote three or four times after that. I don't know why they were never received."

Emily tied off the last knot on James's wound. As she inspected the dressing, she glanced over and saw that Mike still bled. "Frank, your reunion has to wait. Bring Mike here."

Frank helped Mike over to the warehouse and leaned him against the wooden wall next to Derek. The puncture wounds to his left hand were squeeze-bled to help cleanse out the dirt, then wrapped. His thigh suffered a deep gash from a bullet, but it was a clean slice that would only require several stitches to close up. In the meantime, Emily wrapped the wound tightly to keep it closed, then packed snow around his thigh to help deaden the pain. Frank held Derek still while the splinters were removed from his face and neck. He removed the fuse cable from his calf so Emily could bleed it and close it with some strips of cloth. The graze on his arm was cleaned with some snow and also temporarily wrapped. Frank gathered some loose wood lying around from the blast, put it into a pile near Mike and Derek, and lit it with a burning piece of debris from the mill. A fire crackled to life and gave light and warmth to those around.

Once Mike and Derek were settled, James, Frank, and Emily walked to the vertical lift platform to tend to the wounded man whom Mike had shot. He was tall and slender with a neatly trimmed gray beard. His wounds were not life-threatening, but did give him quite a bit of pain. Emily contained the bleeding from two bullet holes, one in the left shoulder and the other in his upper right arm. Once dressed and hauled to his feet, James and Frank helped him to the fire to warm up.

After they lowered the injured man next to the fire, Frank put his hands on James's shoulders. "I still can't believe you're alive. We thought you were killed during the war. Then, ten years later, Dad receives a telegram from a sheriff in a town called Silverton saying you were killed in a mining accident. What's that all about?"

James laughed. "You can't get rid of me. Derek and I were in a mining explosion but we managed to escape. I think Baxter wanted to eliminate us because we started digging too deep into their plan. We thought it best at the time to let him think we were dead. We had no idea that anyone would come looking for us."

Emily motioned to Frank. "Give me a hand straightening Derek. I want to give him some water."

"On my way," Frank acknowledged.

James watched his brother leave. The fires from the office caught his attention and he remembered the two men that he and Mike had left in the snow. He went to check on them. They were unconscious, but otherwise fine. He checked their pockets for any papers or information that might shed some light on the situation. There was nothing of vital importance. He called to Frank to drag them over to the fire when he was finished.

He went next to the blown-out wall of the office. The body of one man was still draped over a pile of debris; the other man lay in the snow gazing toward the sky in a death stare. James sighed, shook his head slightly, and proceeded to search their pockets. He also removed their silver jewelry and placed it in his pocket. It was too dark to read the contents of what he found, so he collected the slips in his hand and then went over to the mine tunnel to check the man on the ground. He, too, was dead after having taken several hits from Derek's rifle. Once again James checked the pockets before returning to the warmth and light of the fire.

"I take it we won," Mike jested as he joined James at the fire.

"Yeah, you might say that," James replied stoically as he scanned the carnage surrounding them. He kneeled near the flames for better light and started reading through the various scraps of paper that he had picked up. The first had a number of hastily scrawled notes on it, similar to a laundry list: extra rope, water casks, food, matches, and other supplies. James tossed it into the fire as he went to the next scrap. It was a bill of lading for supplies that were shipped to the mine office a week earlier. James snickered as he saw the crate of dynamite among the inventory. He handed it to Derek so he could appreciate the irony.

"I guess that's why it blew up so violently," he commented as he perused the list. "It was fresh."

James nodded his head in mock agreement. He unfolded another note. "Hey, this one is from Everett Steele." He held it closer to the fire for better light. "It's sent to Joseph Baxter." He lowered the paper and scanned his surroundings. "You know, I don't remember seeing his body in any of the debris."

Derek said, "Let's see, there was another man in the mine shaft who fell when you hit him. Maybe that was Baxter."

James glanced over at the bearded man leaning against the barn and asked, "Was that man with you named Baxter?"

"No, his name was Harry. He was the mine foreman. Baxter never came off of the mountain."

"What do you mean?" James asked.

The bearded man replied, "Three of the wagons slipped off of the pass in the blizzard and tumbled into the canyon. We went up to find the survivors, but were only able to find one man in the snow. The other two drivers were lost."

"And the gold shipment?" James inquired.

"We retrieved a number of gold bars," he answered. "But we didn't know how much was originally on the wagons. They were destroyed and what we found was in the scatter line where they rolled down the slope. The man we found jumped off when the wagon started to slide. He never went down the canyon, but had hit his head on a rock when he landed. He was unconscious when we found him. It was so cold and windy that I can't imagine anyone else surviving." He paused for a moment in silent reflection and then continued almost in a whisper. "We never did make it to the bottom of the gorge. It was too dangerous."

James pondered the man's account, then returned to the telegram.

"Found way to take care of Grant Stop Send bullion to Golden for smelt and trade Stop Be at Legislature Building on Saturday at ten Stop Gold must be processed by Saturday noon Stop Don't delay Stop Steele."

He handed the telegram to Mike, who also wanted to read it. "Which body did you get this telegram off of?" he asked.

James replied, "The red-bearded one. The one called Seth. I remember him all the way back to Andersonville."

"Yeah, I do, too," Mike replied. He handed the telegram on to Derek, who read it, then set it aside on the snow.

"It looks to me," Derek said, "like the revolution that feller talked about back at the church in Fairplay is about to start. I'd wager that Grant's murder will be the opening topic at that meeting on Saturday, and then secession as an independent country will follow."

"I'd certainly like to be there for that meeting," James interjected. He reached for a long stick of wood, stirred up the coals, and tossed some more wood on the fire. Then he analyzed the situation. "What are we going to do with these other three men?"

"It wouldn't do any good to take them into Georgetown," Frank said. "That entire town is under Steele's control."

James nodded in agreement and said, "All I know is that we need to be at that meeting." He looked at Mike and Frank and added, "Now, how are we going to get there?"

CHAPTER 54

Friday afternoon was coming to a close when Evangeline, Sarah, and Johann rode into Central City. The city had an "out-of-kilter" air about it. Many of the merchants and miners were assembled in lodges, in saloons, on street corners, or under store canopies. An undercurrent of subdued chatter coursed in whispers up and down the quiet streets of Central City as if a long-awaited plan was about to unfold. Militia guards were posted around the banks, postal agency, government buildings, and telegraph office. Many of the men stood at attention. Their anxious eyes betrayed their dignified stance. They found themselves serving in a position they had never anticipated. Evangeline quietly wondered who commanded the loyalty of these nervous men charged with the responsibility of maintaining order.

Evangeline led the way through town. The mounted trio rode past the Teller House and the newspaper's headquarters, and on toward the telegraph office on the edge of town. As they approached the building, two militiamen armed with rifles intercepted them. They wore an official-looking insignia on the upper sleeves of their coats with the words "Jefferson Militia" emblazoned in red letters that arced around a mountain peak with a pine tree and a bar of gold at the center. One of them, a tall, sandy blond-haired man with a neatly trimmed goatee and wire-rimmed eyeglasses, spoke to Evangeline. "Pardon me, ma'am. May I inquire as to your destination?"

Evangeline stopped her horse even with the man's shoulder so she could look down on him from her perch. She looked him over from head to toe and responded with a smile. "Why, sir, we are on our way to the telegraph office to see if there is word from a relative en route for a visit to our fine community. He was detained in Longmont and we are checking his itinerary."

The man absorbed her information for a moment, then replied, "I'm sorry, ma'am. An emergency has taken place and all messages in and out of Central City have been suspended until a time designated by Mr. Everett Steele."

"Oh, I see," Evangeline replied. "And what is this emergency about?"

"You haven't heard?" the guard quizzed.

"No, sir. My niece, nephew, and I live far from town and have just come in this morning," she fibbed. "Tell me, sir, what is the crisis?"

"The president has been killed," he responded.

Evangeline feigned distress in her reply. "Oh, my goodness. What has happened?"

"The president was on a tour of the gorge when the platform cart he was riding on lost all braking control and collided with the train to Floyd's Hill."

"Was his body found?" Evangeline asked.

"No," the guard replied. "The body of one of the drivers was found in a tributary flowing underneath the tracks. The investigators think the president might have tried to jump off the cart into that same tributary, but was then caught in the strong current of the river and drowned. They are still searching down river but haven't found anything. I imagine that's why all communication at the telegraph office has been suspended, so the lines can stay open for any news that comes in from down river."

"So, when will the office be open for normal telegrams

again?" Evangeline asked.

"Don't know," the guard replied. "I'm afraid you'll just have to wait like everyone else to find out."

Evangeline noticed out of her peripheral vision a small lad running out of the telegraph office up the road. He sprinted down the dirt street and disappeared around a corner into an alley that led toward the sheriff's office. He clutched a crumpled piece of paper in his grip as he kicked up dust behind him. Evangeline thanked the guard, turned her horse around, and motioned for Sarah and Johann to follow. They retraced their path back toward the Teller House, but turned on the first available alley to the south. They came out on the next road over, dismounted, and found a hitching post where they secured their horses. Then Evangeline sat on a rocking chair in front of the hardware store and indicated to Sarah and Johann to do likewise.

"What are we going to do now?" Sarah asked.

"One moment, young lady," Evangeline responded. "You two stay here." She got up and went into the store. After some minutes she returned with a smile on her face and sat down.

"What was that all about?" Sarah again asked.

"Patience, my dear," Evangeline replied. "Patience."

They continued to rock for another ten minutes. Soon the delivery boy from the telegraph office came running up the street again. "One moment, son," Evangeline coaxed. She held out a gold coin that she pulled from her pocket. "Would you kindly deliver a message for me to the telegrapher?"

The boy stopped momentarily and puffed a reply. "I'm sorry, ma'am. But no messages are being sent at the moment."

"Ah, I see," Evangeline replied. "Then might you know the man in charge at the moment? His name is Ambrose McHenry."

"Yes, of course," he replied. "He took over the office earlier this morning. He's the one who shut down all messages in and out of Central City."

"Now this is of the utmost importance, young man," she instructed. "Give this box to Mr. McHenry, and no one else. Here is a gold coin for your delivery. Mr. McHenry will want to see me immediately. So there is another coin just like that one," she held up another coin that she removed from her pocket, "for you when you return. Do you understand?"

The boy thought for a moment, looked up and down the street to see if someone should be watching, then reached up and took the coin and box. "Yes, ma'am. I will follow your instructions exactly as you said." He started to take off running again, then stopped and turned around with a smile. "I'll be back again in a jiffy, ma'am. Keep that coin warm for me!"

Evangeline smiled in return and said not too loudly, "I shall, dear boy. Now hurry on your errand."

The young lad spun around and took off at a full sprint again. He ran past the alley that the trio had come down, continued to the next block, and rounded the corner. In his haste, he lost his footing and slid to his knees but, just as quickly, was back up again and off. He came to the next corner and ran by the militiamen. They smiled and waved as he whizzed by, growling like a running bear. He ran past three more guards sitting on the boardwalk in front of the telegraph office, and rushed through the open doorway. "Here, sir." He handed Monty the telegram from the sheriff.

"One moment, son," a deep, resonant voice interjected. "Let me see that first." A large man with a long, black mustache gently held out his hand. Monty gave him the message. He opened it, read it, and asked, "Any activity on the lines?"

Monty looked over his shoulder and listened for a second. "No, sir. None."

"Okay," the large man replied. "Go ahead and send it." He handed Monty the note and looked at the delivery boy. "You seem out of breath, son. How about some water?"

"Yes, sir. That would be great, sir," he politely replied.

"Come along, then." The large man looked at Monty for a moment and said, "If there is anything—anything at all—I'll be in the back."

Monty nodded his head. Then he pointed in the direction of the back room. "The cups are in the upper cabinet, Mr. McHenry. There is water in the pitcher in the ice cooler below the far cabinet."

"Thank you, Monty," he said. "I appreciate it."

Ambrose and the boy moved to the back room, where he opened a tall cabinet, removed a couple of mugs, and set them on the countertop. Then he shouted to the front room, "Monty, did you want something to drink?"

"No, thank you," the reply came. "I'm fine."

Reaching to the far cabinet, he opened the ice cooler, removed a metal pitcher with ice-cold water, filled the two mugs with water, and handed one to the delivery boy.

The boy absentmindedly set the box on the countertop as he took the mug from Ambrose, who noticed it immediately and asked, "What's in the box, son?"

"Oh, yeah, I forgot," the boy responded. "A lady asked me to give that to you." He paused a moment, looked around, and then added, "Only to you."

Ambrose raised an eyebrow at this last phrase. Putting his mug down, he reached for the box. Glancing around to make sure they were alone, he untied the twine holding it closed. He pulled open the lid and removed a piece of folded paper. Upon unfolding it, he read, "Mr. Ambrose McHenry, in this box you will find President Grant's ring. He told me to give it to you with the words, 'Lyss expects compliance.' Please follow the boy alone to my location so we can talk." Ambrose's eyes grew large and his brow wrinkled in consternation as he reread the note's contents. Then he looked into the box and withdrew Grant's ring. He quickly dropped the note and ring into his breast pocket and put the box in the trash bin. He looked momentarily at the lad, then turned and yelled to Monty, "I'm going out for a breath of fresh air. Keep the men nearby in case something comes in."

"Okay," came the faint reply. "How long will you be out?"

"Twenty or thirty minutes, I suppose," he answered. He heard a grunt of affirmation as he directed the delivery boy out the back door.

Ten minutes later, Ambrose and the boy were walking up to the entry to the hardware store. Evangeline was casually rocking in her chair as the boy made impromptu introductions.

"Here you go, Mr. McHenry." Then he turned to Evangeline, but she already knew what he wanted.

She tossed him the other gold coin and said, "Go get yourself a soda, my dear. And tell absolutely no one about me being here. Understand?"

He caught the coin, gleefully agreed to her terms, and took off excitedly in a small cloud of dust.

Evangeline rose to her feet, extended her hand warmly, and said, "Mr. Ambrose McHenry. Please, come sit with us. We have urgent business to discuss."

CHAPTER 55

Joseph Baxter couldn't believe his eyes when he topped the western ridge overlooking the slope above the Silver Plume Mine and Milling Company. He stared in disbelief at the debris field strewn before him where the once premier mining site in all the territory had stood. His frustration and anger, previously held in check through immense patience and determination, was on the precipice of being unleashed like an enormous mountain snow bank showing the stress cracks of excessive heavy snow.

It wasn't so much that he had slid off the mountain two days earlier. He was lucky that the deep snow from the freak springtime blizzard had cushioned his tumble into the gorge. But it was unfortunate that he had not been able to climb directly back out from where he had fallen, and had to follow the steep canyon with all its boulders and crags downstream. After many hours of stumbling around in the darkness, the storm's wind and cold and his lack of progress finally forced him to seek shelter in a small natural cave about a mile below the wagon ruins. Packed snow against the cave entrance gave him a degree of protection and warmth. He succumbed to exhaustion from many days of working nonstop. His strength depleted, he fell into a deep sleep, so deep that he did not revive until only a few hours before dawn on Friday. Sheer grit carried Baxter in the cold temperature without food or warmth until he found a narrow passageway leading out of the canyon. Once on top of the plateau, he made his way back to where he thought the mine should be. As he grew closer, he wondered about the sudden appearance of three loose horses roaming the hillside. As soon as they spotted him, they trotted up to him, hoping for some oats or feed of any kind. Baxter's level of concern rose when he noticed the cut ends of the working bridles and the balance of the harnesses still attached to their sides. He rounded them up, and continued on his way to the camp where he topped the ridge overlooking the mine.

Baxter released the horses and fell to the ground. He squinted against the glare of the white snow and canvassed the scene. On the other side of the first warehouse, a small column of smoke floated lazily into the air. He could see no other activity in the ruins of the camp. He slowly rose, gathered the horses again, and descended the long slope that leveled out near the vertical lift. Cautiously, he looped what was left of the horses' harnesses around a bracing timber and then delicately picked his way down the tracks toward the mine tunnel. Arriving behind the office ruins, he peeked toward the warehouse and saw four men cooking some eggs on a skillet. One of the men was missing an arm, but seemed undaunted by his injury. Baxter recognized him and called, "Bill? Bill, what happened here?"

Bill turned in the direction of the voice and exclaimed, "Baxter! Baxter, we thought you were dead!" He set the skillet down, but made no attempt at rising to meet him.

As Baxter moved toward them, he realized why they hadn't gotten up. "What's with this?" he cried.

Three of the men were chained together with a riveted shackle connecting their left arm and legs. The chain, in turn, was securely attached to the vertical timber of the warehouse. Bill had only one leg iron since he was minus an arm to begin with. A nicely coaled fire with an ample supply of wood lay within arm's reach of the first man. Near Bill, a hefty cache of food

271

and water was stacked in a number of crates. The men lay on a thick layer of straw that protected them from the freezing ground. Bill sheepishly pointed at the chains and shackles and then responded, "They found this stuff in the blacksmith shop. It was either shoot us or secure us until they could send some federals from Denver to arrest us." Bill shrugged his shoulders and shook his head. "At least they gave us food and water and some blankets." He sheepishly added, "Want an egg?"

Baxter's eyes bulged in disbelief. The blood veins at his temples pulsated as he groped for words. With a great effort, he regained a degree of self-control and composure, approached the fire, warmed himself, and muttered, "Okay, tell me what happened."

It took almost an hour for Bill to relay the story. Baxter listened intently to the details, but yet, in spite of his anger, had kindness enough to permit the continued cooking of the morning breakfast. After the story was finished and the bellies were satisfied, a renewed vigor to correct the wrong incurred fueled the men. Baxter went to the blacksmith shop and returned with a small anvil, chisel, and hammer. After an hour of experimentation and execution the shackle fell to the ground.

"Gather the horses," he spoke directly to one of the un-wounded men. "And you," he spoke to the other uninjured, "go to what's left of the stable and see if there is anything we can use." He turned to Bill and added, "Go to the mine and see if any of the rifles are left. Bring back all the ammo you can carry."

Baxter looked down at the man James had shot. "Walter, will you be okay here by yourself for a day or two? I'll send help as soon as I reach a telegraph office. I need Bill, Willy, and Art to ride with me to Denver."

Walter deeply sighed and replied, "I'll be all right, boss. Just move those crates and that wood a little closer so I don't have to move too much. That lady healed me up pretty good for what she had to work with. I'll do okay."

Baxter's eyebrow rose. "A lady, you say?"

"Yeah, that's right," Walter confirmed. "She was probably in her late fifties, early sixties. Said she had some medical training from the War Between the States." He pondered for a moment and continued, "Seemed quite at home around blood and bullet holes."

Baxter listened as he took care of Walter's requests. Art and Willy changed the gear on the horses and slipped new rifles, fully loaded, into the saddle holsters. They also secured fresh provisions in the saddle bags, which also included many additional rounds of ammunition.

"We've got only three horses," Baxter noted. "Art, you and Willy ride together until we find another one. We should be able to pick one up in Georgetown." They mounted up and began to leave the compound. Almost as an afterthought he turned to Bill and asked, "You okay?"

"I'm okay," he responded.

Baxter wheeled his horse around and yelled, "Then let's get going. We have a train to catch at Floyd's Hill!"

CHAPTER 56

Everett Steele drew the black tie around his neck into a tight bow and pushed it up against his white shirt collar. He leaned over his desk, reached into his top drawer, and pulled out a gold pocket watch. He popped it open and checked the time. It was six o'clock, Saturday morning. "Lots of time," he thought. The train leaving for the two-hour ride to Denver didn't depart until seven. As he snapped the watch closed, he noticed two envelopes on his desk. He picked them up together, opened the first one, and read it. It affirmed that his secretary had arranged for his private carriage to take him to the territorial legislature building from the train station. It also verified that the Jefferson militia was in place and that, as of midnight Friday, the telegraph wires and railroads were under his total control. It finished by saying that the body of President Grant had not been located, but that he was certainly dead. He turned toward the mirror on the opposite side of the room, let out a whoop, and merrily danced a jig over to its large glass face. A wide smile broke across his face as he unconsciously folded the notes up and placed them in his hip pocket. He checked himself one last time in the mirror, and congratulated himself on the successful final stages of his plan. In another few hours, his dream of an independent country would unfold before an unsuspecting world.

At that moment he heard a knock on the oak door of his office. Startled, he regained his composure, walked over to the massive entry, and opened it with all the air and confidence of a head of state. "Why, Sydney Williams," he welcomed. "Is it time to board the train already?"

"Yes, it is," Williams replied as he grasped Steele's outstretched hand. He didn't immediately release it, but instead looked him squarely in the eye and with seriousness asked, "Are you ready for this?"

"Yes, of course," Steele smiled without a thought. "I've been ready for two decades."

"Two decades," Williams wondered out loud. "You say you've been ready for two decades? I don't understand."

Steele's face grew cold and his eyes narrowed as he retreated into the past. "Yes, in fact, over two decades ago," he corrected himself as he turned and walked to his desk. "Ever since that repugnant California legislature decided not to consider our plans for dividing up the Oregon Territory and northern California into a Free State of Jefferson." Steele picked up a few sundry items from the desktop and stowed them in his pockets. "They missed a grand opportunity," he snapped.

He straightened up and stared out of the window toward the mountains for a few moments and then continued in a softer, almost reflective, tone of voice. "And then it happened again back in 1859, right over that pass in Georgetown." He motioned with his hand toward the distant mountains rising above the nearby foothills. "We followed all the protocols. But the government wouldn't recognize us as a legitimate entity." He turned, faced Williams, and growled, "Well, now they will."

Williams maintained his posture, but his eyes betrayed an inner apprehension at Steele's expression. "What do you mean by, 'we followed all the protocols'?" he inquired in an attempt to better understand the other man.

Steele's eyes grew wide with hate. "R.W. and I did all the ground work. We unified the miners and merchants as we did back in northern California back in 1848. All we wanted was a self-sustaining country that could make its own rules and govern its own people. It was ludicrous to think that an impartial central government that was months away and clear across a continent could tell us how to live our daily lives." His voice slowly rose in pitch as he spoke. "They ran us out of California! We were labeled renegades to the state because we thought that local people should control their own destiny. When we heard about the rich gold deposits in Georgetown, R.W. and I moved here with what was left of our banking interests.

"Then it happened again. There was no control, no vision for the rich and vast lands that we were developing. We tried again to form a separate, governing state out of the territory." He spun on his heels and pointed at Williams's face. "And for a year and a half we did it! But the federal government stepped in and forced us to conform to the laws set down by a group of idiots half a continent away." He walked back to the window, waved his hand at the mountains again, and sighed. "We conformed again." There was another pause. "We agreed to become a part of the Kansas Territory rather than be an independent entity. All our work was useless." He sadly shook his head and vacantly stared at the drapes. "Our work was in vain and my brother was the one who paid the price."

"Paid the price?" Williams prodded.

Steele was quiet for another full minute. Then he turned to Williams and continued in an almost patronizing voice. "That's why I sought you out, Sydney."

Williams's eyes narrowed as Steele elaborated. "I knew that the plan we devised for the financial attrition of the North and South during the War Between the States would leave vast amounts of capital unaccounted for. Sure, we set aside plenty for the rebuilding of the South, but there was also an abundance left for creating and funding a new country. When the initial plan fell through, that left all the gold available for us. I convinced you and your investors to change your goals to complement mine. And now, with the trading of the gold for depressed silver, and then trading it back for gold when the price of silver rises, we will have secured the future of not just this new country of Jefferson, but the security and prosperity of your investors for years to come."

Steele paused for a moment, straightened himself to his full height, and finished. "Now I don't have to follow the protocols. I don't have to rely on a central government to fund us. We can do as we please. I will create this country and nothing can stop me." His eyes gazed unblinking into Williams's. "And you, Sydney, are here with me to watch it happen."

Sydney Williams better understood the turmoil in Everett Steele's heart. His motivation to succeed in forming this new land of Jefferson was grounded in two failures in the past along with some hidden price tag that his brother seemingly had paid. Williams's only real concern, though, was getting a high return for his investors who had trusted him these eleven years with a risky plan . . . a plan, though, that was ready for harvest.

CHAPTER 57

Sydney Williams's train made exceptional time from Golden to Denver. It arrived at 8:30 Saturday morning with Everett Steele and his bodyguards on board. As planned, a black carriage drawn by a single horse awaited him at the stationhouse. The two men disembarked the train, walked across the graveled walkway, and acknowledged the driver.

"Josh," Steele said with an extended hand, "good of you to meet us this morning."

A skinny young man in his early twenties grasped the bear-paw hand of Mr. Steele and firmly shook it. "Yes, sir. It is a fine morning at that," he replied. "I take it, sir, you are heading to the state house downtown?"

"Yes, that's correct," Steele answered. "We have plenty of time, so drive easy and let us enjoy the beautiful, growing city of Denver."

They got into the carriage and leaned back in the cushioned seats. Williams pulled two cigars from his breast pocket and offered one to Steele. Williams reached across the space and lit it for him. He filled his mouth with smoke, savoring the flavor, before exhaling to saturate the interior with its aroma. Small wisps of smoke floated from the carriage windows as it rolled through the streets of Denver.

As the buggy rounded a corner near one of the telegraph offices, Williams noticed three men in uniform standing at attention by the front door. "I see your men are on duty," he stated.

Steele casually looked over at him and replied, "They are not my men, sir. They are part of the militia of Jefferson. Denver alone has four hundred and ten of them on duty. Each of the mining towns has a certain percentage of its populous as active-duty members."

Steele looked them over as they drove by. "They are more than just soldiers. Each respective member knows his own particular countryside. He knows where the secret places are in which to hide, where the water is, where the best roads are located, and who owns the fastest horses. They blend into the land by knowing the land. Only men familiar with their home areas could have this knowledge. I've heard it said that the hardest army to fight is the one that is fighting on its home ground. These men know their home ground, and are equipped with the best military arms that money can buy so they can defend it."

Williams merely nodded his head in affirmation as the buggy continued down the street toward the state house. As they came closer to their destination, they noticed that the number of people on the streets increased. "Ah," Steele surmised, "word has gotten out about our emergency meeting. I imagine the chambers will be overflowing with staunch supporters ready to cheer us to victory!"

The buggy rounded one more bend and pulled up in front of the state house. The two men disembarked and worked their way through the pressing crowd to the entrance of the wood building. Steele shook many hands as he entered the doorway and made his way through the portico, across the surrounding hallway, and into the debate chamber where he and Williams took their seats on the left side of the first row.

Representatives throughout the territory availed themselves for the emergency meeting in response to Steele's urgent telegram of Thursday night. He was sure they considered it a mere coincidence that the session was timed with President Grant's sudden and tragic demise on Friday. After all, Grant was the epitome of a distant controlling government bent on using the territory's resources for its own purposes. What better recompense than his being killed by the very scenery and resources that he sought to subjugate. His tragic death would certainly be an asset in demonstrating that a distant government thousands of miles away should not govern this dangerous, rugged land.

Everett Steele tapped his foot in endless succession as he waited for the session to start.

The hammering boom of the speaker's mallet pounded repeatedly on the large oak table at the front of the chamber. A loud voice pierced the noisy room. "Gentlemen, let us begin."

The drone of many voices dispersed as the meeting was called to order.

"In light of the seriousness of the situation, the committee has decided to dispense with normal protocol," the speaker began. He shuffled some papers on his lectern as he continued, "I would say at the start that we are all grieved at the tragic passing of the president." A deep silence pervaded the audience. Many lowered their heads and silently whispered prayers. "As many of you already know from the papers, he was killed when the platform cart he was touring upon lost control. Investigators have concluded that he and his companions tried to jump off the runaway cart into the river that paralleled the tracks. One body was recovered; the other three are still missing. Our prayers are extended to the president's family."

Remarkably, nothing more was said concerning the loss of the president and greatest Union general of the past war. Instead the speaker directed the meeting toward a different forum. "In light of this accident, it would appear timely that the issue of creating a sovereign state out of Colorado Territory should come before the council. The unfortunate demise of the president is merely another example of how a distant government cannot dictate safe and proper laws for our new republic."

He paused for a moment of reflection, and then banged his gavel on the lectern and shouted, "They can't tell us how to run our lives!" Most of the audience responded with clapping and loud cheers. "We want autonomy to govern ourselves!" The miners and merchants crammed into the aisle ways and across the back of the room cheered and whistled. The speaker talked for another few minutes driving his point home to a receptive crowd.

Then he pointed to Everett Steele and said, "Let me introduce the man who has led the drive for this new status of sovereignty." He motioned for Steele to ascend the podium. A rousing response from the listeners roared through the halls like the echoing report of a cannon down a deep canyon.

Steele rose from his chair, habitually straightened his tie, raked out the small wrinkles in his coat, and then stepped up onto the stage. He grasped the speaker's hand and pulled him in for a one-armed hug. The two of them turned and waved at the cheering crowd. When the speaker took his seat, Everett motioned with his hands to quiet the audience.

"Gentlemen of the state," he began. "One hundred years ago the fathers of the United States fought for freedom from a government across the sea. They recognized the ineptness of having their lives dictated by a king thousands of miles away. It was inefficient and it was overbearing. So it is with us.

"This land that we live in has the richest resources on the continent. But we have no control over where it goes and what it is used for. Eastern capitalists distribute the labor of our hands for the benefit of their investors. The wealth of the land doesn't remain here, but is moved to the East where it is used for education, the building of cities, and the development of transportation. And what kind of return do we get? A pat on the back? A smile for a job well done? All while our children go hungry from inflated prices and remain uneducated because the profits of the conglomerates are sent to investors back East instead of placed into schools and cities here. My friends, I am tired of this neglect by the United States." Once again cheers erupted from the audience as Steele smacked his hand on the lectern.

As the crowd continued its ovation, three men inconspicuously slipped into an empty space in the chamber. They worked their way through the crowd to an open spot underneath one of the huge windows on the right side of the room, folded their arms, and watched the pandemonium unfold before them.

Steele continued his oration. "My friends, this land now known as the Colorado Territory is rich in many ways. We don't only have the physical resources available to us to build cities and financial institutions, but we have the basic fiber of determination found in people of high quality who can recognize a vision, a dream, and be loyal to its fruition. Let's take the initiative to shout as one voice to bring the dream of an independent country to pass."

More shouts and clamor fanned the vitality of his speech. Steele once again quieted them. "Gentlemen, I propose that we keep our wealth. I propose that we set up our own government to dictate out of experience the harsh realities of watching over the lands that we have developed from the sweat of our brow. I propose building the necessary schools and universities to train our children. I propose investing money to develop our mining towns and communities with the finest infrastructure and communication, to expand the industries of timber and mining and exporting them to the surrounding United States at a price we dictate. My friends, we are the captains of our own ship. We alone can decide what is best for our people and our land. I propose a sovereign country of Jefferson to fill all the needs of our people!"

Cheers from the crowd rose to such a feverish pitch that Steele had to calm them again. "I see only prosperity for our people," he enjoined. "A prosperity that will last for generations to come." When the crowd quieted once more, he posed a simple question. "I have but one question for this council and for the people who struggle every day to make ends meet. Is there anyone who would disagree with my proposals?"

The gallery grew silent. Steele's question seemed to resonate up and down the aisles like a lost echo. He searched the crowd, scrutinizing each face. After some moments he slammed his fist against the podium and shouted again in a thunderous voice, "Is there anyone who would disagree?"

As his stern face scanned the audience, a scratchy voice from the right wing of the stage squawked like a rooster with a sore throat. "Yeah. I disagree!"

Everett Steele spun around on his heel to see the source of the raspy voice. As he focused on the person, his eyes grew wide, his head dropped a bit, and the blood rushed from his face. "What are you doing here?" he gasped.

The audience in the auditorium fell cryptically silent as a gray-haired man leaning on a cane moved forward. His posture was somewhat stooped, but he still towered over Everett. He straightened his back, lowered his steel-blue eyes upon Everett, and asked, "What's the matter, Evie? Forget what your older brother looks like?"

CHAPTER 58

Jack motioned to the small group of travelers to halt. Below them, the lights of Denver twinkled in the dusk as the sunlight on the eastern plains swiftly disappeared into a violet hue. "This is our last chance for a break," Jack remarked. The horses had performed magnificently on the narrow trails and deep ravines. They had maintained an incredible pace to reach their present position in such short order. Jack dismounted and gave his horse an opportunity to drink from a lazy brook to the side of the trail. Henri and Grant did likewise.

"You're quite the rider," Grant complimented Henri.

"Thank you, sir," he replied. "It's been a long time since I've ridden like that. It brings back memories of my youth." Henri pursed his lips and gazed at the ground for a moment before continuing. "It's rather unusual, sir."

"What's that?" Grant asked.

Henri's gaze met Grant's as he said, "When I came to Denver, I thought I was at the final twilight of my life. This entire experience has breathed new life into my old bones and has given me endurance that I thought I'd lost forever." He sighed and smiled. "I guess all I needed was to have purpose again."

Grant smiled and patted Henri on the back. "I believe that's all anyone needs," he responded. "To be needed."

After some moments, Jack looked at the president's face and broke the silence. "You appear used to rough riding, too, sir."

Henri interjected on Grant's behalf, "I believe you'll find Lyss an accomplished rider, Jack."

Grant smiled and added, "Yes, I'm afraid I am. I started riding when I was four. Have enjoyed it ever since." He walked over to a large tree near the brook, sat down, and leaned against it. "My body just isn't used to it," he laughed as he stretched his legs and arms. "But it helps keep me young!"

Henri came over and sat on the ground beside the president as Jack took the horses' reins and led them to a patch of rich grass. Then he sat down next to Henri and enjoyed the cool breeze that blew over the knob.

After a few relaxing moments, the president asked, "Tell me, Jack. What do you know about Everett Steele?"

"Well," he began, "I suppose you already know about his accomplishments in politics and banking. And you're certainly aware of his influence and control of the wires and rails." He thought for a moment, then continued, "He's into mining and lumber."

"Yes, yes," Grant interrupted. "I know about all that stuff. Tell me about the man. What you've observed, learned, and discovered. Anything particular or unusual that I might be able to use."

Jack lowered his head to his breast as he pondered. After some moments, he said, "He's determined."

"Determined about what?" Grant responded.

"He's determined to make this territory a sovereign land," Jack said.

"Why?" Grant asked.

"Well," Jack said, "I suppose it goes all the way back to the late 1840s. He and his brother were successful in northern California in the mining and banking arenas. They felt, though, that the isolated mining areas were left out of the governmental legislation process." Jack kicked his feet out and lay back. "I made a trip up to the northern part of the state and did some inquiring while I was chasing some leads on another issue."

"What are you talking about?" Henri interrupted.

Jack looked at Henri and smiled. "Henri, there's a lot you don't know! Rather than wander off on a tangent about what I've been doing the last eleven years, let's stick to the president's question!"

Henri grinned. "Please, don't mind me. Continue!"

"Anyway," Jack went on, "back around 1849 or so, just before California became a state, there was this movement to make a new independent state out of a chunk of northern California and the then-southern Oregon Territory. The settlers and miners, led by Everett and Robert Steele, took legislation to the California leaders. They were ignored and all but expelled from Sacramento." He thought for a moment. "You could say they were run out of town. A few months later California became a state. Their movement remained active until the early fifties when Oregon also became a state. It created hard feelings for the two brothers, but they returned to Sacramento and operated their merchant and banking interests anyway. Business slowly declined because of their dubious reputation, and when the gold strike in Georgetown happened, they closed their holdings and moved out here."

Grant shifted his body around to get more comfortable, but still listened intently. That was one admirable quality about the president; he gave his full attention when one was giving information that he could use.

Jack also shifted his position. "The two brothers ended up repeating themselves. They were successful in mining and retailing, and then opened a bank. Robert got involved in politics again and started a campaign to create a separate territory apart from Kansas. I'm sure he wanted more than that, but after the California ordeal, he felt it best to stay within the parameters of the law. Everett, on the other hand, wanted to withdraw from United States influence altogether. There was a bit of strife between the two, but Robert prevailed as the older brother. They were able to gather enough support in the broad locale to create and keep an independent Territory of Jefferson alive for almost eighteen months. Eventually the federal government caught up with the situation and laid down its will to align their administration to its territorial laws. Robert and Everett fought furiously between themselves whether or not to conform to the government's will. Robert finally made the decision to disband his miniature government and peacefully become a part of the extended Territory of Kansas."

"So, what happened after that?" Grant inquired.

"Well," Jack thought, "shortly after the new territorial government was in place, Robert had a mental breakdown. Everett placed him in an institution in Denver, and he went on with his life as a banker, merchant, and politician in Golden. As time went on, he became influential in about everything that went on in the territory. He felt that his brother would not approve of his business tactics, so he worked hard at keeping him confined to the asylum."

"I see," said Grant as he pondered the story. He got up and walked to the Denver overlook. The sparkling lights below glittered like yellow diamonds in the deep hue of early nightfall. After some time, he whimsically asked, "What was the name?"

Jack looked at Henri with wondering eyes, then asked Grant, "Name of what?"

Grant replied, "The name of the sovereign state they wanted to make in California?"

"Well, there were two suggestions," Jack answered. "The first was Klamath."

"And the second?" Grant asked.

"The second was Jefferson," Jack replied.

"Ah," Grant nodded. "Jefferson." He stroked his beard and said, "And what of Robert?"

Jack searched his memory. "As far as I know, he is still in Denver."

"Hmm," Grant mused. "Would it seem to you two that Robert, as the elder brother, had more authority when it came down to the brass tacks of an important decision?"

Jack and Henri didn't offer a reply, but paid closer attention to what Grant was saying.

Grant contemplated some more, then asked, "I wonder how much Robert is incapacitated. If Everett always acquiesced to his brother's wishes, and Robert was the one with a moral compass, then what would happen if he showed up to challenge Everett?"

Jack and Henri were silent. Henri finally gave a short, terse reply. "Perhaps we should pay Robert a visit."

Grant turned around and looked Henri in the eye. "That sounds like a good idea."

CHAPTER 59

Night had fully fallen when the three men entered Denver. "Do you remember where the colonel lives?" Jack asked the president.

"Yes, I do," he replied.

The general had a particular knack for remembering small details about people and places. It was an interesting attribute that was a considerable aid in the war that found him a special place in many a Union soldier's heart. To be spoken to by name in the midst of a long tiring march, or in the heat of a raging battle, commanded a soldier's respect and admiration. "It's the next street to the left," he continued. "Then it's the fourth house on the right."

After a few minutes, they stopped their horses in front of a large, three-story Victorian mansion. Grant asked Henri and Jack to stay on their horses while he dismounted and walked to the front door of the house. He knocked four times, then stepped back to wait. A light in one of the upper windows lit, then disappeared, probably in the hallway outside the bedroom. A few moments later, the tall door opened and revealed a man in a nightshirt holding an oil lamp. He looked on the face of Grant for a moment, and then fully realized who it was.

"Lyss!" he exclaimed. "They said you were dead! What are you doing here?"

Grant smiled and replied, "Ah, Colonel Douglas, reports of my demise are greatly exaggerated. But, please, my benefactors and I must have immediate quarters. Can you assist?"

"Most certainly, sir." Douglas peered beyond Grant at the three horses and two men at the end of the walkway. "Have your associates put the horses in the stable behind the house. We'll meet them at the back door." He put his arm behind the president's shoulder and directed him inside, then motioned to the riders to proceed around the house. Then he closed the door, turned, and faced Grant. He extended his hand in warm hospitality and said, "Lyss, it's so good to see you!"

Grant returned the greeting and replied, "I'm really glad to see you, too, Willy."

Colonel Willis O. Douglas saw the weariness and strain in the president's eyes. "Please, sir, come sit down in the library." He ushered Grant into the nearby room and offered him a chair by the fireplace and a glass of brandy before going to the rear entrance to the house to retrieve Henri and Jack. Willis served them likewise and saw to their comfort. "Gentlemen, what else can I do for you?"

Grant answered, "Please, sit and listen. We have very little time, and secrecy is necessary."

"Yes, sir." He pulled up an additional chair, sat down, and waited for his instructions.

Grant finished his glass of brandy and asked, "Do you know where Robert Steele is?"

Douglas cocked his head a little to the side and replied, "Why, yes, sir. R.W. is at the Denver Institution for the Sick."

Grant raised his eyebrows and quizzed, "R.W.?"

"Yes, sir. Robert William. He has been a patient at the Institution since late 1861. He's not a high-risk patient, mind you. The physicians consider him a little confused. His brother, E.S., keeps him there for his own safety."

"Excuse me, Colonel," Henri asked. "How do you know this information?"

"It's common knowledge, of sorts, sir," he replied. "But, in addition to that, my wife's sister has worked at the institution for over ten years. She has mentioned him to Emma on more than one or two occasions. With all the talk about E.S. Steele's plan for a sovereign state, it's been R.W. that has pumped Emma's sister for information."

"I see," Grant said. His eyes seemed to glaze over as he retreated to deep thought for some minutes. This was the general's habit. He would listen to the information and facts, retreat into thought to seek his own counsel, decide, and then act. He looked up at the colonel and ordered, "I want to see R.W. now."

The colonel started to suggest waiting until morning, but then some distant military memory cleared his mind. He stood up, snapped his hand in salute, and replied, "At once, sir."

Grant stood, embarrassed by his tone. He reached for Willis's hand, cradled it in his own, and replied, "I'm sorry, Willy. For a moment I was back in the war. I appreciate your loyalty, but the war is over. Now we are friends, not soldiers. May we see R.W. tonight?"

Willis shared a smile and acknowledged Grant's request. "Why don't you and your friends rest. I'll make the necessary arrangements." With that, he left the three companions alone to enjoy another glass of brandy and the comforts of the colonel's library.

It was a full three hours before Willis returned. In the interim, the three men had nodded off and were slumbering comfortably in their respective chairs. Willis walked up behind the president and shook his shoulder. "Excuse me, sir. All the arrangements have been made. If you'll come with me, I'll accompany you and your associates to the institution."

Another innate ability of the general was the unusual trait of survival on catnaps. During the war, his soldiers would comment that Grant could sleep anywhere at any time. Some of his soldiers had noticed him asleep on a horse while marching southwards after the Wilderness Campaign. The "sleeping" general had immediately responded to a snide comment by a passerby. It was decided that he could sleep and be awake at the same time.

Grant at once opened his eyes and rose from the chair. Jack and Henri were a little bit slower, but did manage to rise and follow the colonel out the back door to a waiting carriage. The night air was typically cold for early spring. The sky was cloudless and moonless, but the brilliant stars offered enough of a faint hue to the night to light the way adequately. Lyss and Willis rode in the front seat while Jack and Henri sat in back. After twenty minutes of travel, they stopped in front of a large limestone building. They got out of the carriage and walked up to the front door. The director of the facility was waiting for them with an oil lamp.

The colonel made the necessary introductions. "Mr. President, this is Director Edwin Berry. Mr. Berry, the president."

Mr. Berry had already been informed of the president's request to visit R.W. so he expressed no excitement or emotion at the meeting. He simply stated, "If you will come this way, sir, I'll take you to him."

They entered the main lobby of the institution and proceeded down a hallway to the right. After fifty feet or so, they ascended a stairway to the third floor and continued down another hallway. At the end, Mr. Berry unlocked a metal door, opened it, and entered, closely followed by the president's entourage. It was a large room, the largest in the facility. In one corner was a brightly lit oil lamp on top of a desk. A white-haired man sat next to it on a chair with his legs crossed. "Good evening," he said. "How may I be of service?"

The president stepped in and examined the eyes of the man sitting before him. It has been said that the eyes are the window to the soul. Better yet is the rare man who can interpret what he sees as he looks through those windows. In Robert's steely-blue iris, the president saw clarity, intelligence, and a desire for integrity. Grant walked forward, sat on the corner of the desk, and replied, "Sir, you may be of service by accompanying me to a meeting this morning."

Robert stared into the president's eyes, and then replied with a giggle, "My brother has caused trouble, hasn't he?"

"Yes," Grant answered. "And I need your help to defuse it."

Robert continued his eye contact, then said, "Can I get my coat first?"

CHAPTER 60

As Ambrose McHenry flicked the whip on the horse's rump for the third time, Evangeline snapped a terse response, "I'm sure the poor beasts are running as fast as they can!"

Ambrose paid little heed to her comment, and gruffly barked in reply, "Just keepin' their minds on the business at hand."

Sarah and Johann grasped the handholds on the back of the carriage as it careened around another turn on the old dirt toll road to Longmont. Their seats were a small bay designed for extra luggage at the rear of the president's personal two-seat buggy, a conveyance that was always on standby to provide an emergency response to any crisis. It was glossy black with plush, leather seats that comfortably cushioned riders from the rough roads of the age. Extra strong wheels with a new, experimental covering, called rubber, quieted much of the noise of the typical steel-clad wooden wheels. As Ambrose predicted, the two black horses, bred and trained specifically for the long, fast runs required in times of emergencies, scarcely noticed the flip of the whip and maintained their incredible pace as they skidded onto a straight-a-way and picked up more speed.

Johann craned his neck over the rail between the baggage section and the travelers' compartment, and shouted to Ambrose, "How much longer?"

"I'm not sure," Ambrose replied. "When the president and I took this road to Central City, we weren't in a hurry." Boards from a rickety bridge clattered beneath the wheels as they crossed over Eldorado Creek. "He was more interested in the scenery than in an itinerary."

Evangeline removed a watch from her pocket and checked the time. "The sun will be down in another twenty minutes," she said. The buggy approached a fork in the road, but Ambrose neither slowed down nor stopped to check for landmarks. "I remember this road, though," she added. "It goes toward Boulder and then on to Longmont. I'm guessing we should be there around three tomorrow morning." She gave a nod toward Ambrose, and then joked, "Unless, of course, the madman at the reins doesn't slow down in the dark. Then we'll be there in an hour!"

Ambrose merely grunted in response, but Johann noticed him take a quick glance at Evangeline, as though he were a track owner taking a second look at a promising racehorse.

At the next creek crossing, Ambrose stopped the buggy at the water's edge to let the horses drink and rest. Evangeline turned around to check on the two extra pieces of baggage clinging to the buggy. "Are you two doing all right?" she asked.

"I suppose," Sarah replied. "Can we get down and stretch our legs?"

Ambrose boomed a simple reply. "No. We've no time. We have to reach Longmont before the train does. It won't wait." While the horses finished drinking, Ambrose removed a piece of fabric covering two brass lanterns which were secured to the iron framework of the canopy. He opened their glass panels, then reached above them and turned a small valve. In a moment, a faint hissing sound could be heard near a small orifice in the center of the lamp. He lit a match and held it up to the sound. Instantly, a yellow flame about two inches long popped on. He did the same with the other lamp. Another knob on the side of each lantern adjusted a concave, silvery reflector into focus. He closed the panels, sat back in the seat, and grabbed the reins. "Hang on!" he shouted as the buggy lurched forward again onto the dirt road. The lanterns emitted a bright light onto the road ahead. Ambrose muttered, "One hour," under his breath as the carriage kicked up a sizeable cloud of dust. He turned and ribbed Evangeline, "Why, I could do the Longmont run in an hour with only a candle to light my way!"

Around eleven at night, Ambrose stopped the buggy at the top of the last pass into Boulder. It wasn't one of the high, snow-covered mountain passes like Guanella or Monarch, but it was a good place to take a short break. The lights from the brass lanterns pierced the inky blackness like a candle looking down a deep well. Evangeline stepped from the carriage along with Sarah and Johann. Ambrose also got out after grabbing some cloths from a compartment under the carriage seat. He moved forward to the horses, and rubbed them down.

Johann noticed how weary Ambrose was looking, so he offered to help. "You know anything about horses?" Ambrose yawned.

"Yes, a bit," Johann replied. He asked for, and received, one of the rubbing cloths.

It was no wonder that Ambrose was showing signs of fatigue. He had been up since before dawn that Friday morning. After tending to the president's needs, he had gone to the rail yard in Central City to manage the next stage of his commander in chief's excursion. His duty was to stay in Central City and monitor the telegraph wires until the president reached his destination safely. Then he would catch up by buggy.

When news of the president's disappearance reached Central City, Ambrose used his authority to secure all wire transmissions within the immediate area to keep communications with the search parties as a top priority. When a message from Everett Steele came across the wire ordering deference to his messages only, Ambrose merely ignored it and passed on the appearance of compliance, while still maintaining control over all communications in his area.

His meeting with Evangeline on the front porch of the hardware store in Central City on Friday afternoon set a variety of sensitive events into motion. The first thing he did was return to the telegraph station. He dismissed the attending guards, sending them out for an afternoon snack, and then asked Monty to send a special message to Colonel Christopher C. Auger, 12th U.S. Infantry at Fort D.A. Russell near Cheyenne, the Territory of Wyoming.

Monty thought it strange that the body of the message was in code form, but he sent it without change or delay. Ambrose also sent a coded message to a remote army outpost in Kansas. He then returned to the Teller House, and requested his assistant to attend the wires while he feigned a trip to the platform car wreck scene to inspect the site himself. He ordered the president's personal carriage to be brought to the front of the hotel, whereupon he took leave to return to the hardware store and pick up his fellow passengers.

A twenty-minute break was all Ambrose allowed. He requested that everyone climb aboard the buggy and they were off. The road straightened out considerably once they descended the mountain. Ambrose smiled at Evangeline as they passed the Mercantile Exchange building near the center of Longmont. The clock showed two o'clock. "Hmm, beat your estimate by an hour," he grinned. "Good thing, too. Looks like the train is also ahead of schedule." He pointed to the rail yard at a large 4-4-0 filling up its boiler by the wooden water tower. Ambrose pulled the carriage up to the first passenger car and called out, "Chris! Chris, are you up there?"

A stuffy, uniformed man poked his head from the first doorway to the car. "Would you be referring to me, sir?"

"Why, of course!" Ambrose bellowed. "You old goat, c'mere

and shake my hand."

The man cleared his throat, straightened up, and descended the steps to the rail car with all the dignity of the King of England. He purposefully stepped up to the carriage and said, "Mr. Ambrose McHenry, I presume. Good of you to come, sir." He held out his hand like a stiff board, whereupon Ambrose grabbed it with vigor and shook it like a terrier playing with a rat.

"Ah, good to see you, too, Chris. It's been a long time." He turned to his companions and added, "This is Colonel Christopher Auger, Commander of Fort Russell. He was good enough to bring some of his men to accompany us to Denver."

"Quite right," the colonel responded as he extended a stiff but warm hand to each of the travelers. "But, please, we must board. The element of surprise must not be compromised. You may leave your buggy in the hands of this man." A small private stepped out of the colonel's shadow and smartly bowed his head in greeting. "He and his companions shall tend to your animals and also ensure that the telegraph lines stay out of service 'til noon tomorrow as you ordered. Now, please, let us board."

"Most certainly," Ambrose replied. He directed his companions toward the waiting train. He eyed the soldiers as he approached the boarding platform, and commented to the colonel, "I like the uniforms. Were those recently acquired?"

"Yes," the colonel responded. "You might say they were recently acquired from a wealthy benefactor of the territory." He uncharacteristically winked at Ambrose. "And I don't think the benefactor knows it yet."

The colonel and private assisted the others on board. Two additional men led the exhausted animals to a nearby stable. The tired travelers were shown seats. The private exited the coach and signaled for a uniformed engineer to get underway.

The characteristic jerk of the train cars signaled that an important part of Grant's plan to secure Denver had begun.

CHAPTER 61

Saturday dawn was breaking across the foothills east of Denver. President Grant was still in council with his men in the library at Colonel Douglas's house. "I still don't like the idea," he grumbled to R.W.

R.W. stared into Grant's eyes as his thoughts reorganized. "Listen, Mr. President," he began. "I've been a direct influence on my younger brother all of his life. I think I can persuade him, and therefore the legislature, to change their minds."

"But you said yourself that Everett kept you at the institution all this time against your will," Grant replied. "I don't see you having much influence on your brother after all these years." He shifted irritably in his seat, let out a frustrated sigh, and stood. He grumbled aloud as he paced the floor of the library. "You don't even know what your brother is capable of anymore. He's changed a lot since you've been in the institution. He's grown powerful, articulate, and dangerous."

R.W. cordially stood up and faced the president. "That may be so, sir. But I still have a very long timeline with Everett that can be used to our advantage. He will either cave in to my ideology, or he will expose his true self. Either way he'll lose his constituents in the legislature and the Jefferson sovereignty issue will be over. I see it as a winning situation."

Grant stopped pacing the floor. He observed the crackling light in the fireplace for some moments as he debated the options in his mind. Almost as an afterthought he asked without looking up, "Colonel Douglas, what is the status on Colonel Auger?"

Douglas immediately replied, "A courier dropped this note off thirty minutes ago with regard to that, sir. Your discussion with R.W. was so intense that I didn't wish to interrupt you with it." He held out his hand and offered a sealed envelope to Grant. He took it, opened it, and read its contents. One could see the slightest smile form under the gray whiskers of the aging president.

"I believe we have an ace-in-the-hole that will complement the risk of approaching your brother, R.W." He pivoted on his heel and pointed to Jack. "You will accompany Mr. Steele to the legislature chamber this morning at ten for the meeting. Make sure that R.W. arrives at the back door of the building, and accompany him inside. Keep him safely hidden until he feels the appropriate opportunity arises for him to make his address. After R.W. is on stage, you can locate a safe place to observe, or simply exit the chamber. I have others in place who will secure the building in case R.W. fails." He turned his head and fixed his eyes on R.W. "Sir, what you are offering, in my estimation, is dangerous. I can appreciate a peaceful solution to this situation and am in debt to your efforts. My men will support and protect you the best we can, but we have our limits. Good luck to you, sir."

With that, President Grant held out his hand to Robert, who took it and returned a warm handshake.

"Now," Grant said, "I believe Colonel Douglas has some fresh clothing for you. You should return upstairs, change, and gather your thoughts. You only have a few hours before the meeting."

R.W. smiled and replied, "I've been rehearsing for years, Mr. President. But I could use a bath and a shave before leaving. Perhaps that would be a better use of my time." He turned and

301

glanced at Jack. "I'll be ready to leave at your request, sir. All I ask is a ten-minute notice." With that, R.W. bowed and exited upstairs.

After R.W. had gone, Grant opened and reread the message from Colonel Auger. Henri appeared at his side and asked, "How many men can he spare?"

"Fifty," was all Grant responded.

"That doesn't sound like a lot," Henri said.

"It should be enough." Grant smiled and winked at Henri. "It's not always the number of men that wins a battle," he gently chided. "It's being where one is least expected at the most opportune time." He sat down at Colonel Douglas's desk, took a pencil from his shirt pocket, and composed a reply on the backside of the message. He refolded it, placed it in the envelope, and handed it to the colonel. "I presume the courier is still waiting in the front room? Give this to him and send him on his way."

Colonel Douglas obeyed without a moment's hesitation.

Grant stroked his beard as he returned again to scan the fire. Henri approached him, almost afraid to interrupt his meditation.

The president caught a glimpse of Henri's face and noticed the deep-set worry lines. "It's okay, Henri. Emily's a resourceful woman. We might not know where she is, but I'm confident she's fine."

Henri admired the instinctiveness of Grant. "How did you know?"

"I've witnessed the faces of many soldiers entering battle. They all wore the same worry lines that you have as they wondered about the wellbeing of their families. Words of comfort always escaped me."

Grant pushed away from the desk and walked around to Henri. He put his hands on his shoulders and gave them a gentle squeeze. "She'll be fine, Henri. We'll find her."

Henri faintly smiled. "You're right, Lyss. We'll find her."

He took a few steps to the side, turned to face Grant, and added, "Okay, then. What's the plan?"

Grant's smiling eyes looked into Henri's. "You and I, sir, are going to address the territorial legislature of Colorado." He pulled out a pocket watch, opened the clasp, and looked at the time. Then, like the punctual general that he was, added, "In five and one half hours."

CHAPTER 62

Everett Steele backed up a couple of paces at the sound of his brother's voice. He blinked his eyes a number of times while Robert advanced toward him. "What have you gotten yourself into this time, Evie?"

Everett Steele regained a portion of his composure, straightened himself, cleared his throat, and replied, "I have grasped what you only dreamt of, Robert . . . a free and independent land of Jefferson."

The older man threw his head back, gave a loud laugh, and then boomed a brusque, bitter reply. "You have no idea what the concept of freedom is until you've had it taken from you!" He scanned the crowd, pointed his bony finger at them, and roared, "You people have no idea what freedoms you have capitulated in order to follow this man and his ideology."

Everett saw the lightning blow that his brother had swung at the hearts of his constituents, and rushed forward to defend his honor. "No, don't listen to this man! His thinking is flawed by years of mental confinement. We have laid plans to rise above the government that takes from us, but doesn't give back. We have struggled to retain our autonomy, our heritage, the labor of our hands and hearts. We've not sacrificed our freedoms; we've sacrificed an oppressive federal rule. Our path leads us to independence and the freedom we deserve."

Robert smacked his hand against the lectern and thundered in response, "Freedom is not deserved; freedom is earned, and with a great price! The people of this land paid for it with sweat, with tears, and with blood. Two hundred years ago, the colonists of the eastern seaboard carved settlements out of a raw land. They shed tears for loved ones lost or killed in that primitive time so they could enjoy religious freedom. One hundred years ago, the founding fathers of this country paid in blood for their freedom from an overbearing and distant ruler. Ten years ago, our country itself paid another toll, not only in blood, but also in economic ruin and in the rape of the land in order to maintain and preserve this unique and priceless experiment in liberty.

"I'd wager that many of you paid a price to come to this country. You left family, friends, a haven or city where you were known. All the things that you counted on for security and peace, you left behind to come here. Why? Because you wanted something better for your loved ones than what you had. You wanted the freedom to express and be who you are. To till and harvest the land the way you wanted instead of the way you were told. To choose to dig for riches in the hard rock of the mountains and the gold-bearing gravel bars of its rivers. To create wealth by becoming merchants and industrialists. To provide jobs for your fellow man and to have the things denied you in your native land. You paid a high price for those freedoms. But the price was worth it because this was the land of opportunity; the only nation on the face of the earth where a man could freely exercise that freedom and reap the rewards from the labors of his hands."

He turned his face to Everett and continued in a dark, scolding voice. "And this man standing here would take it all away from you. He would take the very richness of opportunity that brought you to this great land and focus it into a small, self-serving country only interested in itself. Sure, the concept of preserving the fruits of your labor all for yourself sounds well-deserved, but it only boils down to a self-centered life of wretchedness and greed, isolated in the midst of the very country that drew you here because of its opportunity."

R.W. walked around the lectern and drew close to the men seated before him on the legislature floor. "My friends, the magnificence of man is to work with his hands and to share the bounty that God blesses him with. That concept is not just for wealth of money, but also for wealth of opportunity. This present territory is a part of something important, something bigger than gold or silver or timber. This territory is part of an exclusive test for all mankind to see if men from different backgrounds, different faiths, different languages, can dwell together as one and to use the opportunities founded in freedom to be united in peace."

R.W. strolled across the front of the chamber. "Peace," he repeated. "That is a unique word. Peace is the commodity most sought after by governments, and it remains throughout history as the most elusive. After four years of civil war, the people of our land have discovered that peace is as costly as freedom. But the two go hand in hand because one cultivates the other. Now, ask yourselves—delegates, representatives, merchants, and laborers—does withdrawal from the United States of America cultivate peace with your neighbors, or does it cultivate strife? And if it doesn't cultivate peace, are you willing to risk another civil war that will inevitably follow?"

R.W. paused as he climbed the steps of the platform and returned to the lectern.

His younger brother was poised to his left, speechless as the hard work of the previous years dissolved before his eyes. Everett glared back and forth across the auditorium as he rapidly deliberated on how to respond. He could see the reaction of the crowd as Robert's words took hold of moral values instead of pocketbooks. Everett never could compete with his brother's eloquence, and he was keenly aware that Robert was just warming up.

In years past it was always the silver tongue of R.W. that greased the wheels of public unity. Everett was a good understudy, but always just that, an understudy. Everett's next move derived inevitably from a hard, fundamental character flaw—poured, set, and unchanging as concrete. He scanned the audience and found the face of his most trusted associate underneath a large window of the west wing. Their eyes made contact, and the quick, easy solution was communicated.

R.W.'s moment of silence came to a close. But as he took a deep breath to encourage and direct his listeners, a shot echoed from the western wing of the chamber. An instant splattering of blood appeared on Robert's shirt. Incredulously, he looked at his breast at the spurting crimson, then at Everett, who stood riveted by what he had silently ordered. The men locked eyes, then R.W. crumpled to the floor.

The report of gunfire brought the legislative assembly to their feet. In an instant, shock from the murder changed into chaos as some men raced for the door to escape, while others sprinted to the stage to lend help to their fallen icon. Those nearby the assailant fought to relieve him of his firearm, and wrestled him to the floor. Many of the representatives stood upon their seats and shouted to nearby companions, adding to the mayhem. In response to the gunfire and confusion, a small group of Jefferson militia soldiers that were closest to the scene burst into the chamber of the Denver territorial legislature building from the front portico. The ranking officer scanned the auditorium, evaluated the situation, and dispatched his forces to strategic stations around the chamber.

The first man to reach Robert's side removed his coat and placed it under R.W.'s head. A second later, another man knelt next to him and tore open his blood-drenched shirt to examine the wound. The man reached into his pocket and pulled out a white handkerchief, balled it up, and forced it into the bullet hole. He urgently asked if a doctor had been summoned. Another voice from the chamber floor responded in the affirmative.

Amidst the chaos, Everett Steele walked over to view his fallen brother. R.W.'s eyes rolled aimlessly in his head as he strove to remain conscious. But soon, they became fixed in a glassy stare as shock and the loss of blood took its toll. Everett mildly scrunched his lips and, almost imperceptibly, shook his head. Then he collected his thoughts, turned to the lectern, and faced the raging turmoil.

"Gentlemen," he shouted above the wild assembly. He took the gavel in his hand and pounded repeatedly on the oak lectern. "Gentlemen!" he roared. "Please, calm yourselves and return to your seats. The situation is under control."

The Jefferson militia officer in charge approached Everett and spoke quietly in his ear. Steele nodded his head and spoke some words in return. The officer acknowledged his instructions with a salute and went to distribute his orders to his men. Everett turned his attention again to the crowd. "Gentlemen, the militia has secured the building. Please return to your seats and regain order."

A burly man with wild hair and a bushy beard hastily entered the chamber leading a doctor and a militiaman. Robert was immediately placed on a stretcher, and carried out the back to a waiting military carriage. In the west wing, three militia members escorted the assailant outside the building and to the sheriff's office. A shaken Sydney Williams followed.

In the space of thirty minutes, Everett Steele was again addressing the representatives. As he did so, he pulled his own handkerchief from his pocket and dabbed his eyes. "My friends," he feigned, "this incident causes me much grief. Yes, my brother and I disagreed on how this region should be governed, but to murder someone as a last resort, as did the assailant from over there," he unsteadily pointed toward the west wing, "is dastardly and unforgivable." He again wiped his brow and eyes before continuing. "I know beyond the shadow of a doubt that if R.W. were still here, the debate would have continued in the spirit of goodwill and friendship."

Steele shifted his weight from one foot to the other as he struggled to continue. "But, alas, the debate has ended. Our time has run out. As hard as it is to continue under such circumstances, my commitment to Jefferson and to its people overrules my emotions and grief for this moment." As he leaned over the lectern his eyes narrowed and his voice grew loud. "We, as representatives of our families, our friends, and our constituents, must make a decision. The situation has not changed. A president has been lost. Our dear friend and spokesman was ruthlessly murdered before our eyes. Our land is being threatened by the consistent and endless siphoning of its riches and resources to a government in which we have no voice. Now is our time!" Everett Steele thundered. "Now is our moment." He paused for effect, and then asked, "Who is with me?"

Restrained voices replaced the earlier cheers and applause. Men didn't look at Everett Steele as they had earlier in the morning, but, instead, softly conferred among themselves regarding the message and events pertaining to R.W.'s oration and murder. A silent wave of awareness spread throughout the auditorium like spilt milk spreading outwards across a table. Everett Steele felt the opposition. He looked to the rear of the chamber, made eye contact with the militia officer in charge, and nodded his head.

CHAPTER 63

James's hand throbbed. He grimaced and wondered how Mike and Derek were holding up. The night ride toward Denver was cold and dark and traveling was much slower than anticipated since the only light was from the moon when it peeked out from behind the rapidly passing clouds. There was enough light to discern the trail, but not enough to see the debris littered on the path or the low and high spots that caused the horses to trip frequently. At around three in the morning, James stopped at a fork in the trail and waited for his companions to come alongside him. On the right, the roadway continued onward to Denver. To the left it descended into the valley where Golden lay.

"At the rate we are traveling," he stated, "I don't think we'll make it to Denver in time for the assembly at the legislature building."

"I think you are right, James," Frank noted. "Perhaps we should split into two parties."

"What do you suggest?" Mike quizzed.

"Seems to me," Frank said, "that the note mentioned the need to have the gold refinement finished by noon on Saturday. Maybe Mike, Derek, and you," as he looked at James, "should rest for a couple of hours; then, when the sun rises, continue to Golden and locate the smelter where Baxter was supposed to take the gold."

"What do we do when we find the smelter?" Mike inquired.

310

"The note mentioned a trade after the gold was smelted," James interrupted. "Sounds like there might be a large quantity of money, or gold, or both at that smelter sometime before noon. If we can locate it, maybe we can intercept the trade and sever Steele's financial pipeline."

"I'm sure a man like Steele doesn't have all his eggs in one basket," Derek said. "After all, he's heavily invested in railroading, mining, and timber, not to mention banking and retail businesses. One gold shipment couldn't have that big of an effect on him."

"That's true," James said. "But the contact in Golden may end up being a major player in the transfer of the gold bullion into useable cash for operating those investments, and for any immediate financing of operations pertaining to his plan of secession. If we can discover the money trail that Steele used, then we can either disrupt it or complicate it beyond repair."

Mike shifted in his saddle. "I think it's a good idea. I'm not sure I can make the ride all the way to Denver right now. My leg is hurting again." He glanced at Derek and added, "And Derek is beginning to look a little wore out, too."

Derek nodded his head. "I'm afraid he's right. I need a little sleep."

"All right," Frank decided, "here's what we'll do." He looked at James. "You three head into Golden at first light. See if you can locate the smelter that was supposed to receive the gold from the Plume. Use your imagination and find out what you can about the process Steele uses to clean up and transfer his money. Try to find out what he needs money for right now. Emily and I will continue on toward Denver and attend the meeting at the legislature building at ten. The two of us should be able to make good time once the sun comes up. At the assembly, we'll gather information to have a better understanding of the situation. Afterwards, we'll ride back and meet you at the main hotel in Golden and re-evaluate our options. It's a sure bet we can't stop what plans Steele has in motion. But maybe we can throw a wrench in the cog and grind it to a halt."

Everyone seemed to be in agreement and proceeded on their set courses.

The trail to Denver from the Golden cutoff was still treacherous. Emily and Frank were forced to pick their way, often leading their horses instead of risking a fall over unseen objects. They were grateful when the shades of black gave way to the lighter grays of dawn. "We've still got a ways to go," Frank observed as they mounted their horses after first light.

They continued their steady pace across the upper mountains and then descended the narrow trail into the foothills. The sun was high in the sky as they trotted into the outskirts of Denver.

"What time do you have?" Emily asked Frank.

"I don't know; I left my watch on Sydney Williams's train back in Golden," he replied.

As they rounded a corner, they caught sight of the large clock tower of the Presbyterian Church near the center of town. Its granite spire rose above the many buildings of the business district. "Looks like it's almost ten thirty," Frank said as he squinted at the great hands on the clock face.

They slowed their pace to accommodate the horses and men moving along the busy streets. As they blended into traffic, Frank noticed out of the corner of his eye some men sitting on a bench in front of the sheriff's office. He leaned over and whispered to Emily, "That man on the bench over there looks familiar."

Emily casually looked in the direction Frank had indicated. A group of men dressed in militia uniforms reclined on the decking and steps of the office. A thin man on the bench was leaning forward discussing something with a man who appeared to be the sheriff. A loosely rolled cigarette hung lazily from his

mouth and his bony fingers curled around the edges of a bunch
of papers. Emily quietly asked Frank, "What is familiar about
him?"

Frank slowly replied, "His name is Baxter. He was the one
who started this mess back in 1864."

At that moment a man with only one arm walked out of the
office door. He noticed the two riders and then exclaimed with
a loud voice, "Baxter, those two were at the mine!"

Baxter looked up and turned his head to see the riders. His
black eyes focused on Frank and Emily like the dark barrels of
two Civil War cannons. "Get them."

The militiamen on the steps jumped to their feet and ran
toward the two horses, while the men on the decking drew their
revolvers and took aim. Frank kicked his horse and rode into
the flank of Emily's horse, thus offering both protection and a
prod for her horse to run.

But the bullets from the revolvers were faster than the horses.
Lead projectiles impacted Frank's left shoulder and arm, forc-
ibly throwing him forward into Emily's side. He reached for her
saddle horn, but couldn't retain a grip. As he slid down the
horse he grasped at the saddle tie downs, but realized his left
arm wouldn't respond. As he fell to the ground he yelled to
Emily, "Go! Go as fast as you can!"

She did.

Frank was left behind. The bullets and fall from the horse
dropped him unconscious to the ground. Three militiamen immediately reached for him, pulled him to his feet, and dragged
him over to Baxter. He rose from his bench seat, walked over to
Frank, and pulled his head up by the hair so he could get a better look at his face. Baxter's eyes narrowed as he faintly
recognized the facial features. "I remember you," he whispered
to himself. "I remember you from a certain bridge in Mississippi." He let go of Frank's head and ordered, "Take him to the

doctor. Patch him up and then I'll deal with him."

As they took Frank away, Baxter smiled and added, "That is, if the doc isn't too busy with other matters!" He laughed a sickening, high-pitched giggle, almost like an off-string of a screeching fiddle, as he returned to the bench seat on the deck of the sheriff's office.

CHAPTER 64

The militia soldiers responded immediately to Baxter's orders. One of the men ran behind the sheriff's office and returned with a horse. The other two men threw Frank over the horse bareback like a sack of flour. One man led the horse, while the other two kept Frank from sliding off the horse's back. The small group meandered through the streets of Denver.

When Emily saw that no one had followed after her, she stopped, and tied her horse to a hitching post in front of a funeral home a few blocks away. Then she doubled back to see what had happened to Frank. She stayed on the boardwalk, under the shadows of the roof overhang, and was able to observe. As the militiamen escorting Frank walked by, she slipped into the Mercantile Exchange and watched through the window. Then, once again, she followed nearby as the men traveled through the streets.

After fifteen minutes, the men stopped beside a black military wagon that was parked next to a building. They pulled Frank from the horse and carried him inside. Emily noticed a simple sign stenciled on the large glass window that read "Doctor's Office." She waited until two of the soldiers came back out, untied the horse, and walked back toward the sheriff's office with their companion.

After they had rounded the block she moved to the back of the building and cautiously peered through a small window. Frank was lying on a cot with a militiaman standing next to him. Across the room, the doctor was working on another patient. One man assisted him, but he seemed a rather unlikely nurse. He appeared unkempt with long hair and a bushy beard. His clothing, not the least bit clean, looked crumpled and dirty as though he had just ridden in from working in the mines. The doctor seemed somewhat edgy about the situation as he continually glanced between the militiaman who stood nearby with his sidearm un-holstered, and the man on the table, who was saturated in blood. She was compelled to intervene.

Emily walked around to the front of the building, reached for the door, and confidently stated as she walked in, "Doctor, did you request a nurse to assist?"

The three conscious men in the room were astounded at the stranger who walked into the room. Emily noticed the soldier reach for his revolver and look at her with bloodshot eyes. The assistant looked over his shoulder at her, wide-eyed, and almost frozen in place. The doctor only stopped for a moment to see the intruder, then hastily returned his attention to his patient. In doing so he snapped, "Get over here, then. Anything is better than this sausage-fingered moron."

Emily moved to the table and firmly, though politely, excused the bearded man by pushing him aside. Her eyes rapidly scanned the layout of the instruments, bottles of mixes, and bandages. In one action, she reached for a brown bottle of alcohol, poured some on her hands, and splashed some on the instruments lying on a platter. "Your instructions, doctor?" she requested.

His eyes gleamed at her quick action and respect. "He has a bullet lodged next to his heart. I'm not sure I can extract it." He paused a moment. "Bullet probe."

Emily scanned the platter and found the bullet probe. She doused it in alcohol and handed it to the doctor. The probe was a long instrument made of surgical steel. At the tip was a small knob made of porcelain. The porcelain made a characteristic sound when it hit the bullet versus the bone. The white coating would also scuff with a telltale gray scratch when it was rubbed against the lead projectile. With the probe the surgeon could tell the location and depth of the bullet.

The doctor carefully inserted the probe into the patient's chest. Emily was surprised to see the depth at which he finally made contact with the bullet. "It's deep," the doctor muttered, cursing under his breath. "And it's right between the heart and main artery." He thought for a quick second, then commanded, "Hand me the Levis bullet extractor. We'll try it first."

Once again, Emily responded with the correct instrument and doused it before smacking it into the surgeon's hand.

It only took a few seconds for the doctor to realize his mistake. "Nope, this won't work. It's not long enough." Without hesitation, he dropped the Levis extractor to the side and ordered, "Scoop-tip dissecting forceps."

Emily did as ordered. The scoop-tip dissecting forceps was over twice as long as the Levis extractor. In addition, it had a sliding wire inside of a smooth bore with which the surgeon could push a lever, thus extending an external clip with which he could grasp the bullet. When the lever was released, the bullet would remain clamped in the spoon-like end of the tool, and could then be withdrawn from the patient.

The doctor inserted the forceps and gently wiggled it into position. "The bullet is turned," he mumbled aloud. Emily noticed sweat beading on the doctor's face. She reached for a towel and daubed his forehead. After some tense minutes, he said, "Got it." He slowly pulled it from the man's chest and dropped the tool on the table. "Quickly," he urged, "give me two arterial clamps."

Emily immediately handed them to him. The doctor tried to insert them into the wound, but there wasn't enough room.

"Here," he handed them back. "Knife."

He took the knife and elongated the entry hole. "Arterial clamps," he snapped.

She took the knife and handed him back the clamps after the alcohol dousing. He took them and reinserted them into the open wound. "Wash the wound and soak up some of this blood so I can see," he said.

She reached for a glass container containing some sterile water and poured it on the wound. Then she reached for some cotton and soaked up the overflow. The doctor promptly put the tools back into the patient's chest and clamped off the bleeding artery ends. Then he called, "Tenaculum."

Emily reached for the tenaculum, a tool designed to hold up the ends of the arteries or veins so the surgeon could ligate, or tie off, the blood vessels with suture material.

"The clamps are in position," the doctor stated. "You hold the tenaculum under this first end and I'll suture it with silk."

Emily inserted the shiny steel tool into the patient's chest and gently nudged the artery ends together. The doctor reached over her to the platter and took the deep suture tool and skillfully threaded the silk suture through the ends with the speed of a professional seamstress. He extended it into the chest cavity and carefully sutured around the artery.

"Rotate it some more," he whispered. She shifted the tenaculum to the right, and pulled gently upward to give the surgeon the room he needed. After some minutes he said, "There's one. Now, remove the clamps and see if the sutures hold."

Emily pulled the tenaculum out and slowly released the arterial clamps. Blood flowed through the artery without leaking.

"Good," the doctor said. "Now, reach underneath again. There are some more vessels we need to sew up. They aren't as critical as that last one so we should be in good shape."

Emily assisted in suturing more vessels. Then the doctor

sewed the muscles back together as well as he could. Then he sewed up the entry wound. "Douse the area with alcohol and then clean it well," he added. Emily did as ordered.

When she had finished, she looked the doctor in the eye and said, "We have another patient on the cot."

"I guess I forgot about him," he replied. He noticed the militiaman looking out the window and ordered, "You, help me move these men." Then he remembered the bearded man still standing off in the dark corner. "You, too," he pointed.

The two men moved the man off the operating table and onto a bed. Then they carried Frank to the table. Emily immediately cut off Frank's shirt with scissors and began to clean the two wounds with fresh water so they could see the damage. The two men retreated into the front room and watched intently out the window.

The doctor, duly impressed by Emily's efficiency, was quick to diagnose Frank's wounds. "He's been shot in the arm." He rolled the arm over and continued, "Looks like it went in and then out. Shallow, that's good. Not bleeding too bad, so it didn't slice anything important."

He rolled Frank onto his stomach and examined the bullet hole in his shoulder. "Judging from the entry hole I would say it went up toward his shoulder socket. I think it will be more painful for him than dangerous, though. The bullet probably stopped inside a bone. Give me the porcelain-tipped locator again, please. We'll see if we can find it."

The doctor repeated the action on Frank. The injuries were not too serious, although they had to resort to using chloroform once during the operation in order to quiet him.

After a tense hour, both men were bandaged and recovering in a bed. As Emily was cleaning up, she noticed the doctor talking to the militiaman and the bearded stranger.

"What do you think is happening?" the doctor asked them.

"I'm not sure," the soldier replied. He kept a steady hand on the butt of his revolver. "It certainly has been quiet." He pulled a watch from his pocket and snapped it open. "12:05," he murmured. "Surely Grant has played his final ace by now."

Emily cocked her head as she heard his last words. She noticed a golden wedding band on the man's finger and commented, "Is that the only jewelry you wear?"

The man thought the question strange and didn't reply. But a weak voice next to Emily did.

"It's against regulation for an officer of the United States cavalry to wear any jewelry over and above a wedding ring."

Everyone's eyes immediately fell on Frank. Once he had their attention, he continued, "And, Jack, when are you going to cut off that awful beard?"

CHAPTER 65

Saturday morning found Mike, Derek, and James riding into the city of Golden. Earlier they had spent two hours catching an unsettled catnap on the mountain after their party split and went separate ways. They spent an additional hour making their way down the mountain in the bleak, dim light of a cloudy dawn. Strong winds from the northwest blew the cloud pack over the valley and seemed to promise a clear day.

The three men entered Golden from the western end of town, where the narrow-gauge tracks began their ascent to Central City. A group of men worked to load a freight wagon with sand and debris that had washed onto the track from the heavy rain earlier in the week.

Derek grunted an affirmation of sorts. His mind was elsewhere. As they entered the city proper, he sullenly asked, "How are we going to find the right smelter? Golden is rapidly becoming the center of the Colorado Territory for reduction and refining of all kinds of ore. There must be four or five large smelters in town, not to mention the small independent furnaces and processors littered in every hollow and canyon."

James responded, "If I were a smelter processing illegal gold, I imagine I'd receive a pretty penny for keeping quiet about it." James continued his train of thought after a short pause. "I think we'll find our smelter with the most up-to-date equipment and the best facilities. After all, a good businessman always capitalizes his extra cash."

"That makes sense." Mike nodded his head in agreement. "Let's stop and ask someone which smelter offers the best services."

Before anyone could agree or disagree, Mike, with his usual impulsiveness, stopped his horse, dismounted, and with no little effort on his part limped into a nearby store. James raised his eyebrows and shook his head in amusement at Mike's spontaneity. He did notice, however, that Mike had entered an apothecary's place of business.

Behind the counter in the apothecary, Mr. Samuels, the owner, was grinding some opiates into a fine white powder. When he heard the telltale jingle of the bell fastened to his entry door, he looked up from his work and saw a ragged man stumble into his place of business. He cocked his head in surprise and blurted, "The doctor's office is four blocks east of here."

Mike smiled and answered from across the room, "Well, thank you. But I'm not looking for a doctor's office."

"You certainly look like you are," the pharmacist replied. He eyed Mike's disheveled appearance and added, "You didn't receive a blow to the head or anything, did you?"

"No," Mike replied with a bigger smile. "Just my hand and thigh. Got too close to an explosion, I guess."

The pharmacist shook his head. "You miners are all alike. You blow stuff up, and yourselves along with it, and then you won't bother seeing a doctor. Then you come to me looking for painkillers." He clucked his tongue like a grandmother chastising a wayward schoolboy and ducked into his enclosure for a moment. He returned with a couple of brown bottles, and then asked, "Okay, which one do you want?"

"No, no, you don't understand," Mike retorted. "I don't want any painkillers, I just want some directions."

"Directions?" the pharmacist replied with raised eyebrows.

"Directions to where?"

Mike limped up to the countertop, leaned heavily against it, and asked, "Why, to the best smelter in town, that's where!"

The pharmacist backed up a step and let out a hearty laugh. "Best smelter in town? Why, you must have a case of gold fever!" His laughter slowed and he added, "You've got some ore you think is rich, don't you? You blasted out an ore pocket in your mine, almost blew yourself up with it, and now, instead of wanting to see a doctor or get painkillers, you want to find a smelter. Now doesn't that beat all?"

Mike merely grinned at the learned man behind the counter. "So, which smelter is the best?"

The pharmacist smiled, looked Mike in the eye, and said, "Everyone knows it's the Harranger and Bailey smelter at the southern edge of town. It's been there for a long time and they've got the most up-to-date processing equipment."

"I see," Mike responded. "I think I'll make my way down there and see what they have to offer. Southern edge of town, you say?"

"That's right," he replied. "Eight blocks east of here, then two south. You'll see it on the west side of the road above the creek." As an afterthought he added, "You'll also pass the doctor's office, you know, in case you wanted to stop in for anything."

Mike thanked him for his information, reiterated his lack of need for a doctor, and began to limp toward the door. The pharmacist stopped him and said, "Just a moment, there." He reached for one of his bottles under the counter, scooped a small dosage into a small cup, put a lid on it, and offered it to Mike. "On the house," the pharmacist said. "I can tell you're feeling some pain. It would be cruel of me not to offer you something for it."

Mike turned and accepted his offer. "Thank you, sir. I appreciate your gesture. And thank you for the directions." Mike left the building and limped back to his horse. Upon mounting, he noticed Derek and James staring at him with open mouths.

"What do you have there?" Derek asked.

Mike fiddled with the small cup and replied, "I guess he felt sorry for me. It's some painkiller, I think. Want some?"

James interrupted. "Did you find out anything about a smelter?"

"Sure," Mike answered while looking at the white powder. "Down the road eight blocks, then right for two. Harranger and Bailey is the name. Has the most updated equipment and processes in the territory." He fumbled with the cup and asked Derek again, "You sure you don't want some?"

Derek shook his head and smiled, "No, I'm fine."

James asked, "You found all that out at an apothecary?"

"Yup," Mike answered as he dipped his finger in the white powder and then sucked on it. "Hmm, not bad. Wonder how long it takes to kick in?"

"Come on, then," James said. "Let's get down there before you eat too much of that stuff."

The three men directed their horses toward the southern edge of town and the Harranger and Bailey smelter.

CHAPTER 66

After riding eight blocks to the east, the men turned south and saw the enormous buildings of the Harranger and Bailey Smelting Company. The three- and four-story structures towered some sixty feet above the slow-moving river. Two massive furnaces, belching out smoke from the two stacks, generated heat for the melting pans. A large, wooden water tower stood ready to either provide cooling water for the reduction process or to fill the boilers of the railroad locomotives that passed by on the tracks immediately behind the facility. When they unconsciously stopped to look at the view, Derek asked the inevitable question, "Who has a plan?"

For many minutes, they sat like statues on top of their horses. No one moved; no one said a word. Each man was deep in thought as to what to do.

Mike abruptly said, "I got one. I'll be right back!" With that he whirled his horse around and took off in a cloud of dust back in the direction from which they had come.

James looked at Derek, rolled his eyes, and said under his breath, "Not again."

Derek bit his lip. "Should we follow him?"

James looked over his shoulder at the wisps of dust settling back to the ground, "No, he'll be back when he's ready." He scanned the buildings to their left. "But I say we should find us something to drink while we're waiting."

"Sounds good," Derek replied as he licked his chapped lips.

They tied their horses to a hitching post in front of the nearby saloon, went inside, and after a few moments, came back out to the front decking where they sat on some chairs with a cool drink.

"How long do you think he'll be?" Derek asked.

"I don't know," James answered. "Guess we'll just wait and see."

After an hour of sitting on the porch, James and Derek were roused from their catnap by the tumultuous rumble of a team of horses drawing a heavily loaded freight wagon. James nearly fell from his chair as the lumbering wagon pulled to a stop in front of them.

"Get on your horses and let's go!" Mike yelled from the spring-mounted wagon seat.

James looked at Derek for a moment, and then back at Mike before he shook his head and said, "I don't want to know. I just don't want to know."

"Where are we going, Mike?" Derek asked.

"Down to the smelter to process the ore from the Silver Plume," he replied with a grin. "Just follow my lead. Now mount up, daylight's burning."

The two men did as he had directed and, in short order, the trio, with the heavily loaded freight wagon, pulled into the unloading zone of the Harranger and Bailey Smelting Company. As soon as the wagon stopped, a small, slender man came out of the office and walked up to Mike. He was well-dressed and had an elegant demeanor about him. "Good morning, gentlemen," he began. "How may I be of assistance to you on this fine day?"

"Top of the morning to you, sir," Mike replied. "My name is Mike and my associates and I have just arrived from the Silver Plume mine with a load of concentrates. I believe Mr. Steele has made prior arrangements for its processing?"

"Ah, yes," the man said as he folded his hands and silently rubbed them together. He glanced at the silver wrist bracelets on their forearms. Smiling, he stepped forward, held out his hand to Mike, and said, "My name is Bailey. I'm the man you need to talk to." He took a step back after releasing Mike's hand and pointed to an open stall. "Pull the wagon up to that opening and my men will unload it. You and your friends are welcome to join me for a cold drink of beer while you wait." He noticed the scruffy appearance of the group. "I hope you didn't have any problems coming through town?"

"Nothing we couldn't handle," Mike winked. "You might say it was an explosive trip."

James turned his head and inwardly moaned.

Mike moved the wagon to the unloading stall, while James and Derek dismounted and traded small talk with Mr. Bailey. They entered the office and were shown to comfortable chairs to rest in.

"As I said outside, let's have a beer," Mr. Bailey said. He went into a back room, probably a kitchen of sorts by the sound of cupboards and ice cooler doors opening and closing. He returned with four mugs of light beer with a thick froth on top. "Give this a try," he encouraged. "It's made by a local kid down the road and across the river from here. Has a place set up in the old tannery on Clear Creek Valley." He passed out the mugs. "Name of Adolph Coors. Friendly chap. Been here a few years. Came over on a boat from Prussia." He held up his mug in a mock toast and added, "To fine beer and good friends to share it with!"

James discreetly raised an eyebrow at Mike, stood up with the others, and held his mug up for the toast. The clattering of the mugs and cheers of the toast filled the plush office as they returned to their seats.

Mike drained his mug. "Mr. Bailey, I realize that we arrived late from the Plume this morning. It was unavoidable." He sat up in his chair, leaned forward, and continued in almost a fearful whisper. "But are you aware of Mr. Steele's timetable for processing this ore?"

"Yes," Bailey answered. "I actually got two cables, one from Mr. Steele and the other yesterday afternoon from Bill saying that you would be running late." He set his empty mug on a table. "The refinement process won't be done until this afternoon. What I've decided to do is to weigh the ore after it's unloaded, then apply an average percentage from the four most recent shipments that we had over the previous year to calculate the finished product." He stood. "I've actually prepared most of the paperwork, all but the shipment weights, final processing tallies, and the exchanges to silver bullion. I'll also include the standard cash amount that Mr. Steele usually requests in the exchange and deduct it from the finalized figures. I should have that all done in another hour." He pulled out a pocketwatch and said, "And that should be thirty minutes before noon."

Mike returned Mr. Bailey's enthusiastic smile and replied, "That's great." He glanced out of the window and noticed that the laborers had finished unloading the wagon. He turned to Mr. Bailey and suggested, "We have to buy some more supplies for the mine while we are in town. If it's all right with you, we'll take the wagon. We can be back here in an hour to pick up the paperwork and cash settlement."

"Sounds like a good idea to me," Mr. Bailey responded. "I like a man who squeezes the most work out of a day." He squinted and lowered his head in mock jest and added, "You men want a job here?"

"No," Mike laughed. "I think you'd be hard pressed to pay us what Mr. Steele does."

Mr. Bailey walked to his desk, pulled out a number of fifty-dollar gold pieces, and tossed a couple to each of the men.

"One never knows," he grinned. "Keep it in the back of your minds, all of you. Good workers are hard to find these days."

They shook Mr. Bailey's hand and left him to his paperwork.

CHAPTER 67

At Everett Steele's unspoken request, additional members of the militia of Jefferson were summoned to the legislature chamber. They marched in and lined the perimeter of the room, arms at bay and loaded, the men ready for orders. Steele descended from the lectern and walked up to the nearest soldier. He glanced at the silver bracelet on the man's wrist and inwardly smiled. "Look at these fine men," he declared as he rested his hand on the shoulder of the uniformed man. "They are the finest we have to offer. It isn't only because they are your sons, workers, and friends, but because these men have vision . . . vision for what this land can and should be." He walked down the line of men and checked uniforms, much like a drill sergeant. "And they are ready to carry out this vision at my request and direction. They are the muscle of our revolution, our enforcers, our protectors, the men who give credence to our will. Each of them has sworn allegiance to Jefferson."

Everett's tone grew cold and deliberate as he turned and growled at the audience. "Each of them has also sworn allegiance to me." He sucked on his bottom lip for a moment, cocking his head at a slight angle. "You see, my friends, I had hoped that a consensus on your part would have elected me president of this vast undertaking for sovereignty. But it isn't necessary. After all, the one who controls the military controls the people. Granted, it is easier and more desirable to govern as an elected and supported official, but a dictator can accomplish the same task."

Steele straightened himself to his full height and scanned the audience. His glaring eyes pierced the deathly quiet atmosphere of the chamber. All eyes were affixed on this master craftsman whose product lay unfinished in the molds of acceptance. Yes, the people wanted a level of autonomy to settle their own affairs. They wanted to be able to decide the future of the farms they wrested from the dry prairie land; the profitable ranches developed from the vast range lands once home to only the wild antelope; the rich mining interests and lumbering potentials. They did want control over the destiny of the land they conquered.

But, the realization of a dictator, a man so bent on forcing his will, struck an ill-fated chord. It was the same dissonance that the king of England propagated one hundred years earlier that sparked the revolution for independence. It was the mindset of the feudal lords of Europe that caused so many to escape to the new land of opportunity. It was demanded by an isolated few, the dictators throughout history who ignited and fueled the rebellion for independence in otherwise good and complacent men.

Many of the legislators in the audience were honest and simple men of labor who represented not only hard-working families, but also the men and women of their mountain and farming communities. Yes, there was money at stake. Yes, there was land and prosperity to think about. Yes, there was the desire for an independent and autonomous state. But what cost were they willing to pay for those things? Many of the men had been ingrained with a foundational morality from youth that reinforced and demanded a full examination for a peaceful resolution to conflict. This characteristic trait was the real backbone of the territory . . . that is, the sense to do what was right.

Up until this point of decision, the future of the land was in what they thought were trustworthy and conscientious hands . . . hands that they thought expressed their own moral value and fibrous backbone of truth. Now, after witnessing the oratory debate and discord of the Steele brothers, and witnessing the psychological determination and breakdown of the man in front of them, a major re-evaluation of their goal was underway. The people of this territory did not want a dictator; they wanted a leader who worked to obtain peaceful resolution of their needs. Their trust in and support of Everett Steele was eroding.

Near the front of the audience, an older man stood up. His bushy eyebrows rose, bristling with indignation, as his wide eyes betrayed his inner thoughts. "Mr. Steele! I don't agree with your assessment of this situation. I withdraw my support."

Another man stood up, much younger than the first. "I have five kids and a farm. I'm not going to war with the United States so you can have a sovereign state!"

A third man just as quickly jumped to his feet yelling, "All we want is just representation for our needs!"

The pandemonium across the cavernous room picked up pace. Two men stood in the back to voice their sudden opposition. Another three in the left wing leapt to their feet in vocal disagreement. In what seemed like a brief moment, most of the men in the auditorium were not just on their feet, but stamping, yelling, and threatening Steele's personal safety. The chaotic rampage fanned the flames of a riot against Mr. Steele's sudden proclamation of dictatorship. The quiet and somber group that Everett Steele thought he had in the palm of his hand had become a people of flinty resolve determined neither to submit to his demands nor to listen to any more rhetoric or threats. After all, this man before them who wished to proclaim a dictatorship had threatened the life core and most deeply held value in the hearts of his constituents . . . that aspect of liberty involving freedom of choice.

Everett Steele pursed his lips, looked at the officer in charge, and ordered, "We have lost this audience. Raise your arms and do whatever is necessary to restore order to this chamber."

Captain Morely nodded his head in response, turned toward his men, and bellowed out his orders. "Attend arms!"

The men in the chamber quieted, responding with disbelief at the order that resounded above the commotion.

The militia of Jefferson around the perimeter of the room responded diligently and promptly to the order to attend the firearms. They raised their rifles and aimed mechanically at the now mute and deathly silent legislature.

Everett Steele mutely scanned his rebellious constituents and shook his head. Then he tersely barked, "Shoot them."

CHAPTER 68

The steady clackity-clack of the train car wheels on the fresh railroad track lulled Johann and Sarah to sleep. After all, the high-speed ride from Central City to Longmont demanded their full attention and strength merely to hang on to the bouncing carriage. It was understandable that once they were safely seated in the train, they would relax and fall into a deep slumber.

But it was not so with Ambrose McHenry. Not a minute after the coach was under way, he put his hand on Colonel Auger's shoulder, got his attention, and asked, "Did you construct a war room in one of the coaches?"

Without blinking Auger replied, "Yes, sir. As you requested." He pointed to the door at one end of the coach. "It is two cars forward. Follow me."

They moved down the aisle toward the front of the Spartan car. These coaches were not like the plush cars of Sydney Williams's train of the future. They were simple wooden coaches with hard-backed benches that seated two to a seat. The floors were dirty and littered with miscellaneous trash. In the forward corner was a wood stove with thin metal sheaves nailed to the wall behind it. The floor had a protective metal plate that extended beyond the stove on which split cordwood was stacked. A black, sooty chimney rose in a haphazard manner from the cast-iron top, and disappeared through the ceiling. An occasional candle, housed in a glass canister, decked the top of the car windows and provided enough mellow light to walk safely down the corridor between the seats crowded with soldiers.

Colonel Auger led Ambrose through the cabin door and into the next car. The room was only about ten feet long. At the far end, a wall and door had been hastily constructed in order to provide a degree of privacy. Heavy, black drapes covering the windows necessitated the use of more candle lamps on the wall than were customarily used in the coach section. Haphazard layers of folded, rolled, and laid-out maps speckled a simple wooden table in the middle of the room. Colonel Auger walked to the table, moved some papers around, and pulled one map in particular to the surface of the pile. As he smoothed the wrinkled map with his hands, he commented, "This map of Denver shows the street layouts, major governmental buildings, and most of the merchant buildings in the downtown sector." He fanned his hand to the outlying areas. "And these squares are the military barracks and ammunition depositories that we think the local militia has control over."

Ambrose studied the paper for a moment, then, without looking up asked, "How do we know the militia is in control of these areas?"

Colonel Auger stood up and motioned Ambrose to do the same. He welcomed a newcomer to the room, replying with an outstretched hand, "This man is Sam Chandler. He has been working secretly within Everett Steele's organization for a number of years. He was in a position of passing secret information that provided a number of reliable clues to our investigators."

Ambrose stretched out his large hand to the man in warm welcome as Colonel Auger continued, "When you informed me of your intent yesterday, I took the liberty of pulling Sam out of service. He caught a train to Fort Collins, met us at the station, and has been briefing me since." He nodded at Sam to continue the session.

Sam was a small, skinny man with wire spectacles and a receding hairline. He wore a plaid vest and white shirt with a black tie looped in tight bows. He responded immediately to the colonel's invitation and began the briefing in a soft, but commanding, voice. "Yes, these barracks and munitions supply houses are under the militia's control. There is one of each at the north and south ends of the city boundaries, and one more about two miles east of the city. They are all near a rail station for ease of transportation."

Ambrose motioned for him to stop for a moment while he found his bearings on the map. After some study he asked, "How many militiamen are stationed at each facility?"

"Approximately one hundred-thirty," Sam answered.

"That's more men than we have on this train," Colonel Auger pointed out. "It would be a challenge to gain control of that many men without significant losses on our part."

"Agreed," Ambrose remarked. "Where is the legislature building located where the territorial council is going to meet?"

Sam moved in and pointed out the main building. He also added valuable information concerning the exterior doors and windows, as well as other pertinent facts. Colonel Auger and Ambrose listened intently as they educated themselves on the geography of their battlefield.

The briefing continued into the night as the train grew closer to its destination. Eventually, Ambrose stood, rubbed his burning eyes, and stumbled to the window. He pulled the heavy drapes aside and noticed the early morning hues of dawn lighting the mountaintops. He let go of the curtain, turned to face the table, and gruffly asked, "How are we going to take control of this situation with what we have to work with?"

A grim silence filled the room in rhetorical response. Ambrose leaned back against the table and wrinkled his brow. As he tapped his fingers in deep thought, a voice rose from behind, and to his left. "Why not change the chain of command?"

Ambrose's blank stare flicked into a couple of spastic blinks as he contemplated the words. He pushed away from the table, turned, and faced Evangeline. "What did you say?"

"Change the command structure," she said again.

"Elaborate," Ambrose ordered.

Evangeline had a simple but profound answer. "Stick a ring in a bull's nose, and wherever you pull it, the rest of the two thousand pounds will follow." She looked at the map. "Change the leadership in the militia, and you have control over the militia."

Ambrose looked into her gray eyes for that moment of understanding. Then a hint of a smile curled up both sides of his mouth. "You're brilliant!" he bellowed. He whirled around and looked at Sam. "What did you do for Steele?" he inquired.

Sam responded, "I was his personal telegrapher. I authored ten or fifteen messages a day for him."

Ambrose's eyes narrowed as he asked, "Can you forge his name?"

"Sure," Sam replied. "I wrote the messages but he signed them. He used a grand script or, depending on how much of a hurry he was in, only initials. I can imitate it perfectly."

"Ah," Ambrose cooed as he rubbed his hands together. He scanned his men with bright eyes and a devious smile. "This is what we're going to do!"

Chapter 69

The early morning sun lit the snowcaps of the western peaks of the Front Range like the yellowish haze of kerosene lamps slicing through the blackness of a darkened theater. The train from Cheyenne had braked twenty minutes earlier, and was fueling the boiler with fresh water. The engineer walked alongside the enormous engine wheels with an oilcan. Every now and then he leaned over and dabbed some fresh oil on some moving part. Inside the locomotive control room, the fireman shoveled fresh coal into the firebox so a level of quick steam could be resumed as soon as the boiler was full.

Ambrose paced the rail yard, glancing periodically at his silver pocketwatch. The soldiers from Fort Russell stood at attention along the rails next to the train and waited. Sarah, Evangeline, and Johann had been ushered into the train station out of sight. The rest of the rail yard was devoid of life. The locomotive and its accompanying cars waited.

In the meantime, Colonel Auger strode assertively into the northernmost headquarters for the barracks of the Jefferson territorial militia. The colonel was a man who understood military procedure and was not afraid to exercise its formality to his advantage. He rapped forcefully on the door of the quarters of the officer in charge. After a few moments, the door squeaked open and a stout man with a bushy, but well-trimmed, beard answered in a simple tone, "What is it?"

Colonel Auger quickly articulated a question. "Captain Marshall?"

The drowsy officer replied, "Yes, I am Captain Marshall. What is it?"

Colonel Auger immediately replied with a snapped salute and stoutly English voice. "I am Captain Morely from the eastern sector near the Kansas line." Without hesitation, and with a deliberate flick of the wrist, he delivered an envelope with an elaborate wax seal into his view. "I've been ordered by Mr. Steele to immediately requisition your militiamen to aid in the interception of a detachment of federal soldiers from Fort Hays. I have brought a portion of my reserves to fill in for your men to maintain order in the city of Denver while you deliver your expertise to the area of conflict."

Captain Marshall's eyes grew large as he tried to understand and then absorb what he heard. But his concentration was abruptly cut off as Captain Morely continued, "I have been instructed to give you a choice, sir. You may lead your troops yourself into the conflict, or I will take command of them while you maintain command of my troops for the security of Denver. A train is waiting at the rail yard. What are your orders, sir?"

Captain Marshall, caught by surprise by the early morning interruption, shook his head and mumbled, "I can't believe the federal government has sent troops against us. Let me think a minute." He rubbed the palms of his hands on his eyes and then raked them through his hair. The envelope was firmly entrenched before his eyes. He glanced at the distinguished officer standing before him in complete militia regalia, took the cotton envelope, broke the wax seal, and opened it. Sure enough, as Captain Morely had stated, the orders were in graceful script on the document. At the bottom was the intricate and distinguished signature of Everett Steele. Captain Marshall let out a sleepy yawn and acquiesced. "Give me a moment to get dressed." He glanced at the silver bracelet on his counterpart's wrist as he left the door ajar but retreated to his room. In a few moments he returned and categorically said, "Let's wake the men. I'll transfer them to Kansas."

The two captains rapidly strode to the barracks, whereupon Captain Marshall bellowed in a loud voice, "Call to arms, gentlemen. Report to the gate in ten minutes, fully armed and ready to travel."

The response from the sleeping men was instantaneous. Covers flew, uniforms seemed to flow onto bodies, and weapons were mustered in a moment. As ordered, the regiment was ready to march in ten minutes.

Captain Marshall looked over at Captain Morely as the militiamen fell into rank. "You say the train is standing ready at the yard?"

"Yes, that is correct, sir," Morely replied. "I will accompany you there."

At Marshall's command for a double-time march, the detachment made quick time to the rail yard. As they approached, Captain Marshall saw the replacements for his men and commented to Captain Morely, "They seem able enough. Are they familiar with Denver?"

Morely answered, "Yes, sir. Many of them are from the area. If there is trouble, we can take care of it."

Marshall nodded in agreement.

As the last of the men boarded the train, Captain Marshall addressed Captain Morely in private. "Your orders for today are to provide protection for the territorial legislature building. The session starts at ten. Post two of your men inside the building as sentries. Have the rest stand at attention along the front walkway to the entrance. If, for any reason, Mr. Steele requests your assistance, follow his orders implicitly and without question."

"Understood, sir," Morely answered. He snapped a salute to

Marshall, who returned in kind, with liveliness that he had not exhibited earlier that morning. As he boarded the train, Morely waved a hand of understanding to the engineer. The belching smoke and whistling steam of the black 4-4-0 wrenched the line of cars into motion as the northern territorial militia began its trek to the western reaches of Kansas.

CHAPTER 70

All eyes of the legislature were fixed on the Honorable Everett Steele as he barked out his final order to the Jefferson militia to open fire. Almost all eyes, that is. In the midst of the tension, nobody noticed two men enter the rear door of the stage and walk to the lectern near the left wing of the proscenium arch. One man with a graying beard was dressed immaculately in a black suit. The other dressed in a more casual mode. As they scanned the situation, their eyes made knowing contact and, in rapid response to Everett Steele's notorious order, the best dressed man calmly, but loudly, commanded, "Delay that order, Colonel Auger."

In disciplined response, Colonel Auger loudly ordered, "At ease," to the militia lining the perimeter of the legislature building. All of the men responded by lowering their rifles, snapping them to their sides, and standing with legs slightly spread with a relaxed appearance to their countenance.

In a fraction of a second, all eyes in the building snapped from Everett Steele, to the soldiers, and then to the stranger at the podium on the stage, who promptly stated almost as an afterthought, "And Colonel Auger, would you please detain Mr. Steele."

Colonel Auger and another soldier secured Steele's arms before he could respond. Then, at the wave of the colonel's hand, half of the security force took up defensive positions at critical points of entry to the building, be it door or window.

The other half strategically dispersed to secure positions protecting the men on stage and as backup to the colonel.

The implementation of orders and speedy response by the soldiers stunned the audience, including Mr. Steele. In mere moments the balance of power had shifted to the benefit and control of the man on stage. As a result he stepped from behind the podium and spoke. "I am Ulysses Grant, president of the United States of America."

Upon hearing these words, something snapped inside of Everett Steele. His face contorted and he cried out, "You can't be Grant! You're supposed to be dead. I ordered it myself. You can't be him. No, you can't be him!" He collapsed to the floor, breaking the contact between him and his retainers, and then broke into sobs and moans as he groveled upon the floor of the chamber. Colonel Auger and other soldiers stared at the sorry state of the man before them. They looked to Grant for directions.

"Colonel Auger, will you remove Mr. Steele from the room so I may address this renowned audience?"

The colonel motioned for an additional two soldiers to remove Mr. Steele.

No small commotion ensued from Mr. Everett Steele as the three soldiers escorted him, to the point of half-carrying him, toward the stage, then through a small exit door that led to a long, dingy hallway, which eventually descended into the basement. After Steele's removal, Grant faced the audience.

"Distinguished gentlemen of the territorial legislature of Colorado, it is with the highest level of respect that I address you this day. I use the word 'distinguished' in describing this assembly because it is men of your caliber that have united this great territory together with one mind and one purpose. I have memories of working with men of such stature in the not too distant past when our land was torn and ravaged by a war of

different ideals. Those were men of conviction, men of direction, men that paved the future for this land. It is with heartfelt
regret that, during this time of reconstruction and implementation of those plans for expansion, certain locales of this country
have felt isolated, polarized, and abandoned by their government. Through my administration's busy-ness we have neglected
to express the gratitude and appreciation for this assembly of
men sitting before me, which has provided its economic
resources toward our country as a whole.

"The Territory of Colorado has been a foundational block
upon which this new vision of rebuilding our battered land has
been grounded. Your plentiful timber harvested from these lofty
hills has rebuilt the houses destroyed by battle. The mineral
wealth dug from the most remote mountain mines has provided
an economic stimulus to the entire country. The railroads that
run north and south along the Front Range and east to the cities of the coast provide reciprocal transportation of goods and
transportation for people desiring to settle, farm, and ranch
these new horizons. Yes, Colorado has been greatly instrumental
in the purpose and expansion of these United States of America.
As a representative of this Union, I commend and thank this
territory for its contribution to this country's growth and stability."

The president stopped for a moment and scanned the quiet
audience. He shifted on his feet and returned to the back of the
podium as he continued, "Gentlemen, let us get to the point. As
the president of the United States, I wish to make the following
proposition to this legislative body. Rather than risk the threat
of further damage to our country's future, I want to extend my
hand in peace, and welcome this territory to its rightful place in
the Union. I propose that this assembly in front of me elect the
appropriate number of delegates as required by law to examine

and prepare the state intent and constitution necessary for statehood.

"I will make it my determination to encourage Congress to review these documents. I will see to it that Congress be addressed at a joint session by your representatives, to explain your documentation and wish for statehood. I will use the power of my office to its fullest extent to motivate Congress to pass legislation giving statehood to the area designated by the federal surveyors to be known as the state of Colorado. As you know, along with this designation comes the authority and responsibility to govern yourselves within the laws and statutes of the constitution of the United States; to set up your own schools; to enter into all the rights of a voting entity in Congress; to be represented by your electorates; to enjoy all the privileges, protection, and duties granted to all the other states. Furthermore, I promise you that I will use all of my influence to execute and complete these plans before the elections of November, 1876."

Grant stopped his oration and motioned for Colonel Auger to come forward. Upon receiving his full attention, he turned again to the listeners and ordered in a loud voice, "Colonel Auger, please remove your men from these premises. This governing body has need for discussion amongst themselves in the spirit of freedom."

The colonel did as ordered and relieved his men, sending them outside.

Grant then completed his discourse. "Gentlemen, I shall be outside with my associates waiting for your decision. I look forward to welcoming you into statehood."

As the president moved forward to leave the chamber, Henri and Colonel Auger, who had remained behind as a security measure, flanked him on either side. They stepped down the few steps to the assembly room floor and boldly walked up the corridor to the rear door. As they passed the first row, a man stood to his feet and slowly applauded. Another did likewise. As the small entourage gained ground toward the rear of the room, more and more aisles of men stood up until, by the time they reached the back doors, the chamber was aloud with, not only an ovation, but also cheers and shouts of support. As they exited, Grant let out a sigh of relief. He turned to Henri and whispered hoarsely in his ear, "I think we have an accord!"

CHAPTER 71

The three soldiers half-carried, half-dragged Everett Steele down the narrow corridor leading to a set of wooden stairs that descended into the basement of the state building. Oil lamps hanging from large nails driven into huge supporting timbers illuminated the passageway with an eerie, yellowish light. The group moved downward and entered a long hallway with a number of individual rooms on either side.

"What should we do with him?" the leading soldier asked of his comrades.

"I don't know," responded the second. He stopped for a moment and opened one of the doors within reach. As it creaked open, the dim light of the corridor rapidly disappeared in the yawning entry. The soldier reached nearby for a hanging lamp, removed it, and held it high above his head as he entered the room. The feeble light revealed a room with three frame walls and one made of heavy stone. The floor was hard lime, aged to the hardness of concrete. Crated boxes lay scattered throughout the room, but only stacked two high at most. A good ten feet above the floor, the heavy timbers supported the first floor of the state building. The soldier returned to the hallway and said, "Let's put him in here and watch the door."

When Everett Steele heard the comment, he jerked his full body weight against his captors' grip, broke free, and careened down the hallway yelling, "No you don't! You're not putting me in that prison!"

The three soldiers, taken by surprise, stood stunned for a moment, then gave chase. But Steele had enough of a head start that he not only had time to snatch a lamp off the wall further down the corridor, but also reached the last door on the right and slipped through it before they could catch him. Once inside, he pitched some crates in front of the door to effectively barricade himself in.

The soldiers reached the door and tried to open it, but with little effect. The leader stepped back and quickly summarized the situation. "Well, I guess it doesn't matter which room he's in as long as he's in one." He put his hands on the shoulders of the other two. "You two stay here and guard the door. I'll relay what happened to the colonel."

Inside the dimly lit room, Everett Steele piled a few more crates in front of the door. "That'll keep them out," he muttered. Then he spun around and scanned the far wall. It was hidden by stacked crates and bound piles of papers. He drunkenly staggered toward the impenetrable piles and started casting them into the center of the room. Gradually he worked his way to the cold stone foundational wall. "I know it's here," he continually reassured himself. "I've seen it before. I know it's here someplace. Keep digging. I'll find it." Sweat beaded on his forehead and his coat became moist from his exertion. But he continued throwing, shoving, and ripping bundles, crates, and containers like the madman he had become. He excavated a pathway along the granite barrier as he sought something only his tortured mind could remember.

The state building actually had its beginnings as a first-class hotel built early in the life of Auraria, the founding town of Denver. The Premier Hotel's foundation and basement were laid with the finest hand-cut granite freighted in from a small quarry to the south. Rough-cut pine timbers brought in from the high country supported the three tall stories that soared above the dirt streets of the growing town. It stood as a monument and pinnacle to the determination of the settlers to extract a city out of the lonely and windswept high plains.

As with most new towns in the west, the buildings were built with wood. Auraria was no different. Construction, hastened by the nearby gold strikes and their insatiable requirement for hardware, lumber, and other supplies, continued at a blistering pace. Feed stores, saloons, assay offices, and other structures crammed the small building lots until block after block of wooden buildings extended from one end of town to the other. But, along with the progress of a growing city came the risks associated with no zoning laws and unchecked construction quality.

The cause of the 1863 fire was never conclusively determined. But, it was surmised that one cold spring evening an overheated stovepipe with inadequate protection around its cherry-red glow caught the wood shingled roof of an unfortunate retailing business on fire. The blustery April winds blew the conflagration from one building to another until a rather large portion of the city flamed yellow and red with a destructive force that couldn't be contained. After one day and two nights, a change in the winds reversed the malevolent threat so as to burn itself out for lack of fresh fuel. The only sections of town left standing were the buildings surrounding the Premier Hotel.

It was unfortunate for these sole survivors that the rebuilding efforts ordered by the city council mandated stone or brick structures in lieu of wooden framing. As a result, the small remnant of the original town left untouched by the flames of destruction carried the stigma of danger, causing property values to fall due to the their wood content. Within a short time after the fire, the Premier Hotel could not compete with the newly constructed and much safer brick places of lodging, and ended up closing its doors to business.

Always on the lookout for a good buy, Everett Steele purchased the Premier in the late sixties. He had it gutted and remodeled into the beautiful state house, a building that he hoped would one day be at the center of his new political endeavor. During the remodeling process, Steele had the basement divided into separate rooms for storage. One day, he was called into the basement by the contractor who had discovered a wooden door embedded in a small section of the stone-laid wall. After much debate, an old mason on the job stepped forward and said that when the Premier was first built, a secret tunnel was dug to connect the hotel with an establishment of questionable repute across the street and down a few buildings. Surreptitious transport of customers and providers could thereby be arranged with discretion. As a rising political figure, Steele was disgusted with the thought, and ordered the entry to the tunnel to be permanently closed.

It was this tunnel that Everett Steele's foggy mind remembered. And, in due course, a rap on the wall with a broken board produced an echo from the hollow behind. Everett Steele smiled and whispered to himself, "Now they'll pay. Now they'll pay."

CHAPTER 72

Everett Steele took the board in his hand and rammed it into the laid masonry patch that covered the tunnel door. He screamed in pain as the sudden impact of the pine plank splintered against the granite and drove wooden slivers into his hands as they scraped along the rough-sawn surface. He slammed the useless wood to the ground, cradled his bleeding palms against his stomach, and commenced searching for another tool.

In the corner was a small grouping of foundational stones left over from the basement remodel project. Everett Steele saw them in the dim light and moved in their direction. He tripped on a crate and instinctively put his hands out to break his fall, but miscalculated his timing and, instead, hit his head on the corner of a freestanding bookshelf. Stars blurred his vision, but only for a moment. He struggled to his knees, and shoved his way through the piles of debris that filled the room. At last his ten fingers grasped the smooth, cold edges of a bulky hunk of granite stone. Everett growled like a grizzly bear as he forced the rock over his head, spun around on his feet, and threw the projectile against the masonry façade covering the tunnel entrance. The ensuing dull thud led him to believe that nothing had happened. Upon crawling to the wall, however, he saw that the rock had done its work.

A misshapen shadow hid a gaping hole in the wall where the boulder had taken a number of stones with it as it hurled through the barrier. He reached into the blackness and raked the remaining rocks into the basement room. Then he stood to his feet and reached for the dimming lantern. He held it high as he scanned the timbers along the walls for additional lamps. Spotting more lanterns, he made his way through the debris to their berths and acquired another four.

Instead of lighting them, he removed their lids and emptied their liquid contents onto the piles of rubbish and papers strewn across the room. Then he broke the glass globe on one of them, and lit it with his first lamp. Everett Steele sauntered to the small opening of the tunnel, turned, and, with a screech of demonic glee, hurled the broken, but lit, lamp into the midst of the paper fuel. The oil-soaked papers burst into flame, and immediately filled the room with bright light and black smoke. Everett Steele's face contorted in a strange devilish laughter as he turned toward the tunnel entrance and moved into the inky blackness.

The two soldiers were no longer guarding the door that concealed Everett Steele's actions. They had grown bored with the dingy basement and rationalized to themselves that since they couldn't enter the barricaded door at the end of the corridor, neither could Everett Steele exit. Consequently, they saw no harm in ascending the stairwell and positioning themselves strategically at the only basement exit, while still maintaining a good view of the great hall where President Grant engaged his audience.

As the false masonry wall hiding the tunnel below collapsed under Everett Steele's single barrage, Grant made his appeal to the audience. As the flames consumed their paper fuel and grew in intensity, so did the applause accorded to the president as he departed the legislative chamber. As Everett Steele burst through the flimsy framing in the basement of the saloon across the street, the influx of fresh air detonated the distant basement room into an inferno, like pitching saltpeter and coal dust onto an open flame.

Fortunately, the representatives were already on their way out of the building to celebrate their unanimous decision of unity with President Grant and his associates. As the last man departed the doomed state house, a deep rumble of unstoppable combustion emanated from the ghostly steps of the basement. Acrid wisps of smoke wafted from seams in the walls. The floor, where only minutes earlier Grant had stood, began to radiate heat. But the cheering and excitement of the moment covered the noise of the growing subterranean terror.

Across the street in the basement of the saloon, Everett Steele was engrossed in smashing kegs of whiskey and bottles of brandy. The alcohol industry in Denver had kept fast pace with the increased number of mining and timber workers looking for weekend recreation. Even the saloons in the oldest sections of town carried vast supplies and assortments of the mind-numbing concoctions that dissolved away men's weekly workloads and problems. Such was the basement of the "Brothers Saloon" that Steele had covertly stumbled into.

Once again, he piled high the wooden remnants of his destruction and scattered liquid fire from the strongest drink on the debris. His warped plan in the state house basement had worked so well that he repeated the process of taking lamps off the wall, draining their contents in strategic places, and lighting them as he exited up the stairwell. He unlocked the rear alley door from inside the saloon, as it was officially closed in light of the legislative meeting across and down the street two buildings.

No one was in the alley as he left the drinking establishment, as the celebration in the middle of the main street had attracted most of the city. As such, it was easy for Everett Steele to calmly walk down the alley and kick open the back door of another merchant's venue. He walked in, set his still-lit lamp on a sill, and scanned his new prospect. It only took a fraction of a second for his eyes to light up and a grin to broaden his face.

The hardware store was a pyromaniac's delight. Clay casks of fresh oil, wooden kegs of gunpowder, ammunition, and all sorts of paints and solvents, not to mention the wooden shelves full of combustible materials, marked a fully stocked mercantile. Everett Steele went into demolition mode. He took a sledgehammer from the tool section and drove it mercilessly through the glass display case, shattering the delicate shelving unit and scattering the contents on the floor. The glass display cases containing the firearms and ammunition were next on his rampage, since they blocked the way to the gated closet containing kegs of black blasting powder. A few swings of the heavy mallet broke open the locked gate, whereupon he succeeded in breaking open the stacked kegs. He spread the blackish powder on the shelves of hardware, the boxes, on crates and cartons of stored goods. Then he found something better—some ceramic containers of petroleum. He opened the first jug, smelled it to check its contents, and then threw it across the room, where it broke into a spray of sharp shards and oil. Maniacal laughter contorted his face as he watched the way the shards spun in circles on the slick, oily floor. He spun around, grabbed some more of the brown containers, and poured their contents around the room.

He moved rapidly and precisely, like a cat pursuing and then pouncing on a rat. When he was satisfied at the level of damage, he made a makeshift fuse by pouring a trail of oil from the broken gunpowder kegs to the alley entrance. He opened the rear door of the store, peeked into the alley, and planned his route of escape. Then he reached to the sill, retrieved his burning lamp, and took one more look at the devastation he had wreaked. A sickly giggle reverberated in his throat and rose to his mouth as he extended the lamp to the full length of his arm, dropped it, and fled out the door.

CHAPTER 73

The joyous celebration of unity was in full swing in front of the state house. Men were shaking hands, laughing, and slapping each other on the back like old friends after the successful campaign of their favorite politician. But, in Henri's mind, something felt wrong. He couldn't put his finger on it. Maybe it was the gentle tinge of smoke he smelled. It wasn't like the sweet aroma of tobacco, but more of a trashy, wooden odor, like that of a campfire using waste wood from a torn-down house. His gaze searched all directions for some clue to the distinctive odor.

As Henri turned to comment about it to the president, his eyes widened as the storefront cattycorner to them abruptly disappeared into a massive ball of vivid white light. He, together with everyone nearby, was knocked to the ground as a vicious maelstrom of wind and heat screamed around them. Fiery shards of lumber, hardware, and debris showered the streets as the old frame hardware store exploded.

Across town, fire chief Amos Aldridge rested on a bench in front of the district fire department. His crew milled around the station cleaning and checking the assorted equipment acquired by the city after the massive 1863 fire. As Amos shifted his feet on the crate in front of him for a more comfortable position, a distinctive rumbling resonating from the old building district caught his attention. He got up and moved to the center of the street to catch a view of the incident.

At first, there was nothing to grab his eye, but after a few tense moments he saw a billowing cloud of blackish smoke rise above the rooftops in the distance. His eyes narrowed as his mind quickly and accurately interpreted the nature of the situation from the explosive sound and nature of the smoke plume.

"Boys, we got a hot spot near the state house!" he bellowed to the men in the station. "Get loaded and move out, now!"

The men burst into a flurry of organized action. Horses from the corral behind the station were hitched to the two-pumper wagons, tools secured and protective gear assembled. In the space of three minutes the highly trained specialists were streaming down the streets of Denver in a dash to contain the fire that threatened their city.

Putting his horse to a full gallop, Chief Amos Aldridge caught his first glimpse of the fire within minutes of his departure. Three blocks ahead of his horse, he could see the spiraling flames and boiling black smoke reaching for the sky where a storefront had once stood. The two neighboring buildings were heavily damaged and on fire. His trained eye scanned the other surrounding structures for heat ignition, when he noticed a thin trail of smoke emanating from the state house door. A quick dart of the eyes also picked up more smoke from a saloon just beyond and across the street. A chill ran up his spine as he recognized the same circumstances from the 1863 fire that initiated the formation of the fire company; that is, a runaway inferno whose heat and energy would disintegrate even the finest of masonry structures.

But the chief had trained his men for this "doomsday" scenario. Although taken by surprise at the strength and size of the fire, they were not intimidated by it. As Amos arrived on the scene, he set about bringing order to the dazed and injured victims of the explosion. Men who were able and coherent pulled those stunned or dead to safe areas away from the flames.

The two-pumper wagons were placed near the watering ditches running under the boardwalks on either side of the street. The fire crew organized the manpower necessary to operate the huge water bellows and to lay the long hoses. In what seemed like moments, four streams of water, two from each wagon, were flowing like fountains onto the burning buildings.

In a frontier town like Denver, security was a common goal of every person, citizen, or visitor. Consequently, when the fire wagons roared through the streets on the way to the state building, groups of merchant men, women, and those not involved in the workings of politics followed like a stampeding herd of buffalo. They rushed to the fire chief to lend a hand in whatever way possible. The survival of the town meant their survival.

Chief Amos took full advantage of this town solidarity, and fired orders to men and women alike. Buckets were passed out from the wagons and equipment storage sheds strategically located every few blocks throughout town. Lines quickly formed to the waterways where buckets were filled, then frantically whisked to the lead firefighter at the hot spot of each line. He then skillfully heaved the precious liquid to the most useful location, tossed the empty container aside, then reached for a new one.

A cluster of school students seized shovels and ran to the many areas away from the main flames where burning debris from the explosion could catch some other combustible, like a boardwalk, on fire. They feverishly worked at smothering the smoking wreckage with dirt dug from the street.

A steady supply of strong men consistently rotated out those that grew tired on the pumps, so as to keep an uninterrupted supply of water flowing to the hoses. At first, all four hoses were aimed at the central area where the hardware store once stood. The chief then redirected two of the hose handlers to soak the buildings on either side. He also ordered the bucket brigade to

357

intensify its efforts in the same area. Hopefully, this would extinguish the side fires and retard the fire's spreading.

Two groups of men were rapidly organized to scout out the other sources of smoke that the chief had noticed on his way in. The first group valiantly ran toward the state house, but as soon as the main entrance door was opened, a large fireball, fed by the sudden influx of fresh air, blew the door framing off the wall and threw the men to the ground. The report instantly caught the chief's attention. He motioned for two militiamen to help the four unconscious men and carry them to safety. At the same time, he glanced at the two smoldering buildings on either side of the hardware store ruins, made his decision, and sprinted to the men operating the hoses on the upwind side. He redirected them to the state house, then rushed to the lead men on two of the four bucket brigade lines and did the same.

It was too little too late. The fireball from the state legislature building blew flaming roofing material high into the air and littered it on nearby roofs downwind. Moments later, the windows of the saloon across the street shattered. Heat and flames rapidly consumed the roofed canopy hanging over the boardwalk, and continued upwards into the blackened sky. The fires spread rapidly.

Fear gripped Chief Aldridge. Worse than the buildings burning all around them, the firemen and bucket brigades were beginning to lose heart. If their courage failed, the entire leeward side of Denver would be lost. Something drastic had to happen in their favor. An insane idea sparked in Chief Aldridge's mind. He made eye contact with his second-in-command, and motioned him to follow. In the midst of the whirlwind and confusion, the two men sprinted through the thick smoke and disappeared up the street.

CHAPTER 74

Fire chief Amos Aldridge stopped to catch his breath after sprinting for two blocks. George, his second-in-command, also paused, and tried to talk, but could only mimic sounds like those of a screeching, angry crow. After a few moments, he regained his composure and snapped, "What's with you, Amos? Why are you running from the people who need you most?"

"It's the only way," Amos croaked back. "We've got to stop the fire from spreading." He motioned for George to follow. "Come on, we're almost there. Just one more block."

Amos took off running again before the other man could protest. As Amos reached the next intersection, he veered to the right and stopped at a shop three buildings down and on the south side of the road. A sign in the window read "Assay and Mining Supplies." He sprinted toward the door, threw his full weight against the glass and wooden barrier, and charged through the shattered remains without stopping.

George reached the splintered doorway a few seconds behind. His eyes were wide as he peered in to see his fire chief, bleeding and bruised, and madly breaking open a secured room in the back. "Have you lost your mind, man?" he screamed. "What in heaven's name are you doing?"

Amos kept rooting through the room as he barked out his orders. "Shut up and give me a hand here."

George moved forward in trained response to following instructions.

"Quick, get that wheelbarrow," Amos snapped as he pointed across the room.

George did as ordered. He rolled the barrow behind Amos just in time to receive a box labeled "explosives." "Hey, what's going on here?" he demanded.

Amos stopped for a second, and uttered a calm and collected response. "The only way to retard the fire's growth is to dynamite the buildings in its path. We have to cut off its fuel supply or it will burn the whole south and east side of Denver."

George blinked his eyes in disbelief. Then he understood. He grabbed the box, secured it in the wheelbarrow, and yelled, "Get another one!"

The wheelbarrow was full with three boxes of explosives, some fuses, and matches. "Take these outside," Amos said. His words were in phrases, but were understandable. "I'll load another one. When you get to the fire line, get help. Tie ten sticks together with a short fuse. Take and throw a dynamite bundle at the supporting corner wall of each building in the fire's path. We have to make a fire break at least one hundred feet wide. I'll be along in a moment." As he moved toward another wheelbarrow he yelled, "Move it, man!"

George nodded and raced out of the store, precariously balancing his dangerous load on one wheel.

The heat of the fire line was so intense that the bucket brigades were unable to approach. Three more buildings burst into an inferno of eerie orange and red light. The ground crews withdrew from the thick smoke and large pieces of hot debris. Only the hose crews were able to withstand the inferno and spray water to where it was needed. But the close proximity of the many burning buildings made them feel like a fat porcupine surrounded by hungry grizzly bears. Only the sharpness of their quills, the wetness of their water, kept the enemy at bay. Groups of men had moved the injured and dead down the street out of range of the flaming fallout, but, because of the fire's intensity, only a few could return to help on the pumps.

As if prodded by a fork of hell itself, a smoldering wheelbarrow, pushed by a wheezing, sweaty, and blackened madman shouting at the top of his lungs, and loaded with charred boxes labeled "explosives," emerged out of the thick black smoke. "Give me a hand, boys!" he screamed. "Give me a hand! We got a town to save!"

Only the fellow firemen knew the voice of their friend through the cryptic disguise. Four of them who were not needed on the fire line ran to George's aid. One took over the wheelbarrow, though he quavered a bit when he saw the lettering on the boxes. Another asked, "What do we do?"

George gave his instructions. The men hesitated only a second, and then did as told. Such was the training of confidence and belief in their leaders. All hands ripped open the boxes, matched fuse lengths, and stuck them in the dynamite ends. Each man then took a box of matches and took off in the direction that George had assigned. At that moment, Amos rolled through with his load. Another group of men sprang to his aid and followed his orders implicitly. Necessary action was in the making.

The various groups of men raced frantically through the streets, dodging explosive debris, and staying away from the hottest licks of flame. Through the dense smoke, they gasped and plunged forward ahead of the fire. The first man burst into a clothing store, threw his burden of annihilation, and then ran to the next location slated for obliteration. The next man took out a saloon, another a laundry shop. On and on the demolition proceeded. The crack of exploding dynamite and the rumble of falling buildings resonated up and down the streets of Denver.

Amos ordered fire crews to relocate to the newly made rubble piles. Once again the streams of water ran and soaked the debris piles into useable fire breaks. The bucket brigades lined up further down the streets as a backup. The brave firemen poured water onto the sides of the remaining structures to keep the tinder-dry wood moist and cool. Shovel crews climbed on the downwind rooftops and stamped out the fiery debris as it fell. Every able body worked beyond exhaustion to stem the horror that consumed their town without partiality. On it came, growing in intensity, creating its own wind as the hot air rose high and was replaced by gusts of cooler air near the ground.

The wall of flames approached the firebreak, but the high flames licking ahead in the wind caught no building in reach. The hellish heat radiated forward, but only found piles of sodden debris. The floating embers cast high into the air fell short of the nearby rooftops. Those that did hit the mark were extinguished by dirty hands wielding flat shovels, and by the thick soles of stomping boots.

The men, women, and children, both residents and visitors—the professional fire fighters and lay people of Denver—had contained the fire.

CHAPTER 75

Sydney Williams crept out of the state house close behind the man in custody that had shot R.W. Once outside the building, he worked his way across the street and then took off at a brisk pace toward the financial center of Denver. He pulled a kerchief from his pocket and wiped his brow as he looked over his shoulder to see if anyone followed. He was visibly upset by the events that occurred at the legislative session. He saw the despair in Everett Steele's eyes as he argued with his brother. And then, unbelievingly, he watched the sinister nod to Baxter to commit blatant murder. Sydney had thought he knew the bounds of Everett's character, but now he was shaken to the bone. This man, whom he had put so much financial trust in over the previous years, was on the verge of destroying all that they had strived to achieve.

Sydney arrived at his destination. The bank was closed in light of the political events, but he knew that one of the assistant bankers of the institution would be working in his office. He rapped on the door a number of times before the curtain on the window drew aside. A man with a well-trimmed beard and spectacles made eye contact with Sydney, nodded, and moved to unlatch the door. Sydney slipped quickly inside.

"Mr. Williams," the assistant began, "why are you here instead of at the state house?"

"Oh, everything's going well," he lied in his best English demeanor. "I just wanted to check on a couple of accounts before I left town. Urgent business, you know."

"I understand," the banker replied. "Come, I'll show you to the accounts file."

He relocked the door and ushered Sydney into a private office. As they walked, Sydney asked, "Has the vendor in Golden updated any shipment transfers this morning?"

"No, sir, I've not received any telegrams today in regard to that," he answered. "Most of those transactions usually don't get credited until after the noon hour, though." The banker opened the curtains covering the barred windows, then removed some file drawers from a cabinet and placed them on a table in the center of the room. "I have more correlating to do, sir. If you please, I'll continue with that."

"That will be fine," Sydney said.

After the banker left the room, Sydney turned up the oil lamps and closed the curtains. Then he started looking through the files. At times, he removed an account ledger or certificate, folded it, and placed it in a pocket of his coat. After some minutes, he replaced the file box and repeated the process with another. Before long he had the information he wanted, and replaced the final box. He closed the cabinet doors and sought out the banker. "I'm finished now. If you could let me out I'll be on my way." He motioned toward the other room. "I went ahead and put the files away and closed the cabinet; I hope you don't mind."

"No, no, not at all," the banker replied. "It saves me a step or two." He led Sydney to the door and let him out. "I hope everything was in order, sir."

"Yes, yes, of course it was," Sydney replied. "Like I mentioned, I only had to check on a couple of accounts before I left town. Thank you for attending to me."

"You are welcome, sir. Have a safe trip." The banker closed and relocked the door.

Sydney stepped onto the street and checked both directions. Satisfied that no one was paying attention, he began to walk towards the sheriff's office. He wished he had a carriage, as he was unaccustomed to walking long distances. The sheriff's was a thirty-minute walk and he dreaded the sweat it would create on his attire. He managed to compensate somewhat for the exertion by taking a more leisurely pace so he could think and contemplate his next move.

Halfway to his destination, Sydney heard ominous rumblings across town. He wasn't sure of their source, but he quickened his pace. In another twenty minutes, he saw the recently constructed sheriff's office. A number of men were on the front porch listening to one of Baxter's couriers. Sydney discreetly walked up and caught the tail end of the conversation.

"I tell you, it's all falling apart," the courier wailed. "We have to get out of town, now."

"Calm down," the squeaky voice of Baxter reassured. "Let me think this through before you throw out crazy ideas." He looked beyond the man and saw Sydney standing at the base of the steps. Their eyes locked, and Baxter silently motioned for him to come inside. He turned back to the courier. "Go back and see what else you can find out while I decide what to do." He pointed at the other three men present. "You two accompany him; there's protection in numbers. And you," he said to the third in a guarded tone, "I want you to absolutely verify that Steele is dead. Understand?"

The men nodded, turned, and left. Baxter was left on an empty stoop. Sydney stepped up, looked at Baxter's strained face, walked by him, and entered the sheriff's office. He sat down at the main desk and waited for Baxter.

Baxter entered the office, approached the desk and leaned on it. "What has happened?" Sydney asked.

Baxter violently wiped his hand across the desk, sweeping

papers and registry books onto the floor. He spun sideways and gazed out the window. Then he replied in a deadpan voice, "The courier says that Steele is dead."

Sydney's face turned white. After some moments he dared to ask, "What happened?"

"Grant," was all Baxter could spit out. He regained a little composure and continued in fragmented thought. "Grant somehow showed up and gained control of the session." He paused again. "He took Steele into custody and confined him to the basement. Then he managed to turn the delegates to his side to work for statehood." His eyes rolled in disbelief. He spun around, glared at Sydney, and blurted, "Now that section of town is burning. Steele was trapped in the basement and didn't get out. Everything we've worked for all these years is gone."

Sydney paused and tapped the side of his head with his index finger. Then his mind cleared. He knew what to do. He looked up into Baxter's face and said, "Now listen to me. I have an idea. But I need some information." He paused and stared at Baxter until he received a responding nod. "Do you still have the location for the last unrecovered cache?"

Baxter seemed caught off guard by the question. Then he suspiciously responded, "Yes, I do."

"Good," was all Sydney said. "Good." He put his head into his hands, thought again, and then continued out loud. "I still have access to some money. And my connections will help us reintegrate the bullion. We can try to recover some of our losses." He looked back at Baxter. "Right now, though, we have to get away from here—just us, mind you. The others are expendable." He looked over Baxter's shoulder and said, "I take it there's a back door out of here?"

Baxter's eyes narrowed and a grim smile curled his lips. "Yes," he hissed. "There is. This way, my friend."

CHAPTER 76

Ambrose McHenry was awakened from a deep slumber by the rumble of what sounded like distant cannon fire. He jumped to his feet but stumbled as the blood rushed from his head and left him between a dream world of the war and reality. Eventually, his mind cleared and he remembered where he was. He scanned the storage room at the train station where he, Evangeline, Johann, and Sarah had sought rest after the all-night carriage and train ride from Central City. Everyone was safe and still slumbering.

Ambrose rubbed his eyes and tried to decide what to do. Earlier that morning, he and Colonel Auger had intensely argued about what Ambrose's next role would be. Once the Denver militia was fooled into boarding the train for Kansas, Ambrose wanted to accompany the colonel and his troops to the state house. The colonel had successfully argued that, because Ambrose had met many of the political representatives at Central City along with Mr. Steele himself and his entourage, it would be best to remain behind out of sight until the foray was completed.

This was contrary to Ambrose's nature, but his fatigue overcame his will and he acquiesced to Colonel Auger's insistence. But now the sun was high in the sky. He moved forward to the door and cracked it open for a look. There was no one in the train yard that he could see. He moved further from the storage building for a better view. A streamlined locomotive with a trail of gentle smoke floating from its stack stood waiting about two hundred yards to the north. The depot next door appeared to be empty, and there were no other train cars in view. He closed the storage shed door, then walked around to the side for a complete view of the area. The rail yard was empty. Then he noticed a large column of black smoke rising from one side of Denver. "Something's gone wrong," he muttered to himself. He ran back to the storage shed, opened the door, and woke up his three slumbering companions. "Wake up, wake up!" he bellowed. "Something's gone wrong with Grant's plan. The town is on fire!"

Within moments they stood gazing at the black plume in the distance. "What should we do?" Evangeline asked.

Johann's sleepy gaze wandered to the other side of the tracks. "Hey, that's Sydney Williams's train," he remarked. "I wonder why it's here."

"Sydney Williams," Ambrose repeated. "Why, that's one of Steele's top men." He looked across town at the smoke. "I feel as though we should help with the fire, but we have no horses and it's too far to run. By the time we got there we would be exhausted and of little good." He took another look at the idle train. "Perhaps we should see if Mr. Williams is home. You three stay here," Ambrose requested. "I'll check the train and motion for you if it is safe."

The three slipped into the shadow of the storage building while Ambrose walked directly to the rear of train, climbed the stairs, and, without hesitation, entered the rear door of the passenger car. A few moments later he motioned for the other three.

The inside of the refurbished car was as exquisite as Johann and Sarah remembered. It literally shone, as the polished silver and ornate panels reflected the noonday sun. They told Ambrose and Evangeline about their earlier abduction. While they related their adventures, Ambrose searched the car, and cautiously moved to the forward exit. He opened the door and peered ahead. "Mr. Williams must be planning a short trip," he mused.

"Why do you say that?" Evangeline asked.

"Apparently, from what Johann said about the earlier train, he's taken off both the caboose and the other Pullman car. The only thing between us and the engine is the tender."

Evangeline had come up to his side while he talked. "I see," she remarked. "And look, the tender has a door on it." She cocked her head a little to the side and continued, "Is that normal?"

"No, I've never seen one like that," Ambrose replied. "Let's take a look." He scanned the surrounding area and saw no one. He exited the car, climbed onto the tender, opened the door, and went in. After a number of minutes had passed, he returned. "It's interesting," he said. "There is a pathway around the inside of the tender. Instead of a chute for coal, it has a large container, like a small boiler. It's full of oil, with some hoses and gauges in a sealed control board. All the lines are heavy steel and are strapped to the boiler with rivets. It's very impressive. At the other end, there is another door that leads to the engine. It's all enclosed and weather tight with some windows to view outside." He smirked. "And get this, it's lit by electricity. A string of glass bulbs emit a yellowish light all the way around the tender." He waited for a response from Evangeline, but only received a blank stare and an imperceptible nod. He faintly grunted. "There's nobody on board. Perhaps they are in town for some supplies."

Johann and Sarah ran to the front of the coach. "Ambrose," Johann gasped. "Someone is coming."

Ambrose moved to Johann's side and looked out the window. A carriage with two men was rapidly approaching the rear coach. Ambrose abruptly ordered, "Quick, everyone in the tender. Hurry!"

The carriage pulled to a stop at the rear of the coach. Sydney Williams and Baxter got out and hurried into the coach. "I hope the sheriff doesn't mind us using his carriage," Sydney remarked.

"I think he has plenty of other things to think about," Baxter sneered, "such as explaining his association with Steele, along with my disappearance."

Sydney placed some articles on his desk, then continued toward the front of the train. "Here's something new," he commented casually. He unfolded a cabinet door and exposed a horizontal shelving unit. It was full of knobs, gauges, and buttons. "It's a control panel," he stated. "It was finished yesterday. I can control the train from here. No engineer, no brakeman, no one to shovel coal. It's all automated by the touch of a button or the pulling of a knob."

Baxter moved forward to gaze upon the board. "How on earth did you think of this idea?" he asked. "It's remarkable."

"Watch," Sydney said. He moved a lever forward. The train gently responded by moving forward on the tracks. "There are pumps in the tender car ahead of us that are electrically run. They transfer oil from the holding container automatically to the firebox. There, it is injected under pressure, then ignited to heat up the water jackets. I use the standard water reservoirs laid beneath the tracks every twenty miles to automatically fill the boilers when needed. It's an ingenious design." Sydney returned to his desk. "But come, let's have some brandy and lay out our plans."

The train gradually picked up speed as Baxter and Williams sipped on their drinks and discussed their strategy. They were unaware of a dark figure that grasped the handrail of the rear car and hauled itself onto the platform.

CHAPTER 77

The stowaways in the tender car were immediately aware of the moving train. "Did you see someone climb into the engine?" Ambrose asked.

Nobody replied. Ambrose grasped the door to the engine compartment and inched it open. There was no one there. "Who is running the train?" he asked Evangeline.

"I don't have any idea," she replied. "Perhaps our Sydney Williams has some magic in his blood." She pushed Ambrose aside and stepped into the engine booth. A smooth hum emanated from the firebox. It wasn't excessively hot since the fire door was sealed. There was no hissing steam or dirty coal dust associated with all other locomotives. A grouping of gauges in a glass box attached to the wall showed all pressures and temperatures in the normal range, indicated by a green stripe in relation to the needle. She looked out the window as the outlier buildings of Denver passed by. "One thing is for sure," she said. "Whoever is running this train is heading out of Denver."

"I think it's Sydney Williams," Sarah said.

"Why do you think so?" Johann asked.

"I saw how well-dressed the man in the carriage was," she answered. "It could only be him."

"How about the other man?" Ambrose asked.

"I don't know," she replied. "I haven't seen him before."

Ambrose sat down in a seat originally placed for the engineer. "Well," he sighed. "I suppose we better figure out what to do from here. Anybody have any thoughts?"

"Perhaps we can figure out how to stop the engine," Johann offered.

Ambrose looked around the cab and said, "You know, I don't see any sort of controls in here." He rose to his feet and scanned the perimeter of the compartment. "There are no levers, no valves, nothing that we could move to find a reaction." He smacked the control box with his hand. "All the gauges are sealed in this heavy glass container. The lines running to the injectors are a heavy-grade, rolled steel tubing. I've never seen anything like it. I'm not so sure there is anything in here to sabotage."

"Hey, did you feel that?" Sarah said.

"Feel what?" Evangeline asked.

"The train, it's slowing down," she answered.

They looked out the window and noticed that the engine was reducing speed. Soon they could probably open a window and jump out. But, just as suddenly, the locomotive gave a decided jerk and picked up speed again. The firebox hummed louder now, as oil poured into the combustion chamber. Evangeline noticed the needles on the gauges rise ominously. The fire door started to glow a dull red. The rhythmic clacking of the rails quickened, and the telegraph poles whizzed by faster and faster. "I've never seen anything go this fast!" Evangeline yelled. "If I didn't know better, I would say this engine was a runaway."

The color disappeared from Ambrose's face. Evangeline noticed, grabbed his hands, and said, "What's wrong?"

He didn't answer, but she pressed him. Finally he said, "This track we're on is heading to the northeast. In about twenty miles it will cross a bridge over the Platte River. The bridge has a sharp turn in the middle of it. At this speed the train will jump the tracks and fall into the river."

He paused, took a deep breath, and his color returned.

"Come on," Ambrose said. "We have to find a way off of this thing." He led the group back into the tender car and moved them to the rear. As he turned the door handle and pushed, the wind caught the steel plate like a sail and slammed it backwards into the tender. "Evangeline, listen to me." He took her shoulders in his large capable hands and looked her in the eye. "If we can get to the Pullman car, I can disconnect it from the engine. I'm sure it has a separate brake somewhere on it. If not, at least we can coast to a stop."

"What about the men back there?" she asked. "How can we get rid of them?"

"I'm not sure," Ambrose replied. "But we have to find a way." He leaned close and whispered in her ear. "We're all going to have to do this. You understand? We'll have to help each other."

Evangeline nodded her head in understanding. Then she smiled at him and said, "I can't think of anyone I'd rather do it with. Let's get on with it."

Ambrose smiled back, gave her a quick peck on the cheek, and swung his massive frame out the door.

She immediately went to the opening to watch so she could follow his example and instruct Sarah and Johann.

He began by holding onto the open end of the door where the hinges were, then slowly slid to the handle of the boiler plate door, where he found a solid grip. The supports to the tender provided another handhold and he was able to thus support himself as he balanced on the narrow catwalk. When he reached the back of the tender, he stretched as far as he could and grasped the handle on the coach door. Fortunately, there was a double step with a rail to grasp onto. Ambrose prepped himself and jumped the rail in a smooth transition, considering the speed the coach was traveling. He looked back at Evangeline, motioned her to wait until his signal, and then he disappeared into the coach.

Surprisingly, he returned to the door in only a matter of three minutes. His face appeared pale, but his determination to get them off the tender covered it. "Okay, send Sarah over," he yelled.

Sarah worked her way to the door, listened intently to Evangeline's instructions, and started out the door. Ambrose was waiting for her by the coach rail. Sarah's feminine traits betrayed her tomboyish qualities as she rambunctiously raced across the tender and leapt across the rail into Ambrose's arms.

He laughed outright. "Where did you learn to dance like that?" Ambrose exclaimed. "That was amazing." Then he whispered into her ear. He looked into her eyes, gave her a hug, and ushered her into the coach. Then he turned to the tender door and yelled, "Where's Johann? It's his turn."

Obediently, Johann listened to Evangeline and managed to do the same acrobatic routine, though not with as much finesse as Sarah. He, too, received a whispered message in his ear before being directed to the coach.

Ambrose bellowed once more, "All right, Evangeline, it's your turn."

It was unfortunate that the train had picked up considerable speed since Ambrose's climb to the coach. It rocked violently on the tracks and the wind made even the simplest of moves difficult. But Evangeline pressed forward and accomplished her goal. Ambrose gratefully received her into his strong arms. As she prepared to enter the coach, he whispered in her ear. "Be prepared, Evangeline. The men in the coach have been horribly murdered. It's awful. Be strong and lend some comfort to the young ones. I'll be in as soon as I manage to uncouple this coach." He helped her through the door and then turned his attention to the car coupler.

The difficult task of disconnecting the coach from the tender weighed heavily on Ambrose's mind. He knew he had to act, but it was a trickier proposition than merely moving from one car to another. The swaying of the cars and the forward and reverse slamming of the coupler units made the timing for removing the securing pin critical. As he prepared himself for the task, he noticed the proximity of the meandering Platte River. It was only a few hundred feet to the left. The bridge was surely close by now. If he was going to act, it had to be now. He drew a deep breath, latched onto the railing at the bottom step with his right hand, and forced his right leg into the opposing rail across the step. Then he swung into mid-air underneath the coach and grasped the chassis rail with his left hand. He moved his right hand to a better position, but had to release his leg at the same time. A momentary drag of his foot on the ground caused him to scream in pain as the tip of his shoe disintegrated on the rugged ties. Instinctively, his grasp turned to iron as he pulled himself up and away from the repetitive pain delivered from the tracks.

He pulled himself forward to the coupler unit and reached for the securing pin. He pulled, but with no result. He watched the cycles of the pin movement as the train jostled forward and backwards. At the right moment he jerked upwards and the coupler released, but not without smashing his hand with the backlash of the spring-loaded release. Once again he grimaced in pain as blood poured from his mangled hand. But a loud clanging noise rewarded his efforts and gave him a measure of relief as the cars separated from each other. Ambrose could only hang on and hope that he could wait out the slowing coach before losing his grip to pain and fatigue.

Eventually, the coach seemed to lose speed. Ambrose raised his head and noticed the engine had picked up more speed. He shifted his grip to take better advantage of the chassis supporting rails and then sighed at the relief to his strained muscles. It took another fifteen minutes for the lone coach to stop. During that time Ambrose heard a muffled explosion further up the tracks as Sydney Williams's spectacular prototype jumped the rails and sailed over the edge of the Platte River Bridge.

That evening the fire in Denver was extinguished. The light westerly breezes from the mountains started to disperse the heavy, gray smoke. Many fatalities were avoided by the quick response of Amos Aldridge's firemen as they worked hard to remove the victims from the initial blast zone. Colonel Auger and five of his men were not so fortunate. They, and seven civilians, were closest to the hardware store when it exploded. The discharge of debris and flames sealed their fates.

Among the wounded were Grant and Henri who, in the midst of the foray, were just two more live bodies not recognized in the mayhem and confusion. They ended up three blocks to the west with the other dazed and unconscious souls waiting for medical care from a certain overworked doctor and his two reluctant assistants. Henri and Grant succumbed to exhaustion as they waited for their turn at the hands of the skilled physician.

Sometime in the middle of the night, Henri felt pressure on his leg and jolted awake. His blurred vision cleared to see a relieved and smiling set of eyes returning his gaze. "Hey, old man, I missed you." A broad smile crossed his face as he recognized Emily. She leaned down and gave him a gentle embrace. "I missed you, too," he whispered in her ear.

Emily pulled back, "Come on, let's get you fixed up."

Grant, silent observer to the reunion, rolled over and grunted, "See, Henri, I told you we'd find her."

CHAPTER 78

A wisp of smoke rose from the charred ruins of the state house. The thick timbers of the basement that had collapsed two days earlier under the intense heat of the fire still smoldered from isolated hot spots. Cleanup was generally in full swing as crews piled the ashes and trash into wagons and hauled them outside of town to a makeshift dump. It would take a number of weeks to clear out all the debris, but at least the chore was started.

Henri and President Grant walked along the edge of the scorched burned zone of town, surveying the damage and reflecting on the events of the past several days. They moved rather slowly, as their bruises and minor cuts from the hardware store explosion still caused bouts of annoying discomfort. Two of Grant's security guards stood quietly in the distance as the two men conversed.

"It's hard to believe how thoroughly the fire burned everything," Henri observed as he scanned the burned-out area. "So many of these buildings have nothing left but a thick layer of fine ash. I imagine underneath there is a lot of metal and such, but it's amazing just how large some of these structures were, and how little left there is."

Grant nodded his head in agreement. "It was providential that we were pulled out of harm's way by the firemen, and, more so, survived the initial blast. We could have died and been part of that ash heap."

After many steps Grant added to his epiphany. "If there was

one good thing that came out of this incident, it is that the city has regained its sense of unity again. This time, though, I believe they will rally in support of statehood and follow through with it, not as a small cluster of special interests, but as a coherent assembly of involved and concerned people." He stopped and looked at Henri in a satisfied manner. "I guess that makes it all worth it, eh, Henri?"

"Yes, Mr. President," Henri said, "I guess it does." Henri wasn't looking at the president, but at the pile of ash and rubble from the state house. "It's a shame that the cost was so high."

Grant followed Henri's gaze to the ash heap. He knew of whom Henri was referring. He reflected for a moment, then spoke almost in a regretful tone, "Yes, it is. Everett Steele had opportunity, but he chose a way that catered to his own ego, and it cost him his life."

"I suppose," Henri replied. "It almost cost the life of his brother, too."

"I know," Grant said. "But R.W. is a morally strong man with good ideas and those ideas are in support of statehood. The people will rally around his natural leadership. Even though he agreed to give governorship to another, he'll be exceedingly helpful in orchestrating the next fifteen months."

The men paused in contemplation. Henri then changed the subject. "Has there been any further information into the murders of Baxter and Williams?"

"No," Grant said. "It was certainly a strange series of events. Neither Ambrose nor any of the others could offer any light on what happened."

"I can't imagine the type of person that would do such a grisly act," Henri observed. "The coroner said that Baxter's head was severed from his body. And he surmised it was done by hand." He looked askance at Grant. "My God, Lyss, who could do such a thing?"

"I don't know," Grant replied. "Morning reports from Golden say that the owner of the Harranger and Bailey Smelting Company was murdered the same way yesterday afternoon in his office. It could be that it's the same man; I don't know."

A distinctly familiar set of voices yelled from the next block. It was Emily and Sarah looking for the two wayward philosophers. Sarah ran in between Henri and Grant, grabbed each one by an arm, smiled, and said, "What are you two gentlemen doing out here all by yourselves?" She grinned at one, then at the other and added, "I think you're looking for a cute girl to have lunch with. Am I right?"

By that time Emily had wandered in and took Henri by the other arm. "Methinks this one is already taken, my dear. You'll have to settle for that old army fellow on your other arm!"

Grant's eyes opened wide before bursting in hearty laughter. "It's time for lunch," Emily continued, "All of our friends are here, so let's be on time."

It was a short fifteen-minute ride to where a semi-private luncheon had been arranged. Conveniently, it was only two doors from the doctor's office. He was unable to be there because of his schedule, but he did make arrangements for Frank and R.W. to attend, with strict orders not to overeat or dance with the ladies. Jack was assigned the task of enforcing compliance.

Mike, James, and Derek had made their way from Golden the day before. It took another half day to become updated on everything that had transpired in Denver. As they arrived, nobody recognized them, as they had bathed, shaved, and gotten new suits with matching derby hats. They also rode on fresh horses with fancy new tack and saddles. It would seem that they had recently come into some money of sorts.

When Henri saw them, he rushed to meet them. "Mike!

James!" he shouted. "I can't believe it's really you! It's been so long!"

The men quickly dismounted and came forward, each in turn giving Henri a welcoming hug. Tears glistened in everyone's eyes at the reunion of eleven years.

"Henri," James began. He ushered Derek to his side. "This is Derek Borden, a good friend of ours from Silverton." He turned to Derek. "And Derek, this is the Henri that you've heard so much about."

The two men clasped hands in instant friendship. President Grant stood to the side in relative solitude, but only for a moment. "Hey, what about me?" he interrupted. "Isn't anyone going to introduce me? Am I not important enough to be part of this party?"

Henri broke into laughter and commented something about the lesser folk. Grant matched his grin and was formally introduced to the others.

From the door of the restaurant came the sound of a bell and the booming voice of Ambrose, a silent, but smiling, Evangeline at his side. "Lunch is on, boys! Come in and let's eat." Johann, who had followed Ambrose to the door, narrowed his eyes at the sight of the newcomers and then recognized James. The joyous reunion of the two brothers was a blessing to all who observed.

The luncheon was a time of greetings, renewing old friendships, talking of adventure and history. It was destined to continue into the night, as no one had any thought of leaving the celebration.

CHAPTER 79

Robert W. Steele finished out the day at the temporary state house. It was late and he was tired. But he was also excited about the progress made toward the first draft of the state constitution. The representatives from throughout the future state were agreeable and highly motivated to accomplish their goal of statehood. But the day was over and R.W. was ready to go home. His attendant dropped him at the front gate of his modest, single-story house. The July evening had already cooled into the upper sixties, and the bright moon overhead lit his small front yard almost more than the gas lamp posted next door. He entered his house, went about his evening routine, and retired for the night.

Sometime later, there was a distinct rapping on his front door. At first, the noise filtered into his dream, and he didn't stir. But, as is often the case, after repeating itself over and over, the noise didn't fit the dream anymore. R.W. opened his eyes, rolled out of bed, and pulled on his robe. As he stumbled on his way to the front door in the dark, he called out, "Yes, yes, I'm coming. Be patient, I'm coming."

R.W. unlocked the entry door and swung it open. The moon had long set, and the gaslight next door radiated an eerie, yellow glow on the front of the house. A young courier nervously stood before him. He apologized profusely for the lateness of the delivery, but stated that the sender was insistent on its immediate arrival. R.W. nodded sleepily, took the message, and gave the boy a tip that he took from the drawer in the foyer table. Then he made his way to the kitchen, blindly dug through the drawer in the sideboard for a match, and lit an oil lamp on the center table. The wick was set too high and when it flared, the bright yellow light made him squint his eyes and rub them. It was a full thirty seconds before he could open them to turn the lamp down. He sat down in a chair, took the message from the tabletop where he had placed it, and scanned the return address. His eyebrows arched up as he read, "Edwin Berry, Director, Denver Institution for the Sick." He recognized the hand script on the address. But it wasn't the usual neat lettering that Berry was known for. It was uneven, as if it had been hurriedly written.

He cracked open the sealing wax and unfolded the rough cotton-laced paper. "To R.W. Steele. Urgent. Come immediately. Edwin Berry."

R.W. reread the short note. It had been many months since President Grant had ordered his rapid night discharge from the hospital. He had only been in touch with Edwin twice since then. Once to retrieve his belongings and the other to officially thank him for his generous care over the years. It was an understatement to say that it was odd to receive such a note at two in the morning. But his curiosity was aroused, and he certainly would not sleep until the mysterious note was dealt with. So R.W. returned to his room, dressed in casual attire, and went to the stable to saddle his horse.

The ride to the hospital was lonely. The gas lamps situated every few houses illuminated the broad dirt roads that he traveled in a sad, yellowish haze. One section of road through town had recently been converted into a cobblestone lane as part of a renovation plan. His horse's hooves made a hollow, clip-clopping noise that echoed down the shaded street like wooden blocks knocking against a granite tabletop. R.W.'s mind raced as he tried to figure out what could be so important as to rouse him from sleep at such an hour of the night.

In thirty minutes, R.W. arrived at the hospital. He tied his horse at the front and walked to the front door of the facility. Remarkably, Edwin Berry was waiting for him. He opened the door, extended his hand in welcome, and said, "Thank you for coming, Robert." After a quick handshake, and with no opportunity to exchange more information, he curtly added in his characteristic demeanor, "Would you follow me, please." With that, he turned and strode down the hallway.

R.W. was awash in memories of the years he had spent in this place as he hastened to follow the director. Memories from his recovery process years ago were fragmented, but others were fresher. He didn't harbor bitterness as a result of his compulsory confinement, but looked on it as an experience of preparation for some task. That realized task, he now understood, was that of leading the future state forward in its admission into the union.

Edwin Berry climbed the stairs to the third floor and paced down the dimly lit hallway to the last room on the right. R.W. recognized the destination, narrowed his eyes, and looked warily at the director as he unlocked the door, opened it, and then stood to the side. R.W. slowly crept to the entryway and cautiously looked in. The room was warmly lit with four kerosene lamps. They were permanently affixed to the wall with protective glass so they could not be tampered with. The same comfortable bed that he had used was still in position along with the desk, dresser, and chairs. His eyes scanned the room. They stopped at the sorrowful figure of a man curled in a fetal position in the corner of the room. R.W. moved forward; Edwin followed a few steps behind.

The man was in a deplorable condition. His clothes, merely rags, looked like the cast-offs of a once-wealthy benefactor. He stank as if he hadn't bathed in years. His gray hair was matted with briars as though he had slept many nights on the open prairie. He was gaunt from lack of food, and had a chronic cough that sent drool down the side of his mouth. Dried dirt and what looked like blood stained his fingers and hands. The man wasn't asleep, but lay on his side, a hollow gaze looking somewhere into the past for consolation.

R.W.'s eyes grew wide with amazement and, perhaps, with fear, as he recognized his brother. Without altering his stare, he whispered, "What has happened?"

Edwin stoically replied, "One of the attendants came through here this evening. No one has been in this room since you left, but he felt a need to check it. He opened the door and found Everett where he is now. He tried to approach, but Everett growled menacingly at him, so he backed off. I was called in, assessed the situation, and immediately sent for you. While I waited, I lit the lamps and locked the door. I have no idea how he got in here. Perhaps, in his state, he didn't know where else to turn."

R.W. nodded his head in quiet understanding and dropped gently to a crouching position. He moved forward to Everett's side, quietly talking as he went. "Everett, it's me, Robert. It's all right now." Tears filled his eyes as the wide, empty stare of his brother remained fixed on some ghostly apparition across the room. R.W. made it to his side and sat down on the floor. He reached out, softly took Everett's head in his hands, and placed it on his lap. He stroked the matted hair and whispered tenderly in his ear, "It's okay, Evie. I'm going to take care of you now. I'm going to take care of you."

AUTHOR NOTES

While researching this book, I ran across many snippets of historical fact that I wove into the fictional storyline. The author notes examine the content of that fabric and offer the reader a richer understanding of the times. For those who are interested in these fascinating tidbits, please enjoy their place in history.

A Little Bit About the American Rail System in the 1870s

The rail system in the mid 1870s was well developed. Even though only six years had transpired since completion of the transcontinental railroad, the amount of railway usage had increased dramatically. In 1874 the rail system comprised 78,609 miles of laid track. That same year saw 246,640,679 passengers travel from somewhere to somewhere else across that rail system. Comfort features for travel, such as the luxurious Pullman cars, sleepers, and diners, were slowly integrated into the train configuration, depending, of course, on one's monetary resources to use such facilities. The wooden-bench cattle cars still comprised a portion of the train reserved for the many poor immigrants seeking a better life on the western frontier.

Steam locomotives provided the energy for moving the boxes of wood and steel. First invented in England, they came to the states via the same boats as many of the immigrants. As the rail system developed, engineers redesigned portions of the locomotives to better fit the needs of America's rail system. The English engines came with fixed front axles that provided rigidity for the British railway system. American operators didn't like the fixed axles, so they created flexible bogies mounted on four wheels. The drive wheels were the next innovation made in the States. Instead of a single drive wheel, dual pairs were linked together to create four drivers. The four wheels on the flexible front bogie along with the four drive wheels identified the locomotive as a 4-4-0, American type. It gave long service, high rail speeds, and stability on turns, and revolutionized long-distance travel. Other innovations soon followed. Joseph Harrison of Philadelphia invented the equalizing beam in 1839 that permitted equal pressure by each driver, even on rough track. Earlier in that decade, Isaac Dripps invented the pilot, or cowcatcher. Such equipment was a necessity on a frontier where few tracks were protected by fencing. Night rail travel, common by the mid 1840s, became safer by the conventional large headlight, which burned kerosene in front of tin reflectors. Other additions included enclosed wooden cabs for engineers, locomotive bells and whistles, and sandboxes, used to provide better traction on the steep rails of the West. All these changes added to the rail revolution that made train travel safe, efficient, and fast.

The Denver/Golden Railroad Route

The railroad tracks from Denver to the town of Golden, about fifteen miles to the west, were not new. They were laid in 1868 by the Colorado and Clear Creek rail line under the oversight of William Loveland, who came from New York in the late fifties to prospect and find his "pot of gold." Instead, he found riches in the ownership of merchant stores, wagon toll roads, and, eventually, rail lines.

His dream in the early sixties was twofold. First, he wanted to provide a rail-supply line to the growing mining camps of Central City, Black Hawk, and Georgetown. Secondly, his greater vision was for Golden to be an integral part of the Union Pacific's transcontinental railroad. He saw Golden competing with the major industrial cities of the East as a major trade center and transportation hub at the base of the Rockies. Over the next ten years he courted the Union Pacific to assist in financing his dream. As part of that plan, he had Edward Berthoud, a Swiss engineer, survey a possible rail route through the Rockies to the western slopes in 1861 so he could provide the Union Pacific with a detailed route to consider for their line. As an additional incentive, he planned the rail line from Denver to Golden. Unfortunately, the Union Pacific ended up running their line across Wyoming due to lower costs. They did set up a written agreement in 1866 to provide materials and supplies for the Colorado and Clear Creek Company, since they considered them a valuable associate.

In 1868, Loveland built the Golden/Denver run as a standard-gauge line in order to provide easy transport for the many tons of mining concentrates being sent from the inner mountains to the refiners back East. In 1869, a formal name change to the Colorado Central helped solidify the agreement with the Union Pacific for further support.

The Little Versailles of Georgetown

The Hotel de Paris had only opened a few months earlier, but it was the talk of the town, if not the territory. It was a large, two-story, white building with a tan façade and red trim around the windows and doors. A gilded deer on the retaining wall and a "lion couchant" guarded the gateway to the garden.

Inside, Louis had imported from Europe the finest in décor and furnishings. Red velvet draperies graced the windows. The parlors, with their thick carpets, open fireplaces, massive furniture, and handsome chandeliers, complete with colored glass globes, reflected the pride and taste with which Louis furnished the hostelry. The exquisite dining area, from its walnut and beechwood floor and wainscoting, diamond dust mirrors, solid silver table casters, and expensive Haviland china, created a premier atmosphere for entertaining and relaxation. The overall opulence and extravagance of the frontier hotel attracted people of status from all over the territory and helped give Georgetown a reputation as a place of culture and refinement.

The Silver Plume Blueprints to Reintegrate the Civil War Gold

In the mining process, a passageway was blasted into the mountain by drilling holes into the face rock of the tunnel, inserting dynamite charges, detonating them, and then removing the blast stone. The waste rock was deposited outside the mine on the tailings pile. When a producing vein was being followed, the blast rock would be sorted by hand and, either put in a cart to be taken for further processing or, if not a high enough grade of mineral, deposited in the tailings pile or the mine dump.

The sorted rock was then carted to the first step of the milling process, the stamp. The mill at the Silver Plume had a five-stamp processor. Each stamp was a long, solid-steel rod around eight inches in diameter and six feet long that rose and fell inside of a retaining bore. A series of drive belts from a steam engine provided the power to rotate a line of eccentrics, one per stamp, that lifted them about two feet in the air, then released them to gravity to crush the rock being fed into the bin at their base. This generally reduced the rock to fist size on down to dust.

The second stage of the process required the crushed stone to be transported, again by gravity, to a large cylindrical canister. Here it was mixed with some large iron balls, like cannonballs, and rotated. The action of the iron balls on the stone further pulverized it into a powdery gravel mix, hence the term "dry mix."

In the reintegration process of the gold bars, it was at this stage that the granulated bars were introduced into the giant cylinder. It was important to crush only the stone that had a natural affinity as gold-producing rock from the mountain. Some rock veins were high in only silver or lead content. One couldn't necessarily mix the gold bars with only that kind of rock because an assayer would recognize that the dry mix shouldn't have gold in it because of the type of vein that it came from.

Even though the Silver Plume mine had strong silver output, it also had some deeper workings that produced an auriferous, or gold-producing, rock formation. It was this type of rock composition that was lacking in the dry mix. Without ample auriferous dry mix, the gold couldn't be adequately and covertly integrated into the refinement process to appear natural.

More Details on the Teller Hotel of Central City

A newspaper article nailed to the wall next to the front door in the lobby contained a story from the June 1872 edition of the *Central City Register*. It described the hotel's grand opening, saying that the "Parlors are perfect marvels of elegance . . . all sleeping rooms to the number of ninety are tastefully fitted with all essential conveniences. The majorities are without transoms . . . guests may, therefore, lie down to peaceful slumbers undisturbed by the apprehensions of getting their heads blown off or by having valuables lifted by burglars."

The building, construction costs, and furniture totaled over $60,000, which Henry M. Teller, the proprietor and senior partner of the hotel, proposed as an arrangement to Central

City, which then provided the ground on which to build the facility.

The Teller Hotel was also noted for its elaborate public dinner parties and exquisitely orchestrated events, especially at special holidays like New Years Eve and July Fourth. In fact, it was well known that the Teller House held gaudy parties and performed exorbitant honors for its prominent patrons.

The honor of the silver brick pavement for President Grant in 1874 was a true expression of the hotel's pomp.

The Fictional Harranger and Bailey Smelting Company and the Early Smelting Techniques for the Time

The Harranger and Bailey Smelting Company actually began under a different name back in the early sixties. In fact, it wasn't really a smelting company at all; it was merely a thrown-together building with an inexpensive, low-temperature furnace inside it called a Scotch hearth. The needs of the prospectors in the new mining area definitely dictated what was built. And, in the surrounding area, those needs changed as the surface gold became harder to find.

The mining districts around Golden, called the Rocky Mountain Cordilleran, were made up of three basic layers of mineralized strata. The first consisted of simple placer deposits found in the creeks and gravel bars. These minerals were easily melted down by low-temperature Scotch hearths that were heated with abundant wood and charcoal.

Miners found the second layer of silver- and gold-bearing ore from ground level to as deep as one hundred feet. It was called the Gossan layer. These ores were relatively simple to mine by standard cribbing and hard-rock methods. The Gossan ores could also be refined in the same manner as the placers by heating them in the Scotch hearths.

By the mid-sixties, however, these two layers of easily

processed minerals were exhausted. That left the third layer of mineralized rock. It contained high concentrations of complex galena and sulfides, named for the heavy sulfur odor associated with these ores. They also didn't respond to normal smelting methods known at that time. The charcoal and wood fuel that heated the Scotch hearths didn't provide adequate heat to break down the multifarious ore structures of the deeply mined rock. At that time in Europe, experiments using blast furnaces fueled by coke and carbon did create the necessary heat to reduce the complex ore into gold and silver ingots. These furnaces were imported at great expense in the late sixties and installed in the newly formed Harranger and Bailey Smelting Company.

In the early seventies, the success of the blast furnaces in the reduction process prodded the owners to expand their operations to include additional facilities, allowing for an increased processing capacity. It was strange that the public smelting reports from the Harranger and Bailey Smelting Company showed a high volume of gold output, when it was thought that the extremely rich auriferous ores in the area were nearly exhausted. More strange was the fact that these reports coincided with the vast and expensive expansions at the smelter.

ABOUT THE AUTHOR

Curtis Von Fange began writing for fun in early 1998. His first article related a memorable experience from childhood about panning for gold with his father. It was published in *Gold Prospector* magazine a year later. Encouraged by his success, he went on to create over one hundred stories in various genres for hard-copy publications and online webzines.

Curt currently lives a few miles east of Colorado Springs with his wife and overprotective Australian Shepherd. He is semi-retired and spends two days a week as a heavy-equipment mechanic for a local contractor. The rest of the week is a potpourri of working on his property, helping his four grown kids with their projects, and spending time keeping up with his wife's busy activities.